Also by Anthony Bruce

FICTION

To Taunt A Wounded Tiger

NONFICTION

Railway Surveyors Handbook - Malawi.

THE EAST WIND

A novel by

Anthony Bruce

GLENDAMBO BOOKS

Canadian Cataloguing in Publication Data

Bruce, Anthony Alexander, 1939-
The East Wind

ISBN 0-9681787-1-5

1.Title.
PS8553.R72E27 1998 C813'.54 C98-910000-6
PR9199.3.B73E27 1998

A Glendambo Book

Published By: Glendambo Publishing
151 Saltair Lane.
Salt Spring Island.
B.C V8K 1Y5.
Canada.

Cover Design by Irwan Kurnaedy / The Alexandra Projects
Cover Photograph by Kathryn Oseen-Senda
Sossusvlei - Namibia 1996

Printed in Canada.

For: ELENA KATERINA MIA

With grateful thanks:

In Africa, to:
Rio Tinto Management Services and Rössing Uranium.
The people of Swakopmund. For their kindness and generosity to an *'Uitlander.'*

In Canada, to:
George and Barbara
Kathleen
Win
Caroline
Laura and Brian
Irwan.

In Britain, to:
Lady Gloria Lawrence.
Andy Bruce.

DESERT: *dez'ert*, adj. deserted: desolate: uninhabited: uncultivated. *-n.* a desolate or barren tract: a waste: a solitude.

Prologue:

Namib Desert - Colin - The beginning of the end

The boy had begun to die, unaware that his lifespan could now be measured in hours. For the first time an eddy of fear stirred in his belly. Again he stared over the shimmering stony plain to where the Chuosberge mountains stood blue in the distance. Nothing moved, except an eagle, a black speck circling aimlessly against the inverted vitreous bowl that stretched cloudlessly from horizon to horizon . . .

As yet he didn't feel very thirsty, though his body had begun to give up precious fluid to keep his vital organs cool; dehydration had started and despite the heat he shivered. A drop of perspiration rolled down his nose from the band of his safari hat. He tasted salt. "Good," he thought. What had Kresfeld said? Something about while there was still salt in the sweat there was a chance. Wishing that he had taken more notice of the old German's words, he tried to recall all that Kresfeld had said, but only the frightening statistics came to mind.

This was the Namib, the oldest desert on earth, known to the Bushmen, those tough hardy survivors from the Stone age, as the land God made in anger. Here time meant nothing. Here the incredible Welwitschia plants, living fossils drawing moisture from the night mist, had been dated to centuries before the birth of Christ.

In the empty silence he could hear his own heartbeat. To hide the welling fear from himself, he began to scream curses against the father who had placed him in this position and the uncle who had done nothing to prevent its happening. Not even an echo came back to mock him, for the desert didn't care. Men had died here before and, if imprudent or unlucky, would do so in future.

Finally he fell silent, exhausted, and the tears came spilling over sunburnt cheeks to evaporate quickly in the hot dry air. More precious liquid was lost and his body died a little more.

Chapter 1

Canada - Beaver /Elk Lake - Bitter Memories

Rafa skipped another pebble across the lake, watching the ripples turn silver in the early morning light. Finally he turned "It was a long time ago Laura, and in any case David should tell you the story. Have you asked him?"

"Several times, but all he says is that it's in the past and he has no wish to open old wounds." The girl turned. "Please Rafa . . . Please. You know the whole story, even Batchi doesn't know it all."

Rafa looked up and for a second saw Kate's face in the child; he sucked his breath in sharply at the resemblance, feeling an icy clamp tighten around his heart. He turned away to hide the distress he felt. The girl, puzzled, watched his face but waited silently. She was used to waiting. Rafa looked at his watch. He sighed. "Very well, I have time before my flight. As you know it was an accident, but accidents don't just happen, usually they are the result of actions so minor that individually they are insignificant but collectively ...."

The Namib Desert.

.......The Unimog growled along the canyon floor, its heavy duty, deep ribbed tires alternately gripping and spinning in the sand and gravel of the dry river bed. The continual change in traction jerked the three men sitting side-by-side in the open driving compartment like puppets on a string. The driver, a young man in khaki work clothes, mumbled an apology to his companions.

"Not your fault." The big man sitting next to the driver brushed a hand irritably across his massive black beard, forcing the myriad of flies to ascend, flies that were trying to drink the perspiration that trickled down his deeply tanned face and disappeared into and over the tangle of his beard. "This bloody place would be hard on a hovercraft." Another jolt brought a grunt from all the occupants and the big man closed his hand on the arm of the driver.

"Stop for a second, let Johnny have a look through the glasses."

The third man addressed as Johnny waited until the Unimog had stopped before climbing up onto the bench seat. He steadied himself with one hand on top of the windscreen while he swept the canyon ahead through high power binoculars for the object of their search. The other two waited, listless, the all pervading heat sapping their energy so that even talk was an effort. A puff of wind blasted sand across the floor of the canyon and the big man spoke warningly.

"You see that? The East Wind is coming, by tomorrow night it will be here in full strength so let's find the bloody camp and get the hell out of here - any luck Johnny?" He looked up at the black man dressed in the same worn khakis as his companions.

"No Boss, but I think we are close. Remember, I was only here once last year."

The man with the beard grunted, "I just wish those bloody geologists had picked up all their drillcore boxes before packing up last year." He brushed the flies away again. "OK, we'll give it another half hour then we'll turn back." He turned to the driver."You want a break? Johnny or I can drive."

"No, I'm fine . . . thanks." The driver, a much younger man than his companions, restarted the truck and they jolted forward.

The canyon walls reared up hundreds of feet on either side of the flat river bed they were traversing. Aeons ago water had roared down this valley from mountains far in the interior. Cutting deep through the softer layers on the plains above the water gouged out this awesome canyon. Then successive upheavals had shifted strata, forcing the river to cut and grind it's way through new obstacles. Finally, long after the land had cooled and eroded into the Namib desert the hot dry winds had piled sand into the river bed. The only water now remaining ran several metres below the hard packed sand and gravel the Unimog rode over. In some places the river bed was hundreds of metres wide but in others narrow enough to cause trouble. They negotiated the occasional tight curves in low gear, the Unimog growling in protest at the jagged rock sections that protruded across their path. For a while there was silence, the brooding sinister heights affected them all. This seemed a place of secrets, of old crimes and grim memories. Here no birds sang, and only the odd lizard glared balefully at the vehicle as they rumbled past. Finally just as Blackbeard was about to call a halt Johnny spoke loudly.

"There . . . I see the camp . . . go to the left". The 'camp' was a misnomer. A year ago, a group of geologists had lived under canvas while they prospected the canyon. Later a small drill rig had been brought in to test out likely looking rock formations and it was the abandoned drill core, left behind by the departed geologists that the three men had come to reclaim. The only indication that this flat, thorn tree studded area had ever hosted human life was a small pile of half-buried cans and debris. Still faintly visible were the raised rectangular outlines where the tents had been pegged down but it needed a keen eye to see even that much.

"Ya, I see it . . . good work Johnny." Blackbeard wiped his face with a large handkerchief as he waited his turn to climb down the metal ladder from the cab.

Quickly, for the sun was past its zenith and they had a long way to return, the three men fanned out looking for the pile of core boxes that should be in the vicinity. Ten minutes later Johnny yelled and Blackbeard walked toward the rock face where Johnny stood. Each long flat box was divided into three longitudinal channels. Each channel contained a long tube of rock core approximately 5cm in diameter. These were the drill cores recovered from the drill tube probing like a hypodermic needle into the granite skin of the canyon. The boxes were piled neatly on top of each other in three rows some four feet high but someone had thrown a dark brown tarpaulin over the pile and with several inches of dust and windblown debris they were almost impossible to find. Johnny had noticed a loose corner of the tarpaulin flapping in the occasional blasts of wind down the canyon. Together the two men pulled the tarpaulin free and each shouldering a box they walked over to where the Unimog stood waiting,

"Ivan can climb up on the back and we'll pass the boxes up to him . . . where is he Johnny?" Blackbeard glanced around, puzzled.

"I haven't seen him since we stopped Boss, I thought he was with you."

"IVAN" Blackbeard yelled loudly, "IVAN, COME BACK TO THE TRUCK." Both men listened intently but the rising moan of wind muffled any answering shout. "Uh-Oh," Blackbeard growled, "Where the Hell can the bugger be?" He stared at his black companion uneasily, "Come on, let's look for him, he must've gone round the corner."

The river bed made a sharp turn about a hundred metres from where they stood and moving quickly the two men strode briskly across the gravel, dust lifting with their desert boots and blowing ahead of them. Rounding the curve, the river bed widened to several hundred metres over several kilometres in length. On the far side against the rearing wall of black twisted rock the missing man was on his knees carefully brushing sand from something in front of him. "What the Hell!" Blackbeard exclaimed, "What's he doing? . . . We have to get moving soon."

The young man looked up and seeing them crossing the river bed waved his arm excitedly, motioning them to join him. Minutes later the two men stood looking down at a partially exposed body of a small adult or teenager. Mummified in the hot dry air, the facial skin was pulled tight over the skull and the lips were pulled back in a snarling rictus that exposed the teeth. The skin had blackened, so that determination of race was impossible.

The kneeling man was carefully brushing sand from the corpse and now the shoulders and neck were exposed.

"Jesus!" Blackbeard exhaled explosively, "What happened here?"

"I was looking for the core boxes along the cliff edge and heard a funny noise in this area, so I walked along and tripped over the head . . . it was partially exposed."

"Noise . . . What d'you mean noise . . . what the hell are you talking about? . ." Blackbeard was obviously rattled by the gruesome discovery.

"Sorry Wessel, but it sounded like someone moaning, someone in trouble . . . it stopped when I fell over the corpse."

"Listen!" Johnny stood stock still and faintly they all heard a soft moan rising steadily in tempo abruptly ending in a series of chuffing grunts. Johnny spun wide-eyed in fear and began to run back towards the Unimog.

"Stop! . . . Goddamn it Johnny it's only the wind . . ." The blackbearded giant that the younger man had addressed as Wessel flung out a massive arm and grabbed a handful of shirt. "Don't panic . . . I've heard this sound before, it's the wind around the rock formations . . . remember the talking sands of the Kalahari?" The big black man relaxed slightly. By nature he was not a nervous man, but this canyon summoned up race memories from times primeval, and with a body lying a few feet away he needed every ounce of discipline to stay.

"Look . . ." Wessel asserted his authority as leader. "We don't have much time before we must start back." Looking up at the canyon walls already inky black on the shaded side as the sun sank lower, he made several quick decisions. "Johnny, go back to the Unimog and drive it over here. I'll help Ivan clear the sand off the body. Then we will look for ID and take some photographs with the Polaroid." He paused, rubbing his beard absentmindedly, "Technically we should leave the body in place until the Police have been informed but now that it has been exposed there is always the chance that a stray jackal could find it and damage it. We will take the body back with us on top of the core boxes and wrap it in the tarpaulin." He stared at the two men who seemed reluctant. "OK . . . Lets get a move on . . . move, move."

Chapter 2

Namib Desert - Ivan

David Mornay slammed the pickup door shut. Anger choked him. He pushed the glass-fronted swing doors to the Main Administration Offices open. He bumped aside and ignored the startled looks on the faces of two Personnel officers in their neat lightweight suits who were about to enter the door ahead of him. Blood pounded in his ears, and he felt an awful tightness in his chest. "Nineteen, the poor little bastard was only nineteen." He could still see the agonized eyes and hear the dying whistle through the shattered chest. David's khaki trousers tucked into desert boots were splotched with drying patches of blood and a large stain on his shirt marked where young Kretchmer's head had lain.

Turning the corner to Waldron's office, he collided sharply with a woman, knocking files out of her hands and pushing her into the partition wall. "I'm sorry, are you all right?" He gripped her arm for a second, then unseeing and ignoring the scattered papers on the floor, he stormed down the passage. Waldron's secretary Rita rose with a surprised gasp as he strode past her and reached for the handle to Waldron's office door.

"Mr. Mornay, what is . . ." but David was past her and into Waldron's office before the sentence was complete.

Peter Waldron's office was situated on a corner of the East wing of the Administration Block, giving it an even better view from its large windows than that of the General Manager. A visitor unfamiliar with the mine could be forgiven for thinking that this was in fact the office of the General Manager. The floor covering was a pale grey carpet that spread smoothly from wall to wall. The walls were a tasteful match of blues and greys which set off a large Pernief print on one of the two walls not covered in smoked glass. The airconditioner hummed softly and the half-closed Venetian blinds gave the room an air of luxurious calm in contrast to the heat and dust outside. Waldron sat behind a large, modern and very expensive desk working on a document and looked up in amazement as David stormed in. He opened his mouth to protest. Even the Construction Manager should knock before entering the office of the Head of Human Resources. David slammed the door viciously.

"You cruddy little son of a bitch." David drew air into his lungs in a shuddering gasp. Waldron sat in his leather swivel chair, both hands gripping the padded arms, his mouth open in silent shock.

"One of my men has just died in the pit." David leaned over the desk, both hands gripping the curved edge until his knuckles went white. "First Aid tell me that you cancelled my requisition for an extra paramedic. Is that correct?"

Waldron found his voice. "David, our manpower schedules don't call for extra staff in the First Aid Department until May; there are other Departmental needs you know."

David Mornay was a big man but now he seemed to engulf the room and Waldron shrank back in real fear. David's voice dropped to a horrified whisper. "You're telling me that you cancelled a priority requisition given to you over three months ago because it didn't fit your pretty little charts and schedules?" He shook his head in stupefaction, as if to clear it. "Young Ivan Kretschmer has just died of his injuries in the pit because the only trained paramedic on this plant was busy on a minor injury in the Ovambo camp and took over an hour to get to the scene. Now you tell me that you took it upon yourself to cancel a flagged requisition."

"Look David, among other items, I discussed the manpower needs with the General Manager and . . ." But before he could continue David shot out both hands, grabbing a handful of Waldron's white linen shirt, crushing his expensive silk tie and wrenching him out of the seat. He dragged Waldron over the desk so that his face was held inches from David's own. He shook Waldron viciously back and forth like a rag doll.

"You bloody little clown," he shouted. "You discussed it with the GM, you discussed it with the GM . . . Who the hell gave you the authority to discuss my requisitions with the GM . . . your job is to carry out my instructions." In his rage David was unaware that the office door behind him had opened and a huge bearded man in dirt stained khakis stood framed in the opening.

Wessel van der Walt flung both his arms around David from behind. "Dave, please leave him, it's not worth it, please Dave . . ." The huge Afrikaner's voice was hoarse. He had followed Dave Mornay's trail up from the First Aid post where the body of young Ivan Kretschmer lay still under a blood soaked sheet. Wessel had made a wrong turn and lost vital seconds in his attempt to stop his chief from tearing the Head of Human Resources apart.

David surfaced from his rage. Strong as he was, he knew he could never break the iron grip circling his chest. He let Waldron go. The shaken Head of Human Resources, his fat face shiny with sweat, slid limply back into his chair. "OK Wessel, it's all right." The strong arms relaxed slightly.

"You're sure now Dave, you won't grab him again?"

David nodded, "Yes . . .no . . . let me go." Bile acid in the back of his throat threatened to choke him. He stared down at Peter Waldron. "I'm going to have your job for this Waldron, I don't give a damn how many managers you suck up to." He paused as if to continue, then without another word he turned, brushed past Wessel and stepped out of the office into the passageway. A knot of office staff had gathered around Rita's desk, drawn by the commotion, and they parted hurriedly to let David through. He paused briefly, nausea rising in his throat as the adrenaline surge faded and he clenched his hands to stop them shaking. It was always like this afterwards, the shakes always started when all the action was over. David felt cold sweat breaking out on his face and forehead. The woman in the white lab coat whose files he had scattered was still standing where he had left her.

She had been waiting for him, her eyes set and cold.

"Do you normally rush around knocking people over?" The top of her head was barely up to his chin. Her eyes glared up at him. "Well do you?"

"What?" Her face disappeared and he shut his eyes to stop the wall from swaying.

"I said do you . . ." Her voice paused. "Are you all right?" For the first time she noticed his pallid complexion and the blood drying on his clothes, "You are hurt!"

"No. Sorry, I . . ." Blindly he stumbled past her through the main doors into the harsh sunlight. He found his pickup and rested his head against the glass of his side window as another wave of nausea surged. He could hear the rumble of Wessel's voice behind him talking to the woman, their indistinct voices muffled by the singing in his ears. They must have followed him outside. He stood oblivious to everything, both hands gripping the half-open door. The nausea slowly subsided and perspiration ran down his temples. The slight afternoon breeze cooled him, his shirt sticking clammily to his back.

"Dave, let me drive." Wessel's huge bearded face showed concern.

"No, . . . It's over . . . Thanks Wessel, just a reaction that's all . . . Meet me back at my office." He wiped his face with a faded handkerchief. "I'll have to go and see Mr. and Mrs. Kretschmer. Go back inside and tell those useless bastards in there not to phone, it's the stupid sort of thing they're capable of . . . Oh dear God Wessel . . . he was an only child."

"Easy Dave, easy now." The big hand gripped his shoulder with enough force to make him wince. "Perhaps it would be better for me to go. He was in one of my crews after all."

David looked up and Wessel saw the emptiness in the normally cool grey eyes. He knew David had seen death before, and that he had fought in Vietnam, but a deeper demon had flayed David's soul this time, causing him to lose the crisp control he normally displayed under pressure.

"Thanks Wessel but it's my responsibility. I'll have to go home and change. Will you look after . . . ?"

"Of course." Wessel spoke gently. "Dave, Ivan was badly crushed, even if the medic had come right away I don't think he'd have lived. You mustn't blame . . ." His voice trailed away. "Drive carefully."

"Wessel, will you tell Survey to draw up a plan of the accident scene for the Inspector of Mines. There'll be an inquiry. Have Gariseb take a roll of Polaroid pictures of the scene. I have a record of the times." He reversed in a swirl of soft powdery dust and bumped down the gravel road between the Engineering and Administration Blocks. Wessel stood for a long moment watching the pickup truck accelerate toward the main gate and the highway into Swakopmund, before sighing deeply and walking back into the Administration Block.

Chapter 3

Canada - Barkley Sound, Vancouver Island,

Water ran down his neck, curling under the collar of his rain jacket. The leaden, angry sky matched his mood and he stabbed savagely at the sea with his paddle.

"Watch it Dickhead! What the hell do you think you're doing Colin? The bloody canoe is going in circles." Brian Talbot's voice was sharp with anger.

Colin Mornay craned his head round to peer at the youth sitting behind him. Even if Brian Talbot was 16 years old, his senior by a year and supposed to be his best friend he was damned if he was going to let the comment pass. The events of the afternoon still rankled and he snapped back. "Dickhead yourself, if you're so bloody good why don't you paddle all on your own."

"Listen Colin, if you want to indulge yourself do it on land. If we flip over here because you've got your knickers in a knot we'll both probably drown before the others realise how far behind them we are."

Angrily, Colin started to reply, then choked as a lump of seawater, whipped by the rising wind splashed over the side of the two-man canoe into his face and open mouth. Coughing violently, he dropped the paddle that floated away until stopped by the tethering cord.

"For fuck's sake Colin, watch out! We're going to broach . . . help me turn, move . . . move!"

Startled by the raw fear in Brian's voice, Colin yanked his paddle back and dug the wide blade deep into the chop that threatened to flood their frail canoe. Panting with exertion, the two boys turned the curved nose of the canoe into the wind and the direction the other members of their party had gone. Neither boy spoke again until twenty minutes later when through the gathering sea fog they saw lights flashing in their direction from the shore of Diana Island.

"Hallelujah!" Brian muttered under his breath, "Bruma's going to have our balls for this."

Colin snorted in disgust, "You're afraid of your own bloody shadow Brian. Try to remember that he's a teacher and needs the job more than we need him."

"You know Colin, there are times when you're more than just an obnoxious prick. Like right now, when you're a stupid, obnoxious prick. Bruma's an expert sailor. He warned us to stay close, that the wind could get up."

"We're here . . . aren't we? What the hell are you panicking for? Admit it . . . a little excitement makes life worth living . . . so I goofed off a little . . . it's not the end of the world." Colin grinned over his shoulder. Brian Talbot was his best friend and he realised that today he might have gone too far.

Brian Talbot stared at the stocky figure kneeling in front of him. He bit back a sharp retort. The contract with Mornay Industries was very important to his father's company and he didn't want to jeopardize anything for the father he adored.

Brian Talbot's father had come up the hard way. When the Talbot family fortune had been lost through bad investments his father was 14 years old. Forced to leave his exclusive Prep school and find work Les Talbot became a logger in the days before new technology and improved equipment removed a large part of the danger from a still dangerous industry. Les had lost his right arm to a steel cable that whipped back after tearing loose from a huge cedar. Not one to whine at the vagaries of fortune, Les Talbot took the compensation money and bought his first logging truck. Slowly, with many setbacks, the indomitable logger built up his fleet of logging trucks then diversified into mining equipment. His company now had branches world wide. Determined that his son was going to have the education he'd been denied, he sent Brian to the most expensive Prep school in Victoria. Brian was not academically gifted, but by dint of hard work he managed to keep a respectable B minus average. However, he excelled at most sports and was the school's leading athlete. Enormously proud of his son's achievements Les was even more pleased when Brian and Colin Mornay struck up a friendship. It was a strange attachment, for Colin in one of his less objectionable periods had helped Brian get through his mathematics course. Brian in turn had taught Colin the rudiments of squash. Three years earlier Brian's younger brother Billy had died of a freak outbreak of meningitis and this terrible loss had more to do with Brian's need to fill an aching hole with Colin's friendship than any academic help Colin could supply.

"Doesn't it ever cross your mind Colin that you might be wrong? You never consider other people's feelings. Hell . . ." He stopped and exhaled noisily in exasperation. "Damn it Colin, I sometimes wonder why I put up with your bullshit." He stared at the broad back ahead of him and went through the events of the afternoon.

Barkley Sound is a large coastal indentation facing the Pacific Ocean on the West Coast of Vancouver Island. The Sound 24Km wide by 20Km deep is broken into three main channels which separate the two main island groups. The main group of nearly 100 islands and islets are called the Broken Group and all of these are part of the Pacific Rim National Park. The Broken Group offers safe canoeing among the many islands protected from strong westerly winds, and heavy swells rolling in from the Pacific. The second group on the southeastern side of the Sound are known as the Deer Group and are reached by paddling across the nine kilometres of open water of the Imperial Eagle Channel. After reaching the Deer Group there is a two kilometre stretch of open water called Trevor Channel before reaching the fishing village of Bamfield on the mainland of Vancouver Island.

The party of eight sea-going canoes had left Toquart Bay on the northwest side of Barkley Sound ten days before. Their plan was to explore the Broken Group of islands; cross the dangerous Imperial Eagle channel to investigate the Deer group of islands before crossing Trevor channel, an equally risky stretch of water to reach Bamfield.

It had been a long awaited field trip for the fourteen boys and two masters from the school. The Headmaster, despite the school's emphasis on adventure training, was initially reluctant to approve such an extended outing. Ben Staines, the assistant sports master, argued that Kurt Bruma had sailed solo around the globe in a home built yacht. And he, Staines, was coach to the Victoria Seagulls rowing club where most of the boys selected were members.

Bruma and Staines pointed out that the trip would have definite academic advantages. If the boys brushed up on the early history of the area and were exposed to the ancient aboriginal Indian dwelling sites on these lonely islands they would develop both their minds and bodies. The Head, a strong promoter of more awareness in the community of the aboriginal Indian heritage reversed his veto.

This morning Kurt Bruma had warned them that the calm conditions they had all enjoyed over the past few days were changing. Staring at the scattered clouds moving slowly across the clear sky, he growled at them in his German accent. "I want you all to stay within sight of each other. By late afternoon, if not sooner we are going to have strong winds. Brian, you and Colin bring up the rear. Don't let anyone straggle and remember we will overnight on Diana island before the final push to Bamfield and our pickup tomorrow afternoon."

For most of the morning it had seemed that Bruma was wrong. The surface of the Sound had been no more than a gentle swell that although increasing slowly, posed no difficulties. The sun shone down brightly. Most of the boys had taken off their shirts and all were enjoying the steady rhythm of paddling across open ocean. Colin and Brian, being the strongest paddlers of the group could afford to rest for longer periods than the others.

It was during one of their rest periods, when Colin, shirtless, leaning back with eyes closed to soak up the warm sun heard Brian say something.

"What - what did you say?" Colin didn't open his eyes.

"How come you never mention your Uncle Dave?"

"Why should I? I've never met him. Hell, I don't know where he lives or if he's alive. Why do you want to know?"

"My Dad knew him years ago and says he's quite a character. Is he really the black sheep of your family just because he fought for the Americans in Vietnam?"

"I guess so, although my parents never discuss him. Whenever I bring his name up they change the conversation. I remember my Grandpa shouting at my Dad one time when Dad said he'd had a letter from Dave. Jeez . . . Grandpa was really pissed and said something about not wanting to hear that man's name mentioned again. I though it funny that he couldn't even mention his own son's name but called him, 'that man'. I guess whatever he did must've been pretty bad."

"Well, if he was my Uncle, I'd want to know. My Dad rather liked him, said that he was a good kid who got shafted by your family. Dad said all the kids at school knew that your Grandpa didn't want him even when he was little. Dave used to stay after school and take extra lessons, played in all the rough sports just to impress your Grandpa. According to my Dad nothing changed. Dave was a lonely kid at school, didn't make friends even though Dad says he tried to get to him. I guess whatever your Uncle Dave did, your Grandpa probably deserved it."

"Who knows?." Colin yawned, "Grandad's dead so I can't ask him and my Dad's never at home. Mom freaks out if I bring him up, she calls the Americans - 'War criminals' - anytime a documentary on the Vietnam war comes up."

"Well boyo, I know where he is, and what he's doing." Brians chuckle reached across the sun dappled water.

"Yeah? How come?" Colin was surprised. He knew that Brian's father and his own father and uncle had attended school together. He knew a little about the dramatic reversal in the Talbot family fortunes that had forced Brian's father to leave the exclusive school and find employment with a logging company. Now he wondered where Brian had gathered his information from.

"You know that my Dad's company supplies mining equipment world wide. Well he got an order for specialised concrete dumpers from a big mining company in Namibia and the name on the order was from a D. Mornay. He did some checking and found out that it was your Uncle Dave. He's a senior construction boss with ConAmGeo, one of the biggest mining companies in the world."

"Yeah, well so what? It's not going to enrich my life knowing that titbit of information." Yet curiously Colin was pleased to hear that his Uncle was out there somewhere. He smiled to himself, he would enjoy the look on his mother's face when he broke this news.

For a long time neither boy spoke, the canoe drifting idly on the swells and the sun warming their half-naked bodies. Colin felt a feather light touch on his forearm resting on the edge of the canoe which rose and fell on the gentle swell. Unwilling at first to stir himself, Colin moved his forearm slightly and the sensation disappeared. Then just as suddenly, the gossamer light brush stirred the hairs of his arm again. Languidly Colin opened one eye, and was startled to see a dragonfly balanced on long spindly legs resting on his arm. The boy and the insect contemplated each other with interest. Staring at the insect's compound eyes glinting like dark crystal facets, it's wings iridescent in the sun, Colin felt a sense of wonder. Carefully, so as not to disturb the insect's fragile anchorage he propped himself up into a half supine position so that he could study this tiny aviator more closely.

The dragonfly, blown away from one of the many islands, or perhaps travelling the wind as a matter of course, exhibited no fear as it appeared to stare back at the boy. Colin examined the insect carefully, impressed that something so apparently fragile could attempt what was, in relation to its size, a major ocean crossing.

"Hey, Brian look what's landed on my arm." He called, gently turning his head half-round to his friend. "A dragonfly . . . all the way out here, quite something, eh! I wonder if we're like an aircraft carrier to it?"

Brian sat up to look over Colin's shoulder and the canoe rocked slightly. It was enough. The dragonfly took wing and for a second it glinted silver against the dark blue sea and then was gone. " Yes, I saw it . . .I read somewhere that they can travel tremendous distances."

"Shit I hope so," Colin retorted, "Poor little bugger is miles from land."

"Talking of miles from land, let's get going." Brian pushed himself into the paddling position and reached for his paddle. Both boys squinted across the expanse of ocean and they could see scattered canoes some distance ahead. It was not unusual for individual canoes to fall out of sight of each other as the occupants rested, riding gently up and down on the swells. Both boys dug their paddles into the sea aware that they had fallen further behind than was acceptable. Still, when everyone stopped at the small unnamed island between Fleming and Tzartus Islands for lunch, the discrepancy in individual arrival times had not been unduly excessive. Kurt Bruma mindful of the cheerful atmosphere decided not to criticise. He was to regret his tolerance later.

After lunch on the shingled beach was over, the boys, sitting and lounging on wave worn logs, were addressed by Ben Staines.

"We made landfall on this island for a reason. While planning this trip I was fortunate enough to have lunch with a friend of mine who is one of the Provincial Archeologists. He told me of a very recent discovery on this island. As you know, Barkley Sound was settled for thousands of years before the arrival of the Spanish in 1774 and Captain Cook in 1778. Recent studies indicate that this area supported one of the largest concentrations of population on the West Coast of Vancouver Island. As you have seen and experienced over the last nine days the people who lived here were a maritime people with a strong culture and spirituality. These were a very hardy and aggressive people who went out into the open sea in canoes. Each canoe carved from a single large cedar tree. You boys have been canoeing for the last nine days in relatively calm water, think what it must take to go 40 to 60 miles into the open ocean, harpoon a whale and then tow the carcase back the same distance to their village."

Here he paused, considering. "You have all studied the historical background of this area and so are aware that many totems and artifacts have long since been removed from their original locations. This particular island marked the boundary between the Tseshaht and the Ohiaht tribes and was assumed to never have been inhabited by either tribe, as any such action would have brought retaliation from the other tribe.

Well the assumption was wrong, a sacred place was discovered recently and in order to protect it from tourists . . ." Here he smiled, " . . . like ourselves, the location has been kept secret. I obtained permission for our group to examine this site by pointing out that you boys by virtue of your backgrounds and education are the future leaders our society. No doubt most of you will end up in positions of authority and you will be the ones to ensure that such areas are protected. I ask that you appreciate the trust that has been placed in us and expect you all to keep the location I will shortly show you, to yourselves."

Staines and Bruma then made sure that each boy pulled on a long sleeved shirt and laced on running shoes before leading the group into the dense undergrowth. Leaving the short strip of beach they encountered a tangle of luxurious growth as plants competed with each other for the sunlight at the beach edge. Once into the green gloom of the forest they splashed up a small stream that afforded the only reasonable access through the trees and undergrowth. Spears of pale sunlight splashed down through gaps in the canopy far above and less than a hundred yards from the shore they encountered a rising wall of rock. The stream they were following splashed down from a point far above them in a series of small cascades. Staines waited until all the group were assembled at the foot of the rock, then moving to the right of the stream he began to climb up the moss covered rocks. Feeling the rock face with a free hand he grunted in satisfaction and moving further to the right began climbing rapidly. Following in his footsteps the boys found that the spaces between each ledge were almost like a staircase and apart from a certain horizontal irregularity, could have been man made. The rock face ended and they found themselves on a flat rock plateau 200 feet above the beach. The plateau was roughly rectangular and about 200 feet wide by 180 feet deep. It was a perfect defensive position. On three sides, apart from the easily defended rock staircase the rock faces dropped steeply to the ground below. The fourth side was a rising vertical wall that would have daunted the most adventurous rock climber. With the surrounding trees removed and viewed from an aircraft or helicopter it would have looked like an enormous chair carved in rock. The seat of the chair being the plateau and the rising wall the chair back. A vertical crack in the rising wall widened as it reached the plateau and formed a large opening.

Staring around the plateau the boys became aware of time-worn wooden posts carved with what appeared to be faces. The posts were eroded by time and nearly hidden in the low brush. Vines wrapped themselves like battleship rope over and around two intricately carved supports with a fallen cedar tree acting like a massive crossbar in front of where they clustered on the edge of the plateau.

Silently, in awe, the boys ducked under the fallen tree and walked around the area, which in the now increasingly cloudy light had an eerie sadness. What appeared to be a small traditional grave house, leaning against a large cedar tree, had only a gaping hole where the roof timbers had rotted away. Other posts leaned drunkenly at odd angles, the original carved figures also eroded by weather and time. Scraggly beards of moss hung dripping from the trees and no animal or bird life was visible.

Approaching the vertical rock face, the boys could see that

the crack led into a small cave. The opening was wide enough to admit two persons at a time and inside the cave cedar burial boxes were piled from the floor to the ceiling. The lower boxes had partially disintegrated with time and those above had slid to lean lopsided against one wall. Out of respect for the dead, and not wishing to disturb anything that the archeologists might find Ben Staines did not allow the boys to enter the cave. Standing at the entrance he permitted the boys to shine their flashlights into the dim interior.

Most of the boys, having studied the Coast Indian culture as part of their trip preparations, were fascinated. They could appreciate the tough, hardy people who had lived and survived on this beautiful but dangerous coast. Now, apart from low murmured comments, the boys were generally silent listening as Ben Staines explained the archeological significance of the site. All except Colin Mornay. Colin was disdainful, pointing out with a sarcastic aside to Brian that the area was exposed to the full force of the southwest winds. And if it had been such a valuable site why had the Indians abandoned it. He continued in like vein for several minutes until finally, exasperated, Brian clipped him lightly on the ear and told him to shut up. Stung by the rebuke Colin stopped talking and relapsed into a sullen silence. Suddenly a roll of thunder caused them all to start and look up. Now the sky had darkened considerably and a steady rain began to fall. Staines and Bruma quickly ended the lecture and organised the boys ready to begin their descent.

While waiting his turn, Colin wandered away from the other boys bunched at the head of the natural staircase and found himself in an area of flat sandstone slabs, some looking like gravestones in Christian cemeteries. Colin knew from his studies that the coastal Indians placed their dead above ground in cedar boxes or a cave such as they had just seen and was intrigued at this seeming anomaly. The slabs of flat rock stuck up out of the ground and after rubbing the surface of a particularly well preserved one, realised that what he had taken for engraving was nothing more than weather marks and these slabs were not gravestones but simply random outcrops. Turning away, his foot in the thin runners kicked against a small boulder. With a grimace Colin sat down nursing his foot. Brian Talbot yelled at him to return as it was time to descend.

"I'm coming, damn it - give me a minute." Rubbing his foot with one hand he picked at the boulder which had caused him to stub his foot, and found that it was a man made object. Quickly he wiped layers of encrusted dirt from the object and was excited to find that it was a one-piece stone dagger about 12 inches long. The pommel was rounded and carved into the grip which then flowed into a rounded guard before continuing into a short thick pointed blade. He waved to Brian who was looking anxiously in his direction. "On my way - stop panicking." He searched frantically for a means of hiding his new found treasure. Realising his camera bag was the ideal hiding place, he removed his camera and slinging it around his neck, slipped the dagger inside the bag out of sight. He scrambled to his feet just as Brian began to walk towards him. "I'm coming - I'm coming, keep your shirt on." He ran back to the staircase and while Brian waited to bring up the rear, climbed down. At the bottom Staines waited and when Brian joined them a few seconds later the three splashed down the stream back to the beach.

At the beach preparations were well in hand to depart. It was a fairly short run to the Northern tip of Diana Island, but Bruma and Staines checked over each two-man canoe carefully. After stashing the camera bag in his canoe Colin turned to help launch an adjoining canoe. Finding that the camera slung around his neck was getting in the way Colin removed it from his neck.

Once again Bruma had asked Brian, as the most experienced canoeist of all the boys, to act as rearguard to assist any stragglers and by the time Brian and Colin had launched their canoe, the rain was slashing down in solid sheets. A hundred feet from the shore Colin remembered his camera on the beach log and yelled that he wanted to return. Without a word Brian dug his paddle into the heaving sea and turned the canoe back the way they had come.

Landing was more difficult this time, as the swell was creating small waves that ran up the shingled beach. Colin jumped out of the canoe and began to search for the log on which he had placed his camera. Brian stood holding the canoe and watched Colin search. Glancing into the canoe he saw Colin's camera bag. Puzzled he pulled the bag free and startled at the weight, opened the double zip. Stunned he stared at the stone dagger. He yelled at Colin, who had by now recovered his camera and was returning to the canoe.

"What the hell is this?"

"It's mine - I found it at the village." Colin pushed his camera into a plastic bag, turning his back on Brian.

Angrily, Brian spun Colin around. "Don't you know these artifacts are protected by law - just picking up something from a site can screw it up for the archeologists. Shit Colin, where are your brains?"

"Bugger off Brian, I want a souvenir of this trip - "

Holding Colin firmly by the arm Brian Talbot dragged Colin in the direction of the stream back to the village. "You don't get it, do you? First it is against the law, second you are compromising the archeological investigation which will start soon, and by the time we return it to where you found it we will be at least 30 minutes behind the group." He shook Colin savagely, "Now move your ass and let's get it back before I break your arm." Colin wrenched his arm free but did not argue. He preceded Talbot to the staircase and they both climbed swiftly back to the plateau. At the top Colin led the way to where he had found the artifact and scraping a small hole buried it at the base of the flat rock.

"Look Colin - when we join the others I'll tell Staines that you found it and where it is buried. I'll say that you didn't say anything because you were afraid that it might take a walk. Ben will get the museum people to come out quickly and you will get lots of credit." He pushed Colin , "Come on now, don't sulk . .

. Hell it's much better in a museum instead of being hidden in your bedroom. You know that as soon as someone noticed it in your house questions would be asked." Colin did not answer but turned sullenly back the way they had come. Shrugging Brian followed the stocky figure and in silence the boys returned to the beach where they launched their canoe into the freshening breeze.

For the next hour they paddled through scattered rain squalls in silence until a group of dolphins raced alongside their canoe delighting both boys. The dolphins disappeared as the cold rain intensified and Colin began to complain about the never ending water that permeated everything on board.

"Fucking rain . . .I hate this bloody climate . . . as soon as I can, I'm going to live in a dry, hot place." Colin disgustedly spat into the sea.

Brian grunted, "Yeah, . . . sure you will . . . you can run away to the Caymans every winter." He did not speak again until the moment when Colin's carelessness had nearly caused them to broach in the heavy sea. Now he wondered why he put up with the annoyance. He grinned to himself, the little bastard needed him just like little Billy had needed him and that was enough.

Chapter 4

Namibia - Tsamma Ridge

The Chieftain rolled smoothly out of the turn. David concentrated, holding the curved control yoke lightly but firmly as Rafa had shown him. The brown desert began to rise. He squeezed the rudder to centre the aircraft on the black strip of asphalt moving towards them and flicked the flap switch down, hearing the hiss as the flaps began to deploy. Now the yoke was pressed back into his hands as the change in attitude forced the nose up. He trimmed forward but overcorrected. "OK Dave, I've got it," Rafa's accented English broke into his concentration and David lifted both hands clear of the yoke to show the stocky Chilean that he was no longer in control of the aircraft.

Rafa grinned at him, "Not bad. Not bad at all. Hey amigo, you will take my job if I am not careful."

David Mornay liked this little South American, who had arrived at the mine two years ago, a battered flight bag in his hand, the peaked baseball cap shading his seamed swarthy face from the fierce desert sun. Rafa Modesto, freelance pilot and one time adventurer, had come in response to an advertisement for a replacement pilot to fly the company aircraft. Not many regular pilots lasted long in this savage environment, but Rafa seemed impervious to the heat, the dust and the often unpleasant duty of airlifting badly injured mineworkers to the state hospital at Windhoek. Looking at one of the few men he considered a close friend, David wondered what had prompted Rafa to come to Tsamma Uranium mine. Certainly, Rafa's obvious skills could have ensured him a comfortable position in the more civilized centres of Southern Africa.

David himself had arrived as superintendent of the initial construction crews four years earlier, when the giant ConAmGeo mining group had decided to develop their uranium concessions at Tsamma Ridge. Discovered in the late nineteen twenties by a lone prospector, the Tsamma Ridge orebody had been ignored by most of the major mining houses, who preferred to work richer and more easily accessible orebodies. A large, low grade uranium deposit in the desolate, waterless wastes of the Namib desert was not attractive. Now in the newly independent state of Namibia, one hundred kilometres East of the nearest settlement Swakopmund, Tsamma Ridge waited to come to full production.

For a long time oil prices had been low and interest in uranium as a fuel had suffered several setbacks, caused in part by the disastrous explosion at Chernobyl and the difficulties of disposing of nuclear waste. Environmental pressure groups had made uranium a dirty word and for a period it was viewed as an energy source whose time had passed. Then came the rise of Islamic fundamentalism, spreading rapidly from its origins in Iran. Fundamentalism that came with a chilling message that, at last, real power resided with the mullahs who had been instrumental in toppling the old order in their respective oil rich countries. In trying to clear decades of mounting deficits, the West had turned eagerly to the peace dividend brought about by the collapse of Communism and had steadily pared their fighting forces to the bone. Suddenly, it became apparent that while the Western powers had been downgrading their armed forces, Arab and Moslem countries had just as efficiently been upgrading theirs. Now, with a series of interlocking treaties they had a modern, well equipped Pan Arab army of five million men. The industrialized nations of the Western World had to frantically reappraise their energy needs and uranium surfaced as a panacea for all the follies and complacency of the past decade. Due to the sharp rise in the price of oil and with uranium rising in price, ConAmGeo had taken another look at its half-forgotten options on Tsamma Ridge.

The difficulties were immense, a road and rail link would have to be constructed 50 kilometres across a baked rocky desert where the daytime temperatures soared above 100 degrees Fahrenheit.

Fresh water to sustain life and run the plant would have to be delivered initially by road tanker trucks. Eventually, a hundred kilometre pipeline from the underground wells at Rooibank on the Kuiseb river would have to be constructed to bring the water to the mine. To enable men to live and work in an environment as hostile as the surface of the moon, camps with more than the bare amenities must be built. The logistical problems were a nightmare. Special equipment and mining machinery from such diverse countries as Japan, Sweden, America, Canada and Great Britain had to arrive in the sleepy town of Walvis Bay, which until then had handled nothing larger than the odd coastal freighter.

But as the price of uranium continued its climb, pulled by the rising price of oil, small groups of men began meeting in London, Johannesburg and Montreal. In the softly lit, richly furnished boardrooms of ConAmGeo, men who had been responsible for initiating some of the Free World's richest mines gathered to decide the fate of 500 acres of barren, sand blasted rock, known to those few Namibians who cared, as Tsamma Ridge.

By this time the geological mapping, exploratory drilling and laboratory test work had been completed. The results were promising but not conclusive. Twenty-three floors above the bustle of London's noonday traffic, the decision to go on or cut their losses was made. Despite their wealth and power, the 15 men sitting around the boardroom table that spring day were kin to the old hardrock miners of a century before, the kind of men who had gambled wealth, health and often lives in the elusive pursuit of the big strike. This aberrant side of their natures they would mockingly deny, but beneath bland faces and polished manners a compulsive excitement quickened to this difficult and challenging gamble. The decision to invest five hundred million dollars in Tsamma Ridge was made and down through the immense organization wheels began to turn.

David Mornay, project manager on the nearly completed Motleng flats canal project in Botswana, was selected to head the construction team. He had arrived in the tiny coastal town of Swakopmund with six hand-picked assistants to begin construction of the access road, develop the temporary water supply and provide living quarters for the main construction crews due to arrive six months later. Conditions were harsh. Mornay's men had to deal with labourers who spoke German or Afrikaans or both, but little English. Men who had never been subject to the strict timetables of high speed construction work were now pushed to labour 15 hour days, six days a week. Railcars were unloaded using inadequate equipment, requiring night-time use of truck headlights to illuminate the scene. In true "Catch 22" tradition, the lack of facilities could not be remedied until David's crews had installed the infrastructure on which to install the facilities.

As in all large endeavours where men and nature collide, there were casualties. Big Ben Koenig died when a D9 Bulldozer, driven by an Ovambo trainee, slammed him against a side cutting on the access road. Boet van den Berg lost his right leg and hand when a section of a blast pattern misfired, exploding unexpectedly as he tried to make it safe. Several labourers were badly injured when their truck overturned, the driver tired and unfamiliar with the road making a wrong turn.

David, driven by the knowledge that large groups of men and equipment were waiting, dependent on his crews to complete primary project targets in time, drove himself relentlessly. One evening, returning to the rented accommodation in Swakopmund that he shared with two of his crew, he fell asleep at the wheel of his pickup truck. He awoke, startled to find himself a hundred metres off the paved road with the front wheels anchored in a small sand dune. Tiredness was endemic, yet despite the gruelling pressure that all the men were under, there was time for relaxation on the weekends in the little coastal town of Swakopmund.

Rafa eased the Chieftain down onto the newly paved runway of the Tsamma Ridge airfield with a barely perceptible bump. He grinned at David, "Not as good as usual, eh, amigo. This new asphalt you've put down has raised the height just enough to throw me off." He chuckled and pulling the throttles back to full idle, stood on his brakes, slowing the aircraft as they approached the turn off to the parking area and hangar. Heat rose in waves from the asphalt, distorting the hangar of corrugated metal which seemed to shimmer and float like kelp in a sullen sea. Leaning forward of the vinyl seat to ease the damp shirt sticking to his back, David snorted in amusement,

"How come you always have a handy excuse whenever you foul up a landing. You obviously haven't heard of pride coming before a fall." He reached back to collect his briefcase. "You coming to Lamberti's party tonight?"

"No, I have another trip back to Windhoek this afternoon. I'll overnight and come back tomorrow morning." Rafa swung the aircraft around facing back towards the taxiway with a burst of power on the port engine, braked, and cut the engines. As the two engines whined down to a stop the two men gathered their papers and exited the aircraft by the rear door. While Rafa was talking to the maintenance chief David climbed into his pickup and drove out of the hangar towards Rafa. Stopping short of the two men he leant out, "I have to go into Swakop. See you tomorrow night at the Hansa?"

"Yes, tell Wessel to join us, I need some info on the best fishing places past mile 22."

David waved and accelerated away from the airfield; turning onto the gravel connector road that would take him to the main Swakopmund highway. Deep in thought as he swung onto the main paved highway he nearly did not see a man waving frantically from the verge. David braked and waited for the hitchhiker to reach his truck.

"Mr. Mornay, sorry to trouble you sir, but can I cadge a lift into Swakop? My lift is late and I have to get to town before four."

"Of course," David slid his briefcase out of the way. He did not recognise the man but with the build up of personnel to cope with the plant expansion he couldn't keep up with all the new faces.

The man climbed in and held out his hand to David, "Jim Butler, Mr. Mornay, I was hired in Jo'burg last week. I'm in Bill Mitchell's crew and he pointed you out."

"I see". David shook the proffered hand. "Well, don't believe everything Michell tells you about the desert. Billy's inclined to exaggerate. How are you settling in?" He pulled back onto the highway and settled his sunglasses comfortably on his nose with one hand.

"Fine, It took few days. I must admit it was a bit of a shock at first." He gestured at the flat rocky desert on either side of the speeding truck. "God knows, I didn't expect anything like this."

"Oh, didn't they brief you? I thought that all new people had a short orientation course."

"Yes, yes they did, but nothing can prepare you for the sheer size, the absolute starkness of it all. Its quite magnificent but bloody scary as well."

David looked at his passenger with interest. "Where are you from?" He knew the mine was recruiting worldwide.

"UK . . . London actually, I was working on the new rapid transit system when I saw the advert for technicians and decided to trade rain and cold for sunshine."

David laughed, "Well you certainly did that. What did you know about Namibia before you left home?"

His passenger shook his head ruefully. "Nothing, nada, all I knew was that it was in Africa and was hot. Still I'm jolly pleased

I came. Swakopmund is lot smaller than I expected but funnily enough I feel comfortable there."

"Yes it has a certain charm. When we first arrived to build the mine I think the people were pretty uncertain how to react. Nothing but the annual arrival of tourists from the interior of the country at Christmas had ever disturbed them. Swakopmunders were forced to face up to the prospect of several hundred permanent residents arriving on a steady basis once the initial infrastructure for the mine was in place." David chuckled at the memory. "Apart from a few minor glitches relations have worked out well. Most new arrivals either like it or hate it. Those who hate it usually leave pretty quickly."

"Yeah, I can see that could happen." Butler sat quietly for a while then asked, "I was told at the briefing that Swakopmund was originally established as a port by German colonists."

"Yes, you Brits owned Walfis Bay just 30 kilometres south of Swakopmund, and a small section of land surrounding the Bay. The British government of that time was very wary of German colonial intentions and didn't want them using Walfis. As you know from your briefing Walfis Bay is the only safe port on this stretch of the Skeleton Coast. The only other coast I know of that has as bad a reputation is around the Queen Charlottes and Northern Vancouver Island."

"Ah, so that is why they built the jetty at the bottom of Brucken strasse. I took a walk on it last night."

David grunted, "The Germans were pretty frustrated and they turned to the dry mouth of the Swakop river to establish their own port. They pushed the steel jetty you walked on, actually its a lot shorter now, several hundred yards beyond the heavy surf. Lighters bringing goods from freighters standing offshore could be loaded and unloaded."

"So when did they stop using it? I remember something at the briefing about British cruisers bombarding the town during the first World War. I wondered about that, what possible significance could a little town on the edge of the desert have?"

"Capetown is not that far away to a determined enemy and Germans are nothing if not determined. A well disciplined and fairly sizeable force could've created havoc in attacking South Africa, Bechuanaland or even Rhodesia. No, the Brits and South Africans weren't about to leave the Germans in place." David gestured to the flat plains on either side of the speeding pickup. "Imagine fighting in country like this. In those days, water was the critical element. In 1915 a large force of British and South African troops attacked from the Cape and Walfis Bay and the outnumbered Germans fell back and defended the waterholes. The Allies used water tankers." David grinned, "In those days quite a revolutionary tactic, and outflanked the German forces. The Germans surrendered in July 1915 at Otavi, that's quite a long way north of here."

"Why shell the town, if the Germans had retreated inland?"

"The Germans were still in place when they did. Actually they were after the radio mast on the edge of town and of course the jetty."

"Didn't the Germans fight?"

"Of course; there were several quite vicious engagements, one quite near here as a matter of fact, at a place called Trekkoppies. But the German command knew they were vastly outnumbered and would be annihilated if they kept on fighting so very sensibly they capitulated." David squinted out of the window at something on the side of the road. He spoke flatly, "It's not often that a military High command is in touch with reality." Something in his voice caused Butler to look at him curiously.

"Hmm, you've whetted my interest, what books would you recommend if I wanted to do a little historical research?"

"If you have some spare time go into the Swakop museum. The curator loves to give lectures on the history of Swakop and Namibia. He'll let you borrow some of his books if you're really interested."

"Thanks, I'll do that."

They sat in companionable silence; broken occasionally as David pointed out particular features that might interest Butler. Suddenly they were swinging over the railway bridge into Swakopmund. David turned down the street leading to the single quarters and dropped Butler off outside his apartment before driving to his own home, a large three bedroom bungalow.

Chapter 5

Namibia - Swakopmund

Kate stopped undressing and stared at her husband in disbelief, "But you knew at least a week ago - why didn't you tell me then?" Jack Richardson did not answer immediately, he continued towelling his hair briskly with a small towel. His back was to her and he was naked save for a large towel wrapped around his hips.

"Jack, I asked you a question . . . "

"I'm sure I told you Kate. Damn it all, what's so important about some contractor's party." He dropped the towel and ran stiffened fingers through his hair, looking around for the hair dryer that he had tossed on the bed before stepping into the shower. Jack Richardson had the slim, well-proportioned body of a gymnast, which as the silver trophies in the cabinet proved, he once had been. Watching her husband, Kate was irritated by the total absorption he was giving to the activity of the moment. Perhaps that was why he had been so successful. Top of his class at university, star gymnast in the college team, snapped up on graduation by the world's premier mining company.

At university Jack had chased her with the same single mindedness that he gave to anything he wanted. At first she had been mildly amused, then intrigued at the lengths that Jack would go to, to get her attention. Once after completing a particularly difficult routine on the pommel horse he had done a brilliant dismount, landing as if glued to the mat, then raising both hands to the rafters yelled, "For Kate." Angry and embarrassed, Kate had left the arena immediately and avoided his company for several weeks. Jack, unused to having his advances rejected and realising that he must change tactics, apologised. He toned down the flamboyant gestures that appealed to other co-eds and entered into the more serious circles that Kate moved in. Irritated, but simultaneously flattered, she began to take more notice of the Economics and Business major. Kate had several other suitors, for she was an attractive woman, but as the youngest in a loving but pragmatic family she was not overly impressed by either rank or wealth. Coming from a wealthy sugar cane dynasty in Natal, Jack found this refreshing and redoubled his efforts to capture this quiet, rather serious beauty. Eventually after a long and uneven courtship they were married.

Now anger rose in her like a tide but she fought it down successfully for she did not want to fight tonight. "If you care to remember you know it's not just a contractor's party." She shook her head cutting off the beginnings of his reply. "You know full well that Josh and Liz invited us for dinner to celebrate their wedding anniversary - only afterward were we going on to Lamberti's party."

"Look Kate, I have too many imp . . . ," he snapped at her, his face blank, then it transformed as he smiled and his eyes danced wickedly. " Believe me I did forget, husbands do that you know - come on - you can make my apologies."

"Oh no, ... no. For once you can do your own dirty work. You treat everyone and everything as subordinate to your career. Don't you care that Josh and Liz really want us there? We're their oldest friends in Swakop."

For a second Jack Richardson's face darkened, and he hunched his shoulders like a bull preparing to charge, then suppressing his anger he spoke. "Kate, I didn't plan this trip to Johannesburg with the old man. He feels it is important that I'm in on this meeting. The project budgets for all of ConAmGeo's Southern African operations will be discussed and Tsamma cannot afford to be absent. I was going to send Dickie Crawford but Mr. Butchert wanted me to go personally."

"Oh . . . so you didn't forget the dinner then, did you? If you were going to send Dickie in your place you must have had a reason, and my guess is that you intended to come to the dinner until Butchert twisted your arm." Kate glared at her husband her grey green eyes bright with anger and frustration. "I've cancelled far too many invitations this year because of your ridiculous schedules. For once you could've stood up to Butchert, especially on something this important. " She took a deep breath, exhaling slowly. "I thought we agreed to come here because it would give us more time together . . . at least that's what you said when I argued against moving from Jo'burg . . . Now I see even less of you. Do you realize that you have been home for a grand total of four days in the last five weeks?"

Flushed, Jack snapped back at his wife. "Not all of us have the luxury of a nine to five job, dammit. You seem to forget that for both of us this is a wonderful opportunity and sometimes sacrifices have to be made. And in any case you have a full time career, it's not as if you were stuck at home all the time."

Kate shook her head resignedly, "It doesn't matter what I say, does it Jack? If it were only so simple, but you keep making promises that you have no intention of keeping and laugh it off when I get angry." She unsnapped her bra and pushed down her panties, kicking them aside as she made for the shower vacated by her husband.

Jack watched his wife's lovely naked body, the high breasts swinging, step behind the opaque glass and felt a sudden surge of desire. Half tempted, he untied the towel around his waist and was reaching for the shower door when the bedroom phone tinkled. Naked he hesitated, undecided, then with a grunt strode across the room to pick up the telephone. "Richardson . . . when? . . . yes of course I understand, I'll get on to it right away. It will be on your desk by eight tomorrow morning. . . . No, no that's quite all right, I don't mind at all . . . quite sure . . . goodnight." He put down the phone and reached for his dressing gown calling to Kate over the hiss of the shower. "Don't wait up for me Kate. The GM has just phoned and wants to see our preliminary figures for Jo'burg first thing tomorrow. I'll go into the study and do some work on the computer. It shouldn't take that long."

Chapter 6

Swakopmund - The Party

David Mornay stood with his back to the wall, a nearly empty whisky glass cupped in his hands. He liked Lamberti. The rumble of conversation was punctuated with laughter and the clink of glasses suggesting that the Italian contractor's party was going well. Hans, the owner of the hotel, paused briefly to ask if he were enjoying himself. Satisfied that David needed no attention, he moved off like a sea-polished seal among the guests. Carvel was saying something and he caught the last few words. " . . . very difficult time."

"I'm sorry, what were you saying?"

"It must have been very difficult in the beginning, your initial construction team did one hell of a job." Carvel was the technical representative of a major Swiss paint firm, and was forever trying to get David to purchase special desert condition paints. David felt a slight ripple of irritation at the obvious flattery, and took a mouthful of whisky before replying.

"Thank you, I had a good team." He spotted little Bill Mitchell, the white hair and whiter mustache a spotlight among the dark suits and vivid dresses. Bill was talking to Ray Cline, the Accounts Manager of Lokpipe and, seeing an escape, David smiled at Carvel, "Excuse me, I think I'm wanted." He began pushing through the press of bodies, holding up the nearly empty glass. Bill Mitchell saw David coming and as the big Canadian popped like a cork into their little circle he murmured *sotto voce* to Cline. "Watch out Ray, old King Kong here will tear your head from your shoulders if your pipe crews fall behind." Cline choked on his drink and spluttered, wheezing in delight. "Say there, Tarzan," Mitchell went on, "why in the hell didn't you finish Waldron off when you had the chance?"

David frowned, the incident of a week ago was still fresh in his mind, and he was not ready to be reminded either of young

Ivan Kretchmer's death or his own lack of control.

Bill Mitchell, one of the six men hand-picked to accompany David as part of the initial construction team, was a Canadian like himself. They had met in Botswana on the Motleng Flats project and a solid friendship had developed. Mitchell was built like a jockey, his seamed brown face a mass of crinkled skin surrounding two of the palest blue eyes possible. He was at least 60 years old, but with the energy and drive of a man half his age. David had watched Mitchell, stripped to the waist, a hard hat with a kerchief tucked in behind to protect his neck, working in the searing heat. He had watched him supervising the installation of galvanised pipe up the wicked grades of a cactus canyon, driving the Ovambo and Damara labourers to greater efforts. Locals called the canyon 'the Devil's Slot.' The men called Mitchell 'Baas Klein Billy' and despite the difference in size, would never dream of arguing with him. He had, in the days when language meant what it said, 'presence', a term now misused to describe TV anchormen and movie stars. Like David, he was single, a failed marriage driving him away from his home in Johannesburg to nurse a wound he never discussed.

Mitchell ignored the frown, "He's making trouble for you Davy, I hear that the old man is hearing a very one-sided version of what happened." Despite his age, Bill was constantly squiring young typists from the pool, and as a result he kept up to date on all the Company scandal.

David flicked his hand irritably, "It's over. How are you Ray?" Cline had recovered sufficiently to answer and he cleared his throat, "Bill's right you know, Waldron is one of the new Head Office types. He won't forgive or forget and if I were you I'd watch my back."

"Gentlemen, your concern is touching. Where can I get a fresh drink, since all that the two of you are good for is gratuitous advice?"

Ray pointed behind David. "Over there, where the light's above the alcove." David turned and heard a gasp as liquid splashed over his hand. A woman in a white evening dress stood frozen, the martini glass tilted in her hand. He must have jogged her elbow and to save her dress she had swung the glass away, splashing liquid over his hand and sleeve.

"I'm terribly sorry." He reached for a handkerchief, "did any spill on your dress?"

"No, I think it's all right, thank you." Recognition flooded her face. "You're Mr. Morning."

"Mornay." He corrected, "David Mornay." She dipped her head, "Kate Richardson, I'm pleased to meet you formally. Our last encounter was a trifle rushed."

David frowned slightly in puzzlement, "We've not met before, have we?"

"A week ago in the Admin block. You were in quite a hurry."

"Oh hell! Of course. You were the woman I knocked over going into . . . " He shook his head. "I do apologize and now I seem to have done it again."

"Please don't, your large companion with the beard explained. It was obvious that you were terribly upset." David could not think of a suitable reply and sensing his awkwardness she handed him the martini glass. "Perhaps by way of restitution you would replenish my drink?" Grateful for her tact, he smiled. "Of course, I won't be a minute, excuse me." and pushing through the crowd he made for the bar. Music was starting and couples were drifting to the dance floor in the next room. He collected the drinks and while walking back through the thinning crowd he studied her. She was talking to Billy Mitchell and Ray Cline. He saw the slow smile at something Ray had said and noted, with a start, how lovely she was. She had an understated beauty only a few women possess, just as a Rolls would always be the best and as an Arabian would outshine any other breed. It was an indefinable quality that raised her above the anorexic models that passed for beauties in today's world. He guessed her age at somewhere between thirty and thirty-five years old. The honey blond hair fell softly to her shoulders. She was wearing a white dress cut simply in classical style and held over one shoulder with a golden brooch in the shape of a tortoise. The other tanned shoulder was bare and for a moment he thought of classical Rome and how the Patrician ladies must have looked. David saw the gleam of a diamond as she moved her hand to illustrate something said and felt a flash of disappointment at the fact that she was married, then wry surprise at feeling any emotion at all. His own marriage had been a disaster; a brief period in his life that he preferred to forget.

He had met Jill at a party in his final year at university. Learning that he had served in Vietnam, she began to lecture him on all the wrongs of American foreign policy. Intrigued by her obvious lack of subject knowledge, but, despite his irritation, drawn by her passionate conviction and stunning 'California girl' beauty, David invited her out. Though it was his final year and his workload heavy, he managed to see Jill frequently. Determined to politically re-educate David, Jill dragged him to all the left-wing and radical meetings on campus. They would argue late into the night, then weary of argument fall into bed and make passionate love.

They married the week David graduated and almost immediately, he was offered a position as junior engineer on a small gold mine in Alaska. From the start Jill hated the remote location, the spartan living conditions and the lack of entertainment. David, on the other hand, revelled in the stark beauty of their surroundings and found that despite the long hours, he enjoyed the work. The strain of their relationship began to affect David, and then the dreams started. Suddenly in the early hours he would wake drenched in sweat, screaming at the demons of his war. Frightened, and unable to help or come to terms with the change in her husband, Jill found excuses to visit her parents in Los Angeles with increasing frequency.

At first David did not mind the short absences, but with every visit, Jill stayed away longer until eventually she phoned to advise David that she would not return to him or Alaska. Catching the next available flight, David was met on arrival in Los Angeles by his father-in-law. Jill's father, a retired bank manager, was very fond of David and knowing his daughter, had sadly predicted an early end to the marriage. The old man steered David into a quiet area of the airport and gently advised him that, as far as Jill was concerned, the marriage was over. For several days David tried to talk to Jill, but apart from a brief meeting monitored by her lawyer, in which she reiterated her desire to end the marriage, he never saw her again.

From that day on, his work in remote areas of the globe and his fear of close attachments after the humiliating disaster of his marriage had combined to keep him single. Once, several years later, a girl had lived with him for a year, but he had felt no deep sense of loss when finally in tears she had left, calling him an "emotional cripple".

Now, as he negotiated his way back to the little party gathered in the alcove, he was startled by the anticipation he felt after such a casual meeting. Billy grinned as he arrived with the drinks. "I was telling Doctor Richardson that you've never been known to beat up ladies and that she's really quite safe."

"Knock it off Bill." He handed her the martini. "Doctor Richardson?"

"Yes Mr. Mornay, I'm a chemist."

"Oh I see, that explains the white coat you were wearing last week." He took a sip of his drink and looking down at the lovely face, felt a sudden surge of pleasure in her company.

At that moment Billy grabbed Ray Cline by the elbow and pointed across the room with his empty glass. "There he is now. Come on Ray, let's speak to him before he disappears. Please excuse us Doctor. Dave, I'll see you tomorrow." With a cheery grin Bill dragged Ray off in the direction he had been pointing.

Kate turned to David. "Goodness, what was that all about?"

"Billy and Ray have been negotiating for a long time with the man who has just come in; he owns a vintage car that they have set their hearts on owning. Apparently, they are having some trouble convincing the owner to sell and even our company is not enough to keep them from having another try." The music slowed in tempo as the band switched to a waltz and Kate half turned to watch the dancers swirling by them. Startled by a slight hollowness in his chest, David asked, "Would you care to dance?"

"I would love to . . . it has been ages since I last danced." They placed their drinks on a small table and walked to the dance floor. Feeling surprisingly awkward, David took her in his arms. He was a better than average dancer but he usually preferred sitting with the men around the bar. Small talk on the dance floor made him uncomfortable, so he avoided it. Yet now, as she moved smoothly to the music, he found himself relaxing. Her head was level with his chin and looking down on her face he was conscious of the soft curve of her breasts beneath the low cut top.

"Mr. Mitchell was telling me . . . The smoky grey-green eyes scanned his face and noticed his sudden flush; like a small boy caught out. She smiled inwardly to herself, yet she was flattered . . . that you were the first men to begin work on the mine."

"That's not strictly true, the exploration crews were here first, and if you drive out past the tailing's pond you can see the remains of their camp."

"How many of your original team are still here, Mr. Mornay?"

"David, please call me David. At our peak there were about ten expatriates, men from outside Namibia. We're down to four now, and apart from Bill Mitchell and myself, the others will be absorbed by Tsamma Uranium."

"And where will you go, when your work here is complete?"

"I really don't know, I've got another six months here and then . . . " He shrugged, "I guess back to head office in Johannesburg until they decide where to send me next."

"Mr. Mitch . . . Bill was saying neither of you have family, it must be a very lonely life."

"Like a sailor one gets used to it." He turned her quickly to avoid a couple demonstrating their need to monopolize the dance floor, "I see that you're married. Does your husband also work for Tsamma?"

"Yes, but on the financial side. He's the Chief Accountant."

"Jack Richardson? Black hair, slim, always in a suit and tie?"

"I see you know my husband. I'd say that is a good description."

"I don't know him well. I've met him a few times at various budget meetings. Seems very good at his job." David looked at her. "Do you have any children?" For a second her eyes seemed to cloud over.

"No, Jack felt . . . we've been too wrapped up in our careers I suppose." And switching the conversation, she continued. "Bill tells me he's going back to Canada on a visit next month. Have you been back recently?"

He looked into her eyes and again felt the sudden hollowness under his ribs. "Damn it all," he told himself, "stop behaving like a schoolboy."

"No, not since the . . . at least not for 12 years or so. I only have a brother but we're not particularly close . . . we correspond intermittently." Now why had he told her all that? Again David was surprised to note how awkward he felt.

Her eyes widened. "Really, that's an awfully long time. Do you ever intend to return?"

Now it was his turn to change the subject. He altered step smoothly as the band changed to a slow foxtrot. "What made you become a chemist?"

"Oh, a natural inclination I suppose, chemistry was the one subject I could rely on to improve my generally poor marks and then I seemed to get in deeper and deeper - I enjoy it."

David nodded and they moved around the dance floor in companionable silence. He pulled her closer and rested his cheek against her golden hair. She fitted comfortably into the curve of his chest and for a few minutes nothing, not even the admiring glances of the other dancers, intruded into their private world. Pushing him back gently Kate broke the spell.

"Sometimes, when listening to music, one forgets everything else, don't you agree?"

"You mean like now?" He smiled at her. "I think the company has something to do with it as well." She coloured slightly, but before she could reply he continued. "Your accent intrigues me, it's not South African, but it's not English either. Where are your roots?"

She studied his face for a long moment. "I was born in Kenya. My parents were farmers in the Highlands and some years after Kenya got its independence my father moved the family to South Africa."

David raised his eyebrows. "I've heard it's a beautiful country. But I was under the impression that many whites stayed on after independence. Was your father worried about a black government?"

"No, he always felt that independence was inevitable, especially after the Mau Mau rebellion. In fact he helped some of the new politicians with money and advice."

"Then what made him move?"

"His farm was expropriated. It was one of the better ones you see . . . a man that he had counted as a friend decided that it should be broken up into small units for peasant farmers." Looking down at the grey-green eyes, suddenly bright with old pain, David cursed himself for probing what was obviously an unhealed wound. He fumbled for something comforting to say.

"It must be very tough to leave something like a farm. I suppose, though, that politicians have sometimes to honour the promises made before an election."

"Yes, I'm sure you're right, and I think that if the peasants had received the land it would have been easier for dad to accept. As it was . . . "

David nodded grimly, understanding at last. "The friend has the farm, I should have guessed. I'm so sorry. I didn't mean to open old wounds."

She squeezed his arm gently. "Don't be silly. It was an obvious question and you're not the first to have commented on it. Dad always hoped that Rodean would remove the South African overlay."

"Rodean?"

"A private girls' school in Johannesburg. It's a sister school to the one in Britain."

David decided not to pursue the topic, his knowledge of girls' schools being nonexistent.

The music ended and he reluctantly let her go. People were moving off the floor, someone had dimmed the lights, leaving only the small side lights to provide illumination along the walls.

"Where are you sitting? I've not seen your husband this evening."

"I came with Josh and Liz Wright. Jack is away in Johannesburg on business . . . there they are, near the band." He led her over to the table where five other couples sat in animated conversation. He thanked her, spent a few minutes in conversation with Josh, then left, striding rapidly to the bar. He needed a drink, and badly. Later, he saw her dancing with Josh Wright and, catching his eye, she smiled; he lifted his glass in return. She must have left fairly early because he did not see her again, and shortly before midnight he left the hotel and walked slowly down Brucken Strasse to the jetty. He needed the cold night air to clear his head.

Chapter 7

Canada - Talbot's car

"Have you read this . . . have you? Damn it all Judith, this time he has gone too far. What the hell did he think he was playing at?"

Nigel Mornay stood with his back to the huge picture windows in the main lounge. The late afternoon sun, filtering through semi-transparent curtains, surrounded his head with a pale halo while shading his face from his wife's gaze. He shook the piece of paper in his hand at his wife and his voice grated with anger.

"Apart from the damage to the other vehicles, we are extremely lucky that no one was killed. Don't you realize how close it was?"

Judith Mornay faced her husband, her head thrown back in order to look at the shaded mask of his face. She was a small, fine boned woman and her husband towered over her by a good foot. From the moment Nigel had received the letter, she had braced herself for an argument.

"Nigel, he's only fifteen, and boys at fifteen want to drive."

"Judith just in case you have forgotten, it's illegal to drive before sixteen years old. In any case what was he doing out at midnight during the week and what the hell was he doing with beer in the car?"

Her face flushed with anger, Judith snapped back. "Don't ask me to control Colin's movements when you're never here. All his friends meet in the evenings. How can you expect him to stay at home, especially when his father is jetting around the world."

"I told him to be in by eight . . . now you tell me that he has been ignoring the curfew."

"Nigel. I'm getting a little tired of this conversation. You give Colin an instruction then disappear to Europe or Asia and expect me to enforce it. Frankly I think eight is far too early for

Colin . . . but if you want him in at eight then I suggest you spend more time at home."

Nigel Mornay lifted both hands shoulder high. "OK . . . OK, let's both calm down. We will solve nothing by shouting at each other."

While his parents argued, Colin stood in the hallway, running his hand absentmindedly over the antique telephone on its marble stand. He could hear his parents' voices but not the words, the heavy wooden door to his father's study muffling them. He had never heard his father this angry before, and suspected that this time his mother wouldn't be able to placate him. He looked around the exquisitely furnished hall and through the curved archway into the living room, an eclectic mixture of modern and antique furniture giving the room a timeless elegance that only great wealth could afford.

Colin Vincent Mornay, 15 years old, descended from the early British settlers that landed on this lovely island off the West Coast of Canada. His great-grandfather, a shipping clerk, arriving in the capital, Victoria, with the first Klondike miners on their way to the fabulous Yukon, decided to forsake the dubious wealth of the frozen North for the real gold the miners spent on fitting out their often ill-fated expeditions. Like many early merchants in this bustling seaport, great-grandfather shrewdly built a fortune. He laid the foundations for the family empire that now encompassed large timber, mining and fishing interests, and was rapidly diversifying into commercial real estate.

His son, Colin's grandfather, then consolidated the original fortune, adding steadily to it. A surprisingly avaricious man for one who had so much wealth, he raised his two sons, Nigel and David, with a rod of iron. David, the elder by five years, bore the brunt of his father's bullying, for inexplicably, the old man disliked his firstborn and favoured the younger son. While the two boys bore a strong physical resemblance, in nature and personality they could hardly have been less alike. David, reserved and careful, a "watcher" someone had called him, could sit motionless for hours while observing with fascination the stealthy activity of bird and insect life in the woods surrounding their summer cottage. Nigel, on the other hand, was full of explosive energy and dominated his peer group through the force of his aggressive personality. The difference in their ages and personalities meant that while the boys did not dislike each other, they had so little in common that they spent very little time together.

Finally David rebelled against the constant harshness of his father's rule. Still a teenager, he quietly slipped away one night to sign on as a deck hand on a freighter out of Seattle that was shipping war material to a little known country called Vietnam.

David, was tall and muscular with cool, direct, grey eyes. He could pass for a youth older by several years. In contrast to his bombastic, aggressive father, he was quiet spoken, keeping his opinions to himself. The shipping company, desperate for crew in a booming economy, did not look closely at the smudged birth date on his passport. It was 1966, and despite the old man's wealth and efforts, David disappeared into the confusion of the times. Arriving in the sprawling port city of Da Nang in Vietnam only two days passed his sixteenth birthday, he was impressed by the build up of American arms and men.

Late one evening, on his way back to the ship, David became detached from his fellow crewmen and ended up lost in the old area of the city. Rounding a corner into a dingy side street, he was attacked from behind by a group of thugs. David's size and strength could not prevent him from being driven to his knees by the sheer weight of numbers. He was desperately trying to protect his head from a rain of blows when a roar of anger erupted from a side door and a burly marine sergeant, swinging a wicked length of chain around his head, charged to David's rescue. The gang, startled by this sudden interruption, paused, then unable in the murky light to discern the numbers ranged against them, broke and ran. Without pausing the sergeant lifted David to his feet and half-carried, half-dragged him down the length of the alley to where it joined the main street and the safety of bright lights and people.

Propping David against a wall, the sergeant began to berate him for his stupidity in wandering in an obviously dangerous area. Pausing suddenly, the marine took a good look at the man he had just rescued and with an oath asked David his age. David mumbled through split lips that he was just sixteen. The sergeant shook his head in disbelief and then, taking a firm grip on the boy's arm, led him to a washroom in a quiet restaurant where he helped David clean himself up. Later, walking the boy back to his ship, he dug enough meagre information out of David to form an impression of a desperately lonely and unhappy youth. The sergeant, sent to Da Nang from his up country base to locate missing equipment, made a point in the days following the attack to spend as much time with David as their respective jobs allowed. In the evenings he took the boy under his wing and taught David how to identify dangerous areas and situations and how to be unobtrusive but aware always of his surroundings. By the time David's ship was ready to return, a strong friendship had developed between these two, wholly dissimilar, men.

On his return to Seattle, David sought out the Marine recruiting office and, using his mentor's name as a password, was accepted for training. As more than a few Canadian citizens looking for adventure were joining the American crusade against Vietnam, David was recruited without comment.

After training he returned to Vietnam with a Combat Engineering unit and served three tours of duty in the grim years between 1966 and 1969. Wounded twice in his second tour, seriously wounded at the end of his third, he survived. The war marked him as it marked all those who served in that sad and bitter land, but from the youngest it extracted a special price. The thunder of Mars denied him the golden days of youth; the hopes, fears, laughter and dreams of being a teenager. Going from boyhood to manhood in that bloody conflict where both sides often forgot their humanity, he survived. However, in order to survive and remain sane, he grew hard and old beyond his years.

During this period his mother died. She had been failing for a long time and her husband's meanness and blighted spirit, added to her sorrow over David's disappearance finally caused her to relinquish her tenuous hold on life. She was a gentle woman, too gentle for the rust in her husband's soul. Yet, in his strange way his father was desolate, and irrationally held David responsible for his mother's death.

Coming home, David was met, not as a prodigal, but as an assassin. In a savage argument that precipitated his final break with family, he told the old man that. "Braver, better men than you died in the mud of Asia to keep your money safe. Use the money that you're so fond of to bring back the dead." Stalking coldly out into the night, he caught the first ferry to Vancouver and three days later registered in the Engineering faculty of the University of Southern California under the GI bill of rights.

Embittered by his eldest son's rejection, old man Mornay turned his formidable talents loose on Nigel to ensure that the younger boy would be capable of running an empire that was growing daily. Nigel proved to be an apt pupil. A propensity for work and a desire to please his father drove him to succeed. At twenty-four, a graduate of Harvard and McGill, he began to take over the reins from his ailing father. The old man, at seventy, failing from a variety of ailments brought on by overwork and self neglect, sullenly surrendered power to this tough capable youngster he had sired and shaped. Growing up in an all male household after his mother's death, then spending several years at an exclusive boys' school, Nigel had little experience of girls, and his affairs with members of the opposite sex at University were generally unsatisfactory, causing him to concentrate almost exclusively on his career.

Nigel met Judith deVere Houston at a bankers' convention in Palm Springs. A pale pretty young woman, wealthy in her own right, she determinedly set her sights on this attractive husky

Canadian. Subtly pursued by this volatile beauty, he fell totally under her spell.

Six months later they were married in a society wedding Victoria would long remember as the most lavish ever seen. The reception at the fabled Empress Hotel was attended by all the movers and shakers of British Columbia. Glitterati and business associates from all over North America flew in to pay due homage to the scion of the Mornay empire.

The first year was happy for them both. They honeymooned in Greece, skied in St. Moritz, explored old castles in England, revelling like puppies in each other's company. But an Empire must have an Emperor, and in Nigel the grooves of duty were deeply cut. He came back to find crises in several areas and flung himself into the fray with a determination that frequently kept him late at the office.

Unaccustomed to being denied her wants, Judith sulked, and then to her dismay found that she was pregnant. Nigel was delighted. He brought a live-in nurse to attend his wife, responding to her tears and recriminations with vague promises to spend more time at home when the workload eased. As her time drew near, Judith became increasingly shrill, caused in no small part by her fear of the pain she imagined awaited her on the delivery of her child. Beleaguered by his wife at home and by financial problems in one of his international divisions, Nigel spent even more time away from home. In due time, Colin Vincent Mornay was delivered, a beautiful, healthy boy, who was indulged from the moment of his birth. In revenge for Nigel's benign neglect, Judith refused to allow Nigel to discipline the child and as he grew older, Colin found it was a simple matter to play his parents off against each other. Nigel and Judith had drifted apart, he to his work, she to her social life. Judith had a brief passionate love affair with a doctor friend and had seriously contemplated leaving Nigel, but caution and the fear of losing Colin held her back. Her lover, dismayed at her hesitation tried to force the issue, but Judith, like a sleeper waking from a dream, escaped on a long cruise with friends. By the time she returned, the affair had cooled sufficiently for her to realize how unwise she had been. Nigel indulged in brief momentary affairs while on overseas trips but neither found the state of the marriage sufficiently unpleasant to initiate a permanent break.

In the few times a week he set aside for his family, Nigel tried to repair the breach. He found his son unpleasantly selfish and mean spirited and confided to an old friend that he was at loss to fathom the boy. Conversely, Judith would not hear a word against Colin, even when requested to remove him from Glenlyon School for his "irresponsible activities," as the headmaster judiciously put it. A detailed report on the reasons for this was sent to Nigel. Reading it carefully, he reluctantly had to accept that the boy was close to being totally out of control.

Waiting now in the hallway, Colin glanced over a group of family pictures in silver frames mounted in a neat group on the wall. His gaze stopped on an old photograph of his uncle. The picture, the only one of David in the house, had been purchased by Nigel from a news magazine doing a pictorial documentary on the Vietnam conflict. The picture showed a tired and drawn David in filthy combat fatigues being decorated by an officer in an immaculate uniform. Behind the two men, helicopters were unloading casualties while others were lifting off in swirls of red dust. Colin wondered idly about his uncle and the split that had caused him to leave Canada. He knew that David had been a soldier in the American army and that neither of his parents was inclined to discuss the shadowy figure. Occasionally, Colin managed to get his mother talking about his uncle, a man she had met only once, but one she instinctively disliked for having fought, in what she considered an unjustified war. His mother, as Colin discovered early, disliked any form of violence. Judith was one of those individuals, who through circumstance and wealth, are shielded from the ugly realities of modern politics and simply shut their minds to what they don't want to know. Despite this lack of information on his uncle, or perhaps because of it, Colin built up a picture of a grim, grey mercenary, a man without scruples or compassion. Staring at the picture he tried to image what could cause a man to leave a comfortable existence for the obvious discomforts of military life. Perhaps his mother was right, his uncle must be an idiot. Shrugging, he dismissed the photograph, folded his arms, and leant back against the wall.

Colin was a carbon copy of his father. Well built, not handsome but with a strong face and pale eyes, he could have stood as an advertisement for the "all-Canadian" youth. He was intelligent, his grades, when he exerted himself, rising into the high A's. Lately, he had begun to miss classes, driving Brian Talbot's car around Oak Bay despite being a year under the legal driving age. He had also begun to experiment with marijuana and had several plants growing under the bench in the potting shed.

Despite the lack of discipline at home, and his mother's indulgence of his often rebellious behaviour, Colin had a natural ability in mathematics and science which he, unlike most of his peer group, enjoyed. At the exclusive University school he now attended, this gift had saved him from another expulsion. The math teacher, recognizing his ability, had made a determined effort to help the arrogant, undisciplined boy. When Colin's behaviour alienated all his tutors, it was his math teacher who spoke up for him. Now his absences from classes and his sulky refusal to explain his behaviour had brought even this advocate to the point of abandoning him.

"Colin!" his father's call snapped his mind out of its reverie.

"What!"

"Come in here."

Here was his father's study, a panelled room in rich dark wood, lightened by several arresting paintings depicting the various facets of Mornay Industries. His father's desk had been imported from Italy at the turn of the century. The legs in hand-carved mahogany supporting a mahogany top inlaid with ivory and covered in ostrich skin. As a child he had often stood on one of the curved feet, his cheek pressed to the cold, polished smoothness of the wood. Now as he entered, he saw his mother, her back to him, staring out of the window into the garden beyond. His father spoke.

"Close the door."

He complied, turning to face his father, truculence obvious on his face.

"Colin, did you know that the estimate for all the work on young Talbot's car and the two others you damaged is three thousand dollars?"

The boy, his head up, stared over his father's shoulders and did not reply.

"Answer me . . . "

"Yes, Mother told me before you came home."

"Very well, your mother and I have decided . . . "

"Leave me out of this Nigel, it is your decision." His mother turned to face them. Stopped by the interjection, his father took a deep breath and continued.

"I have decided that as you have been totally irresponsible you are grounded until further notice. I will have to pay for the damages but you are losing your summer allowance . . . No wait a moment." He raised a hand as Colin, stunned, was about to protest. "There will be no argument do you understand?"

Judith gasped, "Nigel, that is grossly unfair. Colin's accident could have happened to anyone."

"It didn't though did it? Neither of you apparently realise how fortunate it was that the accident happened on the new subdivision that Talbot is financing. Had Talbot not managed to placate the other two vehicle owners and had the police been called, Colin could have been in serious trouble. The story I hear is that our son was falling down drunk . . . is that true?"

Colin stared at the carpet but did not answer.

Nigel looked at his son, despair in his voice, "What the hell's wrong with you boy? It's not as if you're stupid. Cresswell tells me your grasp of maths and science is well above average, but you refuse to apply yourself."

Colin turned to his mother, his voice thick, "I've put my summer allowance down on a motorcycle. I can't change it. It's a deal . . . an agreement."

"I see," his father's face was cold, "you have committed money that you don't have yet."

Anger flared in Colin's eyes, but he didn't look at his father. "What else can I do?"

His mother interjected. "Nigel, stop this. Colin didn't deliberately crash Talbot's car, and it's natural for a boy of his age to want a motorcycle."

The protest went unheeded. "Colin, let me be clear, you are going to pay for the damage you caused. Perhaps this time you will understand that stupid behaviour has penalties."

Colin stared at the floor, his voice tight, "I have an agreement. I can't break it."

Nigel Mornay looked at his son with anger. "You will break it . . . " he paused, searching for the right words, then enunciated with exaggerated clarity. "As you have shown no sense of responsibility towards other peoples' property, it is unlikely that you will be any more responsible on a motorcycle. So . . . until I am satisfied that your schoolwork has shown a drastic improvement, you will not be allowed to purchase the motorcycle. Furthermore, you will be home by eight o'clock every evening. Is that understood?"

Sullen-faced, Colin nodded. He knew that to argue now would be futile. Later, when the dust had settled and his father was preoccupied at the office, he would work on his mother. Just at that moment, Maria knocked on the door, "Mr. Mornay, I am sorry, but there is a telephone call from Mr. Ross at the office, and he says it's urgent."

With a grunt, Nigel walked to the door. He paused, his hand on the brass knob, then shaking his head he walked into the hall.

Namibia - Swakopmund

Kate Richardson splashed cold water on her face. Reaching for the towel she found that her hands were still shaking. Her anger had subsided but now she felt slightly nauseous. Damn him, why did she let him do this to her? She went over the argument in her mind trying to analyse it's root causes and failing, knowing that her usual cool objectivity was overridden with a complex swirl of emotions. Once again Jack was going to get his own way. So, no trip to Europe as planned. A trip promised and looked forward to with all the simple enthusiasm of a child. As far back as she could remember Florence had been the one city she longed to visit. Damn him. Damn him. He was becoming totally obsessed with his work; nothing else seemed to matter anymore. She felt the anger rising again and firmly pushed it down, her mouth pulling into a hard line. No, she was not going to give him the satisfaction of seeing how much she was upset. Rubbing her face with the towel she admitted to herself that Jack would probably have hated the trip, but why promise? Did he really think that she believed the silly rumour of another woman at head office? And was the trip to Florence meant to placate her? Jilly Turner had been so quick to give her the bad news which later turned out to be wrong. Jack had been in Capetown when he was supposed to have been seen with a woman in Johannesburg. Kate knew Jack had no interest in anything not connected to his career and an extramarital affair would most certainly affect his prospects.

Staring into the mirror, she wondered if they were two unsuitable people locked into a marriage of convenience. Her mind drifted to Lamberti's party and dancing with David Mornay. The construction boss had moved with polished grace for such a big man but what had taken her by surprise was the quiet intelligence and sense of latent power behind the grey eyes. She smiled at her reflection and scolded herself, now she . . .

Jack called from the living room, "Kate, do you want a drink?

I'm making myself one."

Kate hesitated a second. Well . . . if he wanted to offer the olive branch . . . Oh, to hell with it, arguing was not going to change the outcome. She sighed, throwing the towel into the washing basket. "Please, a glass of white wine; there's a half bottle in the fridge."

Chapter 8

Canada - Drugs

Miss Burgess waited for a brief second, then depressed the intercom switch.

"Mr. Mornay."

"Yes Sybil, what is it?"

"Mrs. Mornay is on the line sir."

"Oh hell! I can't stop now. Would you tell her that I'll call back in 10 minutes?"

"Mrs. Mornay is very upset. She is insisting on speaking to you immediately."

"Upset? Very well, put her through."

Miss Burgess, a tall, plain, angular woman, her greying hair drawn back in a tight swirl and held in place with implacable firmness by a large tortoiseshell clip, spoke softly,

"I have located Mr. Mornay and I am putting you through. Please hold."

Sybil Burgess was of that indeterminate age at which certain women, having had neither sparkle nor beauty, eventually arrive. They become resigned to their condition and remain totally convinced that marriage would have been for them, a most unhappy state. Visitors to this luxurious office complex, perched on the top floor of downtown Victoria's highest building, were often startled by the cold severity of her gaze. Once inside the sanctum of Nigel's office they might raise questioning eyebrows. Smiling faintly, Nigel would explain that Ms. Burgess was efficient and then he would turn smoothly to other matters. What Nigel neglected to add was that Sybil Burgess was worth twice the very considerable salary that he paid her; she forgot nothing and could recall in an instant the main points of a discussion or comment of two or three years before. She was totally incorruptible and would state, when Nigel asked, her opinion of a subject or person without equivocation. Her judgements were based on lucid and dispassionate assessments and he relied heavily on her skills. In the upper echelons of Mornay industries, Nigel found that some of his senior executives considered a shapely secretary an extra to the many generous perks he had introduced since the old man died; and were chagrined to find that they were mistaken. Above all, Nigel valued efficiency. Finding one memorable day that a snap request was beyond the capabilities of a plastic blonde gracing the reception desk of the VP (Timber), he suggested acidly at the next weekly meeting that if looks were preferred to efficiency, then perhaps he should apply the same criteria to his next promotion list. The hint was taken and, as an unexpected bonus, Nigel found himself very popular with the wives of his senior staff. Now, as Sybil Burgess connected Nigel to his wife a small frown creased her forehead, for Judith Mornay rarely phoned.

"Nigel!"

"Yes Judith, what's the matter?"

"Nigel," her voice was pitched high, "please come home at once. Colin . . ." Here, her voice broke and he could hear her weeping and trying to regain control.

A cold chill touched him and his fingers tightened on the telephone. "Judith, what about Colin? . . . Judith, answer me."

"I'm sorry Nigel," She took a deep breath. "Colin is in trouble, will you please come home? I need you to deal with this."

"What sort of trouble? What has he done this time? .. Judith can't this wait until tonight? I'm very busy."

"Nigel, the police are here. I . . . " She began weeping again. Aghast, Nigel stared unseeing at the group of Japanese developers who were examining a large plan on the boardroom table.

"Police! What the hell has he done this time? Judith, I'll be there as soon as I can get clear, say . . . fifteen to twenty minutes." He pushed an amber light on his desk.

"Sybil, have my car brought round right away. Gentlemen," he turned to the group now studying the model of the Harbour development, "I'm afraid I must leave on urgent family business

. . . Would you please excuse me?" He smiled distractedly. "My executive director has arranged lunch and perhaps we can meet later today if that is convenient?" With a rumble of assent, the Japanese began to file out of his office.

"I don't believe it. " Nigel stared through the widow at the gates where the police car had departed ten minutes earlier. Shaking his head he turned to his son. "After your last escapade with Talbot's car I thought you'd learnt your lesson. Now I find that you've been selling marijuana on the street to raise money for a motor cycle?"

Colin did not raise his head. Still frightened from the circumstances of his arrest on a downtown street earlier in the day he wanted nothing more than for this disastrous day to be over. His father had grilled him remorselessly after the policeman had left and revelation after revelation had left both parents speechless with shock.

"And those two unsavoury characters with you, do you honestly think that they wanted nothing more than the pleasure of your company? You stupid little idiot. Don't you understand anything? Haven't you ever heard of blackmail?" Nigel paced the floor seething with anger. Judith sat red-eyed and silent on the elegant sofa. For once she knew that Colin had gone too far and that Nigel's anger was justified.

"Go to your room and stay there. I want to talk to your mother. Go on - get out of my sight." Colin walked stiffly from the room and Nigel waited until the door closed before turning to his wife. "Colin is going to have to leave town until we can sort this mess out. I'm very concerned that this time Colin is in way over his head."

"But why? The policeman said they would not press charges."

"You heard Colin. He has been growing pot in the old greenhouse on this property in fairly large quantities. Fortunately the police don't know that, as they assumed the little that Colin had in his possession today was his whole supply. For God's sake Judith, think . . . growing marijuana for the purposes of trafficking is a serious criminal offense. Colin could be sent to Juvenile prison for a long time. And what about the two men arrested with Colin? Both have long criminal records and what if they had some form of blackmail or worse in mind."

For a while Judith did not answer. She was not a stupid woman and the logic of her husband's argument was not lost on her. "Where would we send him?" she asked. Nigel exhaled, recognizing that a note of resignation had crept into his wife's voice. Unconsciously he had been holding his breath and gripping the arm of the chair. "What about your parents in Vermont? It's almost vacation time and I'm sure Cresswell will allow him to leave school a few days early."

"Nigel, why do you never listen to what I tell you? My parents left on a Far Eastern tour a month ago."

"Oh yes that's right, sorry, I had forgotten . . . what about your sister Ann?"

"Ann is still getting over her divorce, I hardly think she'd welcome Colin at a time like this. If only your brother David was closer."

"David? What on earth made you think of him? It must be two years since he last wrote."

"I don't know, I must have mentally been shaking the family tree . . . No, you're right, he's too far away and in any case we don't even know if he's still where he was, wherever that is."

"Hold on, I think you may be on to something, Judith. Parradine keeps track of him just in case something should happen to me. He's entitled to 5 percent of the Company, although he never shows up at board meetings. The last time Parradine sent me his report, David was still in Namibia working on that uranium mine. It's near some small town." He gripped Judith's elbow, "It's a great idea. He'll have several months in Africa, a chance to get to know his uncle and experience a little of the real world. It will get him right out of this environment for a while. Judith you are a genius!"

"Wait a minute Nigel, I'm not so sure I like the idea of him going out to Africa. Isn't there a war going on in that part . . . where all the UN soldiers went just recently?"

"No Judith, that's thousands of miles away. David's last letter said that it was very peaceful where he was based, but obviously I'll have it thoroughly checked out by my office before we send Colin."

Judith nodded. Not totally convinced, she was unhappy with herself for bringing her husband's brother into the conversation. "How do we know that David will agree to have Colin? He has been a bachelor ever since that nice girl left him. He's probably living in a flophouse. God knows what sort of company a man keeps in a mining town."

"Judith, I know that ConAmGeo provides all its senior people with excellent accommodation, so room is not the problem. But, yes, he might not want Colin. Look, let me get a long fax off to him right away. I'm sure we can have the answers by tomorrow night."

"Nigel I'm still not certain about this, but very well, contact David - I just wish he were closer."

Nigel was striding to the door when he stopped. "Don't mention this to Colin until we make sure it will work. And keep an eye on him. I'll get back early." He walked back to Judith and kissed her on the forehead, "Don't worry, I'm sure everything is going to work out." He smiled. "After all, it's not as if he were going to prison."

Caroline caught up to David just as he was climbing into his pickup. "Mr. Mornay, the reports are ready for checking and a fax has just come in." His secretary was a 19-year-old bundle of energy who always had a crowd of young engineers and machine operators around her desk. Not really pretty, she had an irrepressible vitality and he suspected that it would not be long before she was snapped up and married.

He followed her back into the office and lifted a pile of reports from her desk thumbing through them irritably. "What's the fax about?"

"I don't know sir. As you can see it's sealed and marked confidential."

David lifted his eyebrows, "Well now, who in head office is after my blood this time?" He slit the buff coloured envelope open with her paperknife, grumbling. "Between the paperwork and the telephone I am never going to get any real work done."

It was a game they played. She knew that David would let his paperwork accumulate if he could, avoiding his office in favour of the construction areas. Despite her youth, she also sensed that the old free-wheeling days were over. Before, where a telephoned request could accomplish anything, now every order had to be in triplicate. She feigned indifference, fiddling with her typewriter while he read the long Fax, and finally when he whistled through his teeth, asked. "More work?"

"Hmm . . . no . . . nothing to do with work. How old are you Caroline?"

"Me!" Her astonishment caused her voice to squeak. "I'll be 20 next May, why?"

"My nephew, who I've never seen, may be coming out here to spend his summer vacation with me. He's nearly 16 and I guess I'll need someone to introduce him to the younger set in town." He chewed his lip reflectively. "I wonder what brought this about?"

"Where is he coming from, Mr. Mornay?"

"Canada . . . Caroline check the time it will take to set up a call to this phone number." He copied a number down from the fax. "I'll be in my office all morning." An hour later the mine switchboard advised that his call was going through. He heard an operator in Montreal speaking French, then switching to

English, she advised him to hold. Suddenly the line was open and Nigel's voice came over the wire, as clear as if he were in the same room, not ten thousand miles away,

"David, is that you?"

"Yes Nigel, I received your fax an hour ago. What is all this about Colin?"

"Dear God, do you know what time it is here, have you forgotten the time difference? Could you not have waited to morning?"

"Where I am Nigel, it is afternoon. I'm sorry if I woke you, but you faxed me -- remember? -- and it sounded urgent."

"Yes, I'm sorry Dave, I'm still trying to wake up. I expected you to reply by fax - actually I wasn't sure if you would reply at all. So thanks for being so prompt, even if it is the middle of the night. Can we have Colin stay with you for a while?"

"I suppose so, but what on earth for? Why does Colin want to come out here? You'd better warn him it's not exactly Acapulco."

"Dave, we want Colin away from Victoria for a while. He's become involved in rather a bad crowd. I suspect drugs and a girl may be involved. You know how it is with teens these days. Both Judith and I feel that if you'll have him it will break the grip of this group on him and a change of scenery will put him back on his feet. He considers you the family hero and it will do him the world of good to meet you. It's about time he found out how other people in the world live. I'm afraid that he's been very sheltered."

"Well, well, how circumstances change. There was a time I recall when you considered me totally irresponsible -- said so in fact -- and now you're sending me your son to be straightened out."

"Please Dave, It's time we let bygones be bygones. I've never been your enemy. I forced the old man to leave you part of the company in his will, and even though you may not want it, it's still here. So please don't make me beg. I have a gut feeling that this trip is just what the boy needs. Colin is basically a good kid, but he's been spoilt." He paused. "Of course if you would rather not have him . . . " There was a long silence. "Dave?"

"Nigel don't play games with me. I've been around a lot longer than you . . . Yes, I'll take him. Actually, I'd like to see the boy. Colin is my only blood kin besides yourself and I suppose I'm getting sentimental in my old age. When are you sending him?"

"Today is Saturday, I'll have my travel department fix up his visas and he'll probably leave on Wednesday or Thursday next week, I'll phone you or fax all the details and time of arrival."

"OK, and what does Judith say to all this?"

"It was her idea."

"Well I'll be damned! Now you do surprise me."

"She always thought well of you."

"Nigel, I warned you about trying to bullshit me, but give her my regards anyway. Are you listening in on the extension Judith?"

"No, she's not awake, when she goes to bed it's a dead sleep till morning, some new medication the doctor has her on for stress. Dave, I really appreciate this and if there is anything I can do in return . . . Why not come home, even for a visit?"

"Home! This is my home," he retorted, then softer, "Thanks for the offer, I'll let you get back to sleep. Cheers Nigel, keep well." The phone clicked and Nigel could hear the singing silence.

"Dave . . . Dave?" With a sigh Nigel replaced his receiver, and suddenly he felt very sad. He and his brother had never been close, the old man and a five-year age difference had seen to that. But now as he sat on the edge of his bed, feet into the soft pile of the carpet, he felt a deep sense of loss. He looked at the digital clock beside the bed and decided to try for a few more hours sleep. Tomorrow would be a heavy day.

David replaced the receiver, a thoughtful look on his face. He rubbed his jaw reflectively, then unscrewed his Thermos to pour a cup of coffee. Nothing came out and he remembered that he had finished the last of his coffee over an hour ago. With a growl he poked his head around Caroline's door, but she had left to go across to the Administration block. David looked at his watch, then called to Berta, the other typist. "I'm going to the coffee shop for five minutes. Come and fetch me if anything important comes up. And tell Caroline where I am." Berta, a local girl, was not overly endowed with intelligence and David wasn't sure how she had managed to get the job in the first place.

Picking up his hard hat, he left the Engineering block and walked the hundred metres along the concrete walkway to the coffee shop. Pushing through the swing door, he stopped. The room was crowded with office employees having their morning break and it looked as if all the tables were taken. Shrugging, he turned to leave when he heard his name called. "Mr. Mornay . . . David, over here." To his right along the wall and in the corner was a small table covered with papers and a large black notebook. Kate Richardson sat with pen still poised. She smiled and moved along the corner bench seat to give him room. He eased himself past a table of Administration types commenting on last night's movie in Swakopmund and drew up a chair across from her. "Kate, how are you?" She was dressed in a simple cotton dress covered by her white lab coat and her hair was pulled back into a severe pony tail, but again he was struck by how beautiful she was.

"Fine, thank you. I saw you come in and realized you were looking for a seat. I haven't seen you here before."

"No, I rarely have time, and in any case I bring my own coffee to work. But today I had a pre-dawn start and used up my Thermos earlier than usual. Is this your break?"

She laughed. "No, my airconditioner has failed and I came in here to try and get some work done. It's a lot cooler than my office. I spread my papers over the table to discourage anyone else joining me." She coloured slightly, "That isn't meant to discourage you. I was just about to fetch myself something to drink. Can I get you a cup of coffee?"

David started to push himself up. "I'll get it. What do you want?"

"No, please let me do the honours, you fetched the drinks last Friday at Lamberti's party. . . remember?"

David sank back in his chair. "Well, thank you . . . coffee, black with a little sugar." He watched her move gracefully to the counter and felt the same tingle that had surprised him at Lamberti's party. He stacked her papers to one side of the table, putting her notebook on top to hold them down. Kate put his coffee down first, then sat down and took a little sip from her own cup.

"Are you very busy at the moment?" She took another sip, looking at him over the rim of her cup.

"No, in construction it's either flat out or dead slow. Right now we're finishing up a bunch of contracts and haven't yet started the new work. Therefore my indulgence in coming down here." He smiled at her. "I'm glad I did." She blushed again, but her eyes were steady and didn't leave his face.

"I asked you the other night if you planned to go back to Canada at the end of your contract and I can't remember what you said."

"Perhaps because I didn't answer the question." He took a long drink from the cup. "I left home when I was very young." He stopped and she saw his knuckles whiten around the cup. "My father and I didn't get along. Apparently, he didn't like me from the time I was born, and for a little boy that is hard. He was also a strict disciplinarian - not physically cruel you understand, but it seemed that I could do nothing right and Nigel could do nothing wrong."

"Nigel?" she interrupted, "your brother?"

"Yes, he's five years younger than I am. Funny thing, he just phoned me today to ask if I'll have his son, my nephew, out here for a holiday. Something must be in the air today, first Nigel and then you. Normally I don't think much about Canada."

She shook her head, still watching his face. "Oh David, that's so sad. I can't imagine how that must have hurt, especially when it wasn't deserved . . . a father-son relationship is so important. My own parents are just so wonderful. I had such a happy childhood even after we left Kenya."

He smiled crookedly, without humour. "You are one of the lucky ones. There's no law that states a father has to love his offspring. Food, clothing and shelter are all that is required."

Impulsively, she reached across the table to close her hand around his. "I'm so sorry. I didn't mean to pry. It must still hurt, even now . . . " She stopped, then letting go of his hand she asked. "How do you and Nigel get on?"

"I left home when he was ten and have only seen him once since then, so you could say that we're relative strangers." He smiled at her, watching the twitch of her mouth as she caught the intentional pun. "Now it's your turn to answer questions. What made you come out to Tsamma?"

"Jack was working for Mr. Butchert on a copper deposit in the Northern Transvaal when ConAmGeo decided to create a new company in Tsamma Uranium. I was working as a research chemist for a small environmental company in Johannesburg. Jack was away from our home in Johannesburg a lot of the time and he felt that if we came out here we'd have more time together." She twisted her lips in a wry smile. "As you saw the other night, that still hasn't happened."

"You don't mind?"

Kate looked down, "No, not really. I have my work which I enjoy and Jack is very happy here. I get back to Johannesburg every three months and spend a few days with my parents and my sister's family"

David shook his head. "Somehow I pictured your life differently. I don't know why. I just saw you. . . ." He stopped, embarrassed. "Hell, who am I to talk. All I seem to do is work, eat and sleep."

Kate searched his face, her own grave. "I like work. Perhaps we're two of a kind. You aren't married, I gather. Were you ever?"

He pursed his lips, then deciding, looked at her directly. "Yes, a long time ago . . . It lasted less than a year. We were both . . " He paused, searching for the right words. . . "We expected different things from each other I guess . . . and we were both very young. I suppose Jill thought she could turn a sow's ear into a silk purse . . . God, I didn't really understand her reasons then . . . still don't . . . but there you have it." He grinned crookedly. "For the longest time I thought I must be using the wrong brand of soap."

Kate looked at him steadily. "Did you never meet anyone else?"

"I suppose I never really tried and then mostly I worked in remote areas. These were all male dominated societies with very little female contact outside of . . . " He stopped. "Well you know the sort of thing. Ships that pass in the night as they say."

"Where did you learn to dance so well? For someone who has lived in construction camps all his life you're very good."

David smiled. "After the Irian Jaya project the company sent me to the London office for two years and I lived with a dancer for a while. She decided that I needed a little polish, so she took me in hand." He stared past her shoulder, his face suddenly sad. "She was a sweet person, too good for me really. Everyone thought that we'd get married but . . . " He shrugged. "In the end she married her producer."

"Were you in love with her? Somehow I can't imagine you letting something you want get away."

The room was emptying as people returned to their desks and, glancing around, David noted that they were the last occupants, apart from a group across the room. He turned back to Kate. "I suppose I learned very early not to care too much. Over the years, that facility has served me well, but it has its drawbacks. She called me an emotional cripple and I guess she was right. Was I in love with her? . . . I don't know, probably not. The last I heard she had a couple of kids and was very happy, so at least one of us won."

"That's a strange way of putting it. Do you look on everything in life as a battle?"

David looked at her closely and then began to rise. "I talk too much. Perhaps it's the lack of female company, but I suspect your niceness has something to do with it." He picked up his hard hat. "In another life, perhaps I wouldn't have let someone worthwhile walk away . . Someone like you for example. Thank you for the coffee." He turned and walked out of the door without looking back. Kate stared after him, her mind in a strange turmoil, and when she picked up her coffee cup, her hand was trembling.

Chapter 9

Namibia - Windhoek

Colin Mornay stared out of the window as the Boeing 747 settled towards the runway - so this was Africa. He felt a curious mixture of excitement and disappointment. The last week had been a jumble of confusing events. His father's announcement that he would be spending his summer holidays with his uncle in Africa had left him speechless. At first he had resisted, simply on principle, but seeing that for once, both his parents were in agreement, he had given in with only a token show of sullen resentment. Actually, Colin was fascinated by his mysterious uncle who had caused so much disruption to the family. He knew his mother would worry, so he spitefully added to her concerns by remarking on the poor safety record of Third World airlines and the various crippling diseases he would be exposed to.

Colin was given no time to retract his grudging acceptance of his parent's plan. A rapid sequence of travel documentation, injections and visa formalities occupied him fully until he was airborne out of Vancouver on a Thursday evening. He flew nonstop to London in a British Airways jumbo that curved high over northern Canada, Greenland and Iceland before landing at London's Heathrow Airport at noon on Friday. Here, a business associate of his father's, alerted by a long distance call, met him in the transit lounge. The associate made certain Colin caught the South African Airways jumbo to Frankfurt and Windhoek barely an hour later.

In Frankfurt, where the aircraft waited for two hours to collect extra passengers, Colin was met by another of his father's friends. By this time Colin was understandably tired and grumpy, but made the cardinal error of swearing at an airport security guard who wanted to examine his hand luggage. By the time Herr Schimmel had returned after confirming that the ticketing was in order, Colin was being hauled off to the security offices deep in the basement of the airport. It took several minutes of tactful diplomacy to get him released into Herr Schimmel's care. It was with utmost difficulty that Herr Schimmel restrained himself from clipping the foulmouthed boy alongside the ear as he led him away to a quiet corner of the First Class lounge. Hans Schimmel dealt heavily with Rimrock Nickel, one of the Mornay group of companies, and had spent considerable time in Canada on business. His dealings with Nigel were always very correct and he had met both Nigel and Judith socially. Now he found himself staring at Colin, wondering how such apparently nice people could have produced such an unpleasant youth. Schimmel thankfully handed Colin on to the SAA stewardess and breathed a sigh of relief as he watched the Jumbo become airborne. Later that evening in discussing the incident with his wife, he reminded her of his "throwback" theory. "Remember Lise, sometimes a bad strain will come out several generations later - the bad seed," he muttered darkly.

By this time, Colin was very tired, the continuous motion and tension made him very irritable and he hardly noticed the Jumbo leaving the ground. He fell into a deep sleep, only to be awakened a short time later as the big jet landed in Zurich to pick up passengers. The pleasant and efficient cabin crew was taken totally aback when Colin exploded on being awakened a second time for dinner an hour after take off from Zurich. It was a wild few minutes and might have been excusable given the boy's tiredness, but his language caused several of the first class passengers to blink in shock. It took a cold threat from the chief steward that he would be removed at the next stop, Lisbon, to finally quiet him. For the rest of the journey he sat in sullen silence.

Word of his conduct had obviously preceded the landing in Lisbon. When the Jumbo lifted off again, after a crew change, on the final legs to Windhoek and Johannesburg, a large, fresh and decidedly unfriendly steward had been designated to keep a close watch on Colin. Curled in his seat, Colin dozed fitfully while the huge jet thundered through the night sky over the South Atlantic. Early in the morning, the 747 began curving back towards the coast of Namibia. When Colin awoke, a beautiful sunrise was turning the clouds into a crimson and gold cloth spreading forever to the horizon beneath the aircraft, and Colin, refreshed by the sleep, held his breath at the spectacle. The Captain's voice advised that the silver ribbon off the port wing was the Cunene River, the boundary between Angola and Namibia.

Staring down an hour later into the harsh sunlight, Colin saw the countryside below dotted with scattered, scrubby trees and sandy rivers lacking water except where pools flashed silver in the sun. A range of mountains crinkled the horizon as the aircraft turned and he could see roads and signs of human habitation. As the seatbelt sign lit up, the steward lumbered up to check that Colin was strapped in. The big jet settled lower, spoilers deploying to kill off lift, the huge wheel bogies rumbling out to lock into the dying airspeed. The runway at Windhoek is at an elevation of 4,000 feet and on a hot day the big jets used up most of the 10,000 feet available. Today was no exception. The wheels touched smoothly and the engines screamed as the Captain went into reverse thrust sending a shudder through the giant airframe.

Colin saw an airport empty of aircraft save for a few light aircraft parked on the apron, with a large glass-fronted terminal and a modern control tower perched on a concrete column. His view changed to a vista of stunted thorn trees and dry grass as the jumbo turned to taxi back to the terminal. He had expected thick forest or total desert, but this scrub country reminded him of the area around Kamloops in central British Columbia, except that thorn and acacia trees replaced the fir, pine and cedar of home. Colin was disappointed. He had expected something different. After such a marathon journey, precisely what he expected he couldn't say but certainly not this dry, uninteresting landscape. When the gangways were clear of passengers disembarking, he left his seat. Clutching his camera, travelling bag and overcoat he walked to the exit and stepped into sunshine so bright that it made him squeeze his eyes shut. After the coolness of the aircraft the sudden wave of heat hit him like a wall.

A stewardess smiled at him. “Thank you sir, enjoy your stay.” He walked down the stairs, feeling stiff from the long journey and his mouth was very dry. Colin hitched the overcoat over his shoulder and made his way into the shade of the terminal where the arriving passengers were being processed through Customs and Immigration. For the first time he had no assistance, but with the feigned assurance of a seasoned traveller, he put his passport down in front of a bored looking official. The official took a long and hard look at Colin before pointing with his thumb to a queue where the last of the passengers were being processed. He made no effort to hand Colin his passport back and the boy was forced to drop his bag in order to retrieve the document. His coat slipped awkwardly off his shoulder and he was about to make a sharp comment when caution made him pause. This didn’t seem to be the place to indulge himself.

He passed through the Immigration booth into the baggage hall without incident. Colin’s suitcase, identified by a large strip of silver duct tape down one side, stood out among the few suitcases still on the turntable. Collecting his case, Colin made for the Customs bench but was waved through by an official busy trying to impress a stewardess.

Once through the partition that separated the baggage area from the main terminal, Colin found himself in a huge hall filled with people embracing and calling to each other. Searching the hall for anyone who might resemble his uncle, he kept glancing at the photograph that his father had found in an old album. A disembodied voice crackling over the loudspeakers in a strange language added to his sense of disorientation. Finally, Colin sat on his aluminium suitcase, wondering what to do next, for the hall was rapidly emptying of people. His increasing concern was interrupted by a voice in English that echoed over the loudspeakers.

“Will Mr. Colin Mornay come to the information desk.” A

pause. "Mr. Colin Mornay, passenger from London on South African Airways, please come to the information desk."

Colin stared around the rapidly emptying hall and was about to ask when he saw the sign. Dragging his suitcase, he reached the counter where a young girl in uniform looked him up and down. "Yes?"

"I am Colin Mornay, you were paging . . . "

"Yes, wait here." She walked rapidly to the end of the counter where a short, tanned man in a battered baseball cap stood drinking a coke. The girl pointed at Colin and the baseball cap turned in his direction. The man's face, Colin noted, was deeply seamed and the eyes under the peaked cap were dark brown, almost black. The face beneath the cap smiled, lighting up the dark eyes with a wicked grin and Colin felt an immediate attraction to this tough looking man.

"Amigo, so you made it!" Hurrying over, he crushed Colin's hand in an iron grip, and lifted the heavy suitcase with an ease that made Colin stare. "I am Rafa, the company pilot - your uncle asked me to pick you up. Welcome to Namibia, let's go, the bloody Jumbo was late as usual."

"Why didn't my uncle come to meet me. . . don't I rate?"

Rafa was already striding to the doors that led back to the apron where the light aircraft were parked. "Your uncle, amigo, works 12-hour days, six days a week. If you don't arrive on a Sunday my friend, tough luck, anyway, he will be waiting for you at the airfield at Tsamma. Now come on, I also have work to do and now I am behind with my flight schedule for the rest of the day."

Colin's mouth dropped. He had rarely been treated in such a cavalier fashion in all his sixteen years. The pilot had not waited to discuss Colin's hurt feelings and was already through the double glass doors heading for the light aircraft apron. With a start, Colin realized this was a different world. He hurriedly picked up his hand luggage and raced after the stocky figure.

Out on the apron stood a twin-engined aircraft. Colin was

greatly interested in light aircraft and recognised the type. It was a Piper Chieftain, similar to those based in Victoria. There was a clear difference however, this aircraft was stained and work worn, the nose and wing leading edges stripped of paint. A long streak of oil feathered back over the port engine cowling. Colin viewed it apprehensively, it was so different from the shiny corporate aircraft in the Mornay fleet. Surprised to see no other passengers, he clambered aboard behind Rafa.

"Sit in the co-pilot's seat." Rafa instructed. "I'll just do a quick walk around, then we will be off." Minutes later, they were lifting off from Windhoek Airport and banking towards the west. "There is Windhoek." Rafa banked the aircraft steeply so that Colin could see the neat lines of streets and houses in the distance. "It's about thirty miles from the airport, there is not much flat land around the city for a big airport."

"How long before we get to Tsamma Ridge?" Colin asked.

"About an hour, we should be there by three, help yourself to the coffee . . . It's in the flask under your seat."

"The name Windhoek, what does it mean." Colin asked, more to keep the conversation going than from any real desire to know. In fact, right then he would have been very happy to be flying back to Victoria.

"Hell, I don't know, hoek is Dutch for hook, but I have not given it much thought . . . perhaps Windy hook . . . probably, though, it's a corruption of an old ethnic name."

The aircraft bounced and Rafa concentrated on flying. "It's the hottest time of day," he explained. "Thermals of air rising from the ground where there is unequal heating cause the turbulence, so as you can feel, we get bumps, but it should end in a few minutes once we get clear of the high ground."

Colin nodded and stared out of his side window. He noted that the rolling, scrub covered hills were giving way to flat, treeless countryside. Ahead and to the right of their track was a massive rock outcrop rearing up from the surrounding flat countryside like a rhino horn punched through a sheet of flat paper from below. "What is that?" he asked, pointing.

"Spitzkoppie, it's an old volcano, extinct now and ground down over millions of years. You will find lots of semi precious stones in that area, especially silver topaz. Dave is trying to organize a trip there for you." He pointed past Colin's face. "That larger group are the Erongo mountains, lots of Bushman paintings in the caves."

"Bushman paintings?" Colin asked, puzzled.

"Yes, you know rock paintings similar to the ones in France. Lots of paintings in the Erongo mountains and of course there is the 'White Lady' in the Brandberg. Today, there is too much haze to see that far, but it's in that direction."

Confused, Colin decided not to pursue this line of conversation any further -- later he would make discreet enquiries of his uncle -- for he didn't want to appear foolish in front of this tough looking pilot. Without warning, Rafa pointed to the control yoke. "Do you want to try your hand at flying?"

Startled, Colin stared at him. When travelling on the corporate aircraft in Canada, Colin had never even been allowed to sit up next to the pilot - "Transport regulations," he had been told. Now here he was being asked if he wanted to fly! "Can I?"

Rafa lifted both hands clear of the yoke. "You have control, take a firm grip, put your feet on the rudder pedals and follow everything that I do." Colin placed both hands on the yoke, following the pilot's example. Rafa snapped a switch on the panel to 'off'. "OK, the auto pilot is off, now follow my movements."

For the next ten minutes Colin was shown how to bank, climb, turn and lose height. At one point, Rafa relinquished total control and Colin found that trying to keep the aircraft level was the equivalent of holding a bead of quicksilver steady on a plate of glass. Laughing, Rafa regained control. "Not so easy as it looks, eh! But you catch on quick, you have good hands, perhaps we will make a pilot of you yet."

Colin swelled with pride. "Can I try a little more?" he asked.

"Not now, we are nearly at Tsamma, but you can come on a

trip with me next week. I have to go down to Mariental to pick up some geologists, and it's a long flight, so you can get in some real practice."

The aircraft began losing height rapidly, and ahead of their track Colin could see the flat desert give way to a series of deep ravines. It was as if a careless giant had gripped the land in two enormous hands and pulled in opposite directions, ripping the desert crust to a depth of several hundred feet. The major ravine ran northeast and southwest as far as he could see, and was at least two miles wide. He learned later that it was the action of the Khan River over countless eons that was responsible. Now, as their shadow slid over the dry river bed, he saw round tanks flash silver in the sun and Rafa was pointing out the mine area.

Tsamma Uranium Plant lay in a long, mile wide valley that was a tributary of the Khan. The flat bottom of the valley housed the entire Plant area. He saw roads, a railtrack with a brightly painted diesel loco pulling a string of boxcars, several office buildings, huge silver sheds housing the Leach and Recovery sections and miles of multicoloured piping connecting the various sections. At the northern end of the valley, he could see the Open Pit with a pall of dust hanging over heavy equipment that looked like bright yellow beetles on the pit floor. Then Rafa was lifting the Chieftain to clear the jagged ridge that gave the mine its name. Despite the spread of its operations up the valley, Tsamma Uranium seemed almost insignificant in this incredible landscape. Colin saw the desert stretching away in all directions to the far horizons. Once over the ridge, the land flattened again and the airfield, a single strip of black asphalt with a small cluster of hangars, merged with the sere brown landscape. Colin stared fascinated. Nothing had prepared him for this. This was the surface of the moon and the landscape tilted as Rafa rolled the Chieftain on to its final approach.

A few minutes later they were taxiing back along the asphalt towards the hangars that stood incongruously against the sky. A small group of men waited in front of the open doors, behind them two Ford pickup trucks and a white Peugeot station wagon were parked. Rafa cut the motors and methodically began snapping switches to the 'off' position, removing his lightweight headset and hooking it behind his seat. "Welcome to Tsamma Ridge, the Devil's garbage dump." He smiled, "It's not so bad after the first ten years."

Colin followed Rafa to the exit door. The Chilean pulled a release lever and the fuselage door opened with steps folding out and down. Rafa yelled something to the waiting men, and a burst of laughter greeted his words. He turned and motioned Colin out. Coming out into the harsh sunshine, Colin met the full force of the heat. The transition from the airconditioned aircraft was like stepping into an oven. For a moment he felt a wave of panic, convinced that he was going to suffocate. Stepping down onto the black asphalt, Colin could feel the heat through the soles of his hand-made Italian loafers. Staring at the unending flat, rocky, sandy waste, he wondered what on earth had persuaded him to give in to his father's demand. This was hell. He knew instinctively that he could not last in this environment and swore to himself that at the first opportunity he was going to phone his mother and demand to be brought back home.

Colin recognized his uncle immediately from the photograph. There was no mistaking the obvious family resemblance. His uncle, a bigger man than he had expected, was dressed in faded khaki work clothes tucked into suede desert boots, with aviator sunglasses pushed up on to his forehead. He broke away from the little group and grabbed Colin's hand.

"My God, it's good to see you Colin." He released the boy's hand and placing both his on Colin's shoulders stared down at him. "Damn, you are the spitting image of your father. How are your parents?" Colin mumbled something, his lips numb and his mouth dry. "Here, Wessel, come and meet my nephew."

A huge bearded man gripped his hand. "Hallo Colin, welcome to Tsamma and Namibia." The accent was thick with a nasal twang. He was dressed in the same khaki as Colin's uncle, but his trousers were short. Thick, tanned, hairy legs ended in black mining boots with calf length socks. Nobody else seemed to notice the heat that hit Colin like a fist. He could feel perspiration trickling from under his armpits, and suddenly the cumulative effects of the last three days hit him. He gagged, held a hand over his mouth and rushed to the edge of the blacktop where he threw up in great heaving gasps.

Astonished, David Mornay stared after his nephew before reaching into his pickup for a plastic bottle of tepid water. He walked to where Colin stood bent over spitting into the sand and poured a generous amount of water over the boy's neck. "Here wash your mouth out." He grinned down at Colin, "Hell, I've met people who don't like this place, but none who objected as violently as you." Colin straightened up. He felt a lot better and reaching for a handkerchief he looked into his uncle's amused grey eyes. "I'm not going to stay, this . . ." he searched for words. "What the hell am I supposed to do . . . " he gestured at the empty landscape.

"Well now, how about if you give yourself a good night's sleep to think things over. You look bushed and in any case the flight from Windhoek only goes once a week." He put his arm around Colin's shoulders and led him over to the blue pickup, motioning Wessel away with a shake of his head. Colin climbed into the passenger side and in order to sit down had to push an accumulation of plans and reports into the space between them. Wessel and Rafa lifted his luggage into the back of the pickup and with a wave of thanks, David swung the truck onto a gravel road that was barely distinguishable from the surrounding desert. "I have to go to the mine for half an hour and then we'll go into Swakop and give you a chance to get a bath and some rest. How was your trip?"

"Terrible, I haven't slept since I left Vancouver and I feel rough. How long before we get to your place?"

"We'll be there by four; what's the time now, two?"

"Why can't we go straight to your place? I can see the mine another time."

"We aren't going to the mine for your benefit, Colin. I have a lot of loose ends to tie up and Rafa arriving late has made it worse . . . Sorry, but I am sure you'll survive a little longer."

Furious, Colin stared out of the window. Six weeks of this? At that moment, he hated his father with a deep and passionate hatred. With a curious glance at his nephew, David concentrated on his driving and did not speak again.

The road from the airfield ran through a series of rolling foothills before sweeping round the flank of Tsamma Ridge to drop in a series of wicked hairpin bends to the valley below. At the bottom of the incline, the road flattened out for several hundred yards. Across the road at this point was a security barrier, a black and white striped steel pole barring entry. A high chain link fence disappeared over the low hills on both sides of the road. David slowed to a halt and a black guard in a neatly pressed khaki uniform topped with a white hard hat bearing the logo of Tsamma Ridge peered into the cab. In a harsh guttural sing-song that Colin learned later was Afrikaans, the language of most of Southern Africa, he questioned Colin's presence. David answered in the same staccato sentences and the guard's face split into a slow grin of delight. He raised his hand to the brim of his hard hat in a parody of a salute and the steel pole swung up to allow them entry. Colin looked questioningly at his uncle.

"I told him you were the new 'Chimbusi boy', that's the man who cleans the latrines. It's the lowest job on the mine. Every time I have someone new I invent a special title. He thinks it's a great joke and I often wonder what point there is in having a gate." Colin did not speak.

Now the pickup was rolling down a wide paved road that ran through the middle of the valley where recently erected buildings sprouted from both sides of the road. To the left were stainless steel tanks and steaming stacks of what appeared to be a miniature oil refinery, and on the right multicolored pipes arched overhead on pipe bridges. Despite himself, Colin was fascinated.

Noticing his attention, David explained, "That's the Acid Plant. We need large amounts of sulphuric acid for the extraction process, so we make our own from pyrite mined here. When you've settled down I'll give you a guided tour. This is the most advanced plant of its type in the world and also the largest. It will be something to tell your friends back in Canada." David swung the truck up a narrow incline to the top of a small hill that had been blasted into a level platform. A low white 'U' shaped building with a flat roof sat solidly like some Foreign Legion fort on the edge of the slope.

"These are the Engineering Offices. Come inside, it's a lot cooler . . . yes, leave your bags, they'll be quite safe." Colin followed David through the heavy glass doors and the change was startling, with the air temperature at least ten degrees cooler inside the building. Colin saw a chrome water cooler and, without waiting to see where David was going, stepped up and drank thirstily from the ice cool stream that jetted up when he pressed down on the release button. Finally, he looked up to the amused eyes of two young typists, crisp and cool in their print frocks and realized that David had disappeared. One of the typists rose and came over, "Hallo, you must be Colin," She put out a slim tanned hand, and Colin shook it warily. "I'm your uncle's executive secretary. My God, you look as if you have been travelling forever. You must be very tired. Oh, I am Caroline." She indicated the other typist who raised a languid hand, "That is Berta; her English is not very good." Colin glanced around.

"Where has my uncle gone?"

"Come with me. You were so thirsty you were only interested in the water." She laughed, a rich, throaty chuckle. "My God, the boys at the Hansa are going to love a drinker like you."

As they started in the direction Caroline indicated, David came back towards them frowning, "What's the problem Colin?"

Caroline scowled at David. "The poor thing was dying of thirst, Mr. Mornay. Not everyone can go for days without food and drink like you." She turned to Colin, "Don't let him bully you. He thinks everyone here is a machine, but one day he will get sick and then - hah!" She flounced off, her stiff back expressing her mock disapproval.

David rolled his eyes, "I see you have met my nemesis. I feel for the man who marries that one." He led Colin into his office. The interior of the office was painted a cool lime green. An air conditioner whined softly, two plastic bottles full of water rested over the cold air exhaust which rattled gently. David dropped into a swivel chair behind his formica and steel desk, motioning Colin into one of the two chairs that stood against a bulging row of file cabinets. The desk was covered with papers, a chunk of ore acting as a paperweight. A large calendar, depicting a massive piece of mining machinery, covered a portion of one wall and various charts and graphs covered the remainder. Colin's eyes swept the cluttered office and disappointment showed in his face.

Noticing his nephew's expression, David grunted, "Not what you're used to I'll bet, but it's functional and that's all that matters here." Without waiting for Colin to reply, David lifted his telephone and punched a number. "Pat? - Dave . . . have you freed the pumps yet? No. . . what's the problem?. . . I see . . . OK, you can use the fifteen ton with the fly jib . . . when?... well tell him I want it before five, . . . I know . . . what? . . . Yes, he has arrived. I'm taking him into Swakop in a few minutes. Can you chase the pipefitters yourself? - Thanks." He dialled half a dozen numbers in quick succession, giving orders and advice before finally replacing the receiver. "OK, Colin, let's get going. I bet a bath will feel pretty good to you, eh?" Colin muttered a reply and rose stiffly to his feet. He felt dreadful, dirty, nauseous and thoroughly unhappy.

The drive into Swakopmund was a blur of confusing images to the tired boy. After 15 minutes, the hard gravel road from the mine joined a wide paved road, the main Windhoek, Swakopmund highway. At the junction with the mine road some seventy kilometres from Swakopmund, David floored the accelerator and pushed the big pickup to its maximum speed of 140 kilometres per hour. He kept glancing at his nephew but did not attempt to talk. Colin closed his eyes and leant his head back against the vinyl headrest. The tires hummed softly and Colin did not see the massive outcrop of an eroded mountain rearing up 500 feet above the gravel plains on their right-hand side. Rossing mountain was a jagged fishhook of dolomitic marble and quartzite, with aeolian sand and calcrete blown up high on the north facing inner curve of the hook.

In eons past, massive shifts in the earth's crust had buckled the surface of this land, pushing and folding layers of rock thousands of feet into the air to form huge mountain ranges. Now, only remnants of once awesome ranges remained. Ground down by the relentless forces of erosion over millions of years only a few outcrops, with cores of iron hard dolomite and quartzite, remained as a testament to the giant forces that had spawned them. The flat plains around Rossing mountain were devoid of vegetation, apart from scrubby low lying bushes scattered in dry washes. As the mountain fell behind the speeding pickup truck the scenery changed to flat calcrete and sand plains that stretched into the hazy horizon. David scanned the grim scenery, remembering his own arrival three years earlier and his fascination with the incredible landscape. Instinctively he had accepted that, however starkly beautiful, this was not a land to be taken lightly.

Thirty minutes later, Swakopmund quite literally swam into view, a desert mirage of towers and minarets, backlit by a twinkling indigo sea, hanging suspended on a shimmering liquid band above the brown of the desert. To the right, a range of high sand dunes appeared and as Colin sat up, some signs of civilization began to appear. They passed the main water reservoir, a truncated white pyramid in smooth concrete, its green Water Affairs logo vivid against the white background. Sweeping smoothly over the rail overpass, David slowed as they drove down Kaiser Wilhelm Strasse towards the centre of town.

The houses were mainly low single-storey buildings in a variety of styles, with a few double storey blocks. Every house was surrounded by a low wall to keep out the pervading sand. Colin noticed flashes of green behind the walls, but the standard colour was sand, sand and more sand. They turned off the main street and stopped in front of a low bungalow surrounded by the ubiquitous wall.

"Well, here we are, come on in." David lifted the suitcase and pushed the gate open for Colin. They entered a shaded courtyard with a cool splashing fountain and an area of bright green grass. Pampas grass threw tall spears against a sunlit wall, and Colin noted that the path they were walking on was made of flat slabs of sandstone, mottled with shadows thrown by sunlight through a wall of breeze blocks. The whole effect was of a glade, away from the arid rock and sand outside the gate. A group of budgerigars darted back and forth in bright flashes of colour behind a fine mesh that enclosed part of the courtyard. David nodded in the birds' direction. "Wessel gave me those, he's a great bird breeder -- budgies, pigeons, everything that flies around here -- you must ask him to show you his bantams."

After crossing the small courtyard, they stepped on to a wide cool open verandah, the slabbed floor polished to a mirror shine, and faced a heavily carved door that was all of two inches thick. David ran his fingers over the curved patterns gently. "The fellow who built this house came from Germany in the early years, and he built the house around this door. I guess it was the only thing he had to remind him of home."

A muffled bark came from inside. David smiled. "That's Bones, my dog. He's a Rhodesian Ridgeback and as soft as they come, so don't worry if he flings himself at you. It's a long day for him and he loves visitors." He inserted a key and pushed the door open. Before they could enter, a huge, honey-coloured, short haired mastiff bounded at them. "Down! damn you Bones, down I say!" But there was no heat in his uncle's voice and his affection for this handsome dog was apparent even to someone as tired as Colin. Colin patted the dog and was surprised at how soft and supple his skin was. He followed his uncle and the dog inside.

The house inside was totally white, curved archways separated the various rooms and the floors were smooth dark concrete covered in a variety of woolen and sisal rugs. Bright paintings hung from the walls. Colin saw one of Tsamma Ridge painted in watercolour and signed by Elizabeth Moller and another of Swakopmund by Christine Marais. Though he was unaware of the prestige of the artists, he had his mother's eye for fine art. It was a man's house, and the battered furniture of mellow teak with cushions in faded tweed had none of the elegance and formal precise placing of his own home. Magazines were scattered around and a bottle of Johnny Walker stood on a much abused Mopani wood sideboard.

"Here's the bathroom and shower, clean towels are in the cupboard." David placed the suitcase on the floor, "This is your room, plenty of space so spread out and make yourself comfortable." He paused. "You must be dead beat. Have your shower then we'll talk."

Twenty minutes later, David tapped on the half-open door of Colin's room. "Colin do you like fried tomatoes with your steak? Hendrik is going to start supper for us in a few minutes." Hearing no reply, David pushed the door fully open. Colin, except for a white cotton towel wrapped around his middle, sprawled naked on the bed . He was fast asleep, his chest rising and falling rhythmically.

"Poor little bastard." Closing the door softly, David went back to the lounge and collected his drink from the low glass coffee table. He walked to the window in a pensive mood and watched the budgerigars flitting to and fro in their aviary. He took a deep pull on his drink and wondered if he had made a mistake in agreeing to have Colin. Suddenly remembering, he picked up the telephone. "Caroline - yes - would you send off a fax to my brother in Canada, as follows - 'Colin arrived safely. Everything fine. Regards David' - you have his fax number in my file, or ask the fax operator, they keep a log in the office - what's that? No he's fast asleep. Thanks." Fondling Bones' soft ears, he walked through to the kitchen to tell Hendrik that Colin was asleep and to go easy on the preparations.

Chapter 10

Rafa's War

He pulled Harry's body off the throttles, letting it fall between the co-pilot's seat and the floor. He heard a flat screeching whistle as yet another burst tore into the fuselage behind him. Ignoring the blood that slimed the throttles, he pushed them full open, kicking the rudder and turning the DC3 towards the runway. Lieutenant Safewick burst into the cockpit. "OK up here? . . . Oh, shit !" He pulled the body out of the way and knelt on the right hand seat, the Armalite out of the side window. "There's a machine gun on a jeep, turn left..left.." The roar of the Armalite filled the cabin. "GOT HIM . . . hot damn, go baby go." Safewick grinned over his shoulder at Rafa, the smile changing instantly to a grimace of pain as a single ricochet spun off the bulkhead and ripped into his upper arm, throwing Safewick over the throttles. For the second time, Rafa pulled a body clear and struggled to hold the bucking DC3 steady.

Safewick pushed himself off the floor. His face was streaked with perspiration and was white with pain, but the wound was minor and he struggled to his feet.

"Anyone hurt back there?" Rafa snapped at Safewick as he kicked the rudder pedals, desperately trying to line up with the runway.

"I don't know, but that last burst came right through the main section."

"Was Marieanna hurt?"

"Shit, I don't know. I'll go back and check." He clasped a hand under his armpit where a red stain was spreading quickly. Rafa felt the old sickness return. What if Marieanna was hurt?. . . No . . . he had things to do and emptying his mind he concentrated on holding the DC3 down until the last moment before lifting it up and over the trees. He heard a savage clank from the port side and suspected another hit. Low cloud saved them from the fighters that must have been called up by now, the white mist swirling round the tops of the trees while he held the crippled DC3 as low as he dared.

"It can't be as bad as all that!"

Rafa surfaced blinking, and the bar swam into focus. Dave Mornay looked down at him, his face showing concern. "Can I join you or is this a private party?"

"Oh hallo, Dave." He struggled upright in the soft chair, rubbing his eyes, "It's been a long day, I guess I must have dozed off."

"Yeah, it's been bloody hot all day. It sucks energy right out of the body, and I expect the East Wind will start blowing soon." Dave lifted his hand to Heimo who was looking in their direction, "Two scotches."

The bar at the Hansa was full, for every Saturday night many of the construction crews came in from their camps, and tonight was no exception. Heimo's small bar was throbbing to the sound of conversations in several languages, with bursts of laughter breaking through the steady rumble. A stocky Italian subcontractor stopped at their table to ask David a question, and while David was engaged in answering, Rafa studied the tall Canadian quietly. They had become friends slowly, almost by accident, a chance meeting at the home of an American couple who had invited the two bachelors for a home-cooked meal. During that first meeting, David had expressed a long-held desire to learn the rudiments of flying and Rafa, needing a four-wheel drive Land Rover to go fishing up the coast to Sandwich Harbour, had laughingly suggested a deal.

At first, he had found Mornay an enigma, but their friendship deepened. On the rare occasions when David referred to his military background, Rafa had come to realize that they both had been badly marked, though in different wars. A tacit agreement to let sleeping dogs lie was the basis for mutual respect. A bachelor like David, Rafa had several girl friends but had yet to see David in female company. He suspected that the Canadian suffered from an early love affair, but despite his curiosity didn't press. David was certainly not gay. Rafa grinned slightly at the thought, and wondered what David would say to such an conjecture.

David punched the Italian lightly on the arm, "Push off Carlo, Monday is soon enough to look at the problem. I'll come by your operation first thing on Monday morning." The Italian smiled his thanks and David turned back to Rafa just as Heimo brought their drinks.

"Thanks Heimo, I'll be here a while tonight so just keep track for me and I'll settle up with you later." David raised his glass to Rafa, "When you doze you make a lot of noise . . . the Black Dog walking through your dreams again?"

Rafa grunted, "You are telling me he does not walk through yours from time to time?"

David's face grew suddenly sombre and he took a deep drink from his glass before replying. "Yes . . . yes he does . . . but not so often anymore. I guess he's getting tired of old wrecks like us and has gone looking for younger blood, . . . God help them!" He snorted suddenly, "Enough of this," raising his glass. "Death to the Black Dog . . . long may he be buried." Rafa clinked glasses, "I'll drink to that, anytime amigo . . . anytime."

"So what do you think of the boy?"

"Your nephew? He seems OK, it's hard to tell. After such a long journey one shouldn't expect too much until he's had a long rest. Where is he now?"

"Sleeping. He's pretty exhausted. I pulled a blanket over him and left food in the oven, but I doubt if he'll wake before morning."

"How old is he?"

"Nearly 16, and there doesn't seem to be much character there. I'm beginning to wonder if it was such a good idea for him to come out here."

"Oh, what makes you say that?"

David massaged the bridge of his nose with his thumb and forefinger. "I don't know, just a feeling, but hell, how am I supposed to keep him occupied? He doesn't strike me as the type to be interested in camping, fishing and messing about in the desert. I can only spend time with him at weekends so what's he going to do during the week?"

Rafa grinned at David, "Hell Dave, give the kid a chance. He has hardly arrived and you're ready to write him off. I'm sure he'll get in with a crowd of the local youngsters. It's nearly time for the school holidays and I'll take him fishing during the week when I'm off duty. Old man Schmidt has been pressing for another trip to Sandwich Harbour and Colin can tag along. I have a spare rod and enough gear."

David brightened, "You're right, he's probably just jet lagged to beat hell . . . thanks Rafa. As you say he'll meet some of the local kids and who knows, he might have a great time. Perhaps I should take him up to Wlotkza's Baken tomorrow and see how he enjoys a little fishing . . . do you want to come?"

"Sure, I haven't done any fishing for a while and the old man cancelled his Windhoek flight for tomorrow so . . . yes it will be fun." He lifted his glass mockingly, "To family!"

David stood ankle deep in the icy surf, his fishing rod arcing up and over his shoulder, eight ounces of lead sinker with a six-inch pilchard-wrapped hook whistling out over the incoming breakers. Rafa was yelling something and he looked up to see the Chilean strike heavily. Colin stood next to the Land Rover parked on the beach, an empty rod in his hands. David ran backwards, feeding line out to keep his sinker fixed out beyond the breakers. "Here, take this one Colin, I'll bait up the spare." He handed his rod over, "Keep the line taut, you'll feel the fish take the bait, let him run for a short while then strike hard."

Colin reluctantly took the rod. Despite being born on Vancouver Island, one of the world's great salmon fishing areas, Colin considered the sport dumb. Standing with his back to the desert on this endless beach that disappeared into the grey mist on either side, he shivered in the cold air.

Splitting from the West Wind Drift that travels the Antarctic from west to east, the Benguela current pushes its cold dark sea along the coast of Southwest Africa, bringing rich nutrients to feed the teeming fish and bird life that abound on this desolate coast. Heavy fog, caused by the meeting of cold sea with the hot dry air off the desert, rolls far inland, bringing airborne moisture to a wealth of plant, insect and animal life whose survival depends on the mist. The gunmetal blue sea teems with pilchards, maasbankers, steenbras and the famed 'Cape Salmon' called Kabeljou.

It was the Kabeljou that they were after and Colin was fascinated despite himself as he watched Rafa playing the bucking fish through the heavy surf. Rafa's rod whipped down then relaxed as the fish made a run towards the beach trying to shake the hook off. Rafa reeled in frantically, trying to keep his line taut and deny the fish the slack it needed to throw the hook. The fish was a big one, from the way Rafa's heavy surf rod was bending. It made a last desperate effort to break free by turning parallel to the beach and using the breaking waves to give it the slack it needed, but Rafa anticipated the move. Running barefoot along the sand he kept a steady pressure on the fish and a few moments later a silver flash rode in on a dying breaker. Walking backwards carefully, Rafa drew the fish in, and as the water receded an eight pound Kabeljou lay quivering in the leaden sunlight.

"What bait did you use, pilchard or squid?" David yelled as Rafa dragged the fish up the beach to where the Land Rover sat perched above the high tide marker.

"Pilchard."

As Rafa reached the Land Rover, Colin was startled by a hard yank on his line. He pulled back and suddenly all hell broke loose. The reel screamed and began unwinding line at a rapid rate. Colin jammed his hand down on the reel, but removed it instantly as the rigid fast-moving nylon line sliced into his palm.

"Hold your rod tip up." Rafa was beside him. "Tighten your drag a little more - the spoked wheel on the right - no - the other way - that's it. Now start to wind in and keep your line taut." The excitement was intense, Colin's heart was pounding, all the misery and disappointments that he had felt subjected to over the last few days disappeared in the raw excitement of the moment. He was convinced that it must be an enormous fish, for his rod whipped down viciously as it began another run.

"Let him run, you have plenty of line," David urged. He had left his own rod fixed into a metal sleeve that was anchored into the sand by a long spike, and had run over to join Colin and Rafa. The line suddenly went slack and both adults yelled in unison, "Reel in - reel in, keep your line taut." Colin forgot the cold damp air, the monotonous landscape, the blue gunmetal sea, everything in fact as he concentrated on keeping this fish. He wound in carefully now and the line became rigid again, but there was no further movement. He looked at the two men questioningly. "Nothing is happening."

David tested Colin's line gently and spoke to Rafa over Colin's head, "It could be a Stingray or a small shark and it's lying on the bottom, or if it is a Kabeljou it could have lodged in a rock." He gave another harder tug on the line. "Keep your tension on, work the rod up and down, and perhaps he'll work loose."

Colin did as David directed and for several minutes nothing happened, then just as he was beginning to lose patience, the fish exploded off the bottom and began another run. The boy tried to check the run but his rod dipped alarmingly and the nylon line sang in protest. "Let him run Colin - you only have 20 pound test line on - take your time."

Colin eased up on the drag wheel and the line hissed out on the porcelain eyelets. Ignoring the blood from his cut palm, and tightening up on the drag, Colin began to walk slowly north along the beach. He kept pace with the tiring fish, with Rafa and David following just behind him.

"OK Colin, start to put some strain on the line, try to turn him," David urged quietly. Colin began to wind in, each turn of the geared Penn bringing the fish a little closer. It made another half-hearted attempt to turn, but Colin continued winding and gradually the reel began to fill with line. "Now watch out in the surf, use the incoming wave to help you wind, and wait until the undertow is over before winding again."

As the fish came into the shallower water within 20 feet of the shore it gathered all its fading energy for one frantic last burst. It took Colin unawares. He felt the line snap tight but before he could compensate, the line parted, causing him to stumble backwards in the soft sand. For just a moment he saw a glittering silver-brown swirl and then the retreating wave took the triumphant fish back to sea.

"It's gone," he said, staring at the sea in disbelief, tears of disappointment welling in his eyes and thickening his voice. "If you hadn't told me to wind in, it would have been OK. If you had left me alone I'd have done it by myself." He threw the rod down at the feet of the two stunned adults, stalked back to the Land Rover and climbed inside.

"And now what?" David said to Rafa. "Hell, if he's going to get upset over losing a blasted fish, what sort of behaviour is he going to show when something serious happens?"

"He's only a kid Dave, let me talk to him. It's probably his first fish."

David picked up the discarded rod, shaking sand from the reel. "Well, I tell you, if that's an example of how modern Canadian youth behaves, then all I can say is God help Canada."

Rafa wiped his fish-slimed hands clean on his denim trousers. "Dave, you said yourself that the boy has lived a sheltered life. Give him time. You saw how excited he was when he was playing the fish. People grow at different speeds."

"Yes, I guess you're right. Come on let's try to jolly him out of it. I'd hate to have six weeks of sulky moods to contend with."

The two men trudged through the soft sand to where the Land Rover sat with its sullen passenger.

Chapter 11

Kate

Their eyes met over the dinner table and again he felt a prickling surge of electricity run through him. "Bloody hell!" He cursed silently, telling himself that he was being ridiculous, behaving like a naive kid. Repeat after me -- "This is a married woman." David lifted his wineglass, candlelight dancing through the golden Nederburg. He pretended to study the wine then turned to Liz Wright. "When do you and Josh expect to be transferred?"

"David, we all know that Lokpipe is a good company to work for in many ways, but they have one bad fault. In all the years we've worked for them we've never had more than 24 hours notice of a transfer."

"Oh, come now Liz, you're just cross at me because I need Josh in Turkey, and so you'll have to put off your soiree to the fleshpots of Sun City," Brack Mishki, the visiting chief of Lokpipe International growled, as a ripple of laughter swept the table.

Two days before, David had just dropped Colin outside the town's main swimming pool, when he was stopped by Josh Wright, the American Superintendent of Lokpipe International. Lokpipe was the main contractor supplying and installing the 1.5 metre diameter water pipe bringing fresh water to the mine from the Kuiseb dam at Rooibank.

"Dave, are you and your nephew free for dinner at our place on Friday night?"

"Hallo Josh, I'm afraid Colin's going up to Windhoek and then Mariental with Rafa in the Company aircraft tomorrow, and they'll be away for a few days."

"But you are free I take it?"

"Well yes, I'll be glad to come. Is it anything special -- Liz's birthday or something?"

"No, nothing like that. My boss from head office is out on an inspection tour and we're having a few people over to meet him.

Also, Liz has been nagging to have you back again; she thinks you don't eat enough "

"Josh, every time I come to your house I need two days to recover from all the great food Liz puts on the table, but tell Liz I'll be delighted. Is it a dress up affair?"

"No, casual as usual. Mishki isn't one to stand on ceremony, so come about eight, or earlier if you wish."

Now, he sat between Liz Wright and June Desmond and directly opposite him between June Desmond's husband Edgar and Brack Mishki, the visiting VIP, sat Kate Richardson. He had been taken by surprise at her arrival and hoped that no one had spotted his confusion when Kate had entered the room with the Desmonds. Her hair was swept up off the lovely fine-boned face and piled in a shimmering golden coil on top of her head, leaving her neck and shoulders bare. A necklace of small pearls set off a simply-cut pale blue dress that fell smoothly to just below her knees. David knew that she was simply the most captivating woman he had ever seen. He stood staring as Josh made the introductions, first to Brack Mishki, then turning to David, "Kate this is . . . oh, of course . . . you met the other night." Kate smiled up at him, putting a slim hand on his arm.

"Hello, David, it's good to see you again." David jerked himself back to the present. He could feel his face flushing under the deep tan. "Mrs. Richardson, it's a pleasure to see you again."

"My, my, we are formal tonight," June Desmond simpered, pressing up to him. He grinned at her, grateful for the distraction. "Down woman, or I'll have your husband deal with you." He turned back to Kate, but she had already been drawn away by Mishki, and the American was holding her elbow as he talked. David felt a flash of irritation, but he turned back to June and began to ask how her son was doing at the South African boarding school they had recently sent him to. Later at dinner, he found his concentration wandering again as June subjected him to various bits of project scandal.

"June, my pet," he finally interjected, "will you please start at the beginning. You always assume I know as much of the local scandal as you do."

Edgar Desmond chuckled. "That's telling her Dave."

David liked this ill-matched pair, June fat and fifty, her Texas accent flat and grating, but with a kind heart as big as the plains she was raised on. In contrast, Edgar was tall, white haired and debonair, with the smoothly polished speech that only an expensive education can produce. They too, were part of the Lokpipe operation and David occasionally played tennis with Edgar. He hadn't seen either of them for several weeks, and although glad to see them tonight, he was frustrated that June's interminable chatter barred his desire to talk to Kate.

The dinner was up to Liz Wright's usual standard. An up-country farmer had given her a leg and back of Springbok and the meat quite literally fell off the fork. Usually David cared little for food. He ate to fuel his body and was always amused at the length to which some people would go in order to eat special dishes in certain restaurants. But now the meal seemed to him the best ever and he startled Liz with a list of compliments."Why David, thank you." Liz coloured. David looked across at Kate and noticed that Mishki was covering her hand with his own while he leaned close to her ear. For the second time in the evening he felt a flash of anger and asked dryly, "Don't you agree, Mishki -- you've not eaten venison as good as this before?"

Mishki was saved from a reply by the telephone ringing loudly. Josh Wright excused himself and left the table, but he was back quickly. "Edgar, it's for you. There's been a breakdown at the plant."

Edgar rose and went to the phone and could be overheard in a brief but agitated conversation, presumably with the shift foreman at the plant. He hung up and pulled his car keys from his pocket. "Liz, everyone, would you please excuse me. I'll try to get back as quickly as possible." He left immediately and had still not returned three hours later when the dinner had finally ended with coffee and liqueurs at midnight. David offered to take June and Kate home, firmly squashing Josh's protest that it was his responsibility.

"Hell no, if I let you take them home, Liz will have me washing dishes. I'll leave that job for you and Brack," David said to general laughter. They made their goodbyes to Liz and Josh, not lingering in the doorway, as the temperature had dropped and thick fog swirled round the tiny bulbs that served as street lights. Once in his truck with Kate and June sitting next to him, David turned to June, "June, you are half way down Dunen Strasse, but where do you live Kate?"

"On Davies street, off Welwitschia." He turned the key and the truck rumbled to life. Turning off Kaiser Wilhelm Strasse a few minutes later, he passed the Antonious hospital, prompting June to exclaim, "Oh David, I heard about young Ivan Kretchmer -- what a dreadful thing. He was such a nice young man."

David sucked his breath in sharply. Pressed against him in the confines of the truck, Kate felt him stiffen.

"Yes, he was."

"What happened exactly?"

"June, let it be. He died in an accident. No doubt the Inspector of Mines report will be made public in due course." He stared ahead, thankful that the darkness hid his face.

"Oh Dave, how thoughtless of me. I am sorry - he worked for you didn't he - it was stupid of me to ask."

"It's all right. Men die on projects like these, but it's always a wrench when someone so young and full of life is killed, especially in such a pointless, irrational way." He swung past the high school and accelerated up Dunen Strasse, stopping outside the Wrights' house. "Here we are. I'll wait until your lights go on -- come to the door and wave if everything is OK." He waited until June reappeared to wave at them before he pulled away from the curb. Kate had moved slightly away to give him more room, but he could feel the closeness of her like an electric current between them. They sat in silence until he had negotiated the junction on to Welwitchia Street, when she spoke softly, "How is your nephew enjoying his stay?"

"Not much I guess. Colin is too used to the bright lights of the city and to the good things of life."

"It takes time to adjust to this way of life, David. It must be very different." The use of his name warmed him and he turned to look at her face.

"It's strange that you should say almost exactly what Rafa said. Perhaps you're right."

"The company pilot? Is that where Colin is tonight?"

"Yes, Rafa took him on a trip to Mariental -- for some reason he and Colin have taken to each other."

"And you find that strange?"

"In a way, yes. Colin is spoiled, self indulgent, everything Rafa is not." He shrugged. "Still, I only hope the boy has a good time. It's a hell of a long way to come and be miserable."

"You sound as though things are not going too well."

"I must confess that after a full week I had hoped to see him settle down more than he has." He paused then went on slowly, "I keep comparing him to young Ivan and wondering how he could have turned out so . . . incomplete. Compared with Ivan's vitality and sense of fun, he's . . . " He stopped. They were outside her house but she did not move.

"Young Kretchmer's death has hit you badly, hasn't it?"

He did not answer immediately, then with a sigh he turned to look at her. "It hit us all hard. Ivan was very popular. Strange isn't it -- here is a kid from a poor family, his father a retired railway employee. A kid who was putting himself through university on guts and hard work. He was a symbol of what all of us would have liked to have been at that age. He was so willing and cheerful, so determined to succeed." David's voice had thickened and he gripped the steering wheel hard. He looked away and his voice was bitter. "I was only Ivan's age when . . . " He drew a deep breath. "I wanted him to win so badly, you see . . . to have all the fun, all the excitement that I . . . then there's my nephew, from one of the richest families in Western Canada, born with a silver spoon in his mouth, spoiled, selfish and totally self-centred. I know he's very young, but the man often shows through the boy and I really wonder." He turned to her, "Why am I telling you all this?"

Her face was ghostly in the misty light from the streetlamp, her eyes luminous, fixed on his. He reached out to touch her as if in a dream. She came into his arms and he kissed her, feeling the softness of her lips and body. They clung to each other, the floor-mounted gear shift digging into his thigh. His hands ran down the smooth, bare, skin of her back and he suddenly felt totally out of control. He ran his right hand under her arm and cradled her breast. She surged against him and blood roared in his ears, then suddenly she stiffened and pushed him back.

"No!" turning her head, "No, David. Please."

"I'm sorry . . . No, dammit, I am not sorry at all. Ever since the dance I've felt . . . I don't know what I've felt except that every time I see you, I want to hold you . . . no . . . it's more than that. I want you."

He turned to look at her and was startled to see the silver tracks of tears running down her face. "Kate, please . . . " He stopped helplessly.

"Oh David, It's my fault, you seemed so sad and alone. You're a very attractive man - - any woman would be physically attracted -- and I hoped that you would drive me home tonight. I even imagined a goodnight kiss . . . but then I . . . wanted . . . ." She stopped, then firmly. "I think we both had too much wine tonight." She rummaged in her purse unsuccessfully and he handed her his handkerchief. "Here."

"Thank you."

She squeezed his hand suddenly and with that simple act signalled the beginning, not the end, of whatever relationship was to follow.

"I hate anyone to see me cry." She dried her eyes and handed back the handkerchief, more composed. "David, I'm married. We both know that. Jack and I . . . It may not seem to be the best marriage, but Jack isn't a bad person and, whatever happened tonight I'm not the type to have affairs." She gripped the curved edge of the dashboard in both hands. "I've never even considered the possibility. I couldn't bear the thought of Jack's pain if . . . ."

He turned her chin gently to face him, "Kate, you're obviously not happy now, and Jack is married to ConAmGeo - Oh yes - since meeting you I've done some digging. Old man Butchert has plans for Jack. No doubt he'll end up in senior management some day soon. Hell, I've found out that he's constantly away on company business. What sort of life does that give you?"

She covered his hand with her own. "David, I'm not desperately unhappy either. I've never even thought of leaving Jack until . . . I've just never thought of it. I have my work. Don't you see, I have no reason or right to hurt him so. I couldn't live with myself and it would poison any relationship you and I could have."

He gripped her shoulders, "Kate, you don't love him do you? Liking someone isn't good enough - God help me, I've never felt like this before, but I think I'm falling in love with you, and I don't know what to do."

"David don't." Suddenly she was crying again, face pressed to her hands. "Please don't make it harder, I'm not as strong as you." He pushed her back, finding the handkerchief again, wiping her tears away gently.

"Very well, if that's what you want, I couldn't do anything to hurt you." He shook his head slowly, "Ridiculous isn't it, I am forty-four years old and find that I have never been in love before - now for the first time - I find someone I can't have."

Kate opened the door and climbed down. "David, try to understand . . . " She was about to continue when a vehicle turned off Welwitschia street on to Davies, the golden yellow beams of its fog lamps lighting up the little tableau. Kate turned and ran up the path to her front door. David sat watching the lights go on in her house. Satisfied that she was safe, he leaned over to close her passenger side door, acutely aware of the faint smell of her perfume that lingered softly. “Oh shit! Goddamn it all to hell.” He cursed at nothing in particular and swung the truck back the way he had come.

Chapter 12

Namibia - Mariental

Rafa snapped the light on and threw his flight bag on one of the two single beds, "Hot enough for you?" He turned to Colin who had entered behind him. Colin's thin cotton shirt was unbuttoned, hanging outside of his shorts and he held a small suitcase in one hand.

"Turn the air conditioning up Rafa, this is terrible."

"No, you must acclimatize, air conditioning will hold you back, here . . . " He opened the windows and the sound of splashing rose from below, "Change into your trunks and we'll have a quick swim before supper."

Twenty minutes later they were back in the room, refreshed. Colin watched fascinated as Rafa towelled himself vigorously, a cluster of white and purple ridged scars on his back and chest, a vivid pattern against his swarthy skin.

"What happened to you?" Colin pointed to the scars.

The Chilean grunted. "An accident -- long ago. Now go and have a shower or we'll be late in the dining room."

"Aw, come on Rafa, what sort of an accident? How did it happen? Did you crash?"

"Crash! Well I suppose you could call it that, but at least it was not through lack of flying skill." He looked at Colin keenly. "Once upon a time there was a war, or perhaps more than one, I no longer wish to remember, but like you I was young then and thought I was immortal." He shivered despite the oppressive heat. "Por Dias, enough of this. Some day perhaps I will tell you a story, but right now we need to eat, so go and shower." Later when they had both dressed in clean lightweight clothing, they descended the stairs to the dining room.

Three men in short-sleeved open-necked shirts and shorts, with nothing but rubber thongs on their feet, yelled a greeting at them and Rafa pulled Colin over.

"Hey, you guys, where is number four, I must leave early tomorrow?"

"Jack Richardson left yesterday. The old man sent a message that he had to go down to O'Kiep and sit in on some conference, and we have at least another day's field work. It looks like you'll have a free day tomorrow. Butchert wants you to wait until we're finished so I advised Tsamma of the delay and asked them to call our wives. So, you lucky bastard, you can buy the drinks. Come and join us." The speaker, a giant of a man with a mahogany suntan and a massive black beard, looked at Colin questioningly.

"Norman, this is my new co-pilot, Colin Mornay - Colin these refugees from the forbidden zone are what passes these days for geologists - watch your fingers when you shake hands." A howl of protest from the others greeted his comment and Norman quickly retorted.

"Watch it, Colin lad, I hate to say this, seeing as we are to put our lives in his less than perfect flying skills, but you must have nerves of steel to fly with old Sancho Ricketyback here." He turned to the others. "I bet Castro sent him to subvert our Western values." More laughter swept the table and Colin looked from face to face. He had never come across men like this before and he suddenly felt uncharacteristically shy.

"Here, sit down Colin." A chair was dragged squealing across the slate floor, "Mornay, not related to Dave are you?"

"Yes he's my uncle."

The speaker looked at Colin with renewed interest and respect, "Good bloke Dave, one of the few managers who has any bloody sense on the plant."

Later that evening, the others having left to see a movie at the local cinema which they called the "Bioscope," Colin and Rafa sat on the verandah outside their room, the only light in the inky evening coming from scattered street lights and the glow of Rafa's cigarillo. Colin felt lightheaded, Rafa had allowed him two beers and he had joined in the wisecracks that bounced around the table, feeling flattered that these men treated him as an adult. From talk around the table, he gathered that little love was lost between the field staff, like these geologists, and the "Paper Tigers" who ran the mine. One of the exceptions, they all agreed, was David Mornay, who they all seemed to think well of.

Colin raised the point now with Rafa. "Norman and the others think my uncle is a pretty good guy."

"Don't you?" the glowing tip of the cigarillo made a slight arc.

"Yes, I guess so, but I hardly see him, 'cause he's at the mine most of the time. Sometimes I think he doesn't like me very much."

"Colin, you must understand, your uncle is a very hard man, believe me, I've met quite a few. He doesn't know how to treat you. He expects . . . "

Colin interjected - "He expects me to like everything he likes and nothing I do seems to please him, but I don't care. I'll be going home in four weeks so it really doesn't matter."

"Perhaps, if I tell you that a young fellow, just a little older than you, was killed the week before you got here . . . "

"I don't see what . . ."

"Wait a minute! You've got a bad habit of not letting me finish a sentence. The young man -- his name was Ivan -- was very popular with the construction crews, but especially with your uncle. Dave helped him get the job and sort of took Ivan under his wing. Dave and Wessel van der Walt spent a lot of time keeping an eye on him and training him." Rafa drew deeply on the cigarillo and in the ruddy glow Colin saw the deep lines of pain. "Ivan was crushed when a compressor broke free and pinned him against a drill rig. Dave and I have both lost friends over the years, but this was different -- unexpected -- and then of course you arrived." Colin said nothing, staring mesmerised at the lean face lit by the cigarillo.

"You see, Colin, for men like us -- Dave, Wessel, myself -- we have no family to speak of. We chose long ago, for whatever reason, to live alone without close ties. But then one day you come to realize -- when you see other men with their sons or daughters -- you realize just what you've given up, and of course by then it's too late. For us, Ivan was special, but for Dave he was like a son and then you, his nephew, arrives and he compares you, forgetting that you're from a different world and aren't part of our world like Ivan was. Do you understand?"

"I suppose I'm a poor substitute." Colin's voice was bitter. "My own father doesn't think much of me, so why should my uncle?"

"Stop feeling sorry for yourself, boy. You are neither a poor or a good substitute, simply different." Rafa's voice was surprisingly gentle. "No one can ever be all things to all people, but perhaps for us, Ivan was. But he's dead and you're alive, and that is what matters now. You are young yet, but as I said before, you have good hands and you have courage. Oh, yes! I watched you when we hit the storm over Windhoek, so don't be too hard on yourself. You still have lots of growing to do."

For a while they sat in silence, then Colin asked,"Does my uncle ever talk about why he left home when he was a little older than me?"

In the gloom Rafa chuckled, "No, he's never mentioned that to me. He's not a man for confidences but sometimes, when the Black Dog walks and he needs to talk, he tells me a little of his time in Vietnam."

"The Black Dog?"

"It's an old mercenary saying and it refers to things you would rather forget - things that should be forgotten if a man is to remain sane. Like a big black dog that must be taken for a walk, he comes when you least expect him and must be dealt with."

"Did you also fight in Vietnam? Is that where you got those scars?"

"No, my wars were in Africa." He sighed, "Why is it that war is so fascinating to the young?" He lit a fresh cigarillo, and Colin waited quietly. "During the Simba uprising in the Congo, I was attached to Colonel Mike Hoare's number 5 Commando, and flew a small spotter aircraft for the mercenaries -- a little Piper Cub -- and my job among others was to try to keep the forward columns informed of ambushes ahead. Among the Commando I was attached to, was an Englishman who like many of the others had come to find adventure, be a hero and make lots of money. The problem was that when the shooting started, he realized he wasn't cut out to be a soldier so he tried to desert. This man, Wilson was his name, was short, fat and smelt of garlic. He was a great whiner and I don't know how he avoided being shot when the Colonel recaptured him.

We were fighting near a town called Bukavu and the Simbas were being directed by regular Cuban troops. The Colonel ordered me to try and spot the location of the artillery that was throwing heavy stuff at us and slowing down our advance. To cut a long story short, while I was airborne over the Simba lines, the Piper took a burst in the engine and started going down. I turned towards our own lines and managed to glide towards where our troops were dug in, but I could see that I was going to land at least 200 metres short. I didn't know that the burst that got my engine had also taken out the port tire, so when I touched down the Piper dug in and cartwheeled and left me trapped in a mess of twisted aluminium tubing and torn fabric. I was conscious but couldn't move, and for good measure the Simbas were raking the road with small arms fire." He drew deeply on the cigarillo, his face Satanic in the red glow. "Our captain, a Rhodesian, yelled at two of the troopers to get me out and they ran across the mealie field to get me."

"What's a mealie field?" Colin interjected.

Rafa laughed. "You call it corn. Anyway, I could see dust exploding around their route as the Simbas tried to get them, and of course our own side was putting down a lot of suppressive fire, but still it was a very brave thing they did. And yes 'Fatty' Wilson was one of the troopers. Between him and Dent, the other soldier, they cut me out and carried me piggyback to safety." Rafa flicked the butt of his cigarillo over the balustrade, to fall hissing in the pool below. "Now the moral of this story is that when I asked Wilson the next day why he had come to my aid he said, and this is interesting -- "Didn't stop to think, mate" -- What he meant though, was that he had stopped thinking of himself long enough to do something constructive."

Colin waited, wondering if there was more and if in some subtle way Rafa was giving him a message. The silence lengthened and finally he asked, "What happened to Wilson?"

"Oh he deserted a week later. He really was afraid of death and that's what made his behaviour on the Bukavu road so surprising. Hah! I talk too much. Come on Colin, it's been a long day."

David roared up to the airfield parking lot, braking in a swirl of brown dust. Van Tonder the maintenance man waved and David heard him yell. "Due any minute now, Rafa's just called in." He nodded and walked towards a small knot of men and women awaiting the arrival of the company aircraft. He felt hot and gritty and with the sun almost directly in his eyes he didn't recognize her until he was 10 feet from the group, then he felt a sudden surge of delight. "Kate! What are you doing here?" The others turned to look curiously at him intrigued by the excitement in his voice.

"I've come to meet Jack. He's due back with the Geological party that Rafa is bringing back from Mariental."

"Oh, I see." His voice went flat and he stared at her, oblivious of the others, conscious only of her presence. She stood facing him, a petite figure in an open white lab coat, her hair blowing softly in the gentle puffs of wind that presaged the coming of the East Wind. "I want . . ." he started

She cut him off quickly, pleading in her eyes, "Are you meeting someone, David?"

"Yes, my nephew. He's been riding with Rafa, seeing a little of the country." David smiled at the others. He knew them all slightly and at all costs he must remain calm. Norman Klienbank's wife, Jill, made conversation. "How is your nephew enjoying his holiday. It must be very different from Canada?"

"Oh, fine thanks, but it certainly is very different to what he's been used to." At that moment, the hum of aircraft engines deepened to a roar and Rafa flashed overhead, banking steeply before Tsamma Ridge, wheels dropping as he turned to run in for the landing. Minutes later, the Chieftain sat silently on the parking area as it disgorged three bearded boisterous geologists who grabbed their waiting wives. Over his wife's shoulder, Norman Klienbanks saw David and smiled, "Hi Dave. He's a good kid that nephew of yours."

David grunted. "I just hope you rednecks didn't corrupt him too much." He watched for Jack Richardson to appear and was about to comment when Norman turned to Kate.

"Oh, Kate, Jack went down to O'Kiep three days ago. Didn't he phone you?" The bearded face struggled with embarrassment as he tried to recover from the obvious *faux pas*. "Of course the lines to O'Kiep are bad, but he did say he would be back next week." David watched her face but it showed no sign of emotion.

"Thank you, well I'd better be getting back then." She turned and David dropped into step with her.

"Kate, we must talk, I can't go on like this." She made no answer until they were well out of earshot of the others.

"David, please, we agreed, it's for the best." He noted that she was trembling and fought down an overwhelming urge to take her in his arms.

"No Kate, it's not for the best," he replied harshly. "I can't believe you're happy. Hell, his job is so important that he doesn't even phone to let you know where he is. Dammit, Kate, I'm not used to begging."

The others were drawing nearer and in panic she whispered. "Very well. I must go to the library tonight. I'll meet you there at eight." He nodded and stood watching as she climbed into the Laboratory Peugeot and drove away.

"She is very beautiful my friend." David swung round to face Rafa, with Colin ten feet behind.

"Hello men, how was the trip? Did you enjoy yourself Colin?"

"OK I guess. Sure is hot down there." Scuffing his foot idly in the dust, Colin didn't look at his uncle and again David felt a ripple of irritation at the boy's lack of enthusiasm for anything that had been done for him. He raised an eyebrow at Rafa who clapped Colin on the shoulder.

"He's turning into a hot shot pilot. He flew most of the long leg from Mariental. Maybe we've found his vocation, hah!"

"Well let's hope so, It will certainly be something to take back with you, although I'm not sure your father will thank me. Do you want to come in to the mine with me or go back with Rafa?"

"Well . . . I'll go in with Rafa and have a shower and clean up."

"Sure, OK with you Rafa?"

The pilot swung his bags into his station wagon. "Of course, come on Colin." Colin walked round the rear of the station wagon temporarily out of earshot.

"How did it go?" David asked.

"Not bad, he is not Ivan but he is OK. Now relax Dave, as Wessel says, 'Alles wil regkom' and he's right, everything will turn out OK."

"Thanks Rafa, he has obviously taken to you and it's a relief to see him interested in something." He punched the pilot lightly on the arm. "I owe you a few drinks, how about we all meet at the Hansa for supper -- my treat?"

"Sure, see you there . . . about six?" He started the station wagon almost as if it were an aircraft, waved a gloved hand casually and drove off, bumping down the perimeter road. David stood for a moment deep in thought, grateful that Rafa was taking Colin off his hands. He wanted time to think about his relationship with Kate, and what he was going to say to her tonight.

TAS to URU. He grew certain that she wasn't coming. The books disappeared, rack on rack to the end of the room. He was about to go when he saw her kneeling in the non-fiction section, a book open in her lap. His heart leapt and he almost ran. "Kate?" She looked up smiling.

"David, help me up, please." She extended a slim arm, and as she rose she held on a fraction longer than was necessary before saying, "I'll check out my books, then we can go and sit in the courtyard."

The library was housed in one of the historical landmarks of Swakopmund. Woermann House, built in 1903 by the Damara and Namaqua Trading company of Hamburg, was used as a trading store, then later as the headquarters of the Woermann shipping line. Originally, no expense had been spared to equip the home of the manager and the guest quarters. The tower was designed by the architect Friedrich Hoft and had served as a water tower, a communication tower for the ships of the Woermann line and as a prominent landmark. A beautiful building, now restored after years of neglect, it housed the museum, the library and the reading room. The buildings in timbered Bavarian style surrounded an open courtyard with plastic-coated wrought iron furniture.

It was a clear night for a change, the weather warmer than usual in advance of the dry East Wind. This yearly phenomenon occurred when moist air from the high interior plateau was drawn down across the desert by a low pressure system offshore. As the airmass descended, it compressed and gave up its moisture, becoming very dry and hot. By the time it reached the coast, the effect was that of a blast furnace and the wind drove clouds of fine dust into every nook and cranny, adding to the general misery. But so far, only the first faint intimations of the wind had arrived and it was a very clear night. David found a table in a slight shadow. The courtyard was empty and in darkness, but light from the library windows splashed yellow on the sandstone cobbles as he pulled a chair out for Kate.

She sat with hands clasped, elbows resting on the table. "I wish I smoked," she began. "It's at a time like this when having something to hold is useful."

"I know the feeling, I had a few drinks with Rafa before coming and even so my hands are still shaking -- look . . ." He held his right hand level above the table. They both laughed, and she held her own hand out, "So is mine."

She clasped her hands tightly again and looked up. "David, I need time. This is a novel situation for me. I thought that I knew myself, but I find that I'm so confused . . . please don't say anything . . . I must speak, it has been with me all day - no, ever since you left last night. Despite what you might think I'm not the wild romantic type." She laughed nervously. "Growing up as the youngest child in a house where my parents adored me, I had so much affection that I became quite self-centred." She dropped her eyes to her clasped hands. "I am . . . that is, I was . . . used to getting my own way a lot of the time and the few men I met in my teens simply didn't measure up. I might never have married and been quite happy in my work. Perhaps that's not fair . . . forgive me, I am not one for pop psychology." She stopped and he waited through a full 30 second silence. Then she continued, "I had very little to do with men, I was always the intense student. You Americans -- sorry, Canadians -- I believe you call such people nerds. In University, I thought I was in love with Jack, not madly, not passionately, but in a comfortable sort of way. Jack did all the pursuing and eventually I gave in, more because he persisted than from any great desire to be married." She took a deep breath. "I suppose I believed, in my arrogance, that his love would compensate for my shallow affections and, anyway, he was considered the prime catch, so no doubt ego had a hand." Someone inside the library passed in front of the window and for a second, darkness hid her face, "But if our marriage has not been wildly exciting, it has not been unpleasant either. I feel so -- dishonourable even thinking about . . . "

David waited again but she didn't continue. "Kate look at me, I didn't ask for this to happen any more than you did, but it has. We can't pretend that our lives can stay the same. Love is not something that can be put in storage until a convenient time."

"David, we hardly know each other. It's possible that we're mistaken."

"Mistaken!" His voice was loud in the quiet of the courtyard, "I'm not mistaken, that I'm sure of, but are you?"

"I don't know. Everything has happened so fast. If Jack had come home today, perhaps I would have felt differently -- Oh, I don't know -- I look at you and I feel . . . Oh, David, I don't know." She shook her head helplessly.

David reached across the table and closed both her hands in his. "Kate, I have never expected much from life, or for that matter even wanted much, but I know that we could be good for each other. I suspect that your life, like mine, has not been totally satisfying, we have both turned to our work as a substitute for what really matters. Now the future can become something that will give us both much joy." He held her hands tightly. "Look at Edgar and June -- they've been married for 25 years. Physically and I guess emotionally they are a complete mismatch, but because they love each other their marriage has grown stronger over the years. You can't say that . . . you can't look ahead and say you expect that from your marriage to Jack. Kindness is no substitute for love."

She pulled her hands away gently and raised them to his face, gazing at his face as if to imprint it for the last time. He felt a dread sense of defeat, for when she spoke her voice was stronger. "David, it must end here, because whatever I think I feel for you, it's not right. I'm not a dishonest person any more than you are and we could not be happy doing this." She stood and he saw the glint of tears in her eyes. "Forgive me, but you are so much stronger than Jack." She made as if to step closer, looking down at his bowed head, her voice was barely audible. "Oh, David, I am sorry, I am so sorry." and with her hand pressed to her mouth she rushed into the passageway leading directly to the street.

For a long time, David sat staring at his clasped hands. He felt lost, the same emptiness he felt when he had the final break with his father and again after listening to the padre calling the names of his men, after the murderous Tet offensive was crushed. He sighed and rose to his feet. Suddenly, he felt his age and wondered if it was time to go home. But where was home? Canada . . . hell, he had spent more of his life in Asia and Africa, but where in Africa was home? Perhaps Zimbabwe, for the early years had been happy and perhaps Winston still had the farm.

As he opened the door of the pickup, he could see the fishermen's lights blink down on the jetty below, their voices carrying on the clear air. Best sleep on it, maybe take a few days off to think what to do. Pulling away from the curb, he was still deep in thought and didn't notice Kate's little Volkswagen parked near the jetty, it's motionless driver staring out over the dark sea.

Chapter 13

The Salt Pans

"Damn it boy, I'm responsible for you. Don't you realize the damage you've done?" David glared down at Colin. "Childish pranks I can understand but this was sheer bloody vandalism." He paced the room, while Colin sat downcast on the sofa not answering. "What possessed you boy, what the hell got into you?"

"It was meant to be a joke, we didn't expect him to get hurt."

"Joke! A joke! A man is in hospital with a broken leg, his vehicle is damaged, and you call it a joke!" Colin didn't reply, sitting sullenly, waiting for the storm to pass, as he had so often done at home in Canada. "You've been here nearly three weeks and in all that time the only thing you've seemed to enjoy was your trip to Mariental with Rafa. It's a good thing he's been away the last ten days. He thought a lot of you, but I wonder what he'd think now!"

David stopped in front of Colin, his face grim. "I've phoned the travel agency in Walvis Bay. The first available seat to Europe is on Saturday, four days from now. You will return to Canada and I will phone your parents when I get confirmation that you have a seat, and in the meantime you will not be seeing your so-called friends in the expatriate community. Do you understand?"

Colin looked up, his bottom lip thrust out. "You are not my father, and you can't stop me seeing Zane and Jimmy." He tried to meet David's eyes and failed. "At least they showed me a good time. Everyone here hates the expatriate kids. No one will even talk to us. Look at those people at Etema."

David sighed. Etema had been a disaster. At first, their trip to the tiny guest farm in the foothills of the Erongo mountains had gone well. He had taken four days off work, much to the relief of his staff who had been worried about the change in his usually cheerful attitude. While demanding excellence from his staff,

David worked harder than the best of them, his philosophy being that one led from the front, not controlled from the rear. He was popular, but the affection was tempered with respect. His anger at shoddy workmanship was fast becoming legendary and no one was exempt from his continual monitoring. Since his meeting at the library with Kate 10 days before, he had become morose and irritable. Finally realizing that he was walking around like a bear with a sore head, he had gratefully accepted Caroline's suggestion that he take Colin on a trip inland to a guest farm from which she and her boyfriend had recently returned. David had heard good reports from various people who had periodically spent long weekends there and he had been intending to visit the Bushmen rock paintings for which the area was famous.

The guest farm "Etema" lies north of the Erongo range, with its northern boundary being the dried out bed of the Omaruru River. Being in the central region, the countryside was not pure desert like the coastal Namib. Vegetation was a mixture of scrub trees and hardy bunch grasses interspersed with wind-worn rock outcrops. The area had once been the hunting ground of the Bushmen, but with the coming of the white men they had moved away into the even more forbidding vastness of the Kalahari. Etema farm consisted of a collection of small bungalows huddled around a main farm house, surrounded by soaring outcrops of fantastically shaped rock hills.

Their trip began early in the morning. Four hours later they arrived after travelling on some of the worst roads David had ever seen. Even at the best of times the LandRover isn't a comfortable vehicle and the final 30 kilometres from the tiny village of Tubussis was, to put it mildly, very uncomfortable. Colin's initial interest quickly waned in the heat and the jolting of the truck, and his continual derogatory references to the standard of local road building in Namibia compared to Canada set David's teeth on edge. He held his tongue only because he was determined not to get the trip off to a bad start.

Colin ignored the scenery which slowly changed from the

treeless rocky desert around Swakopmund to low scattered thorn trees interspersed with tufts of rough grass. Dust billowed behind them after they left the paved highway at Usakos and fine powder seeped through the many openings in the old LandRover. David who was inured to the heat and dust hardly noticed as Colin squirmed and coughed in the fine dust that lay over everything. David's commentary on items of local interest were answered only with a noncommittal grunt.

At Etema, Colin managed to find fault with almost everything. The food was lousy, the water in the pool was too cold, and mindful of his license the manager refused to serve Colin beer -- the list seemed endless. David, on the other hand, was enjoying the break from work. He had agreed with Colin that the farm was not exactly five star but had observed that a lot of work and thought had gone into the layout. Gardens tended with loving care in this harsh environment were home to a variety of brightly coloured birds flitting among the low trees. Accommodations were spartan, but clean and comfortable.

On the second day they left the farm and, following directions given to them at breakfast, drove to a group of rock outcrops called the Gramadulla where many excellent rock paintings could be found. The rock paintings were arresting in their simplicity, the only testimonials to the race of Bushmen now long gone. Depicted on the curved underfaces of huge granite boulders protected from the elements were paintings of elephant, rhino and a myriad of antelope. David was completely fascinated and was disappointed when Colin refused to accompany him on a climb to a higher cave, complaining that he had seen enough and wanted to return to the guest farm swimming pool. David tried unsuccessfully to awaken an interest in this unique and long dead art form, but finally gave up in disgust and they descended in silence.

On the third day, a young German girl asked Colin to accompany her on a horseback ride down the Omaruru river bed to search for signs and perhaps the sight of game. Colin was at home on a horse, his father owning several on their farm near Victoria, but had to be prodded and finally agreed with ill grace. They cantered off, disappearing among the thorn trees and David retired gratefully to the bar where he engaged the hotel manager in idle conversation and a game of liar dice.

Half an hour later they were attracted by a roar of laughter from outside the building and on investigating found that Colin and the girl had returned. Colin, however was on foot. The girl, a sweet fourteen-year old, was regaling the group of laughing guests in German how Colin had been thrown while trying to force his horse through a particularly soft patch of sand in the river bed and how the horse had run away leaving him sitting deep in the sand. Except for his pride, Colin was unhurt, but he was clearly the butt of the good-natured laughter. Enraged, he let loose a volley of foul language that left everyone stunned, before storming off to the sanctuary of his room.

This gentle establishment did not easily tolerate such behaviour. At dinner that evening, uncle and nephew were ostracized by the other guests and both retired early. The next day they left, the manager suggesting coolly that Colin would not be welcome in future. It was a strained drive back to Swakopmund, but David managed to remain pleasant to Colin despite his disappointment at the way the trip had turned out.

The real problems began later, when Colin was left alone during the day while David was at work. He encountered a group of boys his own age lounging outside the Portuguese delicatessen, their leader, Zane Dobbs, a 17 year-old American whose father, a uranium extraction specialist on loan to Tsamma Uranium, was well known to David. Like Colin, Zane Dobbs and Jimmy Hicken were temporary sojourners in Swakopmund and like Colin, they missed their own preferred environment in America.

At first David had been delighted at the change in Colin. The boy was obviously enjoying himself, spending hardly any time at all in the house. But Swakopmund is a small town and reports began to filter back to David of some disturbing behaviour by the three boys. He tried to pin Colin down, but the boy denied any involvement in charges of speeding, or of removing pets from the walled gardens of houses and then setting them free to wander bewildered around the business district of town. David did not press his enquiries. For one thing he was very busy at the mine, the ammonium nitrate storage bins were being extended and as usual the completion time for construction was ridiculously short. He hadn't seen Kate since their parting at the library and thinking of her didn't improve his concentration.

At lunchtime, David had received a call from Jack Dobbs the American consultant on loan to Tsamma. David had met Dobbs at various meetings and once socially, and found the dry-humoured Minnesotan a likeable person. Now he listened, surprised, as Dobbs requested that he come back to Swakopmund.

"What's going on Jack? What's so urgent that I must come in now? I usually get back around six?"

"Dave, it concerns Colin and my boy Zane. Young Jimmy Hicken, Brian Hicken's son is also involved. The boys have been up to some mischief and the police are holding them at the station on the corner of Garnison and Bahnhof. Brian and his wife are away in Windhoek for a few days and Jimmy has been staying with us. I'll act for Brian but the police want all the parents or guardians to go and see the Chief. As you know, I don't speak the lingo and I'm not sure how good the Chief's English is, so thought it best I wait until you arrived and we can go in together."

"The police are involved? This sounds more serious than you're letting on - OK, I'll leave right away and meet you at the police station in about forty minutes." He turned to Wessel. "You heard that Wessel," he shook his head in frustration, "Colin has managed to get himself arrested, so I have to go in right away - will you speak to Kobus about the concrete?"

Jack Dobbs was waiting when he arrived at the police station and the two went straight into the Chief's sparse office. The

Chief, who knew David slightly from his association with old man Smit, began quickly, after a courteous handshake. "Your son, Mr. Dobbs, took the other two, Hicken and Mr. Mornay's nephew out past mile eight in your dune buggy. They raced along the beach annoying several fishermen before parking near the pump station, you know the one, near the end of the bird sanctuary." Both men nodded. "Anyway, after smoking a marijuana cigarette -- we've got a witness on that -- they noticed a coloured fisherman on the beach, where the outcrop of rock makes a bay, the place where you and Smit caught the big steenbras last year, Mr. Mornay."

"Yes, I know where you mean."

The Chief continued the recitation, in the clipped, precise manner of a police report. "This fisherman, Abrahams, had his Land Rover parked on a dune above the high tide mark, facing the sea. It appears that a person or persons, crept up, engaged low gear, set the hand throttle and started the vehicle. At first Abrahams did not notice his vehicle moving -- the surf is loud in that area -- and when he did, it was almost to the water. Of course, Abrahams dropped his rod and ran to try and stop it, but by the time he got there it was in the sea and when he tried to open the door he slipped and fell under the vehicle which rode over him and broke his leg."

Here the Chief picked up a sheet of paper and, looking at the two men, continued -- "Fortunately, Piet Heimstra, the shark fisherman, came over the hill and saw what was happening, and I quote." He looked at the sheet in his hand. "I picked up Mr. Abrahams who could not stand and was crawling up the beach and put him in my bakkie and brought him in for treatment right away."

The chief hesitated for a minute, cleared his throat and continued. "While driving away from the pump station, I came across three boys in a dune buggy. They had driven into a salt ditch, one of the ones that takes the brine water from the salt pans and were stuck. Abrahams told me that they were the people that had started his Land Rover. I apprehended them and brought them in for questioning."

Here the Chief looked at both men and David noticed that he seemed slightly uncomfortable. "Heimstra is a very large man and I gather he had to use some force."

"Some force, what do you mean some force?" interjected Dobbs, his voice rising.

The Chief stared at the paper in front of him, "Well . . . your son, Mr. Dobbs was knocked unconscious, young Hinken has a broken tooth and your nephew, Mr. Mornay, has what will turn into a black eye. The injuries are minor."

"Minor! Beating up kids, you consider that minor." Dobbs was white faced, shaking with rage. David gripped his arm, "Wait a second, cool down and let's hear the whole thing."

Chief Pieterse shot a strange look at David and turned to Dobbs. "I agree that force should not have been used. Mr Heimstra was enraged by their behaviour, but I believe would not have hit them if they had not cheeked him, using foul language. He admits that he lost his temper."

David winced inwardly, he remembered only too well Colin's outburst at Etema. "What proof does anyone have that they were responsible?" he asked. "After all, you've just said Heimstra came across them in the runoff ditch. Well that's a good half mile from the rocks where it's supposed to have happened."

"Mr. Mornay, apart from the fact that Abrahams swears that he saw them drive off, and theirs was the only vehicle in that area apart from Heimstra's, several fishermen have confirmed that the only vehicle going south along the beach was the dune buggy, and as Piet came from the northeast there seems little doubt as to their complicity."

Dobbs, his voice shaking, said viciously, "It seems to me, Captain, that you're basing your case on a lot of very circumstantial evidence. I want to put it on the record that I want Heimstra charged with assault. I will not have my son beaten up and, speaking of my son, where is he?"

"I sent all three of them to the Antonious Hospital for a check over -- they should be back shortly." Chief Pieterse replied evenly.

As if on cue, a tall sergeant in the uniform of the Namibian Police entered, followed by the three boys. Colin's eye, as Captain Pieterse had predicted, was closed and turning black, and the swelling extended down his cheekbone. Zane Dobbs, a big rawboned youth was wearing a sweatshirt encrusted with mud and salt, with TEXAS U in black letters on a yellow field on the front and back. Evidently, he had ended up in the ditch, but apart from his muddy clothes, he appeared none the worse for wear. Jimmy Hicken emerged last through the door holding a blood stained piece of hospital gauze over his mouth. They were all painfully subdued and sat quietly on the wooden bench to which the sergeant motioned them. The sergeant came clicking across the parquet floor.

"Alles reg Captein, daar is nie a probleme nie, die groot seun - " He stopped, "I am sorry, I was saying that the Doctor is satisfied that they are in good health, no broken bones or anything." He smiled. "It is good - Ja?"

David thought Jack Hobbs would explode and he moved quickly to cut him off. From much longer experience in Africa, he knew that one kept a civil tongue in one's head when dealing with the police.

"Jack, I think that we should ask the boys for their version of what happened," he said quietly. "Perhaps it will shed some light. He grasped the American's elbow firmly and drew him across to where the three boys sat. Zane Dobbs stared at the floor. Just looking at him, David became sickeningly aware that the three boys were as guilty as hell. He left Dobbs talking earnestly to his son and turned back to Captain Pieterse, hearing, as he turned, Zane say, "We were just driving around."

David motioned the Police Chief to one side out of earshot of the others.

"What will happen now, Frikkie?"

"Well, Abrahams has said that he will press charges. No doubt a charge of malicious damage to property, damages for the injury sustained by himself, hospital costs, loss of earnings and if he gets a good lawyer he'll probably sue for pain and suffering."

"The Land Rover is a write off?"

"Oh no, as soon as it went into the surf the waves shorted out the ignition and it stopped. Fortunately the beach shelves very slowly there."

"Where is it now?"

"In Kluger's garage, we pulled it out with the police four by four."

"Look, Frikkie, this is off the record, I'm inclined to agree with you that they were probably responsible, but your evidence is largely circumstantial and a good lawyer would have this case thrown out of court."

"Perhaps so, but we must let the courts decide."

"Captain, nobody's going to gain if it goes to court. If Dobbs decides to sue Piet Hiemstra for assaulting his son it could run into a substantial sum."

"And you, Mr. Mornay, do you intend to sue?" The Captain was obviously not impressed with the message he was hearing and the green eyes were cold.

David kept his temper. "No, the boy has needed a belt for some time, but that is beside the point. I have a suggestion to make."

"And what is that?"

"Persuade Abrahams to drop all charges, I will have his Land Rover completely overhauled and pay all his expenses, costs and time off. I, that is, we . . . " He indicated Jack Dobbs with his head. "We will also make a substantial cash sum available as compensation to Mr. Abrahams."

"Money!" the police chief's lips twisted."Very well, I will speak to Abrahams, but if he insists on laying a charge I will not discourage him."

"Captain, there is one other point . . . "

"Yes I know, but that is your problem, you will have to convince Mr. Dobbs not to sue Piet, otherwise all deals are off."

David tried to read an expression on the brown face, but it was difficult to see behind the neutral expression. He knew that Heimstra was a friend of the Chief and regretted the next step he was having to take. Jack Dobbs was a loose cannon and could create all kinds of complications. Colin could be delayed for months while the case dragged on and if Colin's father became involved, with all the Mornay money and power, heaven only could predict the outcome. He turned to Jack Dobbs who was talking to his son and Colin.

"Jack, we need to talk."

The American straightened, anger showing in his eyes and in the bright red flush on his cheeks. "Over here, I think we can straighten this mess out quickly."

He explained to Dobbs the discussion he had just had with the police chief, concluding, "If you don't press charges against Piet Heimstra, the Chief will attempt to talk Abrahams out of laying charges against the boys."

"Do you really believe that I'll drop charges," Dobbs hissed. "You said yourself that their evidence is circumstantial and Zane assures me that they did not start Abraham's vehicle. Hell no! I will not tolerate some bloody ape beating up my son. You can do as you please, but don't tell me what to do." He turned to go, but David caught his arm.

"Listen very carefully Jack. Their evidence is more than circumstantial. I overheard the sergeant saying that they had managed to lift prints off the door of Abraham's vehicle - - these guys aren't stupid." David lied uncomfortably. "And, as certain as the fact that I am standing in front of you, those three boys are in a lot of trouble. Whatever satisfaction you'll get from suing Heimstra, it's not going to help your son."

Jack Dobbs face drained of colour, "Are you certain?"

David brushed the question aside. "Now, if we agree to split the costs on this, the chances are that Abrahams will agree to a settlement. Face has been saved by the thumping the boys got from Heimstra and Abrahams only saw them run off afterward. If Pieterse puts our suggestion to him he'll go along."

"But the fingerprints?"

"Pieterse won't mention them to Abrahams. He doesn't need the hassle and he doesn't want you launching an assault charge against Heimstra." Dobbs stood undecided, his shoulders sagging. David understood how Dobbs must be feeling, but remembering what the boys had done, his anger overcame any feelings of sympathy.

"OK, Dave, I agree, but only if Zane admits to starting the Land Rover. I'll talk to him again, give me a minute." Dobbs drew his son into a corner while David and the rest watched. Their conversation was whispered, but it was obvious from Jack Dobb's face that confronted with the fact of additional evidence, Zane had confessed. The boy hung his head and would not look at his father. Grim-faced, Dobbs returned to where David stood waiting.

"Yes, he admits it now. I'm sorry David. Will you deal with Abrahams? I agree to anything you decide."

David proceeded to make the necessary arrangements that afternoon. He drove directly to the hospital where Abrahams agreed to a cash sum and the repair of his vehicle, his wizened, dark brown face creasing in a wry grin as he recounted chasing his Land Rover into the sea. Before retirement, he had been a respected carpenter in Swakopmund, but currently he was known more for his ability to catch fish, and the excessive amounts of alcohol he could consume over an evening. Considering that his right leg was now encased in plaster, the old man showed surprisingly little rancour. "Boys will be boys, Mr. Mornay - I was a bad one in my time too," he cackled through toothless gums. "Oh yes, I was a bad one too." David was grateful for the old man's tolerance, for Pieterse's contemptuous remark about money still rankled. Colin was next on the agenda, and uncle and nephew faced each other in the living room of David's house. A clock whirred and banged unhurriedly in the kitchen, while budgies flashed across the window in streaks of blue and green.

"Colin, I am telling you to stay away from Zane Dobbs and Jimmy Hicken, and you will do as you are told. Be absolutely clear, I'm not asking or suggesting, I'm telling you. Do you understand?" Colin responded with only a slight nod and David continued. "Tomorrow you are going on the day tour into the desert with Namib Safaris. I know you're not that interested in the countryside, but the least you can do for your parents is take some photographs back with you."

He stretched his shoulders, feeling the tension pull at the tight muscles in the back of his neck. He glanced at Colin and wondered if he really was getting through to the boy. What he didn't realize was just how practised Colin was at playing such a scene. The boy was a master of manipulation. He had learned well the art of no -- or very little -- response. Let the storm rage and wear itself out. They'd ultimately tire and even start feeling guilty. Yes, he had learned well, and David was just another authority figure.

David heaved a deep sigh and softened his tone as he got up to leave. "I'm going to have a shower, then we will go down to the Zum Zee Teufel for dinner." He disappeared down the long corridor leaving an unrepentant Colin staring into space.

Chapter 14

The Cauldron

The long wheelbase LandRover station wagon bumped slowly over the rocks. Kresfeld eased her down slowly, the incline was steep and the track they were following was barely wide enough for the truck. Pulling the transfer gear into low range, he anxiously watched the temperature gauge. "Damn it all," he thought, Heinz should have installed the new radiator last week. He cursed his luck. Once again, he had to bring out this lemon. The tourists sat quietly on the three rows of seats behind him. In the main they were a good group, mostly tourists from Germany but there were also two Tsamma employees. His one irritant had been the young boy who insisted on making stupid wisecracks about everything. Fortunately, during the last hour, the boy had been distracted by a young German girl his own age who was obviously attracted to him. Hermann Kresfeld would be 65 in three months and he had promised himself that, from that day on, no matter what the others said, he would no longer drive tourists. He was bored with the routine, the sameness of the questions and now he had to put up with a over-indulged brat.

He pulled the LandRover to a stop, glancing again at the temperature gauge, which had risen past the centre and was moving towards the upper part of the dial.

"Ladies and gentlemen, we will stop here so that you can stretch your legs. This is the site of a skirmish between the German and South African forces during World War One."

He waited until the tourists had gathered expectantly around him.

"Over there, the South African forces came," he explained, pointing to a line of burnt, rocky, dolerite ridges, broken and crusted with scattered boulders. "Here the German Schutztruppe waited." He could not keep the ring from his voice and several of the German tourists smiled. He went on to describe in graphic detail the events of almost 90 years ago. The rocks seemed to come alive with the whine of ricocheting bullets and the hoarse cries of wounded and dying men. Then he pointed to the flat valley between the two broken ridges.

"Here the German commander was heavily outnumbered and withdrew up the Khan canyon, only to meet the Union forces at the battle of Trekkoppies." One of the tourists said something in rapid German and Kresfeld laughed. "Nien."

He broke into English again. "If you wish to look for mementoes we will be here for a half hour. The last time I stopped here one of my parties found a soldier's belt buckle in very good condition."

The party split up, fanning out in every direction, heads bent down and eyes glued on the ground. They reminded Colin of a bunch of chickens pecking at grain. It was hot. God, it was always hot, Colin thought. He watched the others leave and he sat with his legs hanging out of the open door of the Land Rover, his body shaded by the panel roof. Kresfeld came around to his side.

"You are not interested in souvenirs Herr Mornay?"

"No - why did we stop here? I thought you said the next stop was to be the rose quartz outcrop."

Kresfeld looked at the boy from beneath his bushy white eyebrows, and rubbed his jaw, scratching the skin with a gnarled finger. "Ja, I said that - but the engine is getting a little hot - you have noticed how hot it is today, ja? So we will wait a little until the engine cools down." Kresfeld lifted the hood, propping it open on the angled retainer rod.

"Is it serious?" Colin peered in, but could see nothing unusual beneath the hood.

"Nien, of course not, but we have come a long way in low gear and it always raises the temperature, but today . . ." he touched the top of the radiator quickly . . . "it is hotter than usual, perhaps because the East Wind is coming."

"East Wind? What's that?" He could feel the perspiration run down his face from the heat of the engine and he backed away, returning to the shade formed by the angle of the vehicle.

"In the Interior," Kresfeld explained following him to the shade, "it is much higher, also much colder and the pressure is higher, while at the coast the pressure is lower, so the air moves from the mountains to the sea, so it is coming verstehen sie?"

Colin shook his head. "I still don't see." He was beginning to show interest.

"Ach, so - if air comes down it is compressed and becomes more dry, also warmer. By the time it reaches the coast it is very hot and very dry. I have seen the surf blown backwards by the wind and it can blow for days, sometimes weeks." He had turned to check the whereabouts of the other tourists, then he faced Colin again. "You must understand, Herr Mornay, that the East Wind is not something to enjoy, it is to be endured. Fortunately, it usually only lasts a short time."

He removed a stainless steel thermos flask from a pocket in the door, poured black tea into a cup and held it out to Colin. "Russian tea, it is ice cold with lemon juice added -- have a drink."

Gratefully, Colin drank deeply until Kresfeld pulled his hand down. "Slowly, always sip your drink in the desert, never gulp it down for it goes very quickly like that."

They sat, savouring the tea and the shade, until Kresfeld lifted his hand, "Did you feel the wind?"

Colin nodded. "Just a puff."

"Ja, by tonight or tomorrow it will be blowing very hard."

Kresfeld pulled himself up, reaching into the cab to press the horn. The tourists began to straggle back and he tooted once more. When they were all back, he gave each one a cup of water from the bags attached to the front of the vehicle, then made everyone board before lowering the hood. Starting the LandRover, he watched the temperature gauge closely and finally satisfied, he slammed the door shut. "OK! Alles in ordnung, we go to the Rosen Quartz hill -- it is not too far and I will take a short cut," he announced to a chorus of agreement. He let the clutch out and for a second or two the LandRover seemed reluctant to move, then all four wheels gripped the soft sand and it lurched out of the sand onto the flat, rocky floor of the valley.

Chapter 15

The East Wind

Rafa cut the switches and they both sat waiting as the plane's engine's whined to a stop.

"I will meet you at the Kalahari Sands about twelve -- you think you will be finished by then?"

David snapped his briefcase closed. "I guess so -- all I have to do is see the architect, then when that's over we can fly straight back."

"Not before lunch we can't. Mr. Butchert wants me to pick up some special mail from the main office and it won't be ready before one-thirty."

"Ah, for crying out loud! I'd hoped that we could make this a quick trip, I have another meeting at Tsamma at three. Hell, if I had known old man Butchert was going to hold us up, I'd have skipped this trip to Windhoek. The architect could have flown back with you."

"Hey, easy my friend." Rafa pushed himself clear of the pilot's seat. "We will get you back in time. What is the matter? You seem edgy today - still worried about Colin?"

"No, he's off for the day with a tour group into the Namib. By the way, before I forget, how about joining us for dinner at the 'Grunerkranz' tonight? Colin will be glad to see you back."

"Sure thing," Rafa closed his flight bag, pulled off his gloves and followed David out of the door. They walked across the tarmac at Windhoek's downtown Eros airport to the waiting rental car.

Three hours later, Rafa sat nursing a cup of coffee in the Tea Lounge of the Kalahari Sands Hotel. He had a clear view of the busy escalators rising from the shopping mall below, but his thoughts were elsewhere. David was late, and Rafa pondered over his friend's recent morose behaviour. He had phoned David late the previous evening after returning from Johannesburg where he had taken the Chieftain for an overhaul. Unaware of the decision to cut short Colin's stay in Swakopmund, he had brought the boy back several books on basic flying techniques. Rafa had expressed surprise at the news that Colin was to be sent home and had tried to talk David out of it. "Come on, Dave. Sure it was bad, but kids do things like that -- give him a belt and forget it," Rafa had urged.

David's voice had been frosty on the other end of the line. "He is going and that's that, I don't want any more episodes like the last one. I just don't have the time to be a nursemaid." David's tone suggested that the subject was closed, at least for now. Rafa had shrugged. He still felt that David was overreacting, but Colin was clearly David's responsibility.

Now he waited for the big Canadian to join him, worried by his friend's behaviour, suspecting that Colin's prank was not the whole problem. He saw David coming up the escalator, waved his menu card, and a minute later David dumped his briefcase and a pile of plans on an empty chair.

"Sorry I'm late, have you ordered?"

"No, I had decided to give you another five minutes - - are you through with your work?"

"Yeah, damned revisions! Every time some head office executive gets his hands on these plans there's another revision. If we're lucky, this is the end of them and we can start construction." He frowned at the menu. "Is this all they have?"

Rafa laughed. "Everything is against you today, no? Perhaps you should have stayed in bed, my friend."

David looked up ruefully. "That bad? It shows, eh?"

"Only two things make a man behave like that -- money or a woman." He grinned impishly. "It cannot be money, for Colin tells me that you have shares in a very big company and, in any case, you are not a man to care much about money. It is none of my business compadre, but if I can help . . . " He spread his hands expressively.

David looked at him silently for a long moment, and for a

second Rafa wondered if he had gone too far. "For a pilot you would make a good fortune teller . . . you guessed right, it's not money." Rafa waited, no longer smiling, the brown eyes expressionless. "I have . . ." David stopped, embarrassed, then in a rush. "I have fallen in love with another man's wife." He paused, staring down at his clasped hands, "so tell me oracle, what do I do now?"

"Kate Richardson?"

David rocked back startled. "Yes, how did you know? Don't tell me that it's all over the Plant?"

"No, I saw you speaking to her the day I brought Colin back from Mariental . . . remember?"

"Oh yes - that's right - well frankly it's been driving me crazy. I'm behaving like a love-sick adolescent."

Rafa studied his friend's face, all the humour gone from his eyes, "And Kate, she feels the same?"

"I think so . . . I am sure so . . . but she won't leave Jack," he replied bitterly. "She will not hurt him . . . hell, he's never home, he . . . " He stopped short. "No that's not fair, it was an accident, no one's fault . . . God knows I never intended . . . "

Rafa spoke sadly, "I told you about Marieanna, so I know how you feel. After she was killed, I spent a long time . . . I am a Catholic, and perhaps that is why I have never married. As you know, Catholics, once committed, even to a bad marriage, cannot break away. I knew that I would always measure other women by Marieanna and that would not be fair. Is Kate a Catholic?"

"I don't know, but I don't think so. You are wrong. It has nothing to do with religion. I am sure of that."

David signalled a passing waitress and the discussion stopped while they ordered. When she was out of earshot, David spoke again. "I have decided to ask for my contract to be rolled up within the next month. Wessel is quite capable of running things and in any case I only have six months to go, so it shouldn't cause too much of an upset."

Rafa whistled, surprised. "What will you do? Jo'burg is the

last place for someone like you."

"I am thinking of going to Mauritius . . . maybe I can lie on the beach and find some female company to take my mind off Kate. I've got enough time coming to me."

Rafa toyed with his knife, making patterns on the linen tablecloth, before he pushed the salt shaker to one side and spoke. "Do not rush into this my friend . . . take time . . . perhaps a holiday will do you good, give you time to think. But do not cut all your boats adrift." He rapped the side of the salt shaker, listening to the tinkle as it vibrated against the knife. "I cannot advise you, but I know from my own experience that it is better not to make any drastic moves when you are upset."

The waitress, a sinuous coloured girl in a short mini skirt, lowered two plates of steaming liver and onions on to the table, effectively stopping their conversation. Later they drove back to the airport, each wrapped in his own thoughts. At the airport, David gripped Rafa's arm.

"You won't mention this to anyone?"

"Dave, normally I would be insulted at a question like that, but I understand. Don't worry, it will remain with me."

Chapter 16

Sand

Colin was sure that something was wrong, Kresfeld seemed worried and continually stopped the LandRover every time they topped a rise, scanning the horizon for something. They had left the rose quartz outcrop an hour before and were returning to Swakopmund by a different route than their outbound track. Kresfeld had wanted to show them some ostrich and springbok on Tinkas flats, but now he seemed unsure of his position.

Their stay at the rose quartz outcrop had taken longer than anticipated, for all the members of the tour group had been keen to select a good sample of the translucent pink rock. The rose quartz outcrop sat in the middle of a shallow depression ten miles wide, like a pink pearl on a huge brown dinner plate. It had been pegged years ago by some long forgotten prospector and then abandoned after a few half-hearted attempts at blasting. Now the outcrop, a half-open pink dome the size of a small house, surrounded by shards of glassy pink debris, was a favourite spot for gem collectors prepared to suffer the uncomfortable journey over wind eroded tracks. Kresfeld unpacked a picnic lunch, and after everyone finished eating, he drew a map in the sand.

"We can go back this way to Swakop, which is the usual route and will take about two hours, but here," he drew a cross, "are ostrich and springbok . . . last week I saw them . . . so if you wish, we can go and have a look, but it will take longer . . . about three hours, maybe four."

He looked at their expectant faces, "It must be decided by you but perhaps the ladies are tired and do not want to drive for so long?"

There was a chorus of opposition. For these temporary refugees from the traffic and frantic pace of Cologne, Berlin and Stuttgart, this was the experience of a lifetime and they were more than willing to prolong it. A lone woman, one of the Tsamma Uranium people, objected half-heartedly to continuing the journey, but was quickly persuaded by the others, and so they set off. The LandRover's temperature gauge, while indicating higher than normal, stayed below the danger mark and they drove over a reasonably smooth surface for the first hour. At the edge of the plateau the terrain quickly changed into a fearsome wasteland of rugged ravines, ground-down ridges and burnt rocks. The countryside in all its misshapen beauty looked as if in eons past some vicious giant had fired up a gargantuan blow torch and seared the land down to its very soul. Brown, black and rust, with only tiny splashes of green where the Euphorbia cactus clung to crevices in the rock and the drab olive of the scattered acacias sat in solitary splendour -- the colours changed to dark shadows as the LandRover dropped deeper into the gorge. Here, as if a scalpel had sliced the skin of the earth away leaving only the bleached bones, the rocks folded and twisted in tortured ecstasy. Giant pinnacles of rock reared up to a cloudless sky, jagged fingers grasping at the plains above.

There was silence in the LandRover. All seemed affected by the strange, sinister beauty of the gorge they were following. Long shadows hung from cliffs, and despite the shade, the temperature was in the high nineties. Sensing the mood, Kresfeld recounted legends handed down by the Bushmen and early white settlers. "During the Herero war, a troop of Schutztruppe, 20 men, entered a gorge like this . . . perhaps even this one . . . and they just disappeared and were never heard of again." A collective murmur ran through the station wagon and a few women shivered despite the heat. "To this day their remains have never been found. It is a strange land, a cruel land, one cannot compromise with the desert."

"Could we get lost?" The woman who had not been enthusiastic about the extended trip, spoke up from the rear.

Kresfeld laughed. "Have no fear good lady. If we fail to return today, several vehicles would follow our tracks and we would be found within a few hours." He pointed to the two 40 litre containers of water that were still half full. "We have plenty of water." He chuckled, "even if we cannot have a shower, ja." The other tourists laughed.

Colin interjected, frowning, "How can they trail us when we've been travelling over rock and leaving no tracks?"

"Herr Mornay, he knows about the desert, ja?" Again a rumble of laughter greeted this sally. "Do not worry, Sir," the 'Sir' heavily emphasized, "the men who will come if we get lost have much experience, and if necessary they will use Bushmen trackers."

Colin seemed about to speak but changed his mind and subsided, slumping lower in his seat. He caught a glance of sympathy from Ingrid, the German girl, who like Colin was not too impressed with Kresfeld's explanation. During the conversation, they had turned up a broad ravine that sloped gently to the height of land above. The surface changing from hard-packed gravel and rock to loose windblown scree and sand. Kresfeld slowed the LandRover to a stop, searching the ground ahead for clues. Finally, he engaged the low ratio gears and the station wagon moved ahead.

They were halfway up the ravine, the engine whining in protest as they surged through the soft sand, when it happened. The front wheels suddenly sank into a much softer section and the vehicle stopped as if hitting a brick wall. For a few minutes there were curses and confusion as the passengers regained their seats and replaced various items that had been flung free. Kresfeld jumped down and inspected the front wheels and Colin quickly joined him. "Are we badly stuck?" he asked.

"No, Herr Mornay, but we may have to turn back . . . the sand ahead may be too soft and at this angle even if I deflate the tires it might not work . . . it is a pity, for over the top of this rise is the ostrich plains and a good road back to Swakop."

Kresfeld left the group that had gathered anxiously to listen to his explanation and walked up the rise, testing the ground every few paces. Satisfied, he returned to the vehicle and told the assembled group. "It appears that this is only a small patch of bad ground and the rest seems to be good. If you all will remain outside the vehicle, I will reverse and take a run at this section." He turned to the men, "Perhaps if you see me slowing down, you will push from behind . . . it is only 20 metres and once through we should have no more trouble."

Colin looked over the assembled tourists. Apart from himself and the German girl, the bulk of the passengers were over 60 . . . The Tsamma woman was in her thirties and might be useful, but he was sceptical.

Kresfeld reversed the LandRover and they all pushed from the front. It dragged out of the sand reluctantly, leaving two deep pits already filling with fine sand where the front wheels had sunk up to their axles. Kresfeld reversed a hundred metres and took aim to the right of his first attempt. He shifted gears and the LandRover leapt forward, gaining speed as it approached the soft area. The LandRover roared past and for a few moments it seemed he would succeed. It was more than halfway across, before it began to slow down. Realizing the danger, Colin raced to help, but it was hopeless. Before he even reached the vehicle, it had stalled and now all four wheels were sunk deeply up to their axles in the fine sand. Kresfeld restarted and gunned the engine, trying to reverse out. The LandRover moved slightly, then jerked, and, as if an defiant protest against such treatment, there came a loud crack from the rear axle. For a moment, the vehicle and its passengers stood motionless, then Colin stumbled through the heavy sand to the driver's side.

"I heard a bang from the back wheels . . . I think something must have broken."

Kresfeld sat stricken, his face grey under the weather-beaten tan, "Gott in Himmel, it must be a half shaft broken." He held on to the steering wheel for support, then gathering himself, opened the door to confront the tourists.

"Are we stuck?" asked Ingrid, her breath coming in gasps,

for she had run behind Colin.

"We will see . . . I have shovels and sand mats and we will dig around the wheels."

Kresfeld walked to the rear of the LandRover. A short metal ladder bolted to the side led up to a tarpaulin-covered roof rack. He climbed to the top and gripped the ladder with one hand, using the other to untie the cord holding the tarpaulin corner. Throwing back the tarpaulin he climbed on to the wooden platform and began searching, but was down very quickly.

"There are no shovels . . . the spare wheels, extra fuel, sand mats, ropes are all in place, but no shovels," he reported in a flat monotone. He seemed stunned.

One of the tourists said something sharply in German and Kresfeld replied in the same language, spreading his hands helplessly.

"Please, what is going on?" the Tsamma woman looked from Kresfeld to the German tourist, a large florid man in designer khaki desert clothes topped with a floppy bush hat, who responded, "It appears that we are stuck, how do you say? Up a creek with no oar." His face was grim. "Mr. Kresfeld did not check his equipment before leaving today."

"The shovels are always in place . . . always . . . I cannot understand this," Kresfeld pleaded. The tourist snorted in disgust.

"How long before we are found?" he asked.

"Herr Mannheim, it is now 2.30 pm and we are due back in Swakop no later than 4.30 pm. When we do not arrive, the search party will set out in several vehicles and they should find us before dark."

The tourist, a banker from Munich, seemed unconvinced and he stared out at the forbidding scenery around them. "How will they know where to find us?"

Kresfeld hesitated fractionally before replying, "Please you must not worry . . . we will be found . . . we have a procedure, first they will follow the path we have taken since leaving Swakop

. . . all of them have driven the route many times before . . . "

Colin interrupted, for he had noticed Kresfeld's slight hesitation. "But I thought you said earlier that this is not a regular route . . . you said you don't normally come this way."

"Yes Herr Mornay, you are correct," Kresfeld replied, "but as I also told you before, ahead over the rise is the main route, for we have come in a circle. I will walk up there and wait for them to arrive, then lead them back to you." He smiled at Colin, his confidence returning. "Perhaps you will assist me to put the tarpaulin up, where it will make a shade for you to wait under."

Colin and Kresfeld attached the tarpaulin to various metal hooks welded to the roof of the LandRover and stretched it out to two poles and a crossbar that had previously been lashed to the roof, forming a shaded area large enough for all to sit under. Kresfeld, Colin and Ingrid pulled the cords attached to the tarpaulin down to the ground and anchored them with rocks. The heat inside the metal body of the LandRover was rising steadily, now that it was stationary, and most of the tourists made themselves comfortable on the seats that Kresfeld had removed. There was only mild concern, for most had accepted Kresfeld's assurances and were probably even relishing the thought of a little adventure that could become an embellished story on their return to Germany. The banker was not so sure however, and he drew Kresfeld away from the others and they spoke quietly in German "How long will it take you to get to the other road?" he asked.

Kresfeld shrugged. "About 30 or 40 minutes of hard walking . . . why do you ask?"

"Because I think you should not go alone . . . perhaps I can come with you . . . it is better in case of trouble."

Kresfeld protested, "Herr Mannheim, what trouble? It is a short walk and a wait, that is all . . . I cannot permit you to accompany me."

Mannheim had not become head of the Grosse Bundesbank because of his accommodating nature and he hunched his heavy shoulders, eyes hardening. "You cannot forbid me. Should anything happen to you before you reached the road, we would be unaware of your problem and the search vehicles might take days to find us. It is settled . . . I will come."

Kresfeld recognized the logic of Mannheim's argument and tried another tack. "Herr Mannheim please, you are not suited to this, for it is very hot and it may be a strain on you . . . please understand, I cannot risk your health."

The banker glared, unappeased, "It does not change my argument that you should not go alone." Colin and Ingrid had unclipped one of the 40-litre water containers and were dragging it under the shade of the tarpaulin. Mannheim's eyes followed them and he turned back to Kresfeld, "Take the boy, the Canadian, at least there will be two of you."

Kresfeld rolled his eyes heavenward, "As you wish . . . I will take the boy, but I assure you, there is no need." He called out to Colin who was drinking from a plastic cup, "Herr Mornay, will you walk with me to the road? Herr Mannheim thinks that I need protection."

Shading his eyes with his hand, Colin came across the sand towards them. "Why me?"

"Because you are young and fit," Mannheim spoke before Kresfeld could answer. "If you are afraid then I will ask Ingrid to go with Herr Kresfeld, but it is madness that one person should go alone."

Colin's face darkened at the suggestion that he was afraid. "Afraid! What the hell am I supposed to be afraid of?" He glared at Mannheim. "How far is this little jaunt supposed to be?"

"It is not far, perhaps four or five kilometres, but perhaps you would prefer to stay?" Kresfeld replied.

"No, I'll walk it with you, if only to prove to this fat man that I'm not afraid of anything. I'll get my sunglasses and a water bottle and we can go."

Mannheim shook his head as Colin walked back to the LandRover. "What is wrong with the young these days?" he asked to nobody in particular, repeating the query in German.

Twenty minutes later, Kresfeld and Colin emerged from the ravine, climbing up a dune of windblown sand. Colin waited while Kresfeld searched the horizon. Nothing moved, even the first, faint warnings of the coming East Wind had faded. In front of them stretched a flat plain, a few low hills fading into the distance. Over the baking landscape, the intense heat created a shimmering haze and mirages, like pools of sparkling water that rose and fell, changing shape constantly. On the horizon a range of ragged mountains merged into the sky. Colin pulled his floppy hat lower over his eyes. Despite his sunglasses, he found the glare harsh, sunlight deflecting back off the surrounding rock. He turned to Kresfeld. "Where is the road?"

For a moment, the German did not reply, then he pointed to his right. "We must have driven up the wrong ravine, for we are too far to the east. We must make for that line where the mountains join with the plain . . . it is not so far now."

The sun blazed down and Colin pulled his sweat-soaked shirt free of his shorts. "Are you sure?" he asked irritably. "That's a hell of a lot of country out there and I don't want to walk all over fucking Africa."

Kresfeld ignored him and began walking in the direction he had indicated. Colin followed, grumbling under his breath. For the next 50 minutes they trudged through patches of soft sand that dragged at their feet, then over slabs of flat rock that reflected the heat as if off a furnace.

Fed up with Kresfeld's non-committal grunts to every question, Colin finally stopped. "How much further, Kresfeld? We don't seem to be any closer to your road. I'm not going to walk any fucking farther, 'cause I'm not sure you know where you are, anymore than I do."

Breathing heavily, Kresfeld sat down. "All right, we will take a short rest, but we must not waste time . . . it is further than I thought . . .I think we have another five kilometres to go."

"Five kilos! Hell, how far have we come already?" snapped

Colin, wiping his face with the cotton handkerchief tied around his neck.

"About three, perhaps a little more."

"Only three?" Colin was incredulous. "You mean it has taken us an hour to do just three fucking kilometres?"

Kresfeld stood. "The first climb up the ravine took longer than expected, but now the ground is better . . . come let us go," he said, trying to keep the growing anxiety from his voice.

"Wait a minute, Kresfeld, I've had it with your fucked-up directions. I'm not walking for another hour and then find out you were wrong again . . . I'm going back to the LandRover before we get too far away. You're on your own."

"Please, Mr. Mornay, it is not so far and we are wasting time," Kresfeld urged. Spurred by his growing uncertainty, he was now convinced it had been a grave mistake to bring Colin, for he was wasting precious time trying to persuade this obstinate boy.

"Like hell, for all I know it could be another 10 or 15 kilos. I've had it. I'll go back and tell the others that I saw you reach the road, that will keep them quiet until help comes."

Kresfeld lifted his hands in despair. "Mr. Mornay, you could get lost on the return journey. . . I cannot be responsible."

Colin knotted his shirt across his stomach, the skin still white despite his three weeks in Africa. "I won't get lost . . . I can see the crack where the ravine begins from here, and I've got the cairns to follow as well." Every 10 minutes on the outward trek Kresfeld had placed a small mound of stones to act as a marker for the search party that would be driving in the dark. The powerful spotlights on the rescue vehicles would illuminate any man-made object and, combined with the compass bearing from the road pickup point, it would be a simple matter to find the correct ravine.

Kresfeld looked at his watch again and lifted his hands in exasperation. "As you wish, I cannot wait any longer . . . my partners will come as soon as it reaches 4.30 and I have to be on the road before that time. I told Herr Mannheim that the flare pistol is under the driver's seat and when you hear our engines fire one flare directly above your position . . . also, put on the headlights and sound the horn. Go quickly now and I will wait here to make sure that you are heading in the right direction."

Colin turned back the way they had come and started walking. Two hundred metres on, he turned and Kresfeld waved. The German watched him for a few more minutes then resumed his march to the road.

Chapter 17

Shutztruppe

Rafa crumpled the telex form in disgust, "What the hell's the matter with them?" he snapped. "I've just come from Windhoek . . . why didn't they call the tower before I left?"

Jake van Tonder shook his head, "I don't know, Mr. Modesto, the telex came just before you landed."

"What's wrong?" David joined them as they stood on the concrete apron of the Tsamma airfield.

Rafa handed him the crumpled telex. "Butchert wants me to go back to Windhoek right now and pick up a party of head office people arriving on the scheduled flight from Jo'burg at five."

"But we've just arrived!" David exploded. "Hell, Rafa will be racing the clock to get them back here before dark . . . why don't they just stay in Windhoek for the night?" David asked, looking at van Tonder.

"Mr. Mornay I'm just the maintenance man. I deliver the messages, I don't write them," van Tonder replied with a shrug.

"It's all right, Dave." Rafa interjected. "When Butchert says jump it is best to listen . . . Van, will you fill her up and check the oil in the port engine? The damned gauge is probably faulty again."

When van Tonder had left them, Rafa walked with David over to his pickup. "Look Dave, give yourself a chance, do not make any sudden decisions. Remember the old saying about acting in haste and then repenting at leisure."

David turned to him with a grin. "Thank you for the confessional, Mother Superior, but I think I'll live."

Relieved, Rafa punched him lightly on the back, "Good, good, anytime my son." He waited until David's truck had disappeared towards the mine before turning back to the Aircraft.

David drove swiftly towards the plant, taking a shortcut that only he, Wessel and a few others knew about, which bypassed the gate and fences that slowed travel on the normal route. The big pickup slithered around corners as he accelerated to stop the rear end from breaking away into a full-fledged skid. Several times in the past remarks had been passed about his reckless driving. Lately he had begun to observe the rules a bit more closely, aware that the era of empty roads and open spaces was a thing of the past. However this afternoon, engrossed in his own thoughts and determined to get to the meeting on time, he drove fast and hard.

Passing the Mill offices he turned sharply to the left, throwing a cloud of stones and gravel in a wide arc. He failed to see the Ovambo flagman waving him down as he breasted the rise that led to the Administration Block. Dead ahead, a 50-foot tractor trailer combination unloading huge pipe sections partially blocked the road. David slammed on his brakes, turning the wheel to cut through the gap between the side of the truck cab and a steel two metre diameter pipe section lying in the ditch. He would have made the gap with inches to spare, but the truck driver, unaware of the rapidly approaching pickup, opened his door to step down on to the road.

Too late, David saw the door open. He threw the pickup over, slamming against the steel pipe section, hearing the tortured scream of metal as the left front fender collapsed. A tire blew with a retort like a cannon shot. Now, travelling sideways, the pickup sliced across the road, missing a fleeing workman by inches, then hit a low concrete head wall and began to cartwheel. David saw the culvert loom, but hitting the pipe had jammed the steering hard right and he could do nothing. The impact drove the air out of his lungs as the steering wheel slammed into his abdomen. His last conscious thought as the horizon began to turn upside down, was that he would miss the meeting.

Men began running before the dust had even settled. The pickup lay jammed upside down, the rear wheels spinning aimlessly. By some miracle, the windshield was intact but the driver's side door and window were crumpled like tissue paper. David's arm hung out of the cavity left by the damaged door. Blood dripping from his fingers raised little puffs of dust as the drops hit the dry sand before congealing into rust coloured balls.

Rafa lifted the Chieftain off Tsamma field, swinging in a wide arc and turning back over the plant before setting course due east for Windhoek. He looked down casually at the activity below. The mine never failed to impress him, despite its relative insignificance in the vast empty landscape. It was a challenge thrown in the face of many odds and in spite of serious setbacks, it had succeeded. He smiled at nothing in particular before pushing the port throttle slightly ahead to synchronize his engines, unaware that at that moment David Mornay was being carefully lifted out of the shattered and blood splashed wreck of his pickup. It would be two and a half hours before Rafa would return.

Colin turned to look for Kresfeld, but the German had disappeared in the haze. The topography was deceptive, small valleys and hills merging into the general landscape until he drew close to them. In the distance he could see the beginning of the ravine as a dark smear on the otherwise drab landscape but, as he continued to plod, it seemed to draw no closer. He had reached the second of Kresfeld's cairns, surprised at how far to the side he had been despite aiming steadily for the ravine. He sat on the small mound, his legs spread. Although the wind had picked up, lifting the fine sand into tiny dust devils, it was no cooler. The sun was lower and he looked at his watch -- nearly 4.30 -- he must be near the ravine . . . he had been walking for a half hour. Cursing the heat, he rose again and trudged on. He felt drained and wondered briefly how Kresfeld was making out.

Nothing moved. The emptiness was as the sea. The sinking sun now outlined the Chuosberge, pushing them into harsh relief, sharp sinister peaks, dark grey against the sky. Colin tried to jog, but the soft sand made running difficult. He slowed again to a walk. He checked the position of the ravine, but the lower angle of the sun had changed the shape of the landscape and shadows appeared where none had been before.

Colin screwed his eyes into slits. He couldn't be mistaken, he thought, surely not. The mark he had used for a reference now seemed different from a few minutes ago. Again, he broke into a trot, his feet pounding into the loose sand. He neared the ravine, his breath rasping harshly in his throat. Something was wrong. He stopped and stared in disbelief, for the ravine he had reached was only a small tear in the side of a hill, starting nowhere, leading nowhere. Shaking his handkerchief free, he mopped his streaming face. A feeling of disquiet moved in him and for the first time he began to feel frightened. That he was on the edge of a series of ravines, there was no doubt, but which was the right one?

Scanning both left and right, he tried to establish the direction from which he had come. He caught a sudden flicker of movement out of the corner of his eye. His heart leaped with relief and he ran yelling towards the source. But there were no answering yells and he stopped, confused, swinging his head in a tight arc as he tried to locate the movement again. Nothing. Yes, there.. a yellow flash low down. He waited, and the flash -- dimmer now -- was repeated. Throwing caution to the wind, he raced over the flat rock toward it, stumbling, falling heavily, skinning his palms and knees on the fractured rock. Tears sprang to his eyes, the cuts burned and he sucked his palm where pinpricks of blood popped through the broken skin. Rising to his feet, he saw the light wink again, but this time it was faint. He frowned in puzzlement, for it had seemed so close. Another five steps and he stopped in horror, a scream rising in his throat.

The rider must have shot his horse, before lying down to die.

A perfectly circular hole in the long white skull showed where the ball had entered. Bones curved out of the sand. The bridle, intact and brittle green with age, had slid down the bleached bone of the head to end like a tattered nosebag round grinning teeth. Wide with shock, Colin's eyes travelled the length of the skeleton. The rider must have lain with his head on the saddle of his dead horse, for his skeleton lay at right angles to that of the horse. One arm bone and leg disappeared beneath the sand as if the ancient rider were struggling to throw the blanket of sand free and rise from his ghostly bed.

Colin, a fist pressed into his mouth, a wave of bile surging in his throat, bit hard on his knuckles, blinking to keep the tears back. He knelt beside the long dead soldier. There was no doubt that the rider must have been one of the German soldiers lost seven decades before, the ones that Kresfeld had talked about. A leather belt, dry and brittle with age like the bridle, girdled the pelvis, the stamped eagle of Imperial Germany still faintly visible on the buckle. The soldier's skull, half buried in the sand, had rolled a short distance from the entwined bones of man and beast. A toktokkie beetle peered warily out of an eye socket at the intruder.

Despite his revulsion, Colin pictured the desperate scene of almost a century ago. After shooting his horse, the rider must have stretched out beside his dead steed, rested his head on the saddle, and waited for death. His rifle was still secure in its saddle scabbard, the brass butt plate scoured to a mirror finish by the blowing sand, golden in the fading light. That was what had caught Colin's eye, for only the late afternoon sun could reflect off the butt plate at just the right angle. The remainder of the rifle was buried beneath the sand.

Where death was concerned, Colin had led a sheltered life. He had never seen a dead body, let alone skeletal remains. He rose to his feet. The sun was sinking and dark shadows peopled the open plain. Fear returned in waves and, shivering, he wrapped his arms around his chest. Backing away from the sad, grim tableau, he turned suddenly and ran across the desert towards where he had left Kresfeld, sand lifting in spurts from his desert boots.

Kate came out of the laboratory, pulling off her white coat. Someone in the corridor was yelling that the bus was about to leave. She hated this rush at the end of the day, everyone pushing and shoving to get good seats for the long ride back to Swakop. She saw a stenographer slip on the smooth floor, skirt flying open, white legs flashing.

"Doctor Richardson, the bus is leaving." Mike was holding the door for her.

"Yes I'm coming, for heaven's sake, why the big rush tonight?"

"The driver wants to have a look at the accident." His young face shiny, a wispy moustache like a fading tide mark on his unlined face.

"Accident? What accident?" She picked up the folder, thinking that tonight she must do some more cross checks, for the resin pellets were not responding correctly.

"One of the Construction fellows hit a pipetruck in the Mill area . . . apparently it's quite a spectacular sight."

Kate had reached the door, and without breaking stride called over her shoulder, "Why do men always want to see the scene of an accident? It's so ghoulish."

The shiny, 50-seater bus sat hard to the whitewashed curb. Stan, the driver, gesticulated urgently for her to run, but Kate slowed deliberately. She had requested a car, but if management wanted her to ride the bus she was damned if she was going to run for it. She turned to Mike beside her, making conversation more to annoy Stan than out of any real interest in the accident. "Who was in the accident?"

"Fellow called Mornay . . . he's the Construction boss . . . apparently drives too fast and this time it caught up with him."

He was past her and held the door for her to get in. She felt the blood drain from her face, the folder slipped from her hand, banging on the gravel, her papers scattering in a wide arc. Momentarily, her knees buckled and she stumbled against the aluminum side of the bus, both hands holding herself steady, trying to swallow, a strange roaring lightness in her head.

Mike was on his haunches picking up the papers, and handed her the folder. "Doc, are you all right?" His voice seemed to her to come from a million miles away and his face was surrounded by a queer halo.

Kate tried to speak, but no sound came.

"Doctor - Kate what is the matter, you look ill." He held her elbow, concerned.

She pushed him off. "It's nothing . . . thanks Mike . . . something came over me . . . just give me a minute and I'll be all right." She stared at the ground, the buzzing in her ears still loud. His face showing serious concern, Mike watched her for any further signs of collapse. To Mike, her behaviour was not unexpected, for recently she had been working ridiculous hours and, as her senior lab assistant, he felt she was pushing herself far too hard. He helped her into the bus, ignoring the caustic remarks from Stan. The bus lurched and they fell into the front seats.

"Was it . . . ? Is it a fatal acci . . . is he dead?"

"Who? .. Oh, Mornay. I don't know 'cause I only heard of the accident a few minutes before I spoke to you."

The bus swung away from the Chemistry Block, waited as a road grader roared past, then turned on the perimeter road leading to the gate. Halfway past the Leach and Thickener sections, Stan cut across a bumpy patch of open ground and then they were grinding up a short rise to the Administration Block. The bus halted a short distance ahead of the crash scene and Stan, looking back, growled in frustration, "It's your fault we're late missy." A company tow truck was busy pulling the overturned wreck upright onto its wheels and into a position to tow it away.

A group near the door pushed their sliding windows open to get a better look. "Holy cow! What a mess!" Mike turned back to her, "Here, look out my window." He leaned back so that she could see past him at the wrecked truck. He heard her gasp and saw her rise quickly from her seat and head for the door. "Doctor, where are you going?" he cried.

Stan looked back at the commotion behind the driver's seat and, seeing Kate reach for the door handle snapped, "No one gets off to look . . . I'm leaving now, so go back to your seat." Kate ignored him, stepping down to the road and walking across in front of the bus to where a dozen construction workers were staring at the wreckage.

Stan rolled down his window and yelled at her, "You'll have to get the late bus missy . . . I am not going to wait." With a sour grin, he revved the bus engine and roared off.

Kate recognized Wessel van der Walt and touched his arm. "Is he dead?" Wessel turned at her voice and the touch on his arm, and realized at once that the woman facing him was on the verge of collapse. He put two huge hands on her shoulders, "Steady now lady. No, he is alive . . . he is in the sick bay, unconscious but alive . . . I don't know how badly hurt." Her gaze had left his face and she was staring past him at the blood-splashed interior of the wrecked cab.

"I must go there." She tried to break free of his hands.

Wessel patted her gently as a rider would calm a nervous horse. "Easy lady, easy! You can come with me . . . I am going there now." He looked at her curiously. So this was why Dave had been so morose of late. It was not the boy as he had first surmised, but this lovely, distraught woman in front of him. "Come, my truck is parked next to those tanks."

He released her, but walked closely beside her, watching for any signs of collapse. My God, he thought, old Dave is a deep one and her a married woman too.

Kate fought to contain the fear that surged through her. All she could picture was David's gaunt face the last time they had spoken. On the days following their meeting at the library, she had tried to put her life back on an even keel, convinced that she had made the correct decision -- in fact, the only possible decision. But life rarely allows neat endings to complex problems and she had found herself daydreaming of what life would be like with the quiet-eyed construction boss.

She and Jack had agreed not to have children -- both had applied the usual cliches to justify their decision. But on reflection, she realized that she had known instinctively that Jack had not wanted to compete for her affection. She also knew with a sickening certainty that a less self-absorbed individual could have persuaded her to have a family. But, she also acknowledged the unfairness of her anger, she was a willing party to the agreement. Since that evening in the library, she had tried to discuss with Jack her fully wakened sense of emptiness, of bad choices made, but he had not been listening. His mind was focused on the great future that he saw unfolding in front of him. "Just think Kate, we'll have a house in Sandton and an apartment on the beach in Durban for our holidays. You can stop working. Do you know what sort of a salary the chief financial officer gets?"

She had reminded him that she liked her work and really didn't care for a house in Sandton, or an apartment overlooking the beach.

He had laughed weakly. "Nonsense, you'll love it," he had assured her, looking at her curiously, "There was a time when that's all you wanted -- why the change?" She had snapped back at him that people do change, pointing out that what seemed the epitome of living in one's twenties could become inconsequential in one's thirties. But he had brushed aside her concerns with a grin, "Kate you've just become a bit bush or rather, desert happy like everyone who spends too much time here, . . .look . . . . . Just trust me, things will work out. Did I tell you that old man Butchert wants me to represent him at the Extraction Conference in Hamburg next month? Why don't you apply for a spot of leave and come along?" The next morning he had flown off with Butchert to a major meeting in Johannesburg.

Now, she sat next to Wessel staring through the dirty windshield, her mind a maelstrom of conflicting emotions, oblivious to the glances he shot at her as they neared the mine first aid station. A white ambulance stood at the entrance with both rear doors still open. Beside it was a pickup truck, badly parked, the driver apparently in a hurry to help the stretcher bearers bring in the injured Mornay.

Wessel slid the truck to a stop, was out of the cab and striding to the doors before he remembered his passenger and turned to wait for her. She suddenly became aware of the grim tenseness on his face and realized with a shock that there were others in David's life who cared for him. They pushed through the swing doors and stepped into the reception room. Several men sat on straight backed chairs along the wall and the receptionist, a fussy middle-aged matron, snapped at them, "You can see we're full and we've got an emergency so . . . DON'T GO IN THERE!" But it was too late. Wessel had opened the door to the emergency room and ushered Kate in.

Kate gasped, for under a bank of bright lamps David lay full length on the operating table stripped to the waist. His upper body was a mass of old scar tissue and a freshly-stitched wound ran from his left nipple to just under the right side of his chin. A wax-like face was framed in heavy bandages. The doctor, his back to them was working on David's left arm. One of the two nurses said something to the doctor and he snapped over his shoulder, "Out of here, I will see you later."

Wessel ignored the command, "Ken, it's Wessel, how is he?"

"Oh, Wessel . . . well, let me tell you, this is one lucky man . . . he must have . . . nurse hold that end." He worked in silence for a moment. "A very lucky man indeed . . . Look, Wes, go out . . . I am nearly finished and I will see you in a minute."

Wessel nodded and, taking Kate's arm he led her back into the reception area, bumping into the receptionist who after extricating herself from behind her desk had come rushing after them. "It's not allowed. You are not supposed to go in there . ."

Wessel walked outside and sucked in a huge lungful of air, blowing it slowly through his teeth. "Damn, damn, damn it all to hell!" Kate saw the glisten of tears in the bearded giant's eyes and realized that relief was breaking down his normally sober reserve. He patted his pockets and found a crumpled packet of cigarettes. He shook one free and gestured to her.

Kate shook her head.

"Same as Dave, he doesn't either," Wessel sighed. "He used to . . . you know that? When we came here from the Motleng job his lungs started acting up . . . he took a bullet through a lung in Vietnam, you know . . . never told us that himself . . . Billy saw his med records by accident in Jo'Burg . . . he ever speak to you about that?"

She shook her head, watching Wessel's face while he lit the cigarette and drew deeply into his lungs. This normally taciturn man had suddenly become voluble, buoyed by the knowledge that his friend was going to survive. He blew out a cloud of smoke, silent for a moment. She waited.

"So old Billy and I bet him a thousand dollars US that he couldn't stop smoking . . . made a challenge out of it, you see . . . The bastard won the bet, then took Billy and me to the Natal coast for a wild weekend." He stared hard at her. "What's Dave to you . . . how do you know him?. . . He is one hell of a good man, you know . . . hell of a good man."

Kate smiled at him, a wave of affection for this gentle bear of a man lighting her eyes. "We met a short while after Ivan was killed . . . remember you spoke to me in the Admin block the day it happened?" Recognition flooded his face.

"Of course. Now I remember where I've seen you before, but you were different."

"My lab coat and headscarf no doubt. I met him at a dance and then later at a dinner party. We talked and he. . ." She stopped, for the doctor had come out of the First Aid station.

"Wes, give me one of your smokes," he said urgently. "Bloody hell, everyone is on a health kick these days." They both waited while the doctor lit up and drew deeply on the cigarette.

"Well first the bad news. He has a bad concussion -- how bad I'm not sure -- he's got a bad gash on his head and you saw the one on his chest -- took 40 stitches that did -- missed cutting his jugular by a fraction. He has a cracked rib -- steering wheel did that -- and a broken arm, but nothing else that I could find. He has no apparent internal injuries and all the signs are good. He is stable, but we will have to watch him tonight. I wanted to airlift him to the State Hospital in Windhoek, but Rafa won't be back tonight, the damned jumbo was late again so he's having to overnight in Windhoek. I'm going to send Dave to the Antonious in Swakop, where they're better equipped for the unexpected than here."

He took another pull on the cigarette. "Damn it all, Wes, what are these made out of . . . goatshit?" Not waiting for an answer, he continued, "Will you ride in the ambulance with him? You saw the queue in the waiting room. Your bloody boss has made a mess out of my schedule and I really would like to let Janine go home. She's been on a double shift. Helena can help me with the backlog if you do the hand-holding routine, I've phoned the hospital, they're expecting you." He looked expectantly at Wessel.

"I'll ride with the ambulance," Kate burst out, "I missed the bus and need to get back to Swakop myself. I had some medical training -- for a while at University I thought I might become a doctor, but switched to Chemistry after a year."

Ken Hassel looked at her much the same as Wessel had, a cool appraising look, then he nodded, "Not much medical knowledge is required . . . you are Kate Richardson, the Chemical Engineer?"

"Yes."

"Well that's settled then . . . I told them to load. Ah, there they are now." Three men were helping the nurses to lift the stretcher into the back of the ambulance. Striding back to supervise the loading, Hassel called over his shoulder, "On your salary, Van der Walt, you can afford a better brand of cigarette."

Kate was stunned that the doctor could be so casual when a man was badly injured, and she turned to Wessel, anger in her eyes, "Is he always so flippant?"

Wessel smiled at the retreating doctor's back. "Yes . . . always . . . in his job it's the only sensible way to behave."

He looked down at her. "Mrs. Richardson, mining is a dangerous business. Every week in Swakop the doc sees all sorts of serious injuries that are sent in by ambulance and when he makes his usual Friday trip out here there is a long line up at the clinic to see him. Dave was lucky that he crashed today, otherwise the paramedic could only have shot him full of painkiller and transferred him to Windhoek or Swakop. Ken and his partner, Gerry van Niekerk, have learned a lot about trauma medicine since the mine opened."

He pointed at the ambulance. "They are waiting for you."

"Please, call me Kate, and I apologize for sounding like such a fool, I . . . " Agitated, her words tumbled over each other, "I was . . . well, I was worried you see."

Wessel's dark eyes were calm now. He searched her face and nodded gravely. "Dave has that effect on a lot of people . . . you had better go . . . I'll check on him after work tonight," he said, walking with her to the ambulance. "Don't worry, if Ken says he is going to survive, then you can put money on it."

He helped her into the white interior of the ambulance and Ken Hassel rattled off instructions, "OK, all you have to do is watch him. The driver has a radio and can call ahead if you have problems. My partner will be at the hospital to receive him. In the unlikely event that he regains consciousness, just talk to him and reassure him and don't let him thrash about, OK?"

Kate nodded vigorously, "Yes. . . Yes, I understand, thank you Doctor."

Closing the doors, Ken Hassel grinned at Wessel, "We all should be so lucky. How come an ugly bastard like him attracts the fairy princess?"

Kate heard a rumble from Wessel, but the exchange was cut short as the ambulance moved off. She looked at David's still form and wondered if the gossip tomorrow would have David and her romantically linked. Poor David! She reached out a hand to gently touch his forehead and was perturbed to feel how hot it was. For a moment she felt a wave of panic, but just as quickly it subsided. There was nothing anyone could do except get him in to the hospital as quickly as possible. She began to talk to him as if he were conscious, telling him of her childhood, the years at college, her work. The tires hummed softly as the ambulance rolled steadily towards Swakopmund.

Chapter 18

Grim Memories

Colin ran blindly across the desert away from the skeletons, his desert boots sinking deeply into the soft sand. A hundred metres away from the grim scene at the canyon entrance, Colin stopped. He was breathing heavily and his heart was pounding. Now darkness was falling faster and he could barely see the mountains towards which he and Kresfeld had set out so confidently a few hours before. Whatever else, Colin was no fool and he realized that flight into the open desert in darkness would be suicidal.

He decided to find a place to sit and wait out the night, so he turned back towards the ravine -- at least that would be a good starting point in the morning. He must be reasonably close to the LandRover and would no doubt hear the rescue vehicles in the still night air. Passing the skeletons, he gave them a wide berth. Ahead in the ravine proper, he could see a fissure in the wall and was relieved to find it big enough to squeeze into. A pile of loose, wind blown scree had formed a soft bed and he stretched out gratefully, realizing how exhausted he was. He checked the water bottle -- it was nearly empty. In his certainty -- prior to stumbling over the skeletons -- that he was almost back at the LandRover, he had drunk deeply. Now only a mouthful or two remained and he resisted the temptation to have another sip. He was not yet uncomfortably thirsty and common sense prevailed despite his growing panic.

Darkness came swiftly, like a blanket dropped suddenly over the desert. He could no longer see even the outline of the skeletons and in minutes the edges of the canyon disappeared into the inky black. A few scattered stars winked through tears in the thin cloud cover, like tiny Christmas lights behind a tattered curtain. Colin was puzzled for a minute -- it was unusual for there to be cloud cover -- then he remembered that the East Wind was due. Kresfeld had said that it could blow for days sometimes and that once it started it was like a blizzard in Canada. He remembered the stories that Jimmy and Zane had told him. How the East Wind was so fierce that when it reached the coast, it blew the incoming surf backwards; motor vehicles driving into the wind-driven sand would have their paint stripped down to bare metal in minutes, their windshield glass would be so badly pitted that vision was totally obscured. Kresfeld had called it a time to endure, not a time to roam about. A time to stay inside and wait out the fury. The super dry air sucked up any and all moisture so a person's need for liquid intake went up dramatically. Contemplating the East Wind and his dilemma, Colin shivered despite the warm night. Huddled alone in the wilderness with very little water and no idea how far from help he was, the magnitude of his problem finally broke through his wall of arrogance. He hugged his knees tightly and sobbed.

Outside the crevice, the wind gusted. It was rising and there was no mistaking the menace in the air. Finally exhausted, Colin slept. His dreams were fearful and his limbs jerked spasmodically.

At almost the same time in Swakopmund, the ambulance carrying the motionless body of Colin's uncle rolled over the railway bridge and turned down a side street on its way to the hospital.

1904

Terrified, the Bushman scrambled up the rock face. He could hear coarse laughter as the horsemen surged up the ravine after him. A bullet whined off the rocks to his right and in an agony of desperation, he flung himself into a wide crack that led to the plateau above. Below, the soldiers milled about in a circle shouting orders to each other. One of the soldiers, under instructions to stay below and prevent the Bushman from escaping back down the way he had come, dismounted and sat on a rock. The Bushman knew that on the plateau above, he had no chance at all.

His chest heaved and perspiration dripped down his body. He did not know why the mounted men wished to kill him, for he had done them no harm. Indeed, when they had first appeared in the canyon below, he had lifted his hand in greeting only to drop his arm with a gasp of pain as a Mauser bullet slammed into the rocks near his head, throwing razor sharp slivers into his face. What he could not know was that these men were part of von Trotha's reinforcements, brought in from Germany to crush the Herero uprising, and for soldiers who were guilty of genocide against the Herero Nation, a lone Bushman was less than human.

For the last hour they had chased him and he had been unable to stay more than a few hundred metres ahead of the pursuing horses, despite his knowledge of the canyon. By a series of clever feints he had doubled back, trying to get to the cave and hide himself. Now with the cave very close, he needed to escape past the lone soldier waiting below.

The Bushman crawled to the edge of the gap and looked down at the soldier. A shadow hid his face from the man below, but he need not have worried. The soldier was busy smoking a cigarette and his back was to the crevice. Moving carefully, the Bushman began his descent, slipping sideways like a small, brown spider, merging with the shadows and slowly gaining the bottom of the cliff. He froze as the soldier finished his cigarette, flicked away the butt and turned to scan the rocks above, his hand shading his eyes from the low afternoon sun.

Fearing to breathe, the Bushman stayed pressed to the rock wall and waited until the soldier turned away before moving the final few feet to the bottom of the cliff. In desperate moments luck often makes the difference between survival or death, and now the luck that had stayed with the Bushman all afternoon finally deserted him. A piece of sun-rotted rock broke free under the little man's weight and he tumbled the last few feet to the foot of the cliff. The soldier whirled around and made a grab for his rifle which fell over into the sand. This slight delay gave the Bushman enough time to scramble to his feet and run towards a bend in the wall. But it wasn't enough.

The soldier managed to fire just one shot before the Bushman disappeared from view. The bullet slammed high into the Bushman's back, pitching him forward onto his knees. With a convulsive effort, he staggered to his feet and made for the cave. The soldier quickly mounted his horse and spurring it savagely, thundered down on the mortally wounded Bushman. . . .

"Doctor van Niekerk?" Kate had waited until David's stretcher had been wheeled down the tile corridor into a private room.

"Yes Mevrou," he used the Afrikaans form of Madam. "What is it?" Gerry van Niekerk, a large florid man, smiled at her and she noticed a wink of gold from his front teeth. He was dressed in a suit and tie, obviously on his way to dinner and impatient to be gone.

"I have to get home, but after supper I would like to come back and sit with him if you have no objection."

"Ag, Mevrou, there is no need . . . there is a fully operational night shift on duty . . . they will take good care of him and I will look in later." He smiled again, obviously proud of his dental work.

"I have heard very good reports of the standard of care in this hospital Doctor, and I am sure he is in very good hands, but I will not sleep tonight and if I sit with him it will release a nurse for other duties." Her nails dug into her palms and she willed herself not to accept a no answer. "As soon as he wakes I will ring for the nurse and get out of the way." She saw him frown uncertainly, but he was late already and so he reluctantly agreed.

"Yes, yes, Mevrou, come back later, speak to the Matron and I am sure that she will agree." He glanced at his watch. "I must go . . . I will look in later." Unsure whether to pat her shoulder or shake her hand, he did neither and with a jerky, "Totsiens . . . er, Goodnight," clipped off down the corridor.

An Ovambo nurse approached from David's room and Kate asked for directions to the Matron's office. She walked back to the reception area and after some difficulty and further directions, found herself outside a cream-coloured door with "Matron" and a name below in black and white lettering stencilled on it. She knocked and entered at the command from within.

The Matron, a middle-aged nun with gentle eyes but a stern face, looked up curiously at her. "Ja, wissen sie?"

"Forgive me, I do not speak any German . . . do you speak English?"

"Yes, my child, what is it you want?"

"Matron, I accompanied David Mornay . . . your latest patient from Tsamma Uranium . . . he is still unconscious and I have been speaking with Doctor van Niekerk who has agreed that I may sit with him until he awakens."

"I see, but Doctor van Niekerk did not discuss this with me . . . we have nurses who will look after him. Why don't you go home and get some rest child? . . . you look exhausted."

"Matron, please, I will not sleep tonight . . . if I sit in the room I can at least alert the duty nurse when he comes round."

Deep in the Matron's eyes, Kate saw a flicker of understanding, "He means much to you?"

"He is my friend, Matron . . . he is . . ." Suddenly she was weeping silently, the tears tracking down her face.

Matron rose quickly from behind the desk, "There, there, child sit down . . . here, take this." She handed Kate a linen cloth and gently sat her down in an old chair against the wall. "What is your name?"

"Kate." She wiped her tears away and crumpled the cloth in her hand, sitting up straighter. "I'm sorry Matron, it is not like me to cry."

"Kate, why don't you go home, have a nice long bath and something to eat, then come back at seven, which is the visiting time anyway. If you still feel like staying, I will have the duty nurse bring you a hot drink at the change of shift."

Kate sat in a deep easy chair that the Matron had somehow extracted from the bowels of the hospital storeroom, quietly reading a novel. David's breathing was regular and deep, but his temperature had not lowered. On returning to the hospital sharp at seven, she had encountered Wessel and Billy Mitchell leaving David's room. A large black man leaned against the wall waiting and when Mitchell had closed the door quietly, the three men had turned to go, only then noticing her.

"Oh hallo, Mrs. Rich . . . Kate, he is still unconscious," Wessel had reported. "Matron says that you are going to sit with Dave tonight . . . do you want us to spell you at all?"

"No Wessel, thank you, it will be better for me here than at home,"

She had smiled at Billy Mitchell and reminded him, "Mr. Mitchell, we met at the contractors' dinner dance." He had caught her looking curiously at the black man.

"I never forget a beautiful woman, Kate," Mitchell had replied with a grin. "This is Johannes Gariseb . . . Johnny has been with us from the beginning . . . he is another poor bastard that Mornay owes money . . . the bugger better survive or we're all going to be out of pocket." The black man was clearly shocked and had stuttered, "Nie, nie, Baas Billy, he does not owe me money. I owe . . . " Wessel had cut him off. "It's OK Johannes, Billy is joking . . . he has a poor sense of humour . . . why don't you and Billy go on and I will meet you outside."

When the two had said goodnight to Kate and gone off down the corridor with Gariseb haranguing Billy in loud whispers, Wessel had turned to her.

"I told you about his hold on people," he had begun. "Well, Johannes had a death in the family six months ago and he was stuck without transport. Dave gave him his personal pickup with enough fuel to reach his home at Omaruru and return. Dave spent the rest of the week riding in and out with me, and nobody was happier than me when Johannes returned. Mornay has absolutely no concept of time when he is working."

He had chuckled at the memory. "Queer thing with Gariseb . . . Dave nearly fired him a little while later over some stupidity and Billy and I had to save Johnny's neck. But old Johannes still thinks Dave can walk on water."

He had squeezed her shoulder. "I will go and see Colin now . . . He hasn't heard the news yet . . . and I will check in on Dave tomorrow morning on my way to the plant. Seeing as it's Saturday, I can leave later than usual. You take it easy now, OK?"

"Yes . . . thank you Wessel."

Time had slipped by slowly and Kate had dozed intermittently, jerking awake guiltily when something disturbed her. Each time she had checked, however, David had not moved, his breathing regular. Now something different wakened her. She glanced at the digital clock beside the bed, which showed two-thirty in the morning. David's breathing was faster and irregular, and he groaned softly as he tried to move against the tightly bound sheets. She hesitated -- was he waking? She was reaching for the bell behind his headboard when he spoke in a whisper.

"Di Di . . . Maulen Maulen!" He groaned again then clearly in a loud voice, "It's no use, Goddamn you, my men are dead . . . do you hear, dea . . . " His voice faded into a series of inaudible whispers. Kate reached for the damp towel that sat in a basin on the night table and softly began to wipe his forehead.

"David, it's Kate, can you hear me?" He calmed as she stroked him, the tension slipping from his tightly bunched muscles and the sheets relaxing as he exhaled.

"Winston, I'm not a bloody farmer you know, I . . . " He slipped back into unconsciousness and again his breathing became regular. Kate sat upright, wide awake now. He was surfacing and it might take some time, but she must not fall asleep again. She went over to the tiny wash basin and splashed tepid water from the cold tap over her face. Outside, the wind rattled the windows in fitful gusts and she remembered it was East Wind time again. Without warning, David spoke again, clearly, "Braver, better men than you died in the mud of Asia to keep your money safe. Use the money you are so fond of to bring back the dead."

Kate rushed to his side, barking her shins painfully on the

bed corner supports. His face was beaded in sweat and his breathing was rapid. He was mumbling incoherently and straining against the sheets. Kate wiped him down again, crooning softly. "It's all right David, its all right my love, I'm with you . . . it's all right . . . you're safe." He relaxed slowly, and she was startled to see tears trickling down his face. He slid back into unconsciousness and his breathing again became regular. Kate waited for a few minutes, then rang the bell for the night sister, who came in quickly. A large nun, she towered over Kate. Kate explained the sequence of events and the nun checked his pulse and temperature, comparing it with his chart. "He is cooler, and yes he is coming out of unconsciousness . . . do you want me to send a nurse to sit with you?"

"No, Sister, when he is fully awake, I will call."

"Ach so! We have two deliveries tonight, babies always come in the early morning, so if at first no one comes, try again, ja?"

"Thank you sister, I will."

She sat watching the ripples run over his face as he dreamed, but in the next two hours he did not move nor speak again and her eyelids drooped lower and lower until she too was asleep.

Suddenly startled, she sat up. Bright sunlight streamed through the window across the bed and David was watching her, a half smile on his face.

"Oh. . . . oh hell, did I fall asleep? . . . I wanted to be here for you." She rose, smoothing her skirt and tucking in her blouse, "How do you feel? Oh what a stupid question, you must feel like death. Look at your poor eyes."

David's eyes were turning black around the cheekbone and eyelids, and in a short while he was going to have two massive black eyes. He lifted his free hand and gingerly felt his face. "How long have I been in here Kate? What day is it?"

"You crashed yesterday afternoon, and you've been here in the hospital since about six last night."

Recollection flickered in his eyes and he tried to sit up, only to slide down with a groan, "Damn it, what the hell is the damage? I feel weak as a kitten."

Kate pushed him down gently as he tried to rise again, "David lie still, you've had a bad bang to the head and the doctor isn't certain how serious the effects will be. You also have a broken rib and arm. You lost a lot of blood before they got you out of the truck."

"Colin! Has anyone been to check on him? Tell him not to call his parents . . . they'll panic."

She kept firm pressure on his shoulders. "Colin is fine, as far as I know. Wessel went to see him last night and knowing Wessel I suspect that he has reassured Colin. Please David, don't fight, just relax. I'm going to ring for the sister." She reached over him and rang the bell.

David reached up and held her arm. "You sat up all night?"

"Hardly. You saw me sleeping . . . I am not a very good nurse," she replied wryly, covering his hand with her own. "You gave everyone a terrible scare . . . Wessel and Bill Mitchell were in . . . Oh, yes and a Johanny something."

"Gariseb, Johannes Gariseb, silly bastard . . . so he came as well, did he. How long do they think I'll be in here?"

Before she could answer, Ken Hassel came through the door, followed by a nurse.

Overhearing the question he snapped, "For as long as it takes . . . you are bloody lucky to be alive, Mornay." He turned to Kate and smiled, "Go and have a cup of tea, Doctor. I want to examine this idiot and no doubt he will be yelling a lot."

Kate released David's hand, blushing as she realized that Hassel and the nurse must have noticed.

"Yes, of course. . . I can come back later?"

"Give me twenty minutes. Wessel has just arrived, so go and wait with him, and if Mornay is still compos when I have finished, you can both come back for a few minutes."

Kate walked down the corridor feeling curiously light-headed. She tried to analyse her emotions coolly and dispassionately, but tiredness washed over her like a wave. All she could focus on was the likelihood that David was going to be all right, and when she rounded the corner to see Wessel sitting in the waiting room, she was unaware that she was smiling.

Wessel's face was grim. He did not rise to greet her and, instead, patted the leatherette sofa indicating that she was to sit. "How is he Kate?"

"Oh, Wessel, he is going to be fine. He is talking coherently and his memory is clear, except that he doesn't remember the accident. He had a restless night and talked a bit while he was unconscious, but he slept solidly from about four and woke up before I did."

Wessel nodded. "I spoke to the night nurse before she left and she thought he was going to be OK." He paused and took a deep breath. "Kate, I have some bad news . . . the tour party that Colin went with yesterday is lost in the Namib. Search parties have been out since late yesterday and there's no sign of them on any of the usual routes. A full scale search is being assembled this morning. As soon as I've seen Dave, I'm going out to Tsamma to catch Rafa and see if we can do an air search. I'll have to tell Dave."

Kate stared in disbelief. Comprehension of what Wessel had just said numbed her senses. She had heard all the terrible stories of men lost in the Namib and cold fear gripped her heart. "No, no, don't. You know what he's like. He'll get up despite the doctor's orders."

"Kate, he has to know. Anyway he'll very quickly put two and two together when Colin doesn't come to visit him. The news is all round the town and one of the nurses is bound to blurt it out."

Kate sat slumped, emptied of all the relief and happiness that David's survival had prompted. Silently, she asked herself why she had chosen to get involved with these hard men and their dramatic lifestyles. The comfort and security of her precise lab work seemed far away. Drawing on hidden reserves, she shook herself like a dog shedding water after a swim and said firmly.

"Of course we must, you are quite right Wessel." She touched his arm. "He is very lucky to have you as his friend. We must combine our forces to convince him to stay in bed."

There was a long silence as they both sat deep in thought, and finally Wessel grunted, "OK, how about this for a story . . . we tell him that the tour vehicle has broken down and that replacement vehicles have gone out to make the switch. Hopefully, by the time he starts getting twitchy about Colin's disappearance, we will have found them and the emergency will be over. After all, the main facts are basically correct . . . what do you think?"

"It should work, and if we can alert Matron to warn all the nurses not to say anything, he'll be more inclined to obey the doctor's orders . . . come let's go back, it's been nearly fifteen minutes."

"Wait Kate, here comes Ken now . . . let me speak to him first." The Doctor saw Wessel as the big man stood up. Handing his clipboard to a nurse, he walked over to where they stood.

"Wessel, I have just come from David and he wants to see you right away. He's convinced Tsamma Uranium will grind to a halt if David Mornay is sick for five minutes. Now listen to me. He is absolutely not to move from hospital for the next two days. There is complete retrograde amnesia from the time he left Rafa at the airport. Now, that is fairly normal in accidents of this kind, but I am not one hundred percent sure yet, plus the fact that his whole system has taken a severe hammering. I had them fax me his medical file from Jo'burg last night and that man is a walking medical textbook." He turned to Kate, "He has to take better care of himself. Try and hammer into that thick skull that he is not a young buck anymore."

"You giving up smoking then, Doctor?" Wessel delivered the comment with a perfectly straight face.

"Piss off, Wessel. Sorry Kate. I am the Doctor, remember. In any case, it's you bastards that drive me to it," he added, glaring at Wessel in mock anger. "Go on, go on. . . . go and see him but don't forget what I said. I gave him a sedative, so don't stay long."

"Doctor Hassel, have you heard about his nephew?" Kate asked quietly.

"His nephew, no. What about him?"

"He is on that tour that is missing in the Namib. We're going to tell David, but only that the vehicle has broken down and repair trucks are on the way. We . . . Wessel and I were hoping that you would speak to Matron and tell her to impose a blackout on the nurses where David is concerned."

Hassel's face was grave. No longer amused, he had grasped the implications as fast as the words had come out of Kate's mouth. "I see, yes . . . he is in no condition to leave the hospital . . . I will speak to Matron right away . . . good thinking, both of you." With a curt nod he strode away.

Wessel opened the door to David's room. Someone had closed the curtains. The room was lit by a low-powered bulb on the wall above the bed. David's eyes opened slowly as the two entered.

"Hi, Wessel. That excuse for a doctor has shot me full of dope and I can hardly keep my eyes open. You must make sure the Weskus Konstruct people don't forget to keep their fresh concrete watered, the . . . "

Wessel interrupted him. "Dave, give it a rest will you . . . everyone knows what to do, including me. All you have to do is get better and the only way is . . . for once in your sweet life . . . is to do as you are told." He raised his hand to forestall David's reply. "I am going out to the mine in a few minutes and will drop back this evening to give you a full report. Oh, before I forget . . . Colin's tour vehicle has broken down and they've sent repair trucks out, so when he gets back, Kate will bring him round." He moved towards the door. "I'll get going now and leave you two alone." He paused as if to add something, then shrugged as he turned away and closed the door softly behind him.

"Colin is OK?" David was lying back with his eyes closed.

Kate steeled herself and replied as casually as she could, "Colin? Oh I'm sure he's fine, probably enjoying the little adventure. Now listen David, Ken Hassel wants you to rest, so I'll go home and do a few things and be back this afternoon . . . you just try to rest." There was no reply and his closed eyes and steady breathing told her that he had drifted into sleep. She bent over and kissed him softly on dry lips.

Chapter 19

Search

Rafa, his mouth set in a grim line, listened to Wessel. He had arrived five minutes before and the Chieftain was now unloading several passengers and suitcases. Old man Butchert had been waiting with a reception committee, and Wessel had filled him in on the events of the last twenty-four hours. Butchert was no fool -- men who run mining companies rarely are -- and he had not hesitated when Wessel requested that the Chieftain be used for an air search. "Keep me informed, van der Walt . . . you are to report in every hour . . . is that understood?"

"Yes, Sir. I will radio the airfield and van Tonder will phone you. It should be fairly easy to see them from above."

Butchert, an old desert hand, had looked at the sky. As a junior geologist forty years before, he had prospected the length and breadth of this land. More than almost anyone else, he knew and feared the Namib. "Watch the wind, it's beginning to blow . . . very soon you will have no visibility and I don't want you to take any chances, so get going quickly. If necessary, put down in Swakop until the wind drops."

Now Wessel was explaining the situation to Rafa. Like Butchert, the swarthy Chilean had looked at the sky. "Coming from Windhoek, Wes, the wind was like a jetstream and we clipped ten minutes off our regular time," he said. "Butchert is right . . . the visibility is going down every minute. OK, let's go. We will need a few bodies to act as eyes."

"Yes, I thought of that . . . I have a couple of my men here and they can sit on each side of the plane."

Minutes later they were lifting off from the Tsamma airfield. The Chieftain rose up like a rocket into the face of the gusting wind. As yet, the sand content was minimal. The East Wind had not yet begun to unleash its full fury and, apart from a very bumpy ride, they were able to see a huge swath of desert below them. Wessel sat in the right hand co-pilot's seat, a boom microphone clipped to his head, the miniature speaker next to his mouth.

Rafa spoke first. "Wes, I am going to set up a square search, using Rossing mountain as one point and Swakop as the other. We will start from Rossing and fly west for five minutes then turn 90 degrees to the south, fly for another five minutes, then turn again to the east and fly for 10, then turn North for a further 10. The sequence is two legs at five, two legs at 10 then two legs at 15. I add five mins every time we complete two legs . . . got it?"

Wessel stared out the side window. "I think so . . . what do you want me to do?" he asked.

"Nothing, except to look for the vehicle, and if you see it don't take your eyes off it . . . look for reference marks in case we're in a turn."

They flew for the next half hour without speaking. The plane was bucking in the thermals and gusty winds as Rafa kept the altitude to 1500 feet and Wessel heard one of his men being violently airsick in the back. Gazing down at the monotonous terrain strained everyone's eyes -- and imaginations. Rock outcrops, stunted clusters of thorn bushes and even shadows cast by windblown dunes caused momentary exultation, then sinking disappointment as the angle changed and the illusion revealed itself.

For the first time, a feeling of unease gripped Wessel. He had been certain the air search would be quick and effective but as the minutes ticked by he began to realize how extraordinarily difficult finding a small vehicle in the vast crumpled plains was going to be. No one had seen anything remotely resembling the vehicle, when suddenly from the rear of the aircraft came a shout and Gariseb came forward excitedly. He leaned over Wessel and pointed. Wessel could see nothing, then yes, a pattern on the sand, unusual in that it was regular. He spoke to Rafa.

"To the right, Rafa. You will need to get down lower, Gariseb has spotted something and I can see it as well." Rafa clicked a stopwatch fitted to the control yoke and turned the Chieftain in a gentle diving turn. Wessel called corrections, "Come right a little more, steady, can you see it?"

"I have it, looks good." Rafa concentrated on the rapidly approaching target and they both let out yells of relief as they flashed overhead at a 1000 feet. People were waving and the LandRover was clearly visible, a tarpaulin stretched out to one side. Rafa rolled the Chieftain in a tight curve, dropping the flaps and going lower so that on the next pass he was barely 200 feet over the people on the ground. "It's them all right . . . great work, Johnnny, that was a hard spot to see, what the hell are they doing here of all places?" He climbed rapidly, speaking into the microphone. "Tsamma, Tsamma, this is Charlie Mike, do you read?"

"This is Tsamma . . . go ahead."

"Van, we have contact . . . tell the ground crews they are at . . ."Here he pulled a map further on to his lap, "Co-ordinates are . . ."While Rafa read out the precise location, all the men on board were yelling at each other with broad grins on their faces. "I will circle their position until I run low on fuel and then go on to Swakop."

"Understood Rafa, congrats . . . how do they look?"

"As far as we could see, they seem fine. Call Mr. Butchert and give him the news. I will fly back to Tsamma from Swakop later this afternoon just in case there is a hitch."

"Roger, Charlie Mike, Tsamma out."

Rafa had a broad grin on his face as he spoke to Wessel. "I bet Colin will have quite a story to tell when he gets back to Canada. You knew Dave is sending him back at the weekend?"

"Yes, Dave told me, I can't help feeling sorry for the boy. He did a stupid thing with those other kids, but hell, you and I probably did stupid things at that age. A clip on the ear would have been sufficient punishment. I gather Dave was really mad at him and that must have been quite an experience."

Rafa sighed. "Yes, I'm sorry too. I tried to change Dave's mind but he was in no mood to argue. It's a pity, because the boy is a natural pilot and I know I could have had him going solo with a few more lessons. Still, que sera . . . " He looked down at the LandRover far below them. "He is a nice kid when you get beneath all that cockiness. How is Dave doing?"

"Well he looks like hell, black eyes, bandages everywhere. Shit, Rafa, you should have seen him on that operating table yesterday. I thought at first he was a goner . . . gave me one hell of a shock. Ken Hassel, cool as a cucumber, stitching him up like a mailbag. Forty goddamn stitches in his chest. This morning he was conscious and talking and, according to Kate, he managed to get quite a lot of sleep, although he had restless periods, but then he settled . . . "

Startled, Rafa interrupted, "Kate! You mean Kate Richardson? She was at the hospital overnight?"

"Yes, I don't know what is going on with those two, but when she saw the crash site I thought she was going to pass out. She rode the ambulance into Swakop and slept at the hospital last night. She's married to the accountant isn't she?"

"Yes, Jack Richardson, he is one of Butchert's rising stars." Rafa stared through the windscreen at the tilting horizon as they turned over the tour site. To himself he muttered, "Well, I'll be damned! So he was right about her feelings."

The high impedance boom mike carried his softly spoken words to Wessel who turned to look at him in astonishment. "You knew about this? What the hell has Dave been up to?"

Rafa struggled for a moment then said wearily, "Wessel, I guessed the problem only yesterday. He asked me not to speak of it, but you are one of his close friends and I suppose you should know. He has fallen in love with this woman. She tried not to let the situation go too far. Now you know why he was so bloody curt to everyone lately . . . she had told him that it had to end. I guess she's not having much success, if last night is anything to go by."

Wessel whistled softly. "Poor old Dave. Did he say what he is going to do? It's not going to be easy when Jack Richardson gets back. Everyone will be talking about them now. Old man Butchert is not going to be happy with Dave. Richardson is tipped to go places in the organization and Butchert will make sure nothing interferes with that." He shook his head sadly and continued. "Butchert got a very one-sided version over that episode with Waldron the day Ivan was killed and he was pretty annoyed with Dave. I heard that it was only because Joe Clifford at head office stepped in that it didn't go any further. Even if Dave is separate from the Tsamma organization, head office can't always keep on protecting him." He pointed through the windscreen, "There they are . . . see the dust?"

Far below, plumes of dust feathered back from two fast-moving vehicles heading directly towards the tour group position. Rafa looked at his fuel gauge and rolled out of the turn. "Just in time, my fuel is down to reserve," he said. "Let's head to Swakop. I want to see Dave and there's not much more we can do here." He looked down and now dust was rolling across the desert in long clouds. "The East Wind has started, those boys on the ground will get there in time but they will have to shift to get back to Swakop ahead of the main storm." He put the nose of the Piper down in a shallow glide and moved the throttles fully open.

1904

. . . . . The dying Bushman could see the tiny differences in the folds of rock that pinpointed the cave position. In grim despair he knew he was still too far to reach the hidden entry before the Shutztruppe soldier caught him. Staggering now, he turned away from the cave, that secret at least he could protect. He fell, a small bloodied brown ball, and lay still on the dried gravel bed of the Khan river. The mounted trooper thundered down on the still form, yipping in exultation. Reining in beside the crumpled Bushman, the soldier raised his rifle for the killing shot. A blast of dust swirled past the tableau, obscuring the soldier's aim and as he wiped dust from his eyes, the Bushman uncoiled in a last brave attempt to die fighting.

Another swirl of dust driven by the rising East Wind again blotted out visibility. The Bushman, on his feet now, slashed with his hunting knife at the soldier, but the horse moved and he missed his target. Instead, his knife drove deep into belly of the horse. Rearing in shock, the horse nearly unseated its rider as it lunged away from the source of its pain. Recovering, the soldier reined the horse in. At a safe distance, he turned and shot the Bushman through the heart. Dismounting, the soldier found to his dismay that his horse had been severely injured and, wild with rage, he kicked repeatedly at the bloody remains of the little desert dweller. His rage finally exhausted, the soldier retrieved the reins and began the long trek to rejoin his companions, his wounded horse staggering uncertainly behind him. A stinging wind blasted clouds of dust down the grim canyon. The East Wind had arrived . . .

Colin awoke to the early light. His sleep had been fitful, for the rising wind moaning through the eroded spires of rock had kept him awake well past midnight. When he had finally fallen into an exhausted sleep, his dreams were confusing and fearful. Now he sat rubbing his eyes, gritty from the sand that was moving in the rising wind. He shook sand from his clothes. Picking up the water bottle, he moistened his lips, then uncontrollably gulped the last of the water down. It was gone too soon and a sick fear rose in him again as he dropped the empty bottle on the sand.

He walked back past the skeletons to the flat plain. Dust lifted in broad billows, hiding the mountains before subsiding, only to be lifted again as a fresh burst of wind rolled over the desert. He looked over to his right, remembering the position of Kresfeld's cairns. He had been too far to the left each time he had reached the cairns, so he reasoned that he must have ended at a ravine that was left of the correct one. Satisfied with his logic, he began walking towards the right of yesterday's line of march.

Several fruitless hours later, Colin realized that he was hopelessly lost. He had entered several likely looking ravines leading down to the valley floor, but each time he had found no signs of human activity. Thirst was already becoming his sole preoccupation and finally in desperation he followed a wide, gently sloping ravine down into the main canyon, hoping that somewhere he might find a pool of exposed water. Kresfeld had said as much, for apparently during the Second World War two Germans who were fearful of being interned as enemy aliens had gone into the desert and hidden themselves for several years. They had found water and Colin realized now that his only hope of survival was either rescue or finding water.

His lips were cracked and dry, his mouth felt like sandpaper and the increasing gusts of wind made walking more and more difficult. Several times he had stopped and screamed for help, but even the echoes that had returned to mock him earlier were now overwhelmed by the rasping whistle of the East Wind.

Kate slipped quietly into David's dimly lit room. Some light filtered through the partially drawn curtains, but the light above his bed had been extinguished. He slept with his face turned to the door, as if waiting for her. His chest rose and fell rhythmically and his face was peaceful and still. An air conditioner hummed softly and the room was cool, in stark contrast to the dry heat entering the town from the desert.

Twice she had slowed to a stop on her way back to the hospital when sharp gusts had rocked the car. Despite dressing as coolly as she could in a fresh cotton summer dress, her back was wet with perspiration where it had rested against the vinyl seat of her car.

She sat quietly, watching the still face carefully. She could no longer evade or pretend that she had options. Yesterday had brought home to her, with dreadful clarity, how much she cared for this quiet, lonely man. She knew now that she was in love with David Mornay and he had said that he was in love with her. She also knew now that, even if she decided to stay with Jack, her life would not and could not ever be the same again. She reached for David's right hand that lay on top of the covers and he stirred slightly, his fingers closing compulsively over hers. Their hands locked and she felt a great contentment wash over her.

For a long time Kate sat. Never before had she felt as complete as she did now, but she also realized that it was probably going to end in sadness for them both.

David stirred slightly, his eyes flickered, opened, then closed and snapped opened again. "Kate?" his voice was hoarse and he tried to clear his throat.

"Yes David, I'm here." She squeezed his hand. "You've been sleeping . . . try to go back to sleep . . . it's good for you."

He grimaced. "No, I want to look at you . . . help me to sit up . . . these bloody sheets are too tight." He started to push himself up but slipped back with a groan. "Kate, what the hell did Ken give me? I've got no strength at all . . . help me up, please."

"No David, you can see me perfectly well from that position." She stood up and leaned over him, adjusting the sheet. He ran his hand up her arm squeezing it gently as if to reassure himself that she was really there.

"What made you come, Kate? I thought after our talk in the library that it was all over."

She coloured slightly, then lifted her eyes to hold his own in a steady gaze, "I thought so too. When I left you that night I knew that a relationship would bring pain to both of us. " She smiled wanly. "But I thought about you often . . . too often . . . Jack would never understand and I knew that I could not bear to inflict such a hurt on him. Poor Jack . . . I took out all my confusion and unhappiness on him. He said I was 'desert happy' and just needed a vacation to get back to being my old self." Gravely she stared at him. "Jack thought that I was mad at him for being away so much and he tried, poor soul, to jolly me along. I was slowly getting back to some sort of routine when I heard you had been hurt, possibly killed . . . " She squeezed her face between her hands . . . "And when I saw your pickup . . . all that blood . . . it felt as if I had been kicked in the stomach. Never in all my life have I ever had such a feeling of loss." She sighed. "I realized then that I cared very much for you." David reached for her hand and she closed both her hands around his good hand. "I thought sitting with you would give me time to sort out my next move, but I'm as confused as ever." She stopped and a single tear rolled down her cheek.

David watched her face. "Please don't cry Kate. I guess ever since Lamberti's cocktail party I've known that I was falling in love with you and when you closed the door on me, I didn't know what to do. I told Rafa . . . God was it only yesterday? . . . that I was going to roll up my contract and take a long holiday in Mauritius. How could I bear to see you at parties with Jack or even on your own and know that it was ended? I don't know what my future holds, but I do know that it has to include you." He gripped her hand fiercely. "I dreamt of you, but it was a strange dream." His brow below the bandages furrowed. "You were catching an airliner -- leaving me -- and I couldn't run fast enough to stop you, my feet dragged in the thick mist, and it was as white as snow but heavy like beach sand. I kept calling but you didn't hear." He smiled at her, "How good are you at interpreting dreams?"

"I try not to, the future is threatening enough without foreknowledge to keep us awake at night." She took his good hand in both of hers. "David, what I said at the library . . . I thought that it would be possible . . ." There was a knock at the door and Kate dropped his hand on the bed, rummaging for a handkerchief in her purse.

"Yes, come in nurse," she responded. But it was Wessel and Rafa who entered and both were in high spirits.

"Hey, amigo, you been having a smashing time?" Rafa choked on his own joke, and Wessel grinned from ear to ear.

David, his face impassive, growled. "You two been drinking?"

Rafa dropped on to the upholstered arm of Kate's seat. "No, no, amigo. Nothing like that. Just a little excitement this morning. Madre de Dios, look at your face . . . you never were handsome, but now?" He smiled at Kate, who had started to rise.

"I will leave you men to talk," she said.

"No, please, we will not stay long." Rafa placed a sinewy brown hand on her shoulder and gently forced her back into the chair. "The East Wind is coming in hard. I expect that the main force will hit us in a few hours. I want to make sure that the Chieftain is sealed up tight in the hanger here. No one is going to be flying in this today." He stared hard at David. "Wes tells me that you made a very good attempt at committing Hari Kiri and that you are going to be out of action for a while. Is there anything I can get you . . . books, cassettes, a new brain?"

David smiled crookedly at him."You still preaching, Father?" He looked at the ceiling and closed his eyes for a second. "Wes, what is the status of the foundation pour . . . and how come you're back so early when it's barely three?"

"Blast it! I clean forgot to check, but knowing Weskus they'll have suspended operations with the East Wind coming."

David rolled his head slightly to look at Wessel. He was clearly puzzled, "Forgot? How come? That was the whole reason for you to go back today."

Rafa broke in. "We had an emergency. The tour bus went missing last night and they had not found it by the time I returned from Windhoek this morning, so I grabbed Wessel and a few of your men to act as spotters . . . "

Before he could finish Wessel broke in. "We found the tour bus . . . silly bastards were miles off course . . . old Johannes spotted them."

David frowned. "I thought you said this morning -- you and Kate -- that the tour bus had broken down and the rescue vehicles were on their way?" His eyes flicked between Wessel and Kate.

"Yes, we did, and if we had told you at that time that Colin was still missing you would have fretted like an old maid and done everything possible to get up. Ken Hassel wants you to stay put for at least two days," Wessel lifted his big hands expressively, "and we were right. We found the bus and when we left the scene the rescue vehicles were almost there. So by this evening they will be back and I will bring Colin in to see you."

Kate quickly put her hand over David's before he could speak, "David, it was my idea to keep the news from you and, as Wessel says, it was the correct decision. You have had a very calm day, which can only do you good." She stood up, smoothing down her skirt. "I must go home and see to the animals and fix tonight's meal." Kate looked at Rafa and Wessel. "Why don't you both join me for dinner and then we can all come back here with Colin at eight?"

Rafa and Wessel exchanged glances, and it was Rafa who spoke, "We would love to Kate. What time?"

"Oh, say six. Colin will have had time to shower and dinner will be something simple so it won't take long." She squeezed David's hand. "Try to get some more sleep between now and when we return." She smiled at Rafa and Wessel. "Don't stay too long."

When she had gone, Rafa let out a long whistle of air. "My God, there goes a woman in love . . . she is lovely Dave, but she is married . . . what is going to happen to you both?"

David stared at the ceiling. "I wish I knew. She is still not certain if she will leave Jack . . . God what a mess! Don't mention any of this to Colin, either of you, please."

Rafa leaned over the bed, resting stiff-armed on the mattress. "Talking of Colin, why don't you let him stay a while longer, that is, if he wants to? I am sure I can have him going solo in a few more days. After his little cock up, he didn't end in hospital now did he?"

David's laugh broke into a croak as his injured chest expanded. "Are you telling me that of our individual stupidities, mine was the worst?"

"Come on, Dave," Wessel broke in, "you can spend some time with him for a change while you recuperate. Hell, he is your nephew after all."

"OK, OK, I'll think about it. But I'm not sure you two are right about this. Wessel, phone Weskus and see if they did in fact pour today." He lifted his hand weakly. "And thank you both." He hesitated, then waved them away. "Now, piss off . . . you heard the lady . . . I need my rest."

As they reached the door, Ken Hassel stuck his head around the jamb. "How is the patient? You must be fairly stiff and sore now that the anaesthetic is wearing off?"

Wessel and Rafa squeezed past the Doctor on their way out. "We will see you later . . . Give him hell Ken, he deserves it." Rafa said over his shoulder.

They walked down the corridor, each engrossed in his own thoughts. Rafa reached the door first and said with surprise to Wessel. "For crying out loud, look at that wind! It's just as well we found them when we did. Can you imagine what it would be like sitting exposed in the desert in that?"

'That' was a cloud of sand and dust driven on the wind, shrieking between the buildings and rattling against the glass outer

doors like hail on a tin roof. Visibility had dropped to a few metres and both knew that simply to reach their vehicle, parked a hundred metres away, was going to be a problem. Suddenly, the wind dropped and through the drifting dust it was possible to see their vehicle.

"Quick, before it picks up again." Holding handkerchiefs against their mouths they trotted quickly across the asphalt to where the Peugeot station wagon was parked.

Head down and his back to the wind, Colin trudged through another patch of soft sand at the bottom of the canyon. For several hours he had stumbled along the canyon floor, a flat gravelly, sandy plain about two hundred metres wide, studded with wire-like tufts of sparse grasses and the occasional thorn tree. The floor of the canyon was several hundred feet lower than the surrounding rocky desert. It had been carved out aeons ago by waters draining from the interior mountains, but now, except in rare times of exceptional rainfall, the water ran at least 20 metres below Colin's boots through the pebble strata that overlaid the true bottom of the canyon. In places where hard dolerite rock had resisted erosion, the water could be forced to within a few feet of the present canyon floor. After travelling for a few hundred feet just under the surface, or in certain rare locations above the sand, the water sank back to disappear under the sands until forced to the surface again, many miles downstream.

Colin knew little about geology, but it was any kind of surface exposure of water that he was seeking. Ironically, he had stumbled past the only pool for miles in either direction, but it was during a particularly severe period of wind-driven sand when visibility was reduced to a few metres. Colin was now in the secondary stages of dehydration. To conserve fluid for the vital organs, his body was shutting down or slowing respiratory activity, but like a monstrous dry blotter, the East Wind kept drawing life-sustaining moisture to the skin's surface. Without water to replace the continuous loss, Colin had only another day to live.

He drifted in and out of delirium. Now he was paddling in the big canoe with Brian Talbot through the Broken islands. Colin felt a gust of rain on the back of his neck and smiling he turned to face the rain, only to have a blast of stinging sand pepper his face and drag him back to reality. Too exhausted to cry, he remembered bitterly his comment to Brian about hating the rain on the West Coast of Canada. Thirst raged in him and with every let-up in the wind he searched desperately for signs of water and a place to shelter until nightfall. Rising steeply from the canyon floor, the tortured, folded rocks had been heaved upward by the cataclysmic forces that had spawned them, to end in eroded peaks close to the plains above. With good reason the Bushmen, the greatest survivalists in Africa, called this place "The land God made in anger." Prior to being driven west and north into the Kalahari hundreds of years before by the expanding Herero and other tribes, they had rarely ventured into this desolate wasteland. Game and other life forms had developed unique methods of surviving. This is the land where the "headstander" beetles stand head down with their backs to the early morning coastal fog and collect precious moisture on their backs. The moisture collects and runs down to their mouths ensuring survival for another day. Other insects, spiders and lizards venture forth only in the cool of the early morning or at night. During the day, the Aporosaura lizard buries itself beneath the sand to escape the heat, as does the golden mole. Nothing in the Namib exists without incredible adaptation to the terrible conditions.

Weaving from side to side like a drunk, Colin staggered on.

It was late in the afternoon and for what seemed to him the hundredth time, Colin fell on his knees. His swollen tongue filled his mouth and swallowing was all but impossible. His lips were dry and cracked in the 50C heat, swollen to twice their normal size. He was in almost constant delirium, but periodically his mind would clear and in those brief lucid moments he knew that he must find shelter. The wind was literally killing him. Despite the searing heat he had removed his shirt and it now adorned a thorn bush several hundred metres behind him. He had been carrying his bush hat in his hand, but in falling to his knees once again, he released his grasp and the hat fell to the sand, abandoned. Once more Colin wearily pushed himself upright. The wind had dropped to almost nothing and ahead and to the left was an overhang of rock with a patch of shadow beneath. No longer capable of emotion, he staggered towards the dark patch against the grey rock walls of the Khan canyon.

Surprisingly, the wind remained briefly calm and throwing himself down in the shade, Colin stared around through bleary eyes. A deeper black area drew him in further under the overhang. He crawled in on hands and knees as the roof shelved sharply down towards the rising sanddrift of the floor. A strange whistling sound penetrated his clouded mind, increasing in intensity as he dragged himself deeper into the shade. He glimpsed the opening just as the wind burst upon him again and the overhang became lost in the canyon's swirling dust. A last desperate surge of energy drove the boy to crawl through the aperture where he collapsed exhausted on the floor of a cave the size of a small house. Inside, it felt at least ten degrees cooler than the oven outside. There was a strange whistling sound and the air was full of flying dust and grit.

Exhausted after this last desperate surge to get into the shade, Colin folded into a fetal position and slept. What he could not know was that the cave had been carved aeons ago by the same storm runoff spilling from the plains above that had carved the Khan canyon. At some time during that era, a small crack, a hundred metres short of the cliff edge, had diverted part of the run off water, which trickling down had finally been halted in its progress several hundred feet lower by a band of iron-hard dolerite. Seeking an outlet, the water had pooled, and finding a slightly inclined band of shale, it began to travel through the softer material like oil along a wick. The shale exited a few feet above the canyon floor and the water had trickled out to rejoin the parent stream flowing down the canyon. Over time erosion had formed an inverted funnel, with the narrow part the crack on the plains above and the wider part forming the cave below.

The entrance through which Colin had crawled was an aperture left by the long since eroded band of shale. The shape of the cave now acted like a giant cooling tower. Air drawn up from canyon floor through the aperture was pulled up by the lower pressure on the desert surface several hundred feet above where he lay unconscious. Increasing in speed through the venturi like funnel above his head, the pressure decreased and the temperature lowered as a consequence. This was the whistling sound that Colin had vaguely noticed. Now he slept, his body occasionally twitching, as frightening dreams gripped his fevered imagination. Outside, the storm lessened as night came and Colin slept on, his body desperately trying to stabilize.

Chapter 20

Losses

Kate frowned at the clock. It was nearly seven and if Wessel failed to arrive soon with Colin, they would have to rush dinner if they were to get to the hospital by eight o'clock. Rafa was already there, but Wessel had gone to the tour company headquarters to collect Colin. "Would you like another drink Rafa?" she asked.

Rafa rolled the half-empty whisky glass between his hands, deep in thought. "What? Oh no, I am still busy thank you." He looked up at her. "What are you going to do? . . Sorry, it is none of my business." He was embarrassed and covered his confusion with another sip of whisky. "The only reason I ask is because he is my friend . . . you understand . . . "

"Of course." Kate played with a table napkin, pulling it nervously between her hands. "To answer your question, I don't know what I'm going to do." She raised her head defiantly. "I did not expect to fall in love with David." Rafa did not interrupt and she continued sadly, "I am, after all, married and I still care for my husband. I am dreading his return . . . I hate to think of his reaction. We have never, in the seven years of our marriage, had any thought that our marriage was threatened." She took a sip of white wine from the slender glass. "Have you ever been married?"

Rafa stared down at the glass in his hands for a long time. "No, once long ago I was in love with a woman . . . she died. Was killed . . . before we really got to know each other." He sighed deeply and Kate saw the pain in his eyes. "I do not understand how or why it happens Kate, but as you and Dave have found out, the attraction between two people when they are truly in love is like a fire in the brain. It burns everything else up - honour, responsibility, duty . . . race, class." He smiled ruefully at her. "If a person is lucky, there are no hard choices, they meet, marry and, God-willing, raise children. For both of you that is not an option. You are going to have to decide and soon. Staying overnight at the hospital has brought your feelings into the open . . . this is a small town and people can be cruel."

"I know, people always assume the worst." A tear glistened on her eyelash. "It is not for myself that I care, but for Jack. He will simply not understand . . . he is very direct and uncomplicated. It makes me feel so . . . so dishonest."

Rafa held out his glass. "I will have that refill now if I may."

As Kate went to the cabinet for the bottle, there was a furious knocking. The door handle turned, but out of long habit Kate had set the latch and the door remained closed. They glanced at each other in alarm, and Kate rushed to open the door. Wessel stood under the porch light, still dressed in his working clothes. As the door opened, he snapped at Kate.

"Is Rafa still here?"

"Yes, come in Wessel, what has happened?"

Wessel came in, stooping slightly. Rafa had risen from his chair at the knocking, and Wessel burst out. "Colin is still missing."

Kate and Rafa stared at him, dumbfounded, "You mean that was not the tour bus we found?" Rafa asked.

"It was the tour vehicle. They returned to Swakop about twenty minutes ago. Apparently the driver and Colin went off to get help and have disappeared." Wessel took a deep breath."The search party spent about an hour trying to follow the route that Colin and Kresfeld, the driver, had taken, but the East Wind is getting very fierce in the open desert and they had to break off the search . . . the tourists were getting very scared." He looked at the glass in Kate's hand. "Can I have a drink? I think I need a stiff one."

Rafa looked out the window. Inside the house the noise of the wind was muted by foot thick concrete block walls, but he could see in the eerie light of the street lamps dust whirling down the main street. He turned back grim-faced. "This can last for days," he muttered. "If the wind dies down we can try an air search in the morning, but I am not confident that it will be any better than it is now."

Wessel continued "They told me that the driver Kresfeld is an old desert hand and they will probably be in a sheltered place for the night. God, I hope so . . . they both had water bottles and they were heading for the road that leads to the old abandoned tin mine. It is not far to the mine, so my guess is that when the wind got up, Kresfeld realized the danger and they made for the mine." Gratefully, Wessel took the tumbler from Kate who also handed Rafa his refilled glass.

"What are we going to tell David?" she asked. "He'll have to know . . . can we try to get to this mine tonight?"

Wessel shook his head. "Not a chance. Fighting the wind is bad enough, but wind and darkness combined is a sure recipe for disaster, and we could lose more people. No . . . we're going to have to sit tight until morning. The police have been informed and there is a search coordination meeting an hour before first light in the Water Affairs offices on the edge of town." He took out a large, brightly patterned handkerchief and wiped his face. "God, it's getting hot. I just hope they're not out in the open tonight."

Rafa smiled wanly at Kate. "Well, I guess we should eat, Kate. It would be a shame to waste your dinner. There is nothing we can do for them tonight and we are due at the hospital in half an hour."

"Yes, of course." Kate went through to the kitchen and they could hear the clink of plates as she laid out the meal. Rafa spoke quietly to Wessel, "What are their chances?"

Wessel took a deep drink from the tumbler in his hand. He stared at Rafa with bleak eyes.

"Not very good I'm afraid. Under normal circumstances it would be about 50/50 but in the East Wind . . . hell, Rafa, you can feel the heat down here at the coast, so imagine another five to seven degrees hotter in the interior. If, and only if, they made it to the mine, would they have a reasonable chance."

Rafa inclined his head towards the kitchen. "Do not tell her that. She has enough worries as it is, and we are going to have our hands full with Dave. He is going to try to come with us in the morning and I don't think we can stop him."

Kate carried two plates of cold vichyssoise soup to the dining table calling over her shoulder, "Bring your drinks to the table if you wish." She went back into the kitchen to retrieve her own and the two men waited until she was seated before arranging themselves on either side of her. "It's not very exciting, but in this heat I don't think hot food would be very appropriate." Both men murmured that cold food was exactly what they needed and then there was a silence while they concentrated on the soup.

Wessel broke the silence. "This is very good Kate, what is in it?"

"Thank you . . . leeks, potatoes, cream and chicken stock, actually the next course is the cold chicken that provided the ingredients for the stock." She lifted the open wine bottle. "Can I fill anyone's glass?"

Wessel drained his whisky glass, then handed her the tall stemmed wine glass in front of him, "Yes I will, I think it is going to be a long night."

Kate looked inquiringly at Rafa but he shook his head in refusal.

"No, thank you. If I have to fly tomorrow I had better not have any more." He forced a smile. "If this damned wind drops I want to be available to fly at short notice." There was silence for a while as he finished his soup. Rafa stood and reached for Wessel's empty bowl and reached for Kate's.

"Please don't Rafa, I will take them," she said softly, as she poured more wine for Wessel. "I need to keep myself occupied and the more I have to do at the moment, the less time I have to think." Rafa saw that the hand pouring the wine trembled. Although her voice was controlled, she was clearly under great strain and exercising strong will power to appear normal.

"Of course. It is a bad habit from living on my own so much." Rafa looked around the room and said to no one in particular, "The Chinese have a saying that, 'When a man marries and has children, he gives hostages to fortune'. I think the same applies when one cares for one's friends." He raised his empty glass in salute. "To good fortune . . ."

The other two hesitated over the impromptu toast then soberly raised their glasses. "Good fortune."

Kate collected the bowls and disappeared into the kitchen, and they could hear her moving around. Wessel looked at Rafa. "After we've seen Dave at the hospital I want to go to the police station and talk with the search coordinator . . . do you want to come?"

"No, I will bring Kate back and then try to get some sleep. You can give me all the information tomorrow at the briefing. If the wind is still bad, I will no doubt be kept on standby here in Swakop, so that when it drops I can get airborne quickly."

Kate returned with plates piled high with cold chicken cuts and potato salad. Her own was a minute portion and, comparing her plate with his own, Wessel jokingly asked, "Are you giving us some sort of a message, Kate?"

She laughed. "Believe me, Wessel, it really is quite good, but I am not hungry."

When they had finished, Kate cleared the table and rejected their offers to help wash and dry the dishes. "Let's not waste any more time . . . I'll do them when I get home."

"Come with me Kate," said Rafa. "Wessel is going on to the police station after the hospital, so I will bring you back afterwards. There is no need to take your car, especially on a rotten night like this." Rafa collected his lightweight jacket from where he had hung it by the door.

"Well that's kind of you . . . are you sure?" Kate was relieved; for she hated night driving and this wind scared her.

Rafa opened the passenger side door of the station wagon and held it for her. Wessel backed his pickup truck out of the short driveway and was gone by the time they had buckled themselves into their seats. The wind buffeted the vehicle sharply as they pulled clear of the protective wall that surrounded the entrance to the house. The Peugeot is not a heavy vehicle and it rocked on its springs as they moved onto the main street. Ahead of them the traffic lights at the intersection were blurred blobs of colour in the swirling sand. Rafa cursed, "It's a good thing we know this town . . . can you imagine arriving in a sand storm? Just look at those lights . . . they are almost invisible." He paused and, convinced that the intersection was clear, inched across.

Kate leaned forward, peering through the windshield. "I'm glad you offered to drive me. Frankly, I was going to ask if you hadn't offered. I'm not good at night driving and this is just awful."

The station wagon rocked again as a stiff gust of wind hit them broadside. By the time they reached the hospital they were both sweating from the heat. As they pulled into the parking lot, they could see Wessel waiting inside the glass doors of the hospital entrance airlock.

"Don't wait Kate, make a quick run for it." Rafa cut the ignition and lights as Kate pushed the door open against the wind that with maniacal fury seemed bent on keeping her trapped in her seat. She ran across the parking area to where Wessel waited, holding her hair down with both hands knowing that the gesture was futile. As she reached the door, Wessel pulled it open and she stumbled in, Rafa catching her shoulders from behind to hold her steady. They went through the next set of glass doors and suddenly they were in another world. Air conditioned coolness washed over them and the roaring of the wind was muted by the double glass doors of the airlock. Kate patted herself down, puffing dust off the cotton slacks she had chosen to wear instead of a dress. She felt gritty and dry. With Wessel already ahead of them, they hurried to catch up, and turning the corner they bumped into Ken Hassel coming out of David's room.

"Well now, what have we here? Slow down for heaven's sake

. . . he's going to live, you know."

Wessel apologized. "Sorry Ken, how is the patient?"

"He's improving, but I'm going to keep him in here for another few days, so don't encourage him. Hmm . . . right now he's on a mild sedative so don't stay too long."

"Ken, we have some bad news for him." Wessel caught the Doctor's sleeve to prevent his leaving.

"Bad news? What sort of bad news?"

Quickly Wessel explained the events of the day. "We are going to have to tell him Doc, because once he sees that Colin isn't here he'll catch on."

"Very well, but he cannot leave the hospital yet. I am going to rely on all of you to convince him that he will be better off leaving any search to the more physically able. I am still concerned over that crack he took on the head and I want him as still as possible, for as long as possible."

Rafa interrupted, "Doctor, if he insists -- and you know what he is like -- perhaps he can fly with me . . . at least he will not be banged around like he would be in a vehicle."

"Damn it all! Is no one listening? He is not well enough to go anywhere at present. He may think he is, but I must insist that he stay put . . . look, I have another patient to see right away, but I will try to get back and have a word with Mornay before I go home." With that, he left them.

They followed Kate into the room. David had heard the murmur of voices outside the door and his face lit up as he saw Kate. "Hi there, how was dinner?"

She bent over him and felt his forehead. "You are still very hot, David."

He caught her hand and said, "Sit down Kate, I want to look at you . . . I have enough doctors, nurses and assorted bodies poking me around all day. Right now, all I want is to get out of here as soon as possible."

"Well we've just been speaking to Doctor Hassel and he isn't going to let you out for a while longer. What do you think you will do outside anyway? You'll have to take some time off to recuperate."

David grunted, "I'm feeling a hundred percent better than this morning. Hell, it's only a broken arm and some stitches . . . where is Colin?" He tried to look behind Rafa.

"David, lie still." Kate sat on the bed holding his hand in her lap and looked up at Rafa who grimaced as if he had stepped on a thorn.

"Dave, when the tour bus returned to Swakop an hour ago, Colin was not on it. Apparently, the driver and Colin left to get help and they are still missing."

David stared at Rafa. "No! . . . Are you telling me he is still out there?" He tried to sit up, but the combination of the sedative and Kate's weight on the side of the bed kept him prone. "What are they doing to find him?"

Wessel broke in. "They did a quick search over the route that Colin and Kresfeld were supposed to have taken, but the light was fading and they had to bring the tour party back. There is a big search planned for tomorrow covering the whole area. The area is not that large and we suspect that they made for the old tin mine to wait out the storm."

"Storm?. . . What storm?"

"The East Wind has started but we are hoping that by morning it will have died down enough to do an air search."

Horrified, David looked from one to the other. "The East Wind?. . . Dear God, I had forgotten . . . How good is this driver, Kresfeld, in the desert?"

"He is an old Swakopmunder, and everyone I have spoken to says he is very good," Wessel replied. "Dave, the situation is serious, but it is not critical yet. A huge search is going out at first light, and as Rafa says, if the wind dies he will do an air search. Kresfeld must have made for the old mine and they were carrying enough water to survive for at least another twenty-four hours. If they are at the mine, they will have shelter."

David closed his eyes. "And if they have not made the mine

and are out in the wind? Wessel, I want you to pick me up first thing tomorrow morning . . . I will come with you. . . Rafa, I assume you'll stand by at the airfield?"

Rafa grunted. "Yes, my own guess is that we might get a short period of calm during the day and the target area is only ten minutes flying time from here. I have a suggestion of my own. You will only be a drag to Wessel, and every bump is going to feel like hell, so why not stay here until I come and pick you up? You can act as a spotter from a comfortable seat."

David shook his head. "No, you know as well as I do that the wind may not die down. It was a good try, Rafa, but I'm going in with the search parties. He is my nephew . . . oh God, what am I going to tell his parents?" He released Kate's hand. "Please help me sit up and pass me a glass of water." His voice was firm now.

Kate put an arm behind his shoulders and David heaved himself to a semi-supine position, as she propped pillows behind his head. Tiny beads of sweat broke out on his forehead. "That's better, thank you," he murmured. "He keeps giving me sedatives, and I feel like a big bag of jelly, but by morning, when this latest lot wears off, I'll be fine." He grinned at them.

Kate said quietly, "David, be reasonable. There'll be lots of people out searching tomorrow and your presence won't make the slightest difference. In fact, as Rafa says, you might well become a hindrance and have to be brought back."

David shook his head. "You must try to understand, he is my nephew. He was put in my care and I have to go . . . Rafa understands. We served our apprenticeship in similar schools."

Rafa's face was sombre, but he inclined his head in acknowledgement. "As you say, amigo, but we were younger then and immortal . . . He paused, considering, then continued, "I will drive you in your pickup . . . let Wessel go with the main group. As you guessed, I do not believe that the wind will ease enough for me to fly tomorrow and I had planned to go with the ground parties. If you come with me, we can cover the area between the mine and the Khan."

David took a sip of his water and squeezed Kate's hand. "Agreed. Don't look so down, Kate. He'll take good care of me."

"I'm coming with you then," she said firmly. "Please don't argue . . . if you can go in your state then I certainly can come along, and another pair of eyes won't hurt." She withdrew her hand and stood up, glaring down at him. "I think you're mad and I'm certain that Doctor Hassel will be very difficult to convince, but if you do go, then I'm coming along."

Rafa laughed, a low throaty chuckle. "I was going to suggest that you come Kate . . . if David has a problem then an extra pair of hands will be very useful."

David shifted his gaze from Kate to Rafa, "Thank you, Doctor Modesto, and what makes the two of you think that I need nursemaids? I have a broken arm, some stitches and a bump on the head . . . they're not life threatening injuries you know!"

Wessel broke in, "Look, I want to go down to the police station to catch up on the latest information." He shook David's foot through the blanket affectionately. "Get well . . . Rafa, I'll phone you tonight with all the latest news and no doubt will see you at the briefing tomorrow." He opened the door and turned back, "Thanks for dinner, Kate, it was delicious."

The door closed behind him and Rafa took a deep breath, "It's time we left as well. We'll attend the briefing tomorrow, then come back to pick you up. Expect us at about six a.m. I will phone Ken Hassel at home later and hear what he has to say."

David was silent for a long moment and they both watched his face for any signs of disagreement. "Yes, that sounds fine, OK," he said finally, "but Rafa, no matter what Hassel says I'm coming with you tomorrow, so please don't fail to pick me up." His eyes were locked on Rafa's, and Kate realized that this was a pivotal moment for both men. She was excluded from some private, silent, battle of wills. His eyes not moving from Rafa's face, David said softly. "You did not leave yours behind. You didn't have to go back, but you did . . . so don't expect less from me."

His swarthy face tense, Rafa spoke as softly, his voice tight and controlled, "Yes and look at the cost . . . my God, you know well enough that I have often wondered if it was worth it."

"You would do the same again tomorrow, even knowing the cost," David replied evenly. "You and I are like horses bred to run, we cannot change our natures."

Rafa raised his hands shoulder high in the time-honoured gesture of surrender. "I'll be here at six." He touched Kate's arm. "I will wait for you in the annex." Shaking his head at David as he opened the door, he added sadly, "Perhaps it is time for us to change . . . no?" The door clicked shut behind him.

Kate looked at David, bewildered. "What on earth were you both talking about? What did Rafa do, and why did you not believe him when he said he would pick you up?"

David took a long time to answer. "He is probably the closest friend I have, and we tend to think alike, so when he mentioned phoning Hassel I knew that he wouldn't come for me tomorrow."

"But what was all the rest about - going back?"

"During the Rhodesian War, Rafa rescued a small group of Rhodesian special forces soldiers who were trapped deep in Mozambique. They had been parachuted in to destroy several bridges and cut off supplies to guerilla forces opposing the Rhodesian Government. Unfortunately, unknown to them, there was a strong Cuban-backed force in the area and after taking several casualties, the Rhodesians fought their way out to a small bush airstrip and radioed for help. On that day, Rafa was flying a civilian transport Dakota into Umtali, a small Rhodesian town on the Mozambican/Rhodesian border, when he heard the message. He knew that the Rhodesian Air force was at least an hour further away than he was, so he offered to try an evacuation. He managed to get all the surviving troopers clear just as the Mozambican and Cuban troops overran the airstrip." David was no longer looking at her. He was momentarily in another world, one of pain, fear, chaos and loss.

Kate touched his arm gently, "You were with him?"

David shivered and shook his head. "Me?. No . . . no, I served in Vietnam, never in Africa, but we had similar situations in Nam."

"But if it succeeded, what did Rafa mean by saying that it was not worth it?"

"Ah, yes . . . well it was a little more complicated than . . . pour me a little more water please." He drank deeply, and wiped his lips with a white napkin from the white enamelled side drawer. "You see, Rafa was going out with a nurse from one of the hospitals in Salisbury. It was her day off and she was flying up to Umtali with Rafa for the day. When the message came in, he was minutes from landing at Umtali but knew he couldn't spare the time to drop her off. According to Rafa she would have refused to leave and . . . remember she was a nurse . . . her skills would certainly be needed. As he flew over the trapped Rhodesians, he saw that a strong Cuban force was approaching the airstrip. The Rhodesians had booby trapped the access roads and laid ambushes to slow down the enemy, but just as he managed to get all the survivors aboard, the vanguard of the Cuban forces broke through to the airfield. They managed to kill his co-pilot and put a burst of machine gun fire through the fuselage before he got away and out of range." David paused and took another drink of water. "Marieanna -- that was her name -- and a soldier were killed by the last burst through the fuselage . . . he still blames himself . . . " David sighed. "We are both tired of losing." He stroked her face gently. "Kate you must understand . . . Rafa and I are sick of losing . . . we have had so many losses -- Vietnam . . . Rhodesia . . . Marieanna . . . Ivan and a lot of others whose names, God forgive me, I cannot even remember."

Kate closed her hand over his and pulled it down into her lap. "And now, he does not want to lose you . . . that is why he tried to keep you here."

"That's partly the reason I suppose, although he knows I'm

not that seriously hurt. But I suspect Colin is also a concern, because he and Colin have established a bond. Did you know that he and Wessel insisted I keep Colin here for a few more weeks? Rafa wants to have him fly solo before going back to Canada."

There was a sharp knock on the door and Ken Hassel poked his head around the corner. "Time out, is it safe to enter this passion pit?" He laughed at the expression on both their faces, "My goodness, you both look as guilty as hell. Come on Doctor, it's time you left. My patient's blood pressure is probably through the roof."

Kate smiled, "I was just leaving," she murmured, bending down to kiss David's forehead. "I will see you tomorrow," she assured him. She smiled at Ken Hassel, her composure restored, "He is a difficult patient, but thanks to you, he seems well on the road to recovery . . . goodnight, David . . . Doctor."

Kate met Rafa in the annex and they walked to the exit doors in silence. Outside, the wind banged and whistled through the parking area. After a quick run to Rafa's car, they were safely out of the stinging, gritty air.

"Damn, imagine if it did this more often than just a few days every year," Rafa said as he started the Peugeot. "You know Kate, it is not a good idea that David comes with us tomorrow . . . I was watching him tonight and I think he needs more time to recover."

"I know, but he is determined to go and unfortunately, even if Doctor Hassel forbids it, he will simply get up and go. I think the best approach will be to humour him and at the first sign of distress, bring him straight back to the hospital."

Rafa was silent for a while, then as they turned into her street he spoke, "Yes, you are right, we really don't have any other options. At least if he is with us, we can . . . or at least you can, make him accept reality . . . you are good for him I think." They turned into her driveway and the calm afforded by the high perimeter walls. Rafa reached across to open the passenger door.

"Thank you for the dinner tonight Kate. It was a pity that we had to share it with bad news. If you don't mind, I will wait here until you are inside the house."

Kate touched his hand. "No, Rafa, I should thank you, for not judging me and for helping me to see clearly. I am . . . " she hesitated . . . "I have some hard choices to make and I only pray that I have the courage." He saw, in the glow from the interior roof light, that her face was strained. She closed the door and walked a few paces towards the house when suddenly something startled her, she rushed at the door, fumbling for her key. Rafa hesitated, then fearing an intruder might be in the house, leapt out of his seat and followed her. Kate was now inside the house and had the hall telephone to her ear as he burst through the door behind her.

"What the hell's going on?. . . Oh I'm sorry. . . ." He turned to go, and heard her say, "Jack, when are you coming? . . . you want me to go to Germany with you . . . when? . . . we have . . ." He pulled the door closed behind him and went back to his car. For a while he sat gathering his thoughts, then shaking his head sadly, he started the car and reversed out of her driveway.

Chapter 21

Parents

The phone tinkled softly and Nigel did not look up from the papers he was signing. Sybil Burgess waited until the second ring and then reached over Nigel's desk to pick up the telephone.

"Mr. Mornay's office, can I help you?" There was a crackle of static and then a heavily accented voice came faintly over the line.

"Mr. Nigel Mornay? Is that the office of Mr. Nigel Mornay please? This is Tsamma Uranium calling for Mr. Nigel Mornay."

"Yes, this is Mr. Mornay's office, please hold." She covered the mouthpiece with one hand and spoke to the top of Nigel Mornay's head. "It's long distance from Tsamma Uranium, Sir. I called them after the CBC news this morning about missing tourists in Namibia. Mrs. Mornay phoned and asked me to check it out. I think Colin must be trying to get through."

"Colin!" Nigel's face broke into a broad grin. "Here, Sybil, give me that phone, I wonder how he's getting along with David?"

Since Colin's departure a month before, Nigel had made a determined effort to reconcile with Judith and they were both rediscovering in each other's company, some of the early excitement that had initially brought them together. Judith was still fretful about the perils she imagined Colin faced in the wilds of Africa. Her phone call to Swakopmund, the day Colin returned from Mariental with Rafa, when she found him still on a high over his new found ability to fly, had convinced her that her son was well and enjoying his sojourn with his uncle. Nigel had prevailed on her to avoid phoning again, for as he put it, "Don't let the boy think that we're nursemaiding him from Canada." Surprisingly, Judith had agreed and for the first time in many years she and Nigel began to communicate without the unspoken barrier of Colin's behaviour souring their attitudes. Nigel had taken Judith on short business trips and had made sure that he kept several days free to travel around with his wife and enjoy the various places they visited.

Now he reached for the phone, "Nigel Mornay here."

Sybil gathered up the signed documents and slipped them into the leather file folder. She was walking to the door when she heard Nigel's voice rise sharply. "Sweet Jesus, is this some sort of a joke?" He looked up at Sybil and motioned her to pick up the other phone on his desk. Sybil heard a man's voice, different from the first caller, and he was saying," . . . I don't joke about things as serious as this Mr. Mornay. I am the Human Resources Manager for the Tsamma Uranium Group and it is my responsibility to advise you of the disappearance of your son. I only wish I could be more encouraging, but up to the present time, despite an intensive search, your son and Mr. Kresfeld have not been found."

"Where is my brother, and why did he not phone . . . what did you say your name was?"

"My name is Peter Waldron," came the stiff reply, "and your brother is in the Swakopmund Hospital after a serious accident caused, if I may say so, by excessive speed through the plant area. He was very fortunate to escape with a concussion and some broken bones and was also very fortunate that no one else . . ."

"Dear God man, when did all this happen . . . can I talk to David . . . can you give me the hospital number?"

"Mr. Mornay, my information is that your brother is still unconscious and has been heavily sedated. I spoke to the doctor who assures me that your brother will recover, but he will still have to spend a few days in the hospital when he recovers consciousness. I will, of course, see that he is advised to call you the moment he is able to do so."

Nigel stared unseeing at Sybil and she recognized the signs. Clearly, Nigel Mornay was getting angry, for his eyebrows gathered into a dark line and his eyes had half closed as if he were squinting at the sun. His voice was quiet, but a more aware listener would have noted the change. "Mr. Waldo, how long has my son been missing and how did it happen? . . . what exactly happened? . . . please be very specific." Nigel motioned to Sybil, but she had already clicked on the telerecorder and for good measure was writing down the conversation in shorthand.

"Waldron, Waldron not Waldo, Mr. Mornay . . . my name is Waldron, Peter Waldron."

Nigel rolled his eyes in disbelief, but when he spoke his voice had not changed. "My apologies Waldron, now please get on with it."

"My information is that your son went into the desert with a tour group which had a mechanical breakdown. Your son and the driver decided to walk to the main road and get help. The following morning we sent the company aircraft to search and in a very short time we found the tour vehicle with the rest of the tourists safe and sound. Of course, by this time your son and the driver -- an old German called Herman Kresfeld -- had been absent for about twenty-four hours. If only they had not been so foolish as to leave the vehicle we would not have the problem that we now have." Waldron stopped, but when Nigel did not speak, he continued. "At the present time there is a large scale ground search in progress with the police and volunteers from the town and the Mine. As a businessman, I don't have to tell you how seriously things of this nature disrupt production . . . we have at least twenty of our staff, some of them in senior positions, out searching."

"Where can they have got to Waldron . . . ? Surely, it must be fairly open country and if you have an aircraft searching . . . what seems to be the difficulty?"

"At the moment, the East Wind is blowing and that has grounded our aircraft. Of course, as soon as the wind drops we will resume the search, but I must warn you that the wind has been known to blow for days, sometimes weeks."

"The East Wind. What the hell is the East Wind? Look, Waldron, I am coming out there right away and I want you to keep in touch with this number. My personal assistant will be available at any time to take your call and she will be able to get me. Thank you for letting me know."

Nigel put the phone down as Waldron started to speak, cutting him off in mid-sentence. Nigel took a deep breath. Sybil Burgess continued to listen and heard Waldron's emotionless response. "Thank you, Sir," she broke in smoothly. "If you will please give me your personal number I will ensure that you have direct access to me at all times . . ." She dictated her office and home numbers. "Yes, of course, I understand . . . and thank you again for informing us." Sybil scribbled a number on her pad and put the phone back into its cradle. She glanced at Nigel, her face worried. "Do you want . . . ?"

Nigel interrupted, "Call the chief pilot, tell him to prepare a flight plan to Namibia and get Travel to research all the visas we will need . . . Oh, and dig out all the information you can find on Namibia, with particular reference to the East wind." He stared down at his hands, and she noticed that his knuckles were white where he gripped the edge of the desk. Almost to himself he muttered, "Judith is going to be devastated." Sybil waited, but Nigel had retreated into himself and she cleared her throat nervously.

"I will get on to this immediately. Do you want Mr. Ross to see you?"

"What? . . . Oh, yes, get Ross up here, explain the situation and give him the file on the Macmillan Bloedel contract. He can look after that while I'm gone." Ross was Nigel's Vice- President of Operations and his direct deputy. Sybil nodded and turned to go. At the door she turned back to Nigel, who had not moved.

"I'm sure Colin will be all right. Twenty-four hours is not very long."

Nigel looked up at her and she saw the fear in his eyes. "God, I hope you're right Sybil . . . I pray that you're right." He levered himself out of his chair and shivered as if suddenly cold. "I'm going home . . . Call Judith. No. No, don't call her. God, how am I going to tell her? Colin is her world." He stared unseeing through the panoramic plate glass window that filled an entire wall of his office. Over his shoulder, Sybil glimpsed bright sunlight glinting on the distant Olympic mountains, separated from Vancouver Island by the sparkling sea of Juan de Fuca Strait.

"I will get George to bring your car around." She hesitated, glancing at the clock. "I'll stay here after work and field any calls."

Nigel was pulling his coat on and he gripped her arm firmly. "Thank you, Sybil, it's what I thought you would say, but this could take quite a long time, so set up a roster, ask for volunteers and put them on triple pay while on shift. That phone must be manned around the clock." He shook his head sadly. "How suddenly things change . . . yesterday we were planning a trip to Cancun." He released her arm and stepped into his personal elevator. Sybil quickly went to the intercom and called down to the basement garage, "George, the Boss is coming down . . . yes home, and George . . . he's had some very bad news, so no witticisms."

Rafa and Kate entered the hospital in the pre-dawn light, Kate carrying a set of clothes that she and Rafa had collected from David's house. The reception area was eerily silent. This was the end of the overnight shift, just before the morning nurses and hospital staff arrived and as a consequence there was no one to impede their progress to David's room. After leaving Kate the previous evening, Rafa had phoned Wessel for the latest update on the search plans prior to calling Ken Hassel. The doctor had been coldly formal. "I cannot tie him to his bed, but you lot evidently did not try very hard to convince him. So, he is adamant about going on the search. Well, I am washing my hands of this. Tell him to try Windhoek if he has complications."

Rafa had calmed Hassel down, explaining the strategy that he and Kate had come up with. "Look Ken, I am not keen on him coming either, but it is his nephew after all, and he is the one who will have to tell the parents if we have bad news."

Finally, after promising to turn back to Swakopmund at the first sign of trouble, Rafa had rung off, leaving a slightly mollified Hassel to brood on the macho mentality. Now he and Kate walked quickly to David's room, each preoccupied with their own thoughts. Kate had attended the briefing at the Water Affairs' conference room with Rafa. Captain Pieterse had wasted no time on preliminaries, for everyone gathered in the conference room was aware that time was precious. On a full scale map of the area, pinned to the wall, Pieterse had shown the probable route that Colin and Kresfeld had taken. After a quick overview of the latest weather, he had formed the assembled policemen and volunteers into teams and assigned each team a colour coded area to search. Each team was made up of several vehicles and each vehicle had civilian volunteers as spotters. The lead vehicle in each team was supplied with a police radio.

Rafa was paired with the tall lieutenant, Pieterse's deputy, and when Rafa had explained to the smooth-faced youngster that David was coming with them, the young policeman had shown no surprise. Coming from a farming community at Maltahohe, the lieutenant knew and understood the desert, but coming from a large family, he also understood the ties of blood. Pieterse had rapped the table sharply to quell the rising tide of voices as individual group leaders conferred with their counterparts. "Gentlemen, please. Most of you know Hermann Kresfeld. He is experienced in the desert and will use all of his skill to keep himself and the young man alive until help arrives, but, as you are fully aware, the East Wind will hamper the search and time is critical. I want you all to check in at regular intervals and try to keep in line abreast as we get on to the plains. My deputy and Captain Modesto will execute a sweep towards the Khan canyon from the old tin mine road." He had paused. "Let us waste no more time. Go, and good luck to us all."

The men had filed quickly from the room and Rafa had left

Kate in a corner while he conferred with the lieutenant. A few minutes later he had returned."OK, he will wait with his men at 'Martin Luther' . . . the old steam engine monument at the entrance to town . . . while we go and fetch David."

The limo, its smoked glass windows hiding the occupants from outside view, swept through the stone pillars of Victoria's Uplands area and accelerated slightly as George concentrated on his driving. Nigel Mornay had not spoken since leaving the office. George Lundquist, an ex- policeman, had been trained in all aspects of high speed driving and also had passed through the demanding courses of Anti-Terrorist evasion. A freak accident had left him with one leg shorter than the other and he had been invalided out of the Diplomatic Security Detail. Unwilling to accept a desk job, he had wandered around for several months until an associate of Nigel's had suggested he try Mornay Industries. Nigel had been warned by the RCMP that a gang of kidnappers was in Western Canada and intelligence suggested that several high profile targets had been selected. As a business leader worth billions of dollars in assets, it was clear that he would be a potential target. George had appeared at exactly the right time and a liking gradually developed between these two wholly dissimilar men.

Usually, George and Nigel held lengthy discussions on the local hockey team, the Vancouver Canucks. They held a mild difference of opinion on the methods their favourite team should adopt to win the prestigious Stanley Cup, and going home each day this bantering had helped Nigel to unwind from the strains of his job. Normally, he allowed George a latitude of behaviour that was lax even by the egalitarian standards of modern Canada, but forewarned is forearmed and George kept his peace this day. He liked his boss but he had been on the receiving end of Nigel's anger on one memorable morning, when, tired after a late night party with old friends, he had misjudged the traffic lights and nearly caused a crash. Now he swung the big limo into the long leafy driveway that led up to the mansion, only the slight sagging of its springs giving evidence that it was armour plated behind the dark door panels. A pair of electronically operated gates opened smoothly as George activated a remote switch near his knee. Nigel levered himself out of the seat as the limo drew smoothly up to the front entrance. "I may be quite some time, but stay right here. Have the cook make you some sandwiches and coffee."

"Yes Sir." George picked up Nigel's discarded briefcase and handed it to him and Nigel walked up the wide stone steps slowly. Usually he would bound up, taking two steps at a time, but now he climbed deliberately, for this was a man going to face something unpleasant, something that could not be avoided. Alerted by an electronic signal when the gates were opened, Maria pulled the massive door open as Nigel reached the top of the stairs.

"Mr. Mornay, you're early, Sir," she said, reaching for the briefcase.

"Maria, please find Mrs. Mornay and ask her to meet me in the library." Nigel pulled his coat off and handed it to the woman. He walked slowly into the richly furnished room where he kept his rare book collection. A remote control handset lay on the coffee table and Nigel stabbed a coded series of numbers. A portion of the wall slid noiselessly back on nylon rollers to reveal a floor to ceiling liquor cabinet, and reaching for an unopened bottle of malt whisky, he selected two crystal glasses from a separate shelf.

"Nigel, what a nice surprise." Judith had entered while his back was turned, but seeing the whisky bottle and glasses in his hands she frowned. "It's a trifle early for a drink isn't it? Then, seeing his face she stopped. "What is it Nigel, something at work? Something has happened . . ."

He shook his head, "No, nothing at work. Sit down Judith, this is going to take some time."

He partially filled the glasses and dropped an ice cube into each. From long experience, Judith knew that Nigel could not be rushed and she sat puzzled on the sofa facing him. She knew he had been having trouble with a series of interlocking contracts but he had said the problem wasn't work. She had forgotten her call to Sybil Burgess, for she knew David would have phoned if Colin had been injured in any way. She had only asked Sybil to check that all was well with Colin more as a knee jerk reaction to any bad news out of Africa, than any real fear that Colin was involved. Nigel handed her a glass and sat alongside her. Uncharacteristically, he took her free hand in his.

"Judy, I have just had a phone call from Namibia..."

Before he could continue Judith interrupted, colour draining from her face, "Colin, it is Colin, is he? . . . Oh God . . . is he?"

"No. He's not dead, or even injured for all we know, but he has gone missing with another man after their tour bus broke down in the desert." Quickly Nigel gave her all the information that Waldron had given him. "It appears that David was involved in a vehicle accident at the plant that left him unconscious at about the time Colin was with the tour group and David is still in hospital. I assume that he is still unconscious or he would have phoned by now. He probably isn't even aware that Colin is missing."

"I knew Colin shouldn't have gone out there. I just knew it. Oh why did I let you persuade me?" Her face was ashen and the hand holding the drink trembled uncontrollably.

"Judy, what happened was a fluke, but right now that's water under the bridge. The Lear has been put on standby with a full crew to fly us out there as soon as it can be cleared. Go and pack a small case and remember that it's hot out there so bring lightweight stuff." He took a large swallow of his whisky and grimaced as the twenty year old malt washed down. "It's more than possible that they've found the two of them already. I've put Sybil in charge of communications, so she'll call us as soon as word comes through." He gripped her hand fiercely. "Do not assume the worst. As I told you, they are mounting a massive search and I'm sure that in open country like that they will find them fairly quickly." He stood, stretching wearily. "Look, I'm going to have a shower and then change. We'll have a meal before we leave and by then we should have all the information and clearances. Try not to worry . . . I am sure they're competent people out there."

"Nigel, it's a desert, don't you understand -- a desert -- Colin said it was like God had used a blowtorch to sear the land. What chance does a boy have in that kind of environment? Oh God, why did I listen to you?"

Nigel knelt down and clasped both her hands in his. His face was ravaged. "Judith, he's my son too. I have to believe that he will be found. Please, let's not fight . . . I need your support . . . we need each other."

Judith collapsed sobbing, burying her face in his shoulder. "Oh Nigel, I'm so scared. He . . ." Her voice was muffled as she clung to him.

Chapter 22

The Long Day

Rafa pushed the door open and Kate walked in behind him. David was already sitting on the edge of the bed in his pyjamas and dressing gown and stood up as they crowded in. "Good, I see you brought some clothes," he said. "Let's get moving."

Kate placed the clothes on the bed and waited outside the door while David dressed. When David and Rafa rejoined her, she gave Rafa a searching look behind David's back. He shook his head, but made no comment. David walked slowly, chatting with Kate in a firm voice. He did not seem unduly uncomfortable and insisted on being given all the details of the briefing. As they reached the door Rafa said, "Wait here, I'll bring the LandRover to the front door . . . I doubt if you can run through that dust."

Minutes later they were driving through the outskirts of Swakopmund on their way to the search area, David in the front with Rafa, and Kate in the back with a young volunteer they had collected on their way to meet the lieutenant. At 'Martin Luther', an old steam tractor that had been restored and placed on a concrete platform at the entrance to the town, the lieutenant's police jeep waited. Seeing them approach, he pulled out with a wave and led the way. Soon, they were off the paved highway, and as the dust made driving difficult, both vehicles were forced to reduce speed.

Despite the early hour, the rising heat inside the vehicles was a further reminder of the conditions that Colin and Kresfeld were facing. Taking another sip of water from a plastic bottle, Kate felt guilty and for the tenth time wondered if the two lost men had enough water. Had the heat forced them to use up their meagre supply and were they now battling to survive in the howling dust? Periodically, the dust storm lessened and as visibility improved, the three of them passed a pair of binoculars around as they scoured the desert for any signs of life.

By mid morning they reached the position where the tour vehicle had been stuck in the sand, and Rafa called up the search leader on the police radio. With the whistling of the wind and the rattling of the whip aerial, which had been pushed through a small gap in Rafa's side window, they could not hear the exchange, but when Rafa pulled in the aerial and turned to talk to them his face was grim.

"Pieterse reports that there is no sign of them at the mine site, the green team has swept the area thoroughly and the surrounding approaches. Pieterse wants to concentrate the search more towards Swakop. He feels that if they did not make for the mine then their next best option was the Windhoek road."

David interrupted and Kate noted with alarm that his face was grey under the coating of dust they all had acquired. "What exactly does he want us to do?"

"Yes, I was coming to that. As we are the furthermost west of the search teams he wants us to head off at a diagonal southwest to Kresfeld's assumed line of march." Rafa unfolded a topographical map heavily marked with china graph pencil. "Here is where the logical route would have taken Kresfeld. Now, we saw nothing on our journey out, so if we cut across the flats towards the Chuosberge on this line . . ." He scratched a new line at a diagonal from the first " . . . we might intersect their line of march if they were trying to get to the Windhoek road. The other teams will leave the mine area and swing in an extended line behind us to cover as much ground as possible." He folded the map and handed it to David. "Let's get a move on. Dave, keep checking the compass and call corrections."

For the next hour they bumped over the rocky plains, the wind blasting on their beam and rocking the LandRover sideways, adding to their already considerable discomfort. Apart from calling corrections to their course and talking over the radio to the lieutenant's jeep several hundred yards to the right, David showed no sign of discomfort. But that changed abruptly with a particularly severe bump and David let out a grunt of pain. The constant howling of the wind, and the heat and worry over David had Kate's nerves on edge and she snapped at Rafa. "Please slow down. Maybe we should break off and take him back to Swakop?"

David reached back and gripped her forearm hard. "No Kate, Rafa is going as slow as he dares, and we're running out of time." He started a smile which turned into a grimace as they hit another bump, "I'm still a bit sore, but nothing too terrible. So stop worrying."

Just then the radio crackled. "Look to your right, there is something on the ground between us." The lieutenant's vehicle was already turning towards a dark bundle on the sandy ground, a bundle that kept disappearing in the blowing sand. Rafa swung right and within a minute they reached the police jeep that had stopped a yard away from a spreadeagled body, face up on the sandy ground. The lieutenant was holding Kresfeld's head off the ground and as Rafa and David reached him he shook his head. "He's dead, probably several hours ago, rigor mortis has started."

Kate came around the front of the police jeep with the volunteer and gasped. "Is he dead?"

"Yes, I am afraid so." The lieutenant lowered Kresfeld's head gently back to the ground and called over his shoulder to one of the policemen standing behind. "Call Captain Pieterse and give him the news and our location." He looked up at David. "I am thinking Herr Mornay that your nephew will have kept going towards the main road, we are very close to the road. If you want to push ahead, I will wait with the body until the main group gets here."

Without answering, David knelt beside Kresfeld's body, and lifted a water bottle from beneath the dead man's arm and shook it. "This is still half full, if he didn't die of thirst, then what did he die of?" He handed the bottle to the policeman. "And why did Colin not take this bottle when Kresfeld died?" He stood up slowly, in obvious pain. "I hope you're right lieutenant, that he did keep going towards the road. As you say, it's not far, but there has been a fair bit of traffic on the main road and if he made it he would have been picked up by now. I have a strong feeling that they split up." He glanced at Rafa. "What do you think?"

"It is possible amigo, but I think first we look forward, it is also possible that when Kresfeld died, Colin panicked and did not think to take the water bottle. If we are wrong then we can come back here and search back towards the ravines."

David held on to the side of the police jeep and stared down at Kresfeld's body, "I just hope he didn't turn back and get lost . . . poor little devil . . . come on Rafa, let's get cracking." He walked back to their LandRover but staggered as he reached the door and almost fell.

"David!" Kate ran to catch him but he recovered before she reached him.

"It"s OK . . . I caught my foot."

Kate held his arm. "David you're in no shape to continue, we must get you back. Rafa please talk to him."

Rafa had reached them, his swarthy face impassive. "We will sweep towards the main road as the lieutenant suggested, then when we hit the main road we will go back into town."

David shook his head angrily. "We will do nothing of the sort. If we find no trace of him we will come back here and backtrack towards the ravines."

"No amigo, You have not noticed but the wind is dropping . . . I am going to get the Chieftain and fly the area. It is the only chance we have. Now that we know the general area, it will be easier to scan from the air and direct the ground people."

Rafa slid in behind the wheel and waved the lieutenant over and explained what he intended to do. After a quick radio conversation with Captain Pieterse they waved goodbye and bounced across the desert in the direction of the main Windhoek road. Their hopes were raised briefly when Kate yelled that she had seen something, but it turned out to be a piece of wind blown plastic wrapped around a scrubby little thorn bush. Even in the wastes of the Namib, man's pollution intruded.

By the time they reached the main road their eyes were strained and sore and David's breathing had become quick bursts of panting, for he was obviously in more pain than he was willing to admit. Rafa stopped and radioed to the police chief the results of their search. He listened intently, then signed off and turned to the others. "Pieterse is going to detach four vehicles to check either side of the track we have just taken, in case Colin turned off the main road heading. The rest of the searchers are going to head for the ravines and work their way up and down the Khan canyon." He stared hard at David. "You are not looking too good, my friend. I think Kate is right . . . we will get you back home and flat on a bed . . . that rib is worse than you thought."

"Don't waste time nursemaiding me," David growled back at him. "I can keep going, just get to the airfield as quickly as possible." But beads of sweat on his forehead belied his words. Now on a wide paved road, Rafa put his foot down and they roared back into Swakopmund in record time. As they drove up to the hangar that housed the Chieftain in Swakopmund, Rafa glanced over at David who was slumped in his seat with his eyes closed. It was obvious that David would not be coming with them and Rafa spoke over his shoulder to Kate. "Kate, you drive David to his house and make sure that he gets flat on his back. I will take our friend here and we will fly the area."

The volunteer who had been silent up to this moment interrupted quickly. "I am sorry, but I am not going up with you . . . I am terrified of flying."

Kate and Rafa gaped at the young man in astonishment. Rafa spoke first. "Well I'll be damned, I have met a few people who are afraid of flying, but why do I have to meet one today, of all days?"

The young volunteer was embarrassed, "I am very sorry, but I simply would not be any good to you up there . . . why not let me take Mr. Mornay home and the lady can fly with you?"

Kate was torn between her desire to see David home safely and the need to find Colin before time ran out for him, but she was saved by David's voice.

"I'm coming with you . . . we're running out of time and another pair of eyes will be needed." Without waiting for a reply, he levered himself out of the seat and stood beside the LandRover for a couple of seconds, gathering his strength, then he walked over to the Chieftain's airstair door that the hangar attendant had lowered in readiness.

Rafa shrugged and did a quick walk around the aircraft, removing the Pitot head covers and checking the exterior for any signs of damage. Seeing no alternative, Kate followed David into the interior of the aircraft. Lowering himself carefully into a passenger seat on the left hand side of the aircraft, David pointed to the co-pilot's seat. "Sit up front, Kate. I think your eyes are probably better than mine and if I slip off again I'll be safely out of the way."

"David, you should be back in hospital." Kate scolded. "Doctor Hassel was right and there's obviously more damage than you realize." She sat across the narrow aisle from him. "I understand why you must come, but what good will it do if you . . ." Her voice trailed off as Rafa came aboard, pulling the airstair door closed behind him.

"Good, sit up front, Kate. Dave has the right idea. If he dozes off again I don't want him falling over the controls." He grinned down at David. "Quite like old times, eh amigo? When there were no options . . . only one course of action . . . and that not a good one." Tapping David lightly on the shoulder, he pushed Kate ahead into the co-pilot's seat. She had never flown with Rafa before and was impressed at the subtle metamorphosis that came over the pilot as he ran through the ground instrument checks.

There were a few bumps as the two hangar attendants and the reluctant volunteer pushed the aircraft out of the hangar into the bright sunshine. Rafa pointed to the port engine and making a circle with his raised index finger, motioning the ground crew to stand clear. He turned the starter and the port engine rumbled to life, belching thick clouds of black smoke for a few seconds before settling down to a steady whine as Rafa adjusted the throttle. Repeating the procedure with the starboard engine, he watched with a small frown, as it spun to life without the black smoke that had been so evident with the port engine. Rafa watched the gauges carefully, running both engines to full power while he stood on the brakes. He shook his head in disgust. "Bloody mechanics! If I told them once, I told them a dozen times to check the port engine oil pressure."

"Is it going to be all right? " Kate couldn't hide the tremor in her voice. Like the young man on the tarmac, she hated flying but had mastered her fear and had flown frequently on commercial aircraft. Still, she didn't like small aircraft and preferred to drive the three hundred kilometres to Windhoek whenever she had to catch the scheduled commercial flights to Johannesburg to see her parents.

"Yes, it will do . . . damned gauge has been acting up for a while now. Tighten your seat belt and keep checking on Dave. Here put this on." Rafa handed her a radio headset with a thin boom microphone that fitted next to her mouth. He opened the throttles gently and they rolled away from the hangar towards the end of the runway. Rafa switched radio channels and Kate heard his flat metallic voice, the accent exaggerated by the radio, warning potential inbound aircraft that the runway was occupied. At the end of the runway he swung the nose to line up with the scuffed and faded centerline and pushed open the throttles smoothly. For a second the aircraft seemed unwilling to move, then it bounded forward and picked up speed rapidly. The drumming on the tires gradually lessened as the wings began to take more of the weight. Kate stared horrified as the end of the runway loomed up. Just as it seemed inevitable that they would overshoot into the rocky uneven ground beyond the runway's end, Rafa hauled back on the control yoke and the Chieftain lifted smoothly off the ground. He spoke quietly into the radio, advising all aircraft that he was now clear and was switching to the police mobile frequency.

"Blue Leader do you read?" Static hissed. "Blue Leader . . . Blue Leader this is Charlie Mike airborne this time . . . do you read?" Static hissed again, then suddenly a voice broke in.

"Charlie Mike this is Blue Leader . . . go ahead."

"Captain Pieterse, we are airborne and leaving Swakop area for your area. Please shoot a flare to aid location."

"Roger, stand by!" There was a gap of a few minutes and Rafa pushed the Chieftain higher. Then ahead and a bit to starboard, a brilliant white flare exploded at about five hundred feet above the desert floor.

"Flare launched, do you have position?"

"Roger, we have a positive fix and will approach your position from the southwest at two thousand feet. What is the search status, Captain?"

Kate listened intently as Pieterse came back to them. Despite the atmospheric clutter on the frequency, the grimness in his voice was clear. "Negative, I regret negative, all search teams have drawn a blank. Captain Modesto, can you do a run parallel to the canyon on the north side? We have two teams in the canyon and three in line on the south side. I am using Kresfeld's final position as the point on an arc that reaches across the canyons to the northern plains of Tsamma Ridge. I do not believe that the boy could have gone much further, given the conditions."

"Affirmative, Captain . . . I agree with your analysis. . . Ah, I have your team's visual."

It was true. Looking down, Kate saw three jeeps in line abreast. They were spread out several hundred yards apart on the plain above the Khan canyon, east of where the Khan joined the Swakop canyon. From the air, it was a massive jumble of tortured, blasted and deformed valleys and hills. The jeeps were ant-like in the vastness of the terrain and despite the heat Kate shivered, imagining what Colin must be going through . . . if he were still alive.

The two jeeps in the canyon were invisible. Long shadows from the lowering sun turning the canyon into an inky pool with jagged sunlit edges.

"Kate, go back and give Dave the news . . . he must be wondering what is going on."

Kate unhooked her headset and seatbelt and holding tightly to the bulkhead she pulled herself back to David's seat. He looked up quizzically and held her arm to steady her as Rafa rolled into a turn to bring the Chieftain on to the correct heading.

"How are you feeling?" she asked, placing a cool hand on his forehead. "You're still very hot, David."

He reached up with his good hand and gently gripped her wrist. "Kate I'm going to live . . . what's the news?"

"We're going to fly parallel to the canyon on the north side. The Police Chief has three jeeps on the south bank and two in the canyon proper and he wants us to cover the north bank and oversee the ground search."

"No sign of him?"

Kate saw the lines of pain cutting deep grooves into David's tired face and with sudden clarity recalled his words of the previous night -- "I'm tired of losing."

"No, not yet, but now we have a better chance . . . Oh, David, please don't worry, I . ."

"Kate, go forward. Rafa needs eyes. If Colin is to have any chance at all, we're it."

Kate hesitated, then swiftly as if thought would cancel the action, she leaned forward and kissed him gently on the lips. She pulled back and her whispered words were almost inaudible, " . . . not lose again." Startled, David reached to hold her but she had turned and was moving back to the cockpit.

Rafa had levelled out at just over a thousand feet and put the aircraft onto autopilot as Kate clipped herself back into the seat and adjusted the headset. The aircraft bucked in the wind and the updrafts from the canyon and Kate could only imagine the pain that David must be suffering from the constant battering. Several times she had looked away from the savage terrain below and had checked to see if David was still all right. He caught her looking at him and raised his thumb, but his face was bright with sweat.

Rafa called the ground teams again. "Blue Leader, this is Charlie Mike. I have reached the Windhoek road. I will return on a reciprocal heading two kilometres north."

"Captain, we copy, what is your visibility?"

"Blue Leader, right now it is good, but varies as the wind gusts."

"Captain, the wind appears to be moderating at ground level, but we are going to lose light in another two hours. When you have completed your run I would like you to return to where we found Herman's body and fly low and slow back towards the Khan."

"Blue Leader, Roger . . . message understood." Rafa turned to look at Kate and his face was grim. "You heard that, keep your eyes skinned."

"Why, what's happening? Why did Pieterse want you to fly back to where we found Kresfeld's body?"

"Because he is running out of ideas. The ground teams have searched everywhere possible, we have been airborne for nearly an hour and nothing has shown up. Pieterse is getting desperate and he is going back to square one in the hope that we missed something the first time." Rafa had completed the turn and now it was Kate's turn to stare down into the canyons.

For the next thirty minutes they droned back and forth over the same terrain. Kate's eyes were smarting from the strain. Below, the scenery gave up illusions and each time her heart leaped, only to realize that what seemed to be a human figure was only a desert bush or trick of light. Frustration gripped the plane's occupants at each sighting and it came as a relief when Rafa finished the reciprocal runs and put the Chieftain onto a course toward where Kresfeld's body had been found. Now tension rose steadily, for they were all keenly aware that within the next thirty minutes they would have to break off the search and return to Swakopmund. The light was fading and Rafa kept eyeing his fuel gauges. Glancing back to check on David, Kate saw him peering out of the side window and with a silent prayer of thanks she turned back to continue her vigil. They reached the point where Kresfeld's body had been found and flew over the crossed aluminium sand mats that Captain Pieterse had placed on the site earlier.

Rafa spoke with the respect of one professional for another, "Pieterse thinks on his feet . . . he must have thought of this option earlier." He flew back towards Swakopmund for a few minutes and just as Kate was about to point out that they were heading in the wrong direction, he rolled the Chieftain into a gentle turn and headed back towards the crossed sand mats and the Khan canyon. He lowered the flaps and wheels, and there was a soft thump as the wheels deployed. The Chieftain shuddered as the speed dropped off and Rafa placed a gloved hand over the throttles to slowly increase power. Watching Rafa, Kate was aware of the total concentration he was giving to his task. Looking ahead, she noticed how much lower they were and realised that Rafa was slowing the plane to the absolute limit of its flight envelope.

Suddenly a flash to the right of their track caught her attention. "What was that?" she asked pointing.

"Where, what was it?" Rafa peered in the direction indicated and almost before the words had left his mouth, the flash was repeated. He dropped the plane even lower. Suddenly Kate yelled. "There . . . there . . . something on the ground just at the beginning of the ravine." It was Colin's discarded waterbottle, blown by the wind until the shoulder strap caught in a scrubby bush. Now with each gust of wind, the sun winked off its aluminium body.

"Blue leader! . . . Blue Leader!" Rafa was unable to keep the excitement out of his voice. "Something on the ground about half a click from where the tour vehicle was stuck. I will circle the location."

"Great work Captain . . . Yellow team, can you hear the aircraft?"

"Yes Sir, we should be there in five minutes, we are climbing out of the canyon on the Sesriem slope as you instructed."

Rafa shook his head in admiration. "Judas priest, that man deserves a medal . . . he gambled that we might see something and positioned one team just in case." They circled the spot where the intermittent flash had been seen and they watched two LandRovers surge up the long slope out of the canyon and turn towards them. The lead vehicle accelerated as it found firmer traction on the hard ground above the Sesriem ravine and reached their turning point in a few minutes. Men spilled out of the doors and fanned out in a skirmish line.

Rafa keyed his microphone. "Yellow leader, hold the man nearest the vehicle stationary, the remainder of the line swing north . . . no, no . . . the other way. OK, now it's about one hundred metres in front of you." The second LandRover braked to a halt and more men ran to extend the line. Rafa levelled off his turn and anxiously checked his fuel gauges. "We are getting low."

Below them, a man was running back to the vehicles and he reached inside. "Captain . . . Sir . . . we have found the boy's water bottle, it's empty."

"How do you know it is the boy's water bottle?" Pieterse's voice was sharp with strain.

"It has 'D.MORNAY' written on the strap."

"And there are no other signs?"

"No Sir, but the boy must have reached this far. We are going to spread out and search the canyon approaches."

"Two men stay with the radio at all times. I am going to recall all the crews to your location." He called out urgently, "All stations, did you copy that?" There was an answering series of affirmatives from the widely separated vehicles, now all turning to intersect the yellow team's location. The searchers were buoyed up with the first tangible sign in a long day of searching, but they were also aware that Colin's survival chances were decreasing hourly.

Rafa spoke to Kate over the aircraft intercom. "Let David know what has happened and tell him that I think Colin would have gone down into the canyon to look for water. I only have ten minutes loiter time left, so I am going to get down into the canyon and see if anything else turns up." He switched channels and told Pieterse of his intentions.

Kate went back to David's seat and gave him the news. He smiled at her. "You see, I said you had sharp eyes, now get back quickly and use them again."

Rafa dropped the Chieftain lower until they were a mere hundred feet above the canyon rim. With the wheels and flaps fully extended, he struggled to hold the aircraft steady in the gusts from the dying East Wind. Kate clipped herself in again and asked Rafa why they were flying away from the direction of the Windhoek road.

"I agree that it is a long shot, but I am banking on the fact that Colin was tired and confused when he came into the canyon," was the reply. "It would be natural for a right handed person to turn right thinking that it was the direction of the road. The search teams have been down the full length of the canyon to the left of where the tour bus was stuck and have drawn a blank."

The Chieftain rocked savagely as a particularly sharp gust caught them broadside, prompting a curse from Rafa as he struggled to correct the aircraft. Kate heard a sharp cry from David and turned to see him gesticulating urgently. She rushed back and he yelled.

"Tell Rafa about half a click back there is something on the canyon floor on the North side."

Wasting no time strapping in, Kate grabbed her microphone

from the seat and relayed David's message. Rafa pulled the Chieftain up out of the canyon and as they reached a safe altitude, directed the aircraft into a wide flat turn to face the way they had just come. Then he lined up with the canyon centreline and they dropped sharply. Kate's stomach rose into her mouth, but her protest died when she heard Rafa swear aloud and then shout, "Kate, buckle tight. We have just lost the port engine."

Looking out, Kate could see the port engine propeller blades windmilling slowly. Rafa pulled the port throttle into the feathering gate and slammed the starboard throttle wide open. Simultaneously, he desperately raised the flaps and wheels, but the Chieftain was dangerously low and the asymmetric thrust was forcing it into a deadly roll. A savage gust of wind slammed into the Chieftain as they barely cleared one of the many ridges. Tilted as they were and with the higher wing exposed to the full force of the blast, the Chieftain started to roll over.

"Madre de Dios!" Rafa swore as he yanked the throttle back to reduce the torque effect of the good engine, and swung the control yoke hard over to counteract the roll. By this time, the wheels and flaps were almost fully retracted, but without power the aircraft sank below the canyon rim. Rafa increased power again on the good engine as he tried to pull the aircraft up and out of the deathtrap they were in. The shuddering aircraft almost made it, but now their luck ran out. The tip of the starboard wing clipped a spire of rock and the nose dipped sharply. Rafa jammed the rudder to port and managed to avoid the wall of rock rushing at them but the Chieftain now was only metres above the Canyon floor. The port wing slammed into a thorn tree and with a grinding scream the plane slid belly down into the gravelly bed of the dry river. A second thorn tree ripped away one wing and the starboard engine and the Chieftain slewed sideways for several hundred metres, shredding bits of undercarriage and tearing the flaps off. Finally, it hit a huge pile of windblown gravel and stopped dead.

Kate had strapped herself in as Rafa had instructed, but in

her haste had not clipped the seatbelt properly. The sudden stop wrenched the clasp open and she had been flung forward into the firewall where she lay crumpled in a shapeless bundle. A dazed but conscious Rafa reached for her, but found he could not move. A slab of rock encountered in the wild slide across the valley floor had torn through the forward belly on the port side, hitting both rudder pedals and breaking Rafa's legs below the knees.

David had fared better. The main wing spar ran beneath his seat and the additional strength this gave to that section of the fuselage kept the structural integrity intact. In effect he was in safety cage, and apart from almost losing consciousness from the savage pain caused by the seat belt snapping tight into his broken rib, he was uninjured. The silence after the cacophony of the last few seconds echoed in his ears and an ominous hissing sound shocked David out of his stupor.

"Kate! Rafa! Are you all right?" He heard Rafa groan and ignoring the fire in his chest, he clawed the seat belt loose. Reaching the cockpit, he was appalled at the scene that greeted him. Kate lay huddled in a heap out of her seat, her face pressed sideways into the firewall. Rafa was trying to lever himself out of his seat, semi-conscious and unaware that his legs were broken. His arms flailed like some broken insect's. Smoke was beginning to wisp through the shattered floor and the hissing grew louder. David reached over the throttle quadrant and with his uninjured left arm took a firm grip on Kate's blouse and lifted her gently back into her seat. Her head lolled forward and blood trickled down her face from a deep cut on her head. "Rafa, can you hear me?" David shook Rafa's shoulder, then realizing that the pilot was in no condition to help he placed his mouth close to Rafa's ear. "Try not to move . . . I'll get Kate outside and then come back for you."

Rafa gripped his sleeve with surprising strength. "Dave . . . fire . . . get out . . . Ahh!" He gave a gasp. "My legs . . . gone. Go . . . go . . ." His head slumped forward and he slid back into unconsciousness. David lifted Kate with his left hand, but the effort caused another explosion of pain in his chest. Sweat broke out on his forehead and now the smoke filling the cockpit was thicker and a dry crackling added to the hissing he had heard earlier. Gritting his teeth, he summoned up all of his strength and dragged Kate's limp form back down the fuselage to the exit door. The impact had crumpled the fuselage and the door was jammed shut. Releasing Kate, David kicked hard at the lock but the only result was a fresh wave of pain as his broken rib rebelled. Frantically casting about, David saw the emergency fire axe clipped above the rear bulkhead. He wrenched it free and smashed it left handed down on the lock. Fear and desperation drove him to raise the axe again and again, and finally he saw the door move slightly. Sinking to his knees, David rolled onto his back, braced both feet against the door and gave a savage heave. The door burst open and David could see the gravel of the riverbed outside.

Gasping with pain, he rose to his feet, gripped Kate's clothing again and backed out of the aircraft onto the dry sand outside. Pulling Kate's limp form, David stumbled backwards and sat with a jolt that jarred his whole upper body. The pain overwhelmed him and for a few seconds he slid into a semi-conscious stupor. He opened his eyes to see smoke curling out of the shattered windscreen and saw a red flame flickering at the wing root. Rolling forward on to his knees he staggered to his feet, but his legs suddenly collapsed and he was down, his face in the sand. Now looking up through a red haze, he saw flame run along the shattered wing and blossom into a crimson rose.

Chapter 23

Bushman

The Lear jet slipped through the night sky high over Greenland. Nigel rose out of his seat quietly so as not to disturb Judith who was dozing fitfully. He opened the door to the cockpit and stepped inside. The two pilots sat illuminated by the soft amber glow of the instruments and turned to watch him as he pulled the jumpseat down and sat between them. "Any improvement on our arrival time?" he asked.

"No Sir, not really, we've picked up a few minutes, but nothing significant." Joel Buchinsky replied. He was a surprisingly young looking fifty-year-old who had spent twenty-five years as a fighter and transport pilot in the Royal Canadian Air Force and had been snapped up by the Mornay organization as soon as he left the Service. His companion, Chris Walker, was half his age, but like Buchinsky a superb pilot. When only nineteen years old, Walker had flown the Tasman Sea following the same route taken by the famous pilot and navigator, Sir Francis Chichester. He had also used a single engine light aircraft and had scorned all modern navigation aids, preferring to use an old sextant in the same manner as his famous predecessor. Like Chichester, he had aimed to the left of Norfolk Island on leaving New Zealand and had then turned ninety degrees to the right at the correct time. As with his hero, the tiny spot in the South Pacific that was Norfolk Island had appeared just as he began to worry about his navigation. This feat had brought his name to the attention of Joel Buchinsky who had offered the young man a slot in the flight team, overriding objections from the Insurance Department. It had been an inspired selection. Chris Walker loved the long distance trips to Europe and Japan and, after an apprenticeship as First Officer, Joel had begun to send him out as Pilot in charge.

Joel pulled a clipboard from the floor beneath the jump seat and handed it to Nigel. "The plan is to change crews when we refuel in England, but Chris will ride as a supernumerary for he has been to Harare several times and knows the procedures."

"Why are you changing in England, is that necessary?" Nigel asked.

"Yes, I'm afraid so," Joel replied, "I'll have exceeded my allowable hours on operations by the time we get to England. Remember, I only returned with Mr. Oliver from Los Angeles this afternoon. Chris is still within limits, but I felt it wise to have Brian Owen of the European Division available with another co-pilot to complete the trip. Chris can sleep on the crew bunk and by the time you get to Harare he can assist Brian with the final leg to Namibia."

"Of course," Nigel agreed, "I keep forgetting how bloody far it is. Have you had any more news from Sybil?"

"Yes, we had a link about ten minutes ago. I was waiting until you woke up to tell you. Still nothing further on the search. Sybil tried to get your contact in Namibia again but without success, so she called a Mr. D'Aquino of Rio Cerro Mining in London who is involved with the Tsamma Project in some manner. He's getting in touch with the Tsamma head office in Johannesburg and should be back to you or Sybil shortly."

Nigel smiled. "Good old George . . . Sybil must have remembered that George D'Aquino was a director of Mornay Mining in Chile before he left us to join Rio Cerro." He rose and touched Joel Buchinsky on the shoulder. "Let me know if anything further comes through even if I'm asleep. Get Jill to wake me." Jill was the flight attendant who now sat at the rear of the cabin.

"Yes, of course." Joel turned back to the radar screen that was picking up a large storm cell dead ahead.

Captain Pieterse sat with one leg dangling out of the command jeep. The ever-present radio in his hand, he watched two more vehicles arrive in response to his recall. He was desperately tired. Ever since the tourists had been lost, he had been operating on almost no sleep. He had organized the search and worked late into the night when it became known that Kresfeld and Mornay were missing. Herman Kresfeld had been a school friend, they had grown up together. Both were married and saw each other only occasionally, but they had still managed to get away for a few days fishing to Mile 105 every year. Now Herman was dead and he would have to conduct the inquiry. What had caused a healthy man -- even one over sixty to drop dead? And now young Mornay, where the hell was he? And why had he abandoned a dying Kresfeld? Why had he not taken the water bottle?

It was almost time to go home, for searching at night through this moonscape was a hopeless non-starter. He hesitated and then the old training asserted itself. One more try, just one more try, he said to himself, lifting the radio. "Green team . . . Wessel . . . are you still in the canyon?"

"Yes, Frikkie, we are almost at the Sesriem slope. Why?"

"Captain Modesto is making a last pass up the canyon. He thinks that it is just possible the boy was disoriented in the sand storm and may have turned towards Usakos. I want you to carry on past the Sesriem and go up the Khan about five or six kilometres towards the Willa junction. If Modesto sees something he will not have much time left before he has to break off and return to Swakop." He drew a deep breath. "It's our last chance, Wessel."

There was a moment's silence then. "Understood . . . I am sorry about Herman, we will see you back in Swakop."

Pieterse wiped his forehead wearily. They had done everything that could be done. As he had said to Wessel, this was truly their last chance. They would try again tomorrow, but every man knew that the chance of finding young Mornay alive was almost zero. He had been on searches before and without exception three days was the maximum. In the East Wind it dropped to two. He raised the radio again.

"All teams but Green report to the assembly point at the top of the Sesriem slope . . . acknowledge please." As the calls came in, his assistant checked them off on a clipboard.

"All accounted for, Sir."

"Good, well let's get over there, Willie." Pieterse pulled his leg into the vehicle and closed the door.

Suddenly an excited shout crackled from the radio. "Blue leader, we have found a shirt on the canyon floor just before where the Willa ravine joins the Khan."

"Captain Modesto, did you copy that?" Excitement crackled over the airwaves as Pieterse waved his driver to a stop. There was no answer, only the hiss of static. Puzzled, Pieterse called again. "Charlie Mike.. Charlie Mike . . . do you read?" He stared at his driver and a cold shiver ran through his spine. "Wessel . . . All vehicles. Has anyone seen or heard the aircraft?"

Wessel came back immediately, "He flew low over us about five minutes ago heading up past the Sesriem. He was very low so perhaps he cannot hear yo....Oh Gott in Himmel."

"Wessel . . . Wessel . . . what is it man!" Pieterse shouted into the handset.

"The aircraft must have crashed! We can see flames lighting up the sky about two or three kilometres ahead of us."

Pieterse stared out the windscreen in the general direction of the Willa ravine, suddenly aware of the crimson glow rising from the darkening canyon. He felt sick . . . there were three people on board that aircraft.

"Go like hell, Wessel. We are following you . . . All vehicles copy, and keep radio silence, Wessel has priority."

Colin awoke to see a wrinkled brown face peering at him. The Bushman sat on his haunches, naked, save for a dirty loincloth of ostrich hide that hung between his legs. He held an ostrich eggshell in one hand and with the other he splashed water from it on Colin's face. Colin closed his eyes, then as realization of what was happening hit him, he sat up and almost fainted as blood rushed to his head. Sitting with both elbows on his drawn up knees, he cradled his head until the spinning stopped. Water dripped on his bent neck and frantically he cupped his hands beneath the drip and sucked the moisture. Remembering the Bushman, he swung his head to where the small brown desert dweller had been squatting. He heard a chuckle and a series of clicks. Looking up, he saw the Bushman sitting now on a ledge about four feet above the cave floor, pointing to where the water dripped from a series of folds above his head. Standing up slowly, and mindful of the dizziness that had hit him before, he peered over the ledge and saw a small pool of water about two feet in diameter in a concave depression. Colin plunged his head beneath the cool water and he knew he was going to survive. He sank his head below the cool water and revelled in the cool wetness over his raw skin. His cracked lips stung where the exposed flesh met the water, but he did not care. Cupping his hands, he poured water over his back and chest, feeling the sharp stings as it met the dry, sunburnt flesh. He looked for the Bushman but he had gone. Surprised, Colin scanned the now almost dark cave. Maybe the Bushman had crept outside while Colin's head had been submerged. In any event he was no longer visible in the cave. Colin slumped down on the floor and stared at his blistered hands and arms, a huge wave of relief flooding over him. Where was his shirt, he wondered, unable to remember losing it. Even now, with his body greedily absorbing moisture, he was just beginning to recover. His eyelids drooped and he fell back into a dazed sleep.

Water splashed over Colin and he dreamt he was in the surf at Waikiki with his parents and that his father was chasing him. He ran laughing through the shallow water, looked back to see if his father was gaining and tripped face first into the surf. Sputtering and choking, he opened his eyes to find the Bushman standing above him again, splashing water into his upturned face. This time the little brown man was agitated and he gesticulated towards the opening, urging Colin to go outside. Shaking his head to remove the water, Colin crawled past the Bushman and through the entry hole out to the river bed.

A hundred feet away, the Chieftain was burning, jammed nose first into a huge pile of windblown scree. Colin gaped for several seconds before he saw a figure burst through the open door dragging a limp body out onto the sand. He watched in shock as the man tried to rise then collapsed face down after nearly getting fully upright. Again, the man got to his knees and started crawling back towards the burning aircraft. Colin tried to yell, but only a hoarse croak came out and he started to run towards the struggling figure, who had almost reached the door when he collapsed again. Colin dropped to his knees as he reached the kneeling man and with a heart stopping shock recognized his uncle under the bandages covering his head and throat. David turned his head and his eyes widened as Colin knelt beside him. He grimaced in a failed attempt at a smile.

"Colin, get Rafa . . . inside . . . get him out, boy . . . quickly."

By now, the flames were jumping six feet into the air and the front of the aircraft was enveloped in choking white smoke. Colin hesitated, fear rooting his feet to the ground. He shook his head. "I can't." He stared wildly around. "The Bushman can help. Where is he?"

David looked up. "Colin . . . for God's sake, boy . . . help him." He gripped the door opening with one hand and tried to pull himself up as Colin backed away. David watched him in horror. "Colin, he's your friend . . . he came here to find you . . . you can do it boy . . . if you are quick you can do it."

David was nearly upright but he was at the end of his resources. With a contemptuous look at Colin, he pulled himself into the burning aircraft but promptly collapsed half in and half out of the fuselage. Colin stood irresolute, then with a wild cry he flung himself forward to drag his uncle out of the aircraft. Pulling David a few feet clear, he leaped into the fuselage and ran up through the smoke to the cockpit. Rafa was dimly visible in the smoke and Colin saw Rafa vainly struggling to push himself out of the pilot's seat. Seeing Colin, he made a fierce attempt to push himself clear of the flames that were licking at the soles of his feet. His lightweight trousers were smouldering and it would be only seconds before his lower clothing burst into flame. He held out both hands to Colin who gripped each of the pilot's forearms and dragged him backward. Rafa screamed and fainted as his broken legs jammed against the sharp angle of the seat and throttle quadrant. A wave of flame licked up through the space left by Rafa's feet as Colin desperately dragged him back down the fuselage. They reached the door and Colin pulled Rafa roughly over the sill and onto the sand outside. David was on his knees moving towards Kate in a jerky parody of a beetle. He called hoarsely over his shoulder. "Get clear of the aircraft . . . it's going to blow . . . bring Rafa . . . I'll get Kate." Realizing the danger, a wildly panting Colin scooped Rafa up under the arms and hauled the unconscious pilot, his legs dragging in the sand, right to the mouth of the cave. Flames were now shooting fifty feet into the air and Colin saw that David was still too close to the aircraft. Stumbling back, he grabbed Kate's limp form and dragged her away while David crawled along on all fours. Flames roared upward along the full length of the fuselage, lighting up the sharp walls of the canyon.

Riding in the leading "Green Team" LandRover, Wessel was the first of the ground party on the scene. He was out of the vehicle and running before his driver could bring the vehicle to a full stop. He pounded past Colin and scooped David up in his arms. He had taken only three steps away from the blazing aircraft, when it blew up with a deafening roar. They were to be his last steps on earth. A tiny piece of the aluminium fuselage travelling at several hundred feet per second, ripped into Wessel's skull, killing him instantly. He collapsed over David, protecting his friend's body even in death.

A long moment of silence was shattered by the flat echo that reverberated down the length of the canyon, a cry of mourning for the dead of a long day. Other men were out of their vehicles now, racing over the sand and gravel to help. Someone rolled Wessel off David and in a shocked voice exclaimed, "Wessel is hurt, help me with these two." Two men lifted David into a sitting position. He tried to stand, but his knee gave way again. Someone was holding him up and there was a babble of voices. A second person was on David's other side and then he was lying flat on a stretcher and he could hear a calm voice saying, "You are going to be fine now, relax." He did not feel the needle and blackness washed over him.

Pieterse arrived fifteen minutes later. He saw the remains of the Chieftain, burning lower now, and the milling crowd of men working frantically to load the injured survivors. The scene was lit by the headlights of a ring of vehicles and the glow of the burning aircraft. He knew what had happened. His lieutenant who had arrived a few minutes after Wessel in the second 'Green Team' vehicle had called him, his voice breaking with the news. Pieterse levered himself out of the command jeep and was walking toward the two policemen who were taking photographs of the scene when the lieutenant saw him and strode over.

"Captain, the boy is in good shape considering. He was babbling and kept trying to get us to find a Bushman. I think he was pretty badly shocked by the explosion as well as being dehydrated, so I gave him a sedative."

"And the pilot?"

"Both legs broken and some burns to his lower leg. I shot him full of morphine and he is next to Mornay in the back of Wessel's vehicle." He looked searchingly at his Chief. "We need to get them into Swakop as soon as possible."

"Yes, I called for one ambulance to meet us at the old tin mine. Hassel is coming out with the ambulance. Where is Wessel?"

"Over here, Sir." He led the way to a small slab of rock, swept clean of sand. Wessel lay on his back his face surprisingly peaceful. There was an absence of blood except for a small dark spot beneath his head. For a long time Pieterse stood looking down at the face without speaking. The lieutenant said something and he turned. "What?'

"The woman . . . Doctor Richardson . . . she is still unconscious." The lieutenant lifted his hands in frustration. "She seems uninjured and I could find no broken bones, but judging by the gash on her head she took a very hard blow to the head and I am worried that she may have internal bleeding."

"Go to my jeep and call the Hospital," Pieterse said quietly, "and tell them to send the second ambulance and let them know the extent of the injuries . . . and Lieutenant . . ."

"Sir?"

"You have done well . . . good work . . . it has been a hard day for all of us."

Embarrassed, the lieutenant bobbed his head. The captain was not noted for giving compliments.

Later, there would be recriminations, the whys and why nots of the armchair experts. Now, Pieterse walked into the sheltering darkness away from the bustle of activity behind. He stared into the dark sky and the ragged edge of the canyon, black against the charcoal sky. He should feel elated, for after all they had found the boy, but at what cost . . . Two dead, three injured, God only knew how seriously. "Damn the Namib, the bloody unforgiving damned Namib," he thought. But even as the thoughts formed in his mind, he knew that harsh as this land was, it was his land. Let others and their kin live in the dirty and overcrowded cities with all the so-called amenities. This wilderness, flayed by sun and wind was where he felt at home and despite the desert's indifferent cruelty, he considered it the last refuge of the truly free. He had been born here and God willing would die here. He snorted, angry with himself -- "bloody sentimentalism" he thought. But he felt better as he turned back to join the convoy already forming up to transport the injured to hospital.

Chapter 24

Requiem

Chris Walker came back down the passageway with a piece of paper in his hand. He sat in the large swivel seat across from Nigel and handed him the newsfax. "The London office has just relayed a message from Tsamma Uranium, Mr. Mornay. Your brother has regained consciousness and has gone out into the desert with the search crews. Apparently, the East Wind has started to ease up and the aircraft is helping with the search. There was no other information except that the General Manager of Tsamma Uranium will meet you on arrival and extend any help you may need." He nodded awkwardly at Judith who was awake and sitting forward, her fingers digging into Nigel's arm.

"Thank you, Chris." Nigel crumpled the newsfax into a small ball. Walker was a taciturn man. He paused, then uncharacteristically blurted out. "With the aircraft helping the ground search their chances are improved dramatically. I think they'll have a good chance, Mrs. Mornay."

Judith gave him a quick, strained smile. "Yes, I'm sure you're right. Thank you Chris."

The aircraft began to buffet as they flanked a storm cell and Chris Walker made his way quickly back to the cockpit. Joel raised his eyebrows quizzically as Chris slid down into his seat.

"How is she?"

"OK, but she must be under a lot of stress. She's looking very tired. What is our ETA for Shannon?"

Joel punched a button on the console, under the electronic distance measuring readout and looked at his watch. "No change, we should be there in less than an hour. Call Shannon and tell them that we'll be coming down to flight level twenty-four in five minutes."

David awoke to find the sun streaming through the window. He was back in the same hospital bed he had vacated yesterday. Outside, the wind was still and the sky was blue. He pushed himself up on his elbow and was surprised to see Colin sitting in the chair that had been brought in for Kate.

"Colin? How are you boy?" He tried to push himself further up. Colin jumped up and leaned over to help him.

"I'm fine except for a bad case of sunburn." He helped David into a sitting position.

David looked at him curiously. Despite the puffy features caused by the sunburn, the boy had a harder look about him, as if he had crossed a personal Rubicon and was no longer a spoiled and pampered teenager. The boy looked away from his uncle's searching gaze and rose to his feet awkwardly. "I'll call the doctor. He said to let him know as soon as you woke up."

"Wait!" David reached out his hand. "What about Kate . . . and Rafa? I remember Wessel helping me." He stopped in sudden fear. Colin's eyes were full of tears. "Colin, what's the matter . . . is it Kate? Is she . . . ?"

"No, no. Let me call the Doctor. Kate is still unconscious, that's all I know." Visibly agitated, Colin dashed for the door and was away before David could stop him.

David sagged back on the bed. "It must be Rafa," he thought bitterly, "but he was alive on the aircraft and unless he suffered internal injuries . . ." David stared at the ceiling and tears blurred his vision. Outside the open window a bird sang and he turned his head to the sound. The sky had been washed clean and was a cerulean blue, innocent and gentle. Staring through the glass, his mind's eye saw Rafa pulling on his pigskin gloves, a battered baseball cap on his head and a lopsided grin on his face. His reverie was interrupted as the door banged open and Hassel hurried in with Colin.

"Colin, leave me alone with your uncle for a few minutes, will you?" Colin nodded jerkily and left David facing a grim, tired Ken Hassel.

"Dave, I'm very sorry . . . I know he was your friend . . . If it is any consolation it was instantaneous." Hassel reached for David's arm. "You seem to have come out remarkably unscathed. I had to redo some stitches, but apart from shock and general . . ."

David interrupted. "I don't understand, how could it have been instantaneous? He was alive after the crash. Colin got him out before the plane blew up. What did he die of?"

Hassel stared at him, understanding dawning on his tired face. "You don't know? You don't remember?"

"Remember what, for God's sake?.. Ken, spit it out . . . what happened?"

"Rafa is alive. He has two broken legs and some bad burns to one leg, but he'll recover."

"Who then . . . ?" Sudden realization hit David. "Not Wessel?" he whispered. "Not Wessel, he wasn't even in the crash." Wide-eyed, he stared at the Doctor whose face was a study in sadness. "How did it happen?"

"A fluke really. A tiny piece of the aircraft fuselage hit him in the head when the plane exploded. But it behaved like a bullet and with the same effect. All I can tell you is that it was instantaneous."

"Oh shit! oh shit! goddamn it all to hell!" David squeezed his eyes shut. "It's always the best ones who get it . . . you know . . . Oh shit! He was carrying me when it happened."

Hassel's voice was sharp. "As I said, it was a fluke, and you are not to blame yourself. Wessel was my friend too and I will miss him just as much. But you, of all men, should know by now how random fate can be."

They both stared through the window remembering the bearded giant who had been their friend. "God knows he won't be in heaven," David said gruffly, wiping his eyes with the back of his hand. "They aren't going to let him play with explosives in the garden of houris." He sighed deeply. "And Kate, how is she?"

"She's still unconscious," the doctor replied. "We have done a series of x-rays and apart from the gash and swelling on the top of her head she seems OK. Nothing is broken and there's no sign of brain damage."

"Surely, if she took a hard knock, you'd expect her to take a while to come around."

Hassel smiled grimly, "It's been nearly two days since the crash. I've kept you under sedation since they brought you in. I don't think you realize how much you drained yourself in breaking out of the aircraft." He paused. "Kate is in a coma. All her vital signs are normal but she doesn't respond to stimulus. It may be a long time before she surfaces."

"But for God's sake there must be something you can do." David retorted impatiently.

"I wish there was, but the brain is still unknown in many of its ramifications -- even for the specialists." He placed a strong hand on David's shoulder. "There's something else. Jack Richardson flew back this morning and he's been told all sorts of stories about you and Kate. I tried to set him straight on what I know, which quite frankly isn't very much, but he wants to see you as soon as I can allow it."

David absorbed the implication of Hassel's words. "I want to see Kate and Rafa first, then perhaps we can meet. I really have no idea what to say to him. How do you tell a man that you're in love with his wife and that she is with you?" He gripped Hassel's arm fiercely. "It has been quite a week for you. I guess you'll be glad to see the back of me."

Ken Hassel smiled, "I'm not going to see the back of you just yet." He held up a restraining hand. "When will you realize that your body has taken some very hard knocks over the years? You nearly died in Vietnam, you still have small shrapnel in your back. This latest series of events has taken a severe toll on your resources, both physical and emotional."

"You saw my medical file?"

"Of course. Johannesburg thinks pretty highly of you, and when I advised them that you were hurt they cooperated . . . David, I served for a short time with the South African forces in Angola in 1988 and I came to realize that it is not the physical wounds, but the emotional ones that are the worst. Look, I am just a small town doctor, but I would like to think that I can help."

"You are a good man Ken, but no thanks. Some demons are best fought alone . . . but thank you all the same." He levered himself upright. "Can I see Kate?"

"Stay here and I will have a wheelchair brought round and Colin can take you over. I think Jack Richardson has gone out to the mine to see Mr. Butchert." Hassel stepped back and opened the door. "OK, Colin, you can come back in. Just make sure that he doesn't try to walk around."

Colin came through the door, his eyes anxious. He closed the door behind the doctor with a gentle click and stood staring at the floor.

"What is it boy? What's the matter?"

There was a short silence, then he turned his head to the window and the words poured out, "Wessel is my fault . . . if I hadn't been afraid . . . I would have got Rafa out sooner." He looked up, his eyes filling with tears. "If we had been further away . . . it was my fault. I'm sorry . . . " He stopped and reached for a handkerchief to blow his nose noisily. David watched him soberly.

"Sit down Colin. Let me tell you something."

"It was my fault . . . I panicked."

"Colin, many times in combat, I saw new recruits freeze up. It happens all the time. The important thing to remember is that you overcame your fear and went into the aircraft. You got Rafa clear and Kate too." David gripped Colin's arm. "What you did took a lot of courage. There are grown men who would not have done the same. Wessel knew the risks, he took his chances with his eyes wide open." David looked past Colin's shoulder and his voice grew very quiet. "He was my friend and I will miss him -- as you will, for he liked you. But if he were here now, he would be proud of you, so stop talking rubbish about it being your fault. You have just found out that fate plays dice with our lives. All anyone can do is play the hand they are given and try to do it with as much grace as possible." He shook Colin's arm gently. "Come on, let's go and see Kate and Rafa."

Colin helped him out of the bed and into his dressing gown. The hospital slippers were too small and they were rummaging through the cupboard for another pair when a knock sounded at the door. Colin opened it to a dark skinned nurse with a wheelchair. Thanking her, he wheeled it into the room and turned it so that David could sit down.

"I can walk."

"No, Doctor Hassel said that you were not to walk around for a while. I can push you."

With a small grin, David acquiesced. He sat in the chair and Colin navigated it down the long corridors towards the women's section. As they rounded a corner they almost collided with the matron, who was hurrying in the opposite direction.

"Oh, sorry Sister."

"And where are you going?" she asked sharply.

David spoke before Colin. "We're going to see Kate . . . Mrs. Richardson. We'll only be a minute."

"She is in a coma, Mr. Mornay, she will not know you." The brown eyes were compassionate. "Her husband has been sitting with her this morning," she continued, catching the flicker of pain that crossed David's face. She remembered Kate's impassioned plea to be allowed to sit with him and despite her training her heart went out to this severe man who now found himself caught in the oldest of triangles. "Very well, but only for a few minutes. Her room is Number 12."

"Thank you Matron, we'll not stay long . . . which room is Captain Modesto in?"

"He is probably in the recreation room. Tell him please, to stop flirting with my nurses." She smiled mischievously. "Being a hero does not entitle him to special privileges."

David smiled in return. "I'll do my best."

Colin wheeled David down the short corridor, both of them counting the numbers until they reached number 12, where Colin held the door open with one hand and pushed David's wheelchair into the room. It was a duplicate of David's room with an outside window. The sun streamed through the partially drawn net curtains and a huge vase of flowers sat on the trestle over the end of the bed. Kate lay on her back with her eyes closed, her arms outside the covers, breathing gently. Not knowing, one would assume that she was only sleeping. Her face was peaceful and, apart from a thick bandage that was wrapped around her head, she looked as if she could awaken at any moment.

David stepped out of the wheelchair to stand over her. "Kate, Kate, can you hear me?" He reached for a limp hand and squeezed her fingers gently. "Kate, it's David. Can you hear me? If you can hear me squeeze my hand." There was no response.

He sat down slowly. "Ken said it could be a long time before she recovers," he said sadly, staring at the lovely face in despair and finally turning with a deep sigh. "Take me to see Rafa now Colin." His voice was empty and flat.

They found the recreation room where Rafa was sitting in a wheelchair reading a novel. One leg was encased in plaster to the knee, but the other was wrapped in gauze bandages and supported on a stiff wooden board. Several elderly long-term patients sat in a far corner watching television. Mildly curious, Rafa turned his head to see who was coming into the room and his face lit up with pleasure.

"Amigos, como estan? How are you my friend?" He scanned David's face. "What is it Dave?"

"Has Ken Hassel spoken to you about Wessel . . . and Kate?"

A wave of sadness washed over the pilot's face, removing the smile of greeting. "Yes, he told me this morning. It is always the same . . . eh, amigo . . . always the same." He stopped and drew a deep breath. "I only wish . . . " Again he hesitated, then continued slowly. "He wanted to go fishing to Sandwich harbour last week and asked me to go along. He was very keen . . . you know Wes and his fishing . . . but I put him off. Wes was quite disappointed and went off on his own . . . " Rafa pulled a handkerchief from his pocket and blew his nose. "Regrets . . . eh, amigo . . . we have more than our share."

David leaned forward and gripped Rafa's forearm. "No, no regrets, Wes would hate that. He never took offence, that's what made him so popular. He is . . . was . . . a big man in the best sense and Goddamn it, Rafa, no one can predict the future." David tightened his grip and leaned close to Rafa. "Talking of the future, why not plan a trip to Mauritius, take Billy, Gariseb and Colin . . . I'll talk to Colin's parents, you can use the pool money to have a really good break."

Rafa looked at David soberly. "And what about you? What are you going to do . . . wait for Kate to recover . . . what are you going to do about her?"

"We have just been to see Kate. Ken says . . . "

"Yes I know, he told me this morning. I am sorry, but look Dave, I have heard of people coming out of a coma suddenly. It has only been two days. I think any speculation about long term effects are just that . . . speculation." He looked past David at Colin. "I am in your debt, amigo, I would not have made it without your help."

David was surprised. "You have not seen Colin before now?"

"Ken Hassel knocked us both out. I only woke up properly this morning and I was told that you would be up soon." He turned to Colin. "As soon as I am out of this place we are going to get you your student pilot's licence. I have a friend in Windhoek who will give you some lessons and before you return to Canada we can have you going solo. Dave did tell you that he extended your stay a few days ago? Didn't he?"

Colin blushed in pleased embarrassment, "No, we haven't

spoken about my going home yet. But I would like that."

"Tell us what happened, how did you come to end up in the canyon?"

For the next fifteen minutes Colin recounted the fateful steps of his long ordeal for his uncle and Rafa. Yesterday, Captain Pieterse had spent several hours coaxing him gently to tell all he could remember. Colin could not believe that Kresfeld had been found dead, and Pieterse realized that the boy was telling the truth and must have separated from Herman Kresfeld at least an hour before the German's fatal heart attack. The story of the Bushman he did not believe but had sent his men to search the cave for signs. They had returned convinced that Colin had been the only occupant of the cave and must have been delirious.

When Colin repeated the story of the Bushman to his uncle and Rafa, the two men exchanged raised eyebrows and David responded carefully. "Yes, now I remember. You said something about getting the Bushman to help you when the plane was on fire."

Looking from one to the other, Rafa spoke to Colin. "There have been no Bushmen in this part of the Namib for hundreds of years. Are you sure you weren't delirious?"

"I saw him," Colin replied firmly, "and if he hadn't splashed water in my face and made me leave the cave I wouldn't have found you. The police captain told me he sent men back to look for tracks and they found nothing, but at least they found the water spring that I drank from." He looked from one to the other."I'm telling the truth. I swear it."

Both men sat in silence, torn between the boy's conviction and conventional wisdom. "I wonder . . . " Rafa started to say something, then stopped.

"What are you wondering?" David asked.

"Look, we know that the Bushmen were driven out of this part of the Namib hundreds of years ago, but I am also convinced that Colin is telling the truth. So either a lone Bushman has travelled five hundred miles from the Kalahari to walk the canyon of his ancestors, which is pretty unlikely or . . . "

"Or what? The only possible explanation is that Colin was delirious or that a Bushman, unlikely as it seems, was in the cave."

"I know." Rafa rubbed a hand along the side of his jaw. "As soon as we are able, I want to go back to the crash site. There is something I want to check out. Perhaps the answer is not so mysterious after all."

Colin interjected. "This was a live man. I told you, he poured water on me."

Clearly puzzled, David spoke gently. "As Rafa says, Colin, it's remotely possible that a lone Bushman hundreds of miles from home found you. But you have told us that Pieterse's men found no sign of human tracks other than your own. Given that you were delirious and near death when you found the cave, isn't it possible that your mind played tricks on you?"

Colin shook his head, but before he could speak, Rafa spoke softly. "Perhaps that is the explanation, but let us leave it for now. There is still a lot to confirm. The insurance assessors will want proof that the engine failed, so the crash investigation team will have to remove the engine for tests to find out what caused it to quit. But if there was a Bushman, I for one, would like to meet him and thank him."

For the next half hour, they explained to Colin how they had searched for him and how David had come to be injured but had insisted on flying with Kate and Rafa on the day of the crash.

"I am glad that he was pig-headed enough to override Hassel and me," Rafa interjected. "I hate to think what would have happened if only Kate and I were aboard." He leaned forward and bounced a gentle fist on David's arm. "I owe you, amigo,"

"Well, you can buy the drinks as soon as they let us out of here. I have to see Jack Richardson this afternoon." He turned to Colin. "Wessel was feeding Bones every day while I was in hospital, so you are delegated to see that he is OK. And I want you to contact your parents . . ." He stopped, for Colin's hand had flown up to his mouth and his face was a study in confusion.

"I forgot to tell you," he said. "Mom and Dad are on their way out here. There was a news flash on the CBC about a party of tourists being lost in the Namib. Someone in Victoria heard it and mentioned it to my mother, so she phoned my father's office. They called Tsamma Uranium and someone told Sybil, my father's personal assistant, that you were in hospital and I was missing. Apparently, Mom went ape and they're coming out here in the company plane. I don't know if she knows yet that I'm safe."

"You haven't spoken to them?"

"No, your secretary phoned the hospital right away, but you had left with Rafa to search for me. I only heard about them coming when your secretary stopped in yesterday to see you at the hospital and she gave me their flight times. I asked her to call Sybil with all the news but I haven't spoken to Caroline since." Colin stood up, patting his pockets. "Here it is." He pulled a crumpled piece of paper from his shirt pocket.

Rafa reached up and took it from him. "Let me see. OK, they are flying from Victoria to Shannon in Ireland. From there they will be following the commercial route south to Nairobi in Kenya and then on to Harare. From there I would guess that they will route direct to Windhoek and Swakopmund. What sort of aircraft is it?"

"A jet, a Lear Jet with long-range tanks. My father often flies to Europe."

"Well even for a Lear it is a long haul," Rafa observed, turning the paper over. "It says that they are due in Swakop tomorrow morning."

Exasperated, David growled at Colin. "Why didn't you call them as soon as you could. Your parents must be going through hell."

"How was I to know that they would hear about it?" Colin's face tightened, and for a moment he was a small boy again. He didn't know if he should feel guilt or anger.

"Hmm, I guess you're right. It isn't your fault, but if there was only some way we could get in touch."

"Your secretary said they were going to phone again, so maybe by now they'll have heard," Colin said, hopefully.

"God, I hope so. Judith in full sail is a sight to behold," David replied, staring soberly at Colin. "You had better phone the mine and ask Caroline what's happening. Tell her to phone Sybil if she hasn't done so already and give Sybil all the news. Also, tell my cook to clean out the spare bedroom and get some more food in. Go on, Colin, you are going to have to be the organizer."

Colin stood up uncertainly and Rafa chuckled, "It is a big switch from being the hero to being the gofer, eh Colin?" He pulled at the pocket of his dressing gown and gave Colin a plastic covered card. "Gariseb has brought my station wagon to the hospital and has a driver on standby. Go and find the driver and show him the card. He will take you around wherever you need to go."

Colin took the card and left the two men alone. David turned to Rafa. "How are your legs, are you going to fly again?" he asked quietly.

"Ken assures me that I will be back at work in two or three months, sooner perhaps if I heal faster."

David gazed at his friend soberly. "Well, thank God for small mercies. What are you going to do in the meantime?"

Rafa grinned at him. "I meant what I said. I am going up to Windhoek with Colin and make sure he gets his private licence to take back with him. He will have to work like a dog to do it in the time he has left, but I am certain he will do it." He slapped David on the knee. "Amigo, amigo, don't look so grim, Kate is alive, and she will recover . . . I feel it in my bones."

David sighed, "I hope you're right. I have to meet with Jack Richardson this afternoon and frankly I am not at all sure what to say to him." He stared at the floor. "Richardson has been given a lot of misinformation and he is bound to be in nasty frame of mind. Still, I can't say that I blame him, considering . ."

"You must not blame yourself . . . these things happen and from what I heard, she felt the same for you."

For the next hour the two men worked over the rescue sequence in detail to determine that their recollections coincided. There would be an enquiry and the experience gained, in this instance, could prompt improvement in the response system should a similar disaster occur in the future. The mine was big on accident prevention and response.

A nurse came into the recreation room, her eyes scanning the little knots of patients scattered around the room. Spotting David and Rafa, she walked over.

"Mr. Mornay, Doctor Hassel would like to see you in your room."

"Of course, sister." David started to rise but was firmly pushed back into the wheelchair.

"I will take you, where did your nephew go?"

David explained that Colin was running various essential errands and that he, David, was quite capable of walking unaided.

The nurse shook her head firmly. "No sir, you will not walk. The doctor was very specific about that." She spun the wheelchair around and pushed David briskly back along the route he had taken earlier. David felt acutely uncomfortable but did not protest, reserving his arguments for the doctor. The nurse briskly one-armed the door to his room open and manouvered the wheelchair in with her free arm. Standing beside the bed with Ken Hassel was Jack Richardson. The contrast was stark -- David Mornay, pale, drawn and unshaven, head bandaged and arm in a sling, and Jack Richardson, stocky and fit, blond and more than modestly handsome in his immaculate Pollock-Delisle suit.

"I will leave you two alone then, but please, both of you, keep this conversation civilized."

Hassel looked at David. "Mr. Richardson wanted a private talk with you and I suggested your room." With a nod at Jack

Richardson, he drew the nurse out of the room, closing the door firmly behind them.

David waited until the door clicked shut. "Hallo Jack, I'm sorry that we have to meet under these circumstances." He remained seated, thinking that getting into the bed would put them both at a disadvantage. "Why don't you sit down?"

Richardson waved his hand irritably. "Don't patronize me, Mornay. I'll stand because this won't take long. Kate is being transferred to the Kenridge Hospital in Johannesburg by ambulance aircraft as soon as it can be arranged. I really don't want to hear about your infatuation with my wife." His voice hardened. "If putting the life of someone you profess to love in mortal danger is your idea of a good relationship then you are a bigger fool than you look, and why she agreed to fly with you, I cannot understand."

David held up his hand. "She insisted on coming along. I tried to change her mind, but she was firm. Look, none of this was premeditated." Here David hesitated, "I can't find an easy way to say this, but I'm in love with Kate, and I believe she's in love with me . . . "

Richardson interrupted angrily. "You stupid prick, what makes you think that Kate feels that way . . . she told you that did she? Perhaps that's why she has agreed to fly to Germany with me on Saturday, and was quite excited at the prospect . . . but, of course, I forget she's madly in love with you."

David gasped, "She's awake, out of the coma? . . . Thank God."

"She is not out of the coma, but four nights ago I phoned her from Capetown and told her I was going to Germany and that she could come along. She was very excited about that and gave me no indication that she was anything but happy with our relationship."

"Four nights ago . . . that was . . . "

"Well, well . . . give the monkey a banana . . .Yes, she had just been to see you in the hospital. She told me all about you and she said you were nothing more than a good friend. She has a habit of picking up strays."

David growled softly, his eyes going hard. "Be careful, Richardson, I can understand how you feel about me, but I am not some junior clerk you're talking to. Neither Kate nor I expected to have events develop this way, but it happened. Kate tried very hard to end it. She in fact did not see me until after my truck crashed. She is, as you must know, a very moral woman and I am not the kind of person who jumps into bed with every available woman."

"Don't flatter yourself, Mornay. I know Kate, and what you took for affection . . . you call it love . . . was just her usual niceness to people she feels sorry for. I can't believe for one minute that Kate was physically attracted to you."

A surge of anger flowed through David's body, but he closed his eyes for a second, concentrating on suppressing his rage. "Look I don't plan to argue with you. My main concern is Kate's recovery. There'll be time enough to sort things out when she is back on her feet."

"Well, at least we both agree on something," Richardson countered. "If Kate wants to get in touch with you when she has recovered, then no doubt it can be arranged. But for the near future I don't want you trying to see her or interfering with her treatment in Johannesburg. If you try to see her, I'll deal with you myself . . . I'll also make a formal complaint to ConAmGeo. You are skating on very thin ice Mornay. You are not indispensable, and in this I know that I have the full support of Mr. Butchert."

David stared at Jack Richardson for several seconds and when he spoke his voice was soft but the anger flickered through his words like distant lightning. "I do not take kindly to threats, Richardson, and I will continue to monitor her progress for as long as she is in a coma. If, when Kate recovers, she -- not you -- tells me that she does not want to see me again, then I will accept that. I will not have you dictate what I can, or cannot do."

There was a long silence as the two men glared at each other, but it was Jack Richardson who looked away and began to leave the room, his face flushed with suppressed rage. At the door he stopped and spat out savagely, "You are going to find out shortly that you are far from indispensable, Mornay. Your supporters at head office are getting tired of your antics and . . . ." he caught himself in mid-sentence and slammed the door violently as he stormed out.

David stared at the closed door. What the hell was Richardson referring to? Billy Mitchell had tried to warn him that Waldron had been stirring up trouble after the incident when young Ivan Kretchmer was killed. Now it seemed that Richardson and Butchert had added their complaints to the chorus. He looked down at his hands. Well, he could always go back to Canada, he had enough money saved and there was always his share of the inheritance. He and Kate could live very comfortably. Suddenly a cold chill swept over him. It couldn't be true, or could it? Jack Richardson had said that Kate had agreed to go to Germany with him. Was her behaviour only to keep him calm and help him heal after the accident? David racked his memory trying to recollect all the nuances of her behaviour. Nothing fitted with what Richardson had said, nothing matched. He must have lied, but the remote possibility gnawed at him and he struggled with the thought that perhaps Richardson was right, Kate only wanted to see him back on his feet. Had he been blinded, and was it really just one-sided? "No!" he slammed his good fist on the arm of the wheel chair. His unpleasant conjecture was interrupted by a sharp knock and Rafa poked his head around the door.

"You in one piece?" He inquired, wheeling into the room and pushing the door closed behind him. "I just saw Jack Richardson leaving and he looked a very unhappy fellow."

"Yes, we had a rather sharp exchange . . . frankly I can't say that I blame him, but something he said really threw me." David grimaced at the memory.

"Oh, what did he say, that he would take a horsewhip to you

or something?"

"What, . . . Oh no, nothing like that. He said the night that you and Wessel had dinner with Kate he phoned her and they were planning a trip to Germany and she was very excited. It just doesn't make sense, because she's not the kind of person to blow hot and cold. But why would he lie about something like that?"

"Ah, now I remember." Rafa pinched the bridge of his nose. "When we returned to her house after leaving the hospital, she heard something and jumped out of the car and dashed inside. I thought maybe there was a burglar and so I followed her in, but I was a bit slower. As I got to the front door she was on the phone and it must have been Jack calling. I distinctly heard her say something about going to Germany." He looked at his friend curiously. "I also don't think she is the fickle type, but let us face facts my friend, neither of us is an expert in the area of women."

David's face went blank and his voice was flat. "I just don't believe it . . . damn it all, Rafa, I am sure of her." But the words sounded hollow to his own ears.

Chapter 25

Home Alone

Brian Owen grabbed Chris Walker by the shoulder, and they both were grinning like schoolboys. Chris pointed to the control yoke and co-pilot Jos Pickstone took over, banking the Lear to make the final turn over the Nairobi beacon while they waited their turn to land behind a Lufthansa Jumbo.

"You do the honours, Chris . . . go and tell them, and I'll help Jos with the final approach," he said.

Chris unbuckled himself from the left seat and squeezed past Brian. He stretched his shoulders and yawned. He had been flying since they had passed over Khartoum, while Brian Owen had been napping. The two Englishmen had replaced Joel Buchinsky at Shannon, but like Joel, they had also been pulled off routine flying operations and were reaching the limits of their allowable airtime. Chris stared into the dimly lit cabin, the only light coming from a small neon strip along the floor. Even that had been dimmed. He walked down to where Nigel and Judith sat in the huge seats that were racked right back to provide a semi-supine position for sleeping. Judith was covered with a blanket that had slipped partially off her shoulder and dragged on the floor. Sleep had smoothed, but not erased the lines of tension and worry that creased her face, and Chris Walker grinned to himself. This news was the best thing anyone could give her. Nigel Mornay snapped awake as Chris touched his shoulder. He had not slept well.

"We are ready to land at Nairobi Sir, but we have just had a call from London."

Nigel was now fully awake. He pushed a button on his seat console and his seat whined softly into the upright position. "What's the time," he asked, brushing his hair back with stiffened fingers.

"It is eight in the morning, Kenya time. The news is that

Colin is safe. He is . . . "

"What! What did you say?" Nigel yelled, half rising out of his seat. The noise woke Judith who tried to sit upright, and Chris leaned over Nigel to punch the seat button to bring her seat upright.

"For God's sake man, stop messing about . . . Judith he's safe! Colin is safe!" Nigel gripped Chris's arm in a painful clamp. "What did they say? What happened?"

"He was found just after we left Shannon. Apparently there was quite a lot of confusion at the time, the search aircraft crashed and there were fatalities. Your brother survived the crash and Colin was located at the same time. The message only said that he is suffering from exposure, but is expected to make a full recovery. Sybil Burgess has been trying to get through to you and finally phoned Nairobi control who have just relayed the information."

Nigel released Chris's arm, and his face was split from ear to ear with a big grin. He reached across to Judith and gripped her by the shoulders.

"By God, Judith, I had given him up . . . I really thought that he was dead. This is wonderful news."

Judith reached into a bag next to her seat and mopped up the tears that were running down her face. "So had I. Oh I feel . . . Oh thank you, Chris." Impulsively she pulled his head down and kissed his cheek.

Startled, but pleased, he muttered that he was also happy for them, but that he must get forward as they were due to land at any moment.

The wheels slid down to lock with a soft thump as the Lear settled lower over the Athi plains and lined up with the centerline of the Jomo Kenyatta Airport's main runway.

"Ken, you have my word that I'll take it easy . . . actually, I'm feeling a hell of a lot better and I really must try to get back to work as soon as possible. Now that Wessel is . . ." He stopped and stared out of the window. "Now that I no longer have Wessel, I'll have to reorganize the construction department."

Ken Hassel shook his head in mock anger. "The last of the immortals, eh? Your recovery has been very fast, but you still have a lot of healing to do." He searched David's face, noting that the bruising around the eyes had faded to a sickly yellow. The grey eyes were bright and alert, and the cut across David's chest and throat was healing. By some miracle, only a few of the stitches had pulled loose during the violent struggle to escape the crashed aircraft. The Doctor smiled. "I will say this for you, you may be a medical pain in the ass, but treating you is anything but boring." He glanced down at the clipboard in his hand and flicked the top page back. "OK Dave, I would rather keep you here for at least a few days more, as you know." He turned to Colin who was standing against the wall listening to the conversation and gripped him by the arm. "You make sure that he does not do anything excessive. Is that understood? No lifting, no stretching, lots of rest periods. I am relying on you to keep him in line, Colin."

David snorted. "Thank you, Doctor, for your vote of confidence. Colin is almost as big a nag as you are. Between the two of you I can see I'm going to have to ask permission to go to the bathroom."

Hassel laughed, and still chuckling left the two men alone.

Colin cleared his throat. "What clothes do you need me to bring from the house? I'll have to let the driver go soon, it's almost his quitting time."

"In the top drawer in my room, you'll find a couple of shirts and my slacks are hanging in the cupboard. You'll find underwear and socks in the bottom drawer. Oh, bring my slip-on shoes. That's all I think, and Hendrik will help you if needed. How are you getting on with him?"

Colin grinned. "Fine . . . I'm teaching him how to make hot

dogs using German sausage. His pizza needs a lot of work, but I'm really not sure how to make them myself."

David grunted, masking the real pleasure he felt at Colin's transformation, "OK, away with you and try to see Rafa on the way out. He tells me that he's dug up some training books for you to study."

"Roy, he will have to go . . . he needs a long break after the accident . . . Yes, I know he's your top construction man, but the main construction phase is over, we have our own teams to do the work." Butchert held the telephone in his left hand while he doodled on a plain pad with his right. Jack Richardson sat across from him, looking over Butchert's shoulder at the mine spread out below the huge window. "Yes, I know he has done good work, but frankly he has outlived his usefulness . . . no, that's not the reason . . . Look Roy, he is your man. I have no authority to discipline him . . . he is only on secondment to Tsamma from ConAmGeo. You could transfer him to one of the other operations . . . Yes, I do think it's for the best . . . Thank you, you will let me know?" With a sigh Butchert replaced the telephone and looked across his desk at Jack Richardson. "They will discuss Mornay's transfer at tomorrow's board meeting. If he is infatuated with Kate, he is not going to be happy with a posting to Chile."

"Chile? Why, that's excellent news." Jack Richardson's face lit up with pleasure.

"Look Jack, I was hoping that you and Mornay could work out your differences, but from what you tell me he has convinced himself that Kate is in love with him. You also are convinced that Kate does not feel anything but friendship for him." He shrugged his burly shoulders and swivelled his chair to look out of the window. "You have a great future in the organization, and I have invested a lot of time and effort in you." He sighed and swung back to face Jack. "Look, right now your main concern must be for Kate. As soon as the air ambulance arrives from Johannesburg, why don't you go along and take a few days in Johannesburg? It wouldn't hurt to call in at the head office and do some networking."

"What about the O'Kiep report? I was hoping to have it finished by the weekend. I could follow Kate down to Jo'burg as soon as it is ready."

He saw Butchert looked at him curiously, and continued quickly, "Kate is in a coma and it could be a long time before she regains consciousness. A few days one way or the other is not going to make all that much difference. If she comes out of the coma soon, I can be in Jo'burg within a few hours."

"As you wish." Butchert replied. "The O'Kiep report is important and I was going to suggest that you take it with you, but it would be faster if you completed it here." He leaned back in his chair and steepled his fingers across his chest. "Something you should remember Jack, sometimes impressions count more than reality." He leaned forward and picked up his pen signifying that the discussion was over.

Jack Richardson rose to his feet feeling slightly uncomfortable. He sensed Butchert's disapproval, but was unsure what had prompted it.

When Richardson had gone, Butchert put his pen down and swivelled his chair to face the window. He chewed his bottom lip reflectively. Why didn't he believe Jack Richardson totally? He liked Mornay, they had had their disagreements, but the Canadian had a wry sense of humour and usually got his way without being pompous. He couldn't believe that a man of Mornay's age and experience could have misread anyone to the degree that Richardson was claiming. And Kate? He had met Kate Richardson socially and at work, and found it hard to believe that her recent, open display of concern over the accident to Mornay was as casual as Jack had suggested. Perhaps she and Mornay were having an affair and . . . Yes, he thought finally,

Jack Richardson is threatened and he's playing rough.

Nigel looked out of the window as the Lear settled lower towards the airfield at Swakopmund. His mouth pulled into a grim line at the vista below him. This was what Colin had been lost in, an endless expanse of wind and sun blasted sand and rock. The harshness was unrelieved by any vegetation with the exception of sparse grasses that stuck up in khaki tufts in the dry washes they flew over. He heard Judith gasp and turned to see her staring at the same terrain he had been eyeing.

"What a horrible country. I cannot understand why David likes it so much," she said. "Poor Colin, can you imagine what he must have gone through." She turned away from the window. "He is coming home with us Nigel. I couldn't sleep after seeing this . . . I'd be imagining all sorts of disasters."

"Well, his term is due to start soon and he will be ready to come home I am sure," Nigel agreed. "I can't believe that David would let him go on a safari in this terrain. David and I are going to have some words about this."

The jet noise rose sharply as they flashed over Swakopmund, the little town perched on the coast like a space station in the vastness of the desert. The cold South Atlantic shimmered steel blue in the sunlight as Brian Owen turned out over the ocean to make his run back to the airfield.

Colin, David and Rafa's driver, Piet, stood on the tarmac and watched the white and silver jet whistle overhead. For a second they lost it in the sun, then the wings flashed as it turned back towards them, the wheels dropping as it lined up with the runway. Minutes later it touched down and the jets rose to a scream as Owen engaged reverse thrust. The long nose dipped as the brakes took hold and then it was turning towards them. Colin stood tense beside David who rested one hand on the hood of the station wagon. A flight attendant ran out to signal where to park and the Lear swung towards the hangars and stopped at the signal, its engines idling down to a whispering whine. For a few minutes nothing happened, then the Airstair door swung down and Judith came out followed by Nigel, both blinking into the bright sunlight. Colin was moving towards them, followed slowly by David, when Judith holding her hand up to shield her eyes, caught sight of him. With a shriek, she rushed over to smother him in her embrace.

"Please Mom, I'm all right, honest I'm fine. Mom it's OK, please don't cry." Frantically Colin looked around and his grinning father, seeing his discomforture, pulled Judith gently back.

"Give him air, Judith, I want to get a good look at him. By God, boy, you certainly gave us a scare." Nigel held Colin at arm's length then wrapped his arms around his son in a bear hug.

David waited until the emotional greetings subsided. "Hello Nigel, Judith, I am sorry that you had such a worrying time."

Wiping her eyes on a hastily produced handkerchief, Judith stared at him. "David? Oh my goodness . . . look at you . . . oh my!" and a fresh burst of weeping had her frantically searching for another tissue.

"David," Nigel turned away from a thoroughly discomfited Colin, "we heard you had been injured, how are you?" He looked at the lean suntanned figure, the left arm in a sling and a white bandage just visible below the floppy sun hat that shaded, but did not hide the massive bruising around the eyes. His brother's khaki shirt was open at the throat and Nigel noted the white adhesive bandage stretching from the Vee to just under his chin. He felt a sudden wave of affection for his battered brother and gripped David's outstretched hand in both of his, the twelve year separation since their last meeting evaporating like smoke in a high wind. Looking at David he was painfully aware how out of shape he was. Despite the visible injuries, his brother stood straight and his loose clothing could not entirely hide the flat stomach and tight muscles.

David's face broke into a slow smile. "I guess I've been better. Come on, let's get you both out of the sun and up to my house." He called out to Rafa's driver in Afrikaans and Piet rolled the Peugeot towards them.

Spotting the three pilots coming out of the Lear, he turned back to Nigel. "I'll have another vehicle pick up your crew and take them down to the Hansa Hotel." Nigel nodded, still bemused by the metamorphosis he sensed in his son who was now back at David's side and looking up at his uncle with a worried look. Nigel felt a flash of envy, obviously the boy was David's puppy dog, hanging on to every word. David pushed Colin towards the aircrew who were unloading the luggage. "Explain to the pilot that I'll send a car for them and as soon as they're cleaned up I'd like them to join us for a drink." Colin was glad to have something to do and trotted over to talk to Brian Owen who acknowledged the message with a wave of his hand. Recognizing Chris Walker, Colin began to tell the pilot of his plan to get a private licence before returning to Canada.

Shepherding them towards the station wagon, David avoided a series of questions that Nigel was shooting at him.

"Nigel, let's save all the questions until we're home." he suggested. "You must both feel travel weary and probably want to soak in a deep bath." He turned to Judith, "I only wish it had been possible to get a message to you sooner, but the damn Doctor put me under for two days."

But Judith wasn't to be put off. She glared at her brother-in-law. "He could have been killed, how could you let him go on such a trip, surely you take your responsibilities more seriously than that?"

"Oh, for heaven's sake Judith, the desert trips are run once a week throughout the year. Hundreds of foreign tourists make them without incident. This was a fluke and what happened to Colin and Kresfeld was pure bad luck. Come on, we can discuss all this at my house. It's too hot to stand out here arguing." David called across to Colin that they were ready to leave and he held the rear door open for Judith. Colin climbed in beside his mother and Nigel walked around the station wagon to sit on the other side of Judith.

The Peugeot bumped over the railway tracks and in a few minutes they were pulling into David's driveway. Bones barked excitedly on hearing their arrival outside the gate and Colin, unbidden, crossed the courtyard and opened the heavy door into the house, grabbing Bones to prevent him jumping up on Judith. The budgerigars chittered and flashed frenziedly back and forth behind the mesh on the verandah that made their cage.

David led Nigel and Judith into his living room and was pleased to see that Hendrik had outdone himself. The floors gleamed and fresh flowers mixed with desert grasses stood on the Mopani sideboard. "Well folks, welcome to Swakopmund. This is not the Ritz, but I think you'll be comfortable."

Nigel murmured that it looked very nice, but Judith obviously was not so sure. She gazed around the room and made no comment. Sensing the tension, Colin took his mother's hand and led her off to see his bedroom. David pointed to a comfortable chair and when they were both seated began to describe the events of the past week. Nigel listened intently, interrupting only to clarify an obscure detail, finally David sat back.

"Well, that's what happened, but you know, Nigel, the boy you sent me -- and quite frankly he was a royal pain in the arse to start with -- has turned into something half decent. Wait . . ." he said, seeing the frown start on Nigel's forehead, "I think that you and Judith spoiled Colin badly, but coming out here and the experience in the desert has forced him to grow up. So in the end your plan worked. Colin wants to stay here and complete the flying training that Rafa has started and I think you would do well to listen to him when he raises the subject."

"Stay here?" Nigel's jaw dropped. "Are you mad? Judith would have a fit. My God, David, have you any idea of what we've been through?" He raised his hands in disbelief. "He is coming back with us as soon as the Lear is refuelled and the flight crew have had a rest."

Colin and Judith reappeared, Judith holding a glossy photographic enlargement of the burnt out Chieftain that had been taken by the police photographer and given to Colin as a souvenir. Colin had pinned it up on his wall and foolishly had advised his mother that he intended to get his pilot's licence.

"Nigel, look at this, Colin has been taking flying lessons in this very aircraft. David, I simply cannot believe how irresponsible you've been." She shook the photograph at him. "How could you." She was crying again. Tired from the long flight and overwrought by the conflicting emotions of the last few hours, she simply could not cope with the rush of new information.

"Judith, go and have a bath," David said gently. "I've put you both in my room and the bathroom is en suite. The aircon has been running for a few hours so the room should be comfortable. Have a rest and we'll wake you for dinner." David stared at his younger brother. "Nigel, I have to go out to the mine for a few hours and Colin has to sign a statement at the police station. We can continue our conversation when Judith is more rested. Make sure you both get your feet up for a few hours." He started for the door, calling over his shoulder, "Come with me Colin, and I'll drop you off at the police station."

Colin retrieved his precious photograph from his mother's hand and placed it face down on the sideboard before following David out of the door.

Outside Colin trotted alongside his uncle. "I signed a statement for Captain Pieterse yesterday. What statement were you talking about?"

"I simply want us both out of the house until they have rested. Your mother is not totally rational at the moment and if you spring your plan on her right now, I know she will flatly refuse. I've already tested the water with your father and right now he's not in favour. I am hoping he won't say anything to your mother until they feel more rested and we -- that is you -- can present a persuasive argument."

"I won't go back," Colin's lower lip was stuck out and he slammed the car door with unnecessary force.

Piet started the car and David spoke to Colin in the back seat. "For someone who is reasonably intelligent you certainly make some stupid statements."

"You said I can stay . . . I won't go back."

"Listen to me Colin, I am only going to say this once. Your parents can -- and will -- take you back unless you can persuade them otherwise. I will do everything I can to help convince them to let you stay, but in the end they will decide. Something you should remember, more flies are caught with honey than with vinegar." Piet navigated the corner and they turned out on to the main Windhoek road. *"Die myn Kantoor Piet,"* David was silent for a moment wondering if he had been too hard on Colin. "Look Colin, I want you to stay, and Rafa is keen to get you through your pilot's licence, but in the end your parents will be the ones who decide. Fighting will only make them more determined to get you back to Canada. Your father thinks that I somehow have alienated your feelings and he will want to get you away from my influence. He loves you and no father wants someone else to replace him in the affections of his son."

"He didn't show much affection back in Canada. Everything I did was wrong."

"If your behaviour on arrival here was anything to go by, then I suspect that most of what you did probably was wrong. Remember, affection is a two-way street. It is not given, it is earned. Your father wants what is best for you. Hell, why do you think he sent you out here. From what you told me you were two steps short of prison. I think your father wants very much to have his son back."

At the mine, David told one of his young Ovambo assistants to take Colin on a tour of the plant, guessing rightly that this time Colin would be interested. In his office, Caroline handed him a batch of mail and told him that Mr. Butchert wanted to see him right away.

"He said as soon as you showed up, even if he were in a meeting."

David frowned. He and old man Butchert had a standard meeting once a week. "Call his secretary. Tell her I am walking over. Did he say what it was about?"

"No, but he was insistent that you see him when you arrived."

Entering the main administration complex, David was subjected to several curious stares and various fingers were pointed and he could hear whispering behind his back. Butchert's secretary smiled at him as he pushed open the glass door to the manager's reception room.

"Mr Butchert is waiting for you Mr. Mornay, please go right in." She depressed the intercom button."Mr. Mornay is here Sir."

The automatic doors slid back soundlessly as David walked into the General Manager's office.

Butchert looked up, and his eyes widened for he had not seen David since before the accident. "Mornay, good of you to come so quickly. I did not expect you back for a few days yet. How do you feel?" He indicated the chair across from the desk. "Please sit down."

"Stiff, I feel stiff, but apart from that, not bad at all." David sank into the leather chair.

"David, your term as Construction Project Manager is coming to an end and I want to make some plans to ensure that there is a smooth transition when the construction department is finally integrated into the Tsamma organization." Butchert pushed his chair back. "Previously, I had hoped that I might be able to persuade you to join us as Chief of Engineering, but apart from the fact that ConAmGeo is not keen to let you go, your involvement with Jack Richardson's wife excludes that possibility."

Nothing like getting to the point quickly, David thought sourly, and started to rise.

"Please sit down." Butchert's voice was sharp. "I am not making any judgements, moral or otherwise. You have done excellent work here, but you must obviously realize that I cannot have one of my most promising managers and the man who is infatuated with his wife working at the same plant."

David started to answer, then decided to let Butchert finish. From the moment that Kate had jumped into the ambulance, the outcome had been inevitable. Butchert looked at him with sympathy and his tone warmed. "I have been told by the board that you are being considered for the Las Esmeraldas Copper project in Chile and I have strongly supported that decision. It is a major step up for you and as the largest project in the ConAmGeo organization, one of the most interesting."

David smiled and rose slowly out of the chair. "Thank you for your support, but I doubt that I will be accepting the offer. I will draft a report outlining my recommendations for the integration, and it should be on your desk in about a week. I need to get back into the swing of things and see who performed while I was away and who did not."

"Very well, but try not to be too hasty about the Chile project." Butchert stared at him from under bushy grey eyebrows. "Don't make any decision until you've thought about it carefully." He hesitated, then continued. "You know that Kate Richardson is being transferred tomorrow evening to the Kenridge in Johannesburg?"

"Tomorrow! I knew the air ambulance had been requested, but not so soon . . . that is good news." David stared out the window, then shrugged and turned back to face the General Manager. "I only hope they can do more for her than Hassel and his staff have been able to achieve. Ken is a good Doctor, but this is outside his experience."

David walked to the doors and they opened soundlessly. Butchert stared at David's retreating back with a thoughtful look on his face. He leaned back in his chair and realized that the interview had reinforced his earlier suspicions.

By four thirty, David had caught up on most of the paperwork and had Caroline fetch Colin from the coffee room. Colin had finished his tour of the plant with the junior Engineer who had taken him to the coffee room where Colin had been surrounded by various typists and office staff eager to hear of his recent adventure. Most of the staff were interested in the romance between David and Kate, for as one plump young typist had put it, "It is the stuff of real romance, hey." Reluctantly, Colin left the admiration of several young girls, barely older than he was, and joined David for the trip home.

Arriving back at David's house, they found both Nigel and Judith fast asleep and David gave instructions that they were not to be disturbed. After supper David rose from the table and pointed at the door to the bedroom. "Let them sleep," he advised Colin. "I want to go to the hospital to see Rafa and Kate, and I also must pop in to the Hansa to see how the pilots are getting on. You stay here in case they wake and want something to eat."

Colin protested, for he also wanted to see Rafa, but David insisted. "You can go and see Rafa in the morning. Right now, I want you to be on hand for your parents. They have come halfway around the world and have had a desperately worrying time. You owe them the courtesy of being here when they wake up." He grinned down at his scowling nephew. "Remember what I said about flies and honey." He called to Piet who had been chatting with Hendrik on the verandah and they climbed into the Peugeot.

"No David, absolutely not, he is coming back with us and that is final." Judith sat in the living room sipping on a mineral water that Hendrik had produced from the back of the fridge. David had just returned from a frustrating visit to the hospital. Rafa had been asleep and there was no change in Kate's condition. He had called in to check on the pilots and found them ready for an early night. They were courteous, but obviously could not wait for him to leave. On his return, David found that Nigel and Judith had wakened and Hendrik had produced a pair of fluffy omelettes which they had washed down with a bottle of chilled Nederburg. They both looked rested and Judith, especially, seemed to have recovered her poise.

"But Mom, it is only until I get my private license. I can be back in two months."

"Colin, your father and I have discussed this and you can just as easily take training at the Victoria Flying Club. You seem to have forgotten that school starts in less than three weeks."

"I will go here, I can make up the difference as soon as I get back. I promise I will work extra hard and will not fail the finals."

Exasperated, Judith turned to Nigel, "Talk to him Nigel, I'm not getting through."

Nigel sat idly stroking Bones' head. The big dog had taken to Nigel and now lay curled up at his feet. "Colin, why is it so important that you stay here? You can get your pilot's licence in Victoria. Your schoolwork has not been so good that you can afford to miss even a few weeks. I'm at loss to understand why it's so important that you stay here."

Frustrated, Colin snapped angrily, "I want Rafa to teach me. He is the best there is. I want to go back with my licence, not get it in Victoria."

David interrupted, "Don't let me influence either of you, but I should mention something that may have a bearing on all of this. I will be leaving Tsamma Uranium in about two months. Originally, I had planned to spend a few weeks in Mauritius at the end of my contract, but I would be happy to fly back to

Victoria with Colin if you agreed to him staying."

"No! How many times must I say it?" Judith stamped her foot. "I am determined that Colin comes home with us."

David nodded. "Well that's settled then. Let's put that aside for the moment. Tomorrow morning I am going out to the crash site. Nigel, why don't you come along? You have to rest your crew for at least another day." He shot a warning glance at Colin who was starting to protest, and turned to Judith with a smile. "This may not be your idea of a great place, but I can have someone take you around the town and show you the sights."

Nigel and Judith exchanged glances. Relieved that the argument had ended, they were eager to compromise.

"Yes, I would like to see the area, and Judith you should stretch your legs."

Colin and David said their goodnights. Judith hugged Colin fiercely. "Please understand Colin, we only want what is best for you." Colin had not answered and now with both parents safely behind their bedroom door he turned to David.

"I want to stay. Why did you have to say that it was settled? I want Rafa to teach me, not someone in Canada."

"Colin, sometimes it is necessary to accept the inevitable. Your parents have made up their minds, and quite frankly you do not have a convincing enough argument. Look, I did some thinking myself coming back from Tsamma and I am not going to be here much longer. Rafa may or may not stay, but he has plenty of vacation time due, and has spoken about going back to Chile. I want to see how Kate progresses, so I will rent a small apartment near the hospital in Jo'burg for the foreseeable future. You go back with your parents. I will persuade Rafa to join me for a trip to Victoria towards the end of the year. The three of us can rent a light plane and fly down to Mexico for a real holiday." He sighed softly. "You have done a lot of growing in a very short time. Now you need to consolidate what you have learned. Wessel mentioned that I should get you interested in Mining Engineering. Perhaps when you get back you will investigate UBC where they have a very good program."

"Mining? Dad wants me to do an MBA. I don't know . . . I want to be a pilot."

"Well keep it in mind. Wes was a good judge of character. But you have lots of time. The main thing is to get your grades up so that you have the option."

"You and Rafa will come in September?"

"Yes, we will."

David and Colin walked down the passage, talking of the plans for the next day.

Chapter 26

The Old Ones

The two jeeps stopped in swirls of soft, powdery dust. Through the windscreen they could see the burnt-out wreckage of the Chieftain and the debris scattered along the valley floor. For a long moment no one spoke, then Chris Walker let out a low whistle. "Holy shit! What a place to put down." He turned to Rafa in the rear. "I only hope I never have to do anything like that. You did a fantastic job."

They climbed stiffly down from the two vehicles -- David, Nigel, Colin and Chris Walker. Despite his broken legs Rafa had insisted on coming and a stretcher had been rigged in the back of the LandRover. Of all of them, Rafa had had the most comfortable ride. The other vehicle had carried two Aviation Ministry inspectors with a representative of the insurance company and a police officer. Gariseb and Piet had volunteered to drive and the little party had set out from Swakopmund after breakfast. They stood in silence, contemplating the now peaceful scene. A light wind ruffled the grasses and sighed through the gutted fuselage of the Chieftain. Rafa sat up on the stretcher and through the open rear door explained the sequence of events that had led to the crash. "What Dave saw before we turned round was Colin's shirt hung up on a thorn bush. Wessel and the police jeeps came on it just as we crashed."

Colin pointed to the wall of rock on the left. "That's where the cave is, come on." He ran forward, ducking under the overhang of rock that had been his original shelter. Nigel followed with David and Gariseb. The entrance to the cave had been enlarged by the police teams searching for evidence of the Bushman and it was an easier entry than Colin had found. They crawled in on their hands and knees and once inside stood marvelling at both the coolness after the heat outside and the clear pool of water that had saved Colin's life. "He sat here," Colin said pointing to the ledge above the water, "and he poured water down on to my head."

Gariseb walked wide-eyed around the interior, muttering to himself in Nama, clicking his teeth and shaking his head. They all turned to watch him and David called out, "What is it Johannes, what's the matter?"

"This place has spirits boss, old spirits from the long ago." He muttered again in Nama and was so clearly uncomfortable that he crawled back outside. David looked around the chamber. There were no Bushman paintings on the walls, nothing to suggest human habitation. He remembered someone telling him that the Nama and the Bushmen had been mortal enemies centuries before. Finally, he joined Graiseb outside.

"You say 'spirits' Johannes, what kind of spirits?" The big black man stared past David, his eyes unfocused. Johannes 'Johnny' Gariseb had been with the initial geological teams and David's construction team had inherited him along with other staff transferred when the exploration phase was completed. David had made Gariseb his foreman in charge of earthmoving equipment and had always found him to be solid, if a trifle unimaginative. Now something was disturbing Johannes and he pointed to a small mound twenty metres further along the rock bluff.

"Aiee, I remember this place. I was here before, I remember now. Boss Wessel, Ivan and I came here to collect some geological drillcore that had been left behind."

Clearly puzzled, David said. "I don't see the connection Johannes, what has that to do with anything."

"No, no, Boss Dave. When we came here, Ivan found a body, the wind had swept the sand away and exposed the head of a very small body at the base of the cliff. It was old, very old . . . the sun had dried the skin and the bones were yellow and brown. When we cleared the sand away we saw that the man had been shot . . .we could see a hole in his chestbone. There was a necklace of shell on the body and an ostrich egg in a leather bag. In his hand was a fighting knife. At first Boss Wessel wanted to take the body into Swakop to the police but then after we cleared away all the sand he said no. He and I dug a grave, that grave there." Johannes pointed to the mound. "We put all the things in the grave and then Boss Wes said a prayer for the soul of the Bushman."

"But why did you not report it?"

"Boss Wessel said no. He said the man was a warrior who had died fighting and deserved a proper burial, and if we reported it, the museum would want the remains because it was from the German time. He said this man's bones should lie in peace."

"Wessel said that . . . I wonder why? He was never particularly religious. And now you think that the Bushman's spirit is around here?"

"I don't know Boss David, I only know that I felt the old ones in that cave." Johannes abruptly turned away and walked back to the jeeps and climbed behind the wheel. Nigel and Colin had followed David out of the cave.

"You surely don't believe that nonsense." Nigel had caught the tail end of the conversation. Colin dusted sand off his hands on his shorts. "I saw a Bushman, and he was as real as you are. I don't know what Johannes is talking about, but I saw a Bushman."

David said nothing. He walked slowly over to the little mound that Gariseb had pointed out. For a long moment he stared down, then squatting he lifted a handful of fine sand which he trickled down on to the grave. "Thank you." he murmured. Then rising and brushing his hands on his shorts, he rejoined the others.

"You really believe that story, Dave?" Nigel was clearly perplexed by David's behaviour.

"I don't know, but this is Africa, old Africa, and there are many things one learns to accept," he replied. "Come on, I want to get back to Swakop before the air ambulance takes Kate to Jo'burg."

David wheeled Rafa down the long corridor towards the women's ward. They turned the corner and saw Ken Hassel coming out of Kate's room.

"Hallo Dave . . . Rafa. Come to say your goodbyes have you?" Hassel pulled the door shut behind him. "The air ambulance will be here in the next ten minutes so you will have to be brief."

"Any change in her condition?" David's voice was tight, the only outward sign of the emotions raging inside.

"No. Several times this morning I thought I saw slight signs, but it could have been my imagination. Anyway, she will have the best specialists look at her in Jo'burg." Ken Hassel opened the door and motioned them in. "Come and see me before you leave, OK?" He walked briskly away down the corridor. Inside the room, nothing had changed. A nurse sat beside the bed and smiled when she recognized David. Kate looked fresh. Her eyes were closed, but her skin glowed and her breathing was steady and regular. David reached for her hand.

"Kate, it's David. They are taking you to Jo'burg but I will not be far away. I am going to get a small place close to you." He rubbed the back of her hand with his thumb.

"Like hell you are, Mornay! Take your hands off my wife." Startled, David turned and saw that Jack Richardson had just entered the room. Rafa spun his wheel chair, effectively blocking Richardson's attempt to get to David and forcing him to go to the opposite side of the bed. Richardson's face was dark with anger and he leaned across his wife's still form to wave a finger at David. "I've told you Mornay, Kate is not in love with you. When will you understand that she is committed to this marriage? I warned you about trying to see her. Fortunately this will be the last time." David chose to ignore the tirade. Silently, he rose from his seat beside the bed and released Kate's hand.

"Goodbye Kate." He placed her hand back on the cover and stood looking down at her, then turned to Rafa. "Let's go and see Ken," and it was as if Richardson wasn't there. The two of them left the room leaving Jack Richardson and the nurse alone with Kate. They moved down the corridor in silence until Rafa spoke.

"Jo'burg is not Swakop my friend. He can stop you seeing Kate very easily I think."

"I know, but I must try to be around when she recovers. I need to know the truth. I just don't believe that she was off to Germany . . . God, what a mess!"

They entered the main Administration area, passing the air ambulance stretcher that was being wheeled up to Kate's room. Ken Hassel's office was empty when they knocked and he popped his head around the Admin counter.

"Go in, I have just had a call . . . let me see . . . I won't be a minute." He walked rapidly back the way they had just come. David and Rafa glanced at each other then entered the office and sat down. David could barely hear the whisper of conversations over the hospital telecom system next door. Rafa looked around for a magazine and, finding one, sat back to read. For the next ten minutes the only sound was the ticking of the hospital clock as they both sat absorbed in their own thoughts. Suddenly the door was thrust open and the nurse that had been in Kate's room burst in.

"Mr. Mornay please come, Mrs. Kate is talking, and she is asking for you."

"What!" David was on his feet and out of the door in one bound.

"Dave wait!" Rafa frantically levered the wheelchair around and the nurse pushed him, following David back to Kate's room. Outside Kate's room the Air Ambulance stretcher and the two attendants stood waiting. The door was ajar and David swung around the jamb with such haste that he cannoned into Ken

Hassel who was bending over Kate. Kate was sitting up in bed, tears spilling down her face. Seeing David, she held her arms out to him. "I dreamt that you were dead. Oh David, I was so desolate. Then I woke up and Jack was here and said you had just left, that you were going to Chile. But I didn't believe him, I had to see you." She gripped David by the arm her eyes bright with joy. David looked across the bed where Jack Richardson stood white-faced, staring at his wife. He opened his mouth as if to say something, then without a word marched stiffly out of the room.

Ken Hassel gently pushed Kate back on the pillows. "Please take it easy, Mrs. Richardson. You have been unconscious for quite a long time and I don't think this excitement is doing you any good."

"Kate, Ken is right, you took an awful crack on the head." David turned to the Doctor. "How did this happen? Is she going to be all right?" He held Kate's hand, grinning like a schoolboy, oblivious of the others in the room.

"I don't know, sometimes it happens, we have no idea what triggers it. But she should rest so I am going to insist that you all leave now. So outside all of you."

"Please Doctor, let David stay for a minute. I want to speak to him privately." Dubiously, Ken Hassel looked at the two of them. "Only a few minutes then." He ushered the others outside.

Kate stroked his arm. "I feel as if I have been reborn. Jack said Colin is safe and that you were not hurt in the crash."

"Kate, Jack told me that you were going to Germany with him. Is that right?" He tensed for her answer as she frowned in puzzlement.

"No, the night I spoke to Jack he asked me to join him in Germany and I refused. I told him that I wanted a divorce, that I was in love with you and that I could not continue with our life together. I wanted to tell you the very next day, but Jack insisted that I wait until he returned. He said I owed him that much. That is what I wanted to tell you."

David exhaled. Without realizing it, he had been holding his breath. "You mean Jack knew that you wanted a divorce? He told . . . " David stopped. "I hope you know that I'll shortly be unemployed and that I'm a poor risk," he said, unable to hide the twinkle in his eyes. "I have some money and my shares in Mornay Industries, but for all that, I'm not sure I'm going to be good for you."

Kate smiled and stroked his face. "You are not getting away this time, David Mornay. For once in my life I'm taking charge of what I want."

Several days later David, Kate and Rafa watched the Lear lift off from Windhoek Airport. They watched until it disappeared with a last twinkle into the gathering dusk.

In the Namib, an eddy of dust lifted over the canyon and settled on the broken fuselage of the Chieftain. Slowly the desert began the age old unending process of assimilation.

-------------------0------------------

Epilogue

"And that's how it was." Rafa rose and held out his hand to the girl, "Come, it's time I was going."

Laura took his hand rising as gracefully as a fawn. She studied the swarthy Chilean's face carefully. "You loved her too, didn't you Rafa?" Rafa took Laura's face in both hands, kissed her on the forehead and chuckled, "Of course, but when you were born I transferred my affections."

The girl punched him in the chest. "You're mocking me, you shouldn't mock."

Rafa grunted, the blow had caught him by surprise. "No, little one, the day you were born you became my special charge. Why do you think I'm telling her daughter ancient stories?" He turned, placing an arm around the girls shoulders, "I know that when you're older you'll be just like her. You'll

catch the eye of some handsome caballero like your father and leave me nursing a broken heart."
The girl laughed, "No I won't. You're my caballero - for ever and ever."
With their arms around each others shoulders they two walked towards the waiting limousine.

FINIS